Books by Robin Reardon

A SECRET EDGE

THINKING STRAIGHT

A QUESTION OF MANHOOD

Published by Kensington Publishing Corp.

# A Question of Manhood

## Robin Reardon

KENSINGTON BOOKS
www.kensingtonbooks.com

KENSINGTON BOOKS are published by

Kensington Publishing Corp.
119 West 40th Street
New York, NY 10018

All Kensington titles, imprints, and distributed lines are available at special quantity discounts for bulk purchases for sales promotion, premiums, fund-raising, educational, or institutional use.

Special book excerpts or customized printings can also be created to fit specific needs. For details, write or phone the office of the Kensington Special Sales Manager: Kensington Publishing Corp., 119 West 40th Street, New York, NY 10018. Attn. Special Sales Department. Phone: 1-800-221-2647.

Kensington and the K logo Reg. U.S. Pat. & TM Off.

ISBN-13: 978-0-7582-4679-0
ISBN-10: 0-7582-4679-X

First Kensington Trade Paperback Printing: October 2010
10  9  8  7  6  5  4  3  2  1

Printed in the United States of America

*Only the dead have seen the end of war.*
—Plato

# PART I

# Good Son, Good Soldier

# Chapter 1

Chris will be home tomorrow!

It was like a silent litany all through the house that November Tuesday, last fall. Mom was making herself a little crazy getting the house ready. It wasn't like the place needed any extra attention, either. I mean, it's what she does. Keep house. And she does it great. I think she just didn't know what else to do with herself. I felt the same way, and I almost wished she'd make me do some of it. I knew better than to volunteer, though; I wouldn't wanna get stuck forever with any household chores that didn't already have my name on them.

What I really wanted was something I could do to make myself more presentable, to make me feel a little less like the kid brother who wasn't old enough to do anything useful. Even though I was sixteen, I had a feeling there would seem to be more than the three years between us when I finally laid eyes on Chris.

I had this scene in my head of what it would be like when he walked through the front door. Chris would drop his duffle and brace himself for the onslaught of Mom's hug. She'd put her whole body into it—nearly squeeze him to death. Finally she'd let go, dabbing with a tissue at her eyes, and Dad would step forward. First he'd just look, taking in the short golden hair, the two days of beard growth, the broad shoulders, the lean body proudly held. And then he'd grin. He'd take Chris's right hand in his and clap him on the shoulder with the other.

"Son, just look at you! You've become quite the man. I'm so proud of you." That's how he'd open.

Chris would say something like, "Yeah, well, you were right, Dad. There's not much that'll make a man out of you faster than the army."

"Did I say that?"

"You did."

"Guess I was right, then. You want a beer?"

I ran through that scene in my head so many times, in the days before he arrived. The words changed a little from one take to the next, or maybe Chris had shaved, and in one take Dad actually told Chris he could start calling Dad by his first name, Andy. One thing that didn't change? It always played out with me off to the side, worried that I was gonna look like some needy little kid if I wanted to be noticed. If I wanted a hug or even a handshake, too.

Maybe the litany itself was silent, but Dad didn't stop talking about Chris coming home from Vietnam. He'd been on the phone with all his cronies.

"That's right! My boy is coming home for some leave. He deserves it, too!" Almost made it sound like he had just one boy. And it wasn't me.

But I understood how important it was. Chris had been over there for months now, and almost every day it had occurred to me that he might not come home. Ever. That he might step on a land mine, or a punji stick hidden in a hole in the jungle floor, or even get stabbed by some double agent pretending to be a whore while Chris thinks he's just having some boom boom time with her. His letters didn't talk about this stuff, because he knew Mom would just about memorize them. But the war had been going on for years by that time, November of 1972, and I'd heard a few things from brothers of friends, and from the newspapers. So just the fact that Chris was still alive was something to celebrate. And when Mom told me after school one day that he was coming home on leave—well, let's just say I had to go someplace alone. I got on my bicycle and rode and rode until I was exhausted. Then I slowed down but kept going until I was far enough into the remnants of what used to be farmland to be sure no one could hear me when I stood in the middle of a field, nearly invisible in the dusk, and hooted and hollered and howled. It was freezing cold—early November in our little corner of southwestern Pennsylvania—but I didn't care.

I started imagining what he'd be like as soon as I was back on my bike heading home. Would he have gotten taller? More muscles? Grown a beard? Would he have changed? I know some guys have come back from 'Nam a wreck. Shell-shocked, having nightmares, drinking like fish to forget the shit that happened to them over there. I didn't want to think what Chris would go through if he'd been in the position of having to kill civilians, especially women or kids. I couldn't even picture him killing enemy soldiers.

When I got back from my solo journey I was surprised by the reaction from my folks. I hadn't really expected anyone would notice that I'd left, but they had, and they weren't happy.

Mom met me at the door, her round face all squeezed into worry lines under her sort-of-blond hair. "Oh, Paul! Where have you been? We were worried sick."

Dad didn't even let me reply. "Fine thing you've done, getting everyone upset when we've finally had some good news!"

"I was just out riding my bike. Jeez!" But by the time they gave me enough space to say this into, they'd both turned away again, Mom to finish getting dinner ready and Dad back to his paper to wait for the meal.

At the table we talked about Chris, of course. Mom kept reciting phrases from his letters, and Dad was obviously trying not to sound like he was looking forward to war stories. At one point I asked, "Dad, didn't they have any wars for you to fight in?"

He got this stony kind of look on his face, picked up his pipe—beside him on the table, but not lit at the moment—and set it down again. "They did, Paul. Korea. I tried to sign up, but they didn't like my leg."

Right. It's funny, you know? You tend to forget, when you see someone all the time and they limp all the time, that there's anything unusual in that. Dad was born with one leg about two inches shorter than the other, and he couldn't run very well. Threw his hip bones off, too, so he couldn't do long marches. Plus, he *makes* you forget; he's a real man about it and never complains. The only complaint I ever heard was that he wasn't able to be a cop, which he'd really wanted to do. Instead he owns a pet supply store.

Dad's big into dogs. I've always thought that if Mom weren't allergic to animals, Dad would've had a pet store, not just a pet supply store. He does sell birds, mice, rats, fish, and some amphibians, but it's dogs he really likes. But at least he gets to see the dogs people bring into the store, and he allows it as long as they're on a leash. And Dad loves it. He likes to talk to the dogs, play with their ears, and he says the owners really warm up when he asks them about their dogs. The next time he sees the people, he always remembers their dog's name. He thinks it makes customers buy more stuff, or at least keeps them coming back to his store. He's probably right.

The fact that he's not a cop is actually just fine by my mom, who much prefers to think of him at the store rather than chasing down criminals. He's been successful, too—had to move the store twice in the last twelve years into bigger spaces as the Pittsburgh sprawl grew. There's talk lately of a big chain buying him out, but he's only forty and says he isn't ready to retire. Besides, he always wanted Chris and me, or at least one of us, to take over the business. The danger of hanging on, though, is that the chain could open a competing store and undersell him until he closes. Then he'd lose everything.

I can't say I really want to take over the business. I had always expected Chris would do it; he'd always been the reliable one.

After dinner, in my room trying to focus on homework, all I could think of was Chris coming home. I stared out the window over my desk half the time, my eyes following the cars that went by the front of the house. Every time I started worrying that he'd be totally changed, some memory from when we were younger would push it out. Growing up? I wasn't just the pest kid brother. Well, at least not all the time. It was like he wanted me to know where he'd stepped wrong so I could make better decisions. Sometimes he even made them for me.

Imagine this scene. My best friend when I was eleven, Charlie, had borrowed my baseball glove. His folks couldn't afford to buy him one. Or so they said. Looking back, I think they had the money, but his dad spent it on booze. Anyway, he lost it. Or, he didn't lose it, actually; his neighbor's dog chewed the hell out of it, but he told me he lost it.

Furious, I marched right over to his house and searched all over the yard, in the basement, in Charlie's room, every place that might conceivably hide a glove. I didn't know whether to believe him that it was misplaced somewhere or whether he might be hiding it to keep it. I mean, you don't just *lose* a baseball glove; it's too big. And too smelly. But I couldn't find it.

Just before I stamped off home again I said, "You better find it, or else!"

I was steaming mad when I got home and was all ready to go to my folks about it. Chris saw me first, though. He was reading some book, lying on the couch.

He looked up as I slammed the door behind me. "Hey, Paul, what's that for?"

"Nothing!"

"You're madder than a wet cat. Get over here." He swung his legs off the couch and sat up.

"It's Charlie. He stole my glove!"

"The fielder's glove you got for your birthday?"

"What other glove do I have?"

"Are you sure he stole it? What did he say?"

"He borrowed it two weeks ago, and I've been asking for it back. I called him a little while ago, and he says he lost it."

"Maybe he did. Did he—"

"Chris, you don't just lose a glove."

"Did he offer to replace it?"

"Ha. He couldn't afford one for himself. How's he gonna do that?"

"Well, let's just think about this a minute. Charlie's your best friend, right? And if you didn't have good reason to trust him in the first place, would you have let him borrow it?"

I was trying to stay mad, but my steam was petering out. "Well . . . no."

"So why don't you trust him now? And why should he lie to you? His thinking is probably more like, if you let him use it once, you'd let him use it again. And wouldn't that be better than losing you as a friend? Why take that chance? Besides, if he's lying and he still has it, he'd never be able to use it any-place you could see it."

I wasn't ready to give in. "How do I know what he's thinking? People change, y'know. Maybe he figured it was the only way he'd ever have one of his own. Take someone else's."

"But it doesn't make a lot of sense, and it isn't something that sounds like Charlie. Think of it another way: What if he weren't your friend anymore?"

I blinked. Charlie? Not my friend? "Well . . . he won't be, if he doesn't replace that glove."

"So that glove was worth more than being friends?"

This stumped me, but only for a few seconds. "All I know is I want that glove back." I was afraid Chris was going to talk me out of my righteous anger, and I didn't want to be talked out of it. I wanted to hang on tight and yell and curse. I stomped up to my room, turned on the radio, threw myself onto the bed, and sulked.

Later I found out that Chris went to Charlie's and talked to him. Charlie showed him the tattered remnants that he'd man-aged to get away from Zodiac, the half shepherd, half Lab that lived next to him. What ended up happening was that Chris lent Charlie enough money to buy me another glove.

I didn't know this right away, of course. All I knew was that I wasn't going to call Charlie, or talk to him, until he did the right thing. But when he knocked on my door a few days later and handed me a brand new fielder's glove—well, I didn't feel that rush of vindication that all my fury had led me to expect. I didn't want to say, "That's more like it." Or "Glad to see you came to your senses."

I stared at Charlie, wondering where the hell he'd got the money. All I said was, "Thanks."

We stood there, staring at our sneakers, until he said, "Well, I should go."

"D'you have to?"

So we went upstairs and played records until dinnertime.

Two years later, just before Charlie and his mom had to move away after the divorce, to go stay with his grandparents for a while, he finally told me what had happened. He was all worried because he hadn't been able to pay Chris back completely, and he didn't know how he was gonna do it now.

"Tell you what," I said. "Whatever's left, I'll pay him."

"But that's not fair."

" 'Course it is. He may have paid for the glove, but you and I both benefited, right? I mean, we stayed friends. Shake?"

"Shake." And we hugged. We'd never done that before, and now we'd never have another chance. I never saw Charlie again, but I feel like I still have his friendship. Chris saw to that.

A few days after Charlie told me all this, I confronted Chris. "How come you bought that glove for Charlie to give to me?"

He chuckled. "Took you all this time to figure that out?"

"Never mind that. He says he still owes you."

"He doesn't owe me. You do."

"Duh. I already told him that. But why'd you do it?"

"You were about to lose a friend. I'd been in that place once. Lost a friend over something really stupid. I vowed it would never happen again. And I didn't want to see it happen to you."

"How did it happen with you?"

He took a deep breath and closed his eyes a second. "This is really embarrassing. But maybe it will be good for you to hear. It was winter, and there'd been this huge snowstorm. The plows had pushed lots of snow to the edges of the playground. I was about the same age as you, when you lost that glove.

"At recess, we were playing King of the Mountain. Only we

had teams. I was on the same team as Dean Pendleton. You probably don't remember him. Redheaded kid. Anyway, I was always really good at this game, climbing up the snow mountains and pushing kids on the other team back down. But this one day they had more kids than our team, and we were really struggling. I managed to claim the top, and I decided I was gonna stay there no matter what. So I was pushing at kids right, left, anybody I saw.

"Now, as you know if you've ever played this, you're supposed to help your own teammates get to the top, too. But I was just thinking, Me: I want to be on the top. At one point, Dean was clambering up—I was looking right at his bright blue wool hat—and he'd nearly made it when someone on the other team got hold of his leg from farther down. Dean looked up and called to me."

Chris took another breath and let it out real slow. "He was reaching out a hand, yelling at me to help him. All I could think of was that if I tried to help him, and if I couldn't pull him away from the other kid, we could both go down. It was him or me, not us. I can still see the strain on his face. A kind of panic in his eyes."

He shook his head like he was throwing water off his hair and then stared down at his hands. "I ignored him. I looked right into his eyes like I didn't know who he was, and I ignored him. And he was pulled farther and farther down the hill."

He stopped. I said, "Did you hold the top?"

Chris looked at me. "Have you been paying attention? Yeah, I held the top. But I lost my friend."

So this was my brother. And for several months now, he'd been an army infantryman, a grunt, fighting the VC. He'd signed up, in fact. Put off college to go. It upset my mom a lot; she wanted him to go to college, the first one in the family who would go. And he's smart; he would've gotten into a good school. But mostly what she didn't want was for him to get hurt. Or worse. Dad was a different story. He sounded so proud, telling his friends that his son had volunteered.

I guess I felt sort of someplace in between. I understood my dad's pride; I felt it, too. On the other hand, lots of guys who go to 'Nam don't come home.

After Chris signed up, Mom started going to church alone. She had always gone, or almost every week anyway, to the Lutheran church she'd been going to since she was a little girl. It was the church she and Dad got married in, and we went as a family until I was maybe, I dunno, twelve? Anyway, at some point I started putting up a fuss, and Dad said he'd stay home with me. A few times after that Mom insisted I go with her, but eventually she gave up trying to force me. To tell you the truth, I think Dad was just as happy to stay home, read the paper, lounge around, whatever. He worked pretty much six-plus days a week, and Sunday was the only day he could sleep in and just vegetate before he started doing paperwork for the store.

Chris kept going, though. That's so like him, you know? I don't even know how seriously he took it, but even if it meant nothing to him he'd go because of Mom. Chris never talked about it, although Mom would sometimes talk during Sunday dinner about something the preacher had said in his sermon. I just remember feeling glad I hadn't had to get up early and then sit through it, on those hard wooden benches, in uncomfortable clothes, hot in summer and drafty in winter, pretending to feel all solemn and contrite and holy. What a crock, was what I thought.

But several weeks after Chris signed up, one Saturday dinnertime Dad said, "Irene, you going to church tomorrow?"

"Of course I am. I always go. You know that."

Well, she *almost* always went, anyway; there was no point in arguing, so I kept quiet. Then Dad said, "Think I'll go with you." And after that he went with her a lot. I was old enough by then to stay home on my own, so that's what I did. I figured if God was going to listen to anyone about keeping Chris safe, it wasn't gonna be me.

That homecoming scene happened pretty much as I'd pictured. Chris looked tall and masculine and strong, but his hair was longer than I'd imagined; guess they don't make them keep it buzz cut. But there was one real important difference. After Dad offered the beer, Chris looked at me before he answered. "How's my kid brother? Too old for a hug?"

He held an arm toward me. This foolish grin slid onto my face from somewhere—I couldn't stop it—and I shrugged and moved toward him. His arms felt so strong around me, like there was nothing he couldn't do. He made me believe he was glad to see me.

All of us wanted to know what it was like, all the stuff there's no room for in letters, all the stuff we wanted to hear him say with his own voice. That first night, though, he was just too tired, barely able to sit at the dinner table, but he was so happy to be eating home cooking. Every so often he'd just sit there, face blank, eyes closed, chewing slowly. You could tell he was committing every texture, every hint of flavor to memory.

At one point he set his fork down and said, "You know, I never expected the food over there to be good. I just didn't know how—different it would be. From good food. From this." He looked like he wanted to say more, but in the end he just shook his head slowly and put another forkful into his mouth.

We'd been sending him care packages. The first one had lots of different stuff in it, like socks and underwear and little goodies. The letter he wrote back was clear: All that stuff was great, but what he really wanted was FOOD. So the next packages all had peanut butter ("choke" is what the guys called it over there), crackers, cookies, candy, Tang, more cookies, more candy, and he loved it. We couldn't send anything that would go bad, like cold cuts or cheese, that sort of thing, but his favorite seemed to be cookies. All kinds. Plus, he said in one letter, they were great for trading with the other guys for things.

"What kinds of things?" Mom's return letter asked. Probably she wanted to be able to include everything he might want to keep *and* everything he might want to trade for. But his response was evasive. "Oh, just whatever. You never know what you're going to be in the mood for."

While he was home, in private, he swore me to secrecy and told me that what he traded cookies for—though he did eat a lot of them—was beer, cigarettes, and koon sa. Marijuana. But he sure wasn't going to tell our folks about those items. I'd always thought of Chris as kind of a Goody Two-shoes, in a lot of ways. He always seemed to do everything right, as far as our folks were concerned, and I always felt like the troublemaker. So, to use one of my mom's favorite phrases, imagine my consternation when Chris told me he smoked pot! It was the first sign, I think now, of the new way I would come to see him—a lot of stain on the pure white—by the time he left to go back overseas.

That first night, though, at the dinner table, Chris nearly nodded off before he could finish his piece of the chocolate cake Mom had made, but he asked for more coffee and that seemed to perk him up a bit. Then he left the room for a minute and came back with stuff for us.

He gave Mom a huge piece of blue and green silk material that she could use to make whatever she wanted. It made her cry, and she worried that she'd get salt stains on the silk. Dad got a really cool pipe. It was made of some special kind of wood they had over there. He wanted to use it immediately and even got up, mumbling about trying it first with the most bland tobacco he had so he could get a sense of the pipe, but Mom made him give it to her so she could wash it first.

When it was my turn, Chris said, "Hold out your hands. Make a cup." And onto my palms he dropped five round metal pellets. "Ever heard of a cluster bomb?" I shook my head. "Those five are from a SADEYE. It's about as big as a baseball. Lots of them get dropped at once, and when they hit the ground they explode. Then all these steel balls go shooting out."

Out of the corner of my eye I saw Mom shudder. But I said, "Neat!" Then Chris handed me something wrapped in brown paper. Dad asked to hold the pellets, and he kind of played with them while I unwrapped the package. I held up a pair of shoes. Sandals, really. They were super ugly. I looked at Chris, confused.

"Those, little brother, are called Ho Chi Minhs. They're made out of cut-up tires. The straps are from inner tubes. We wear them around camp when it's hot, or when it's muddy or wet. You can't hurt 'em." He grinned like they were a real treat.

"Thanks!" I said, trying to sound enthusiastic. I was thinking I'd just have to give them a try; Chris didn't steer me wrong as a rule.

Mom wasn't so patient. "Good Lord, Christopher! What do you want to go perpetuating that man for? He's dead, and that's where he ought to be. Why name a shoe after him?"

Chris just shrugged. "Well, we walk on 'em, don't we? We wear them when we need to walk through stuff we don't want to touch, right?"

This shut her up, though she did cross her arms and make some noise of disgust. I looked at them again, with a little more respect this time.

Coffee or no coffee, Chris had to crawl upstairs to sleep right after dinner. I took my steel balls and my tire-tread sandals into my room, and at first I was thinking I'd stay up there. It was nice to think of Chris in the next room, and I pictured him in his bed for the first time in what seemed like forever. His bed and mine had just the wall between them, and I pictured him lying in there, head near the wall, feet pointing toward the window that looked out onto the backyard . But pretty soon I heard him snoring through the wall, and I wondered if Mom and Dad were talking about the war and about Chris, and I wanted to be a part of that.

They were at the kitchen table, finishing their coffee. When they knew I was there, Dad stopped talking and they both looked at me. I grabbed a soda, flipped the top, and made my-self comfortable, waiting for him to go on. Finally he shrugged and finished what he was saying when I came in.

"Anyway, forget that idea, Irene. There's no way he isn't going back to finish his tour. They expect him back, and back he'll go." ·

"But why?" Mom's voice sounded almost whiny, and her plump face went into this little girl pout. "The war is ending! Henry Kissinger said so. Why can't our son stay home, now that he's here?"

The war was ending. At least, that's what we'd been hearing. Just recently the news was all about how the Linebacker operation was over. Chris wasn't directly involved in that, since it was air force and navy carrying it out, but it was this huge offensive, and it sure put a dent in the Vietcong's battle capabilities. And it probably cinched the election for Nixon the week before, though people like my dad believe he would have beat McGovern, anyway. Dad's a real Nixon supporter. But my friend Terry Cavanaugh's dad had some other opinions, and I'd heard some of them.

I chimed in, "Mr. Cavanaugh says that was just an election ploy, saying the war was ending."

Dad turned a hard stare on me. "President Nixon was in no need of falsehoods to win this election. It was no contest. Kissinger wouldn't need to lie just to win the election for the president."

I shrugged like it didn't matter to me. And, really, as long as the war ended and Chris was okay, I didn't give a shit who won the election. Or how.

Mom wasn't done. "But it's nearly Thanksgiving!" she almost wailed. "He should at least be allowed to stay with us for that!"

"Irene, stop it. The boy volunteered, very bravely"—here he turned back to me, as if to underscore silently what he thought of Terry's brother, Ron, who'd gone to Canada to escape the draft—"and he will finish his work. He will not let his squad down. No son of mine backs out of his commitments."

Mom got up in sort of a huff and started collecting dishes to wash. We have this portable—though that hardly seems like the right word—dishwasher that you can roll over to the sink and attach to the faucet while you run it. Mom nearly dented the counter in front of the sink, she hauled it over so fast and hard. She made as much noise with the dishes as she could without breaking them, but flatware is less fragile, and she had her way with it.

Dad tried once more to get her to see reason, as he would have put it. "Imagine, would you? Just for a second? What would he feel like, sitting here with us having turkey and gravy

and potatoes and pumpkin pie, knowing his platoon was over
there having rations? Imagine how he must feel every day he's
here, when one of the guys who may have saved his life at some
point, maybe last week even, is in danger now."

She didn't even look at him. A fork hit the floor, I think by
accident, and then another landed next to it and bounced and
clattered with the force of her throw.

Dad got up and stomped unevenly out of the kitchen, leaving me there sucking on my soda can and feeling like some
piece of luggage no one had enough hands to carry. Fine. So I
headed back to my room.

I got as far as the foot of the stairs when Dad came up behind
me. "And as for you," he said in this angry tone, pointing a finger at me, "don't you go listening to anything that dove Cavanaugh says. He should be ashamed of that boy of *his*, instead
of making excuses." He turned on his heel and headed for his
recliner in the living room.

"What'd I do?" I called after him. *Goddamn it, why does he always assume I've done something wrong? It's like all the shit Chris has-
n't done, all the stuff a kid usually gets blamed for, is what I get
accused of double. I'm no angel; wouldn't want to be. But if they think
they have trouble with me, they should think again.*

I sat staring out the window in front of my desk, ignoring my
homework, telling myself sourly that I'd even have Saturday
night for schoolwork, though that was something else I was
angry about, actually. My allowance was puny compared to
most of my friends, so paying for dates was an extra challenge
on top of just getting them. I'd asked for more money in September, but of course the answer was no. That had felt like a
slap in the face, with the store doing as well as it was.

So parties were one place I could take a date that didn't cost
anything. Saturday there was gonna be this really great party at
my friend Kevin's house, and I had already asked Laura
Holmes, just about the cutest girl in class. I've always thought I
was okay looking—dark blond hair with just a little wave to it,
gray-green eyes, decent build—but even so I would have
thought Laura would be out of my league. It took guts, or arro-

gance, just to ask her. And she'd said yes! But when it came out that it was the weekend Chris would be home, my mom was all over me.

"Young man, you can't possibly think anything in this world is more important than spending time with your brother! He's been over there risking his life every day, and anything could happen to him at any time. He'll be here only a few days, and you think you're going out with your friends?" She stood there, dust rag dangling from the hand that wasn't planted on her broad hip, glaring at me.

"Ma, it's not just 'going out with my friends.' It's taking this really"—I'd almost said hot—"sweet girl, someone every guy wants to go out with, to, like, the biggest party of the fall!"

She wagged her finger at me, the rag flopping around in the air. "Do you want me to pull your father's weight into this? You're not going, Paul. I don't care how important it seems to you now. In the overall scheme of things, in retrospect, it will pale in comparison with how important spending time with your brother will be."

We stood there, kind of facing off, a test of wills. Sometimes this works for me. She doesn't always have what it takes to stare me down; she's a softy, really. But not this time. She was ice. And the look on her face told me she would pull Dad into it if necessary. And there was no way I could win with him, once he set his mind on something. I'd need Chris for that. Chris was always the only one of all of us who could move my dad with reason or anything else, he's that stubborn.

*Go ahead, tell Dad. Let him do his worst. I'm going to that party!* It was on the tip of my tongue. But my jaw clenched tight shut, almost against my will, my hands balled into fists at my sides, and I turned and stormed off. The worst of it was that I had to call Laura and tell her. When I did, I couldn't really get a bead on her reaction. I mean, she didn't pout or whine or anything, but it didn't feel like sunshine and roses. What a freakin' mess. Who could blame her if she never agreed to go out with me again?

And now, even though Chris was actually home, just thinking

about missing that party this weekend made me steam. Lying there on the bed listening to Chris snore in the next room, this feeling of resentment started to bubble up. When you thought about it, I sort of had a lot to resent Chris for. He was the favorite son, no doubt there. And if he'd been some kind of monster, or at least if he'd been mean to me, I could have gotten angry with him and felt good about it.

But he never gave me a chance like that. He'd never done anything to get me into trouble, and in fact, he'd stood up for me so many times in one way or another, getting my folks to ease off on some punishment Dad was sure I deserved for whatever, getting both of them to see that something I'd done was just horseplay and not a sign of evil taking over my life and theirs. He'd always been able to calm Dad down—he was the only one who could—and he'd always done his best for me.

But I wasn't in the mood to think of what a great brother he was. Even so, as I lay there on my bed, music playing quietly, staring at the treads on one of my Ho Chi Minhs, I could feel the steam leak out of my attempt to stay angry with Chris about missing the party. And a chance with Laura. I tried to shift the focus, be angry with Mom, but I couldn't keep that up. I knew why she'd thrown the fork. I understood. As long as Chris was here, he was safe. Staying for Thanksgiving would be great, but really it was the staying that mattered. The being home, away from the danger, away from the possibility that one of those casualty reports could include him. Away—far away—from the knock on the door when some stateside colonel, hat in hand, might come to tell us the last thing we wanted to hear.

But I knew what Dad was saying, too. Maybe Mom couldn't— or wouldn't—imagine the tug Chris must feel from over there all the while he was home, but I could. And I knew that if I were Chris, I couldn't really enjoy that terrific meal. And even if I did, I'd feel guilty.

Christ, this whole fucking mess had everyone fighting. Just the previous week in school, Terry Cavanaugh and this other kid, Bobby Darnell, got into it but good. I didn't catch the whole thing, but it sounded like Bobby was talking up his brother Ken's escapades, how many VC he'd killed, that sort of thing. I heard Terry shout something about certain people having messiah complexes, thinking they could go over there and save the world, which of course set Bobby off, and we had to pull them apart.

"Easy, man, easy," I mumbled into Terry's ear as Kevin Dodge helped me hold on to him and back away. Two other guys were taking charge of Bobby. We barely got things quiet before a teacher or somebody saw, so no one got in trouble, but it just goes to show you. War is war, and it spreads.

That little episode got me thinking about loyalty. I mean, Terry was trying real hard to be loyal to his brother Ron, but Ron—hell, he fucking skipped the country! So guys like Chris and Ken, they went over, and damn it, Chris was no martyr. He didn't think he was Jesus Christ. And I don't think Ken thought he was, either. But to be honest, I was a little angry at Ron, and maybe even at Terry for sticking up for him. But I was also mad at Chris for going.

And before too long, I'd be mad at Dad for making him go. This was something I didn't allow myself to think about. Not even that night, meditating on the tire-tread sandals. But now? Now I do.

# Chapter 2

The whole time Chris was home, we all kept pumping him for stories. Sometimes he really didn't want to talk, and Mom would shoo us away. Other times he talked, and he did his best to walk a line between satisfying Dad's thirst for guts and glory and Mom's reluctance to think of her favorite child in danger. He was always good at that—keeping everybody satisfied. So he tried to let us know what his day-to-day life was like and tried not to paint too grim a picture.

Over Thursday dinner he told us about this one mission his squad got sent on, where they had to be lookouts for some other guys sweeping for mines. The VC are always coming into areas where the mines have just been found, and replanting them.

There were a couple of guys, not Chris's squad, walking down this dirt road, swinging metal detectors around and watching for spots that looked like they'd just been dug. Behind them there was an armored dump truck, loaded with dirt, that was retrofitted to drive backward, and the driver was way up high above the truck in a special little cab. This truck followed the two minesweeping guys a couple hundred feet behind, and some guys in Chris's squad were way out in front of the minesweepers, and some stayed well behind the truck, and they were all watching for snipers. The idea was that if the minesweepers missed anything and the truck ran over it, the truck would set it off. The dirt was to keep the truck from getting blown far, and the driver was supposed to get thrown to safety from the cab.

Chris said the trouble with this plan was that the driver was so far above ground that unless he landed in water, he was probably gonna get hurt pretty bad. So, as Chris put it, it took a special kind of guy to drive the thing. Chris walked behind the truck one day and in front for two days, and they never saw any snipers. But he said the driver was always stoned. I guess you'd kind of have to be.

Mom didn't like that story, because it worried her that someone Chris might have to depend on was high. In more ways than one! So the only stories he could really tell her were about life in base camp or when they were away on a mission but weren't fighting, and even then he could talk about only the most benign stuff. Nothing about what they did to get beer, or koon sa, and sure as hell nothing about girls.

But when she wasn't around, or if us guys were hanging out in the backyard trying to pretend it wasn't cold, Dad wouldn't let him get away without at least some of the gory details. He'd ask, "How many men did you lose in that encounter?" or "How bad were that man's wounds? Did he make it?" And always Dad wanted to know, "Did you hold?"

Did they hold the ground. Was Chris King of the Mountain. And how many friends did he lose.

One story was about when they were on their way someplace—I forget where—in this big truck. They were driving along this road that was typical, all dirt and not very wide, going through an area of rice paddies with farmers working in them. The farmers had tools and baskets and sometimes hats that they would set on the ridges between the paddies when they weren't using them. But then about a mile farther Chris said they noticed that the tools and baskets were there, but no farmers. Chris said no one ever left things like that; tools were too scarce. So the farmers had to have left because something was very wrong.

As it turned out, the VC had mortared the area to frighten people who lived in a nearby village. Chris's group didn't figure this out, though, until they got to the village, where they noticed mortar holes in the ground, and there was one old man there who hadn't fled. He told them the attack had happened about half an hour ago.

Chris said his friend Mason would sometimes point out how the spookiest part of being in a situation like that was that no one really knew what to do. The guy driving the truck didn't know any more about what might be wrong than the guys he was driving, didn't know what it might mean to them, or what to do about it. They had no guidance, so all they could do was look to the ranking officer and pray like hell that he had a good head on his shoulders.

My favorite stories were the ones where Chris and one or more of the other guys took care of each other. Made sure everyone was okay, that they all got out of whatever they were in. Chris told a few of these stories, and they usually included his friend Mason.

There was this one story he told Dad and me on Sunday afternoon. Mom was home putting dinner together, and the three of us drove off to this fishing spot on Parson's Lake, where we'd go in the summer. It was too cold to sit outside, so we stayed in the car. Dad cracked his window so he could smoke his pipe, and I was in the backseat straining to watch Chris's face while he talked. I couldn't see much more than a silhouette, there was so much light coming through the windshield from across the water. His voice was flat, and from what I could see of his face he wasn't allowing much expression to show there, either. He was looking almost but not quite at Dad, his gaze falling someplace off to the side of the car.

"We were away from base on a mission. It was night, and we'd made camp. There was jungle on one side of us and rice paddies on the other, and just as we were getting ready to turn in we heard the shrill sound of incoming. A whistle, then boom. And the boom was really close. But we couldn't tell where it was coming from. So all we could do was wait. And then there was another. It landed just past the edge of our camp. This time we could tell it came from the direction of the rice paddies, so we grabbed what we could and headed for the jungle.

"We hadn't come this way, we'd come up the road, so we had no idea how bad this section of jungle would be. Booby traps, mines, that kind of thing. It's hard enough to watch for trip wires even in the daylight. And from the sounds around us, I could tell some of our guys were setting off traps. There's booms and screams and shouts, the place is a hellhole. We figured out later, those who survived, that the VC must have set the place up and then fired on us to scare us into this patch. They never came across the rice paddies. They didn't come anywhere near the trap.

"But we didn't know this yet. So I'm crawling, feeling with my hands. Mason is with me, but he has this thing about snakes and won't crawl unless he's ordered to. So he's sort of bent over, following next to me. Both of us are trying to use the light from mortars and rockets to watch ahead, make sure we aren't touching anything we shouldn't. And suddenly I see something right ahead of me, something I wouldn't have seen if I hadn't been crawling, that tells me there's been activity right there. I freeze.

"Just then, someone not twenty feet from us trips a wire. There's a flash, and a scream, and he's down and silent. Mason sort of jumps, and I grab his ankle, but his other foot goes right into the area ahead, where I know there's something waiting. I just grit my teeth and hang on.

"He falls, but somehow he falls toward me and lands right next to me, but he's sliding away at the same time. It's a pit, and I know there'll be a punji stick at the bottom, probably covered with shit to make sure whoever lands on it gets thoroughly infected. 'Grab my clothes!' I yell at him. He hangs on, and I'm pulling back with everything I've got. We scramble, clawing at the ground, and by the time I've pulled him up next to me the shelling has stopped.

"We'll never know whether it was necessary to run for cover, 'cause we never found out how many VC were there. Too many guys had been killed or wounded to return an attack, so the radio guy called for a dustoff, which means Hueys would come in to take out the wounded. Mason and I found our way to the edge of the jungle with the other guys who made it, ready to provide some cover from the VC across the paddies if we needed to. We took cover by the side of the road while a couple of Hueys landed behind us. One of them was just lifting off when we heard this grinding, scraping noise. Mason and I wheeled around, not knowing what the hell might be happening, and we saw the rotor blades had come off one of the Hueys; the Jesus nut had let go."

This was too much for Dad. He didn't often interrupt Chris, but he asked, "What the hell's a Jesus nut?"

"It holds the whole rotor mechanism to the top of the helicopter. If it comes off when you're in flight, only Jesus can help you. But the copter had just started to lift off, so the guys inside weren't hurt badly—except for the ones they were supposed to be carrying off, of course. Anyway, the blades had been moving, so they had some momentum, and when they went sliding off they were still going around. The blade piece rose into the air a little, drifted sideways and came down like a twirly toy. Then it hit this guy and took his head right off."

We were all silent for several seconds. Then Chris said, "Thank God it was dark." I knew what he meant; he wouldn't have wanted to see that too clearly.

Chris turned in the seat so he was facing out the other way. I couldn't see his face now. We sat there, maybe a minute, and then Chris got out of the car. As soon as his door slammed I started to open mine.

"Paul." Dad's voice was sharp. "Let your brother have a minute."

Sometimes after one of these stories I'd go someplace by myself. Maybe my room, or if I didn't want to be found, into a corner of the basement near the furnace, where it was warm enough to hang out for a while. In my mind I'd go over some of the scenes Chris had painted.

Chris had gotten an air rifle one Christmas, I think when he was ten, and although I never got one of my own he gave me his when he got tired of it. I found it and took it into the furnace corner, trying to imagine what it would be like to stalk through jungle, watching for trip wires and disturbed brush, anything that might give away the location of a mine or a booby trap or a pit with a punji stick in it. The air rifle became a machine gun.

Chris had told us that a machine gun isn't a rifle. You don't really take aim with it, and when you fire it's a burst of five rounds at once in the general direction of where you think your target is. There's this arc of light when you shoot, because every fifth round has magnesium on it, and it burns real bright so you can see where the rounds are going, even in daylight. The thing is, you want to pelt the area with as many bullets as possible.

In country, Chris said you often couldn't really see the enemy, you just sort of knew where they probably were. And they weren't likely to sit still while you fired at them. So this technique of raining bullets over a whole area, creating a sort of death zone where nothing could survive, was supposed to have more effect.

But Chris said you'd never know it was effective from the number of VC they kept seeing. It was like when you shot one, several more sprang up out of the ground. So one evening I sat there, pointing the old gun across to the other side of the basement, and I imagined what it would be like to fire hundreds of bullets in a few minutes at an enemy that kept growing in number. And every time I fired, there were more and more enemies swarming toward me.

I didn't last very long. I started shaking, dropped the gun, and backed farther into the corner.

I guessed Chris must have lost quite a few friends by now, trying to hold this ground.

Mom made an executive decision about Chris's time with us. Maybe she couldn't stop him leaving when he was supposed to, but she could move Thanksgiving if she wanted to. He'd arrived home on Wednesday, and he had to leave on the Tuesday before Thanksgiving. So Monday night was Thanksgiving in our house.

Mom declared that I was staying home from school, and she tried to get Dad to close the store, but he wouldn't. He said too many people were contemplating giving pets at Christmas, and lots of them started shopping early for all the stuff that went with the animals, or buying books to figure out what pet they wanted to buy.

It was fun, actually. Mom let Chris and me do some of the cooking. I cut up the stuffing bread and the onions and things that go into stuffing, while Chris made the pie. He'd always been good at pies, and Mom could never figure it out. "I didn't teach him much," she'd say. "If I had, my crust would be as flaky as his!"

It felt a little like old times. I always liked this best, when it was just the three of us. When I was younger, I used to imagine that Chris was my dad, and he and Mom were married. They always got along so well, you know? Laughing and making silly jokes. Chris always laughed at Mom's jokes, and she made more of them when Dad wasn't there.

I hope this doesn't sound like my folks didn't get along. They were fine, for the most part. It's just that when Dad wasn't around and Chris was, Mom was almost like a girl. She was fun and silly and giggly, and Chris was somewhere between her best friend and her boyfriend. And when they teased me, which was their way of including me since I couldn't always keep up with their joking, it felt good.

So we put dinner together, the three of us. We took our time, since Dad had said he wouldn't be home any earlier than a usual work night. But he surprised us and showed up at three-thirty. He'd asked his assistant manager, Carol Burns, to come in on her day off so he could spend more time with Chris.

"Where's this turkey dinner you promised me?" he bellowed, and he pretended he'd told us to expect him early when he knew he hadn't, and he strutted around despite his limp, acting like he was annoyed and making silly faces. Mom put him to work polishing glasses and setting the table. He refused to iron the tablecloth, so Chris did that. Then Mom shooed us all into the living room while she finished things up.

"How about another one of your war stories, son?" he asked Chris, handing him a beer. I was thinking we'd probably heard enough of those, but obviously Dad wanted more.

Chris sat on the floor, his back to the sofa, and took a swallow. "You know, I have to go back there tomorrow. I'd rather not think about it. I'd much rather hear one of your stories. Something crazy somebody bought for their dog or their cat."

Dad sat back and looked thoughtful for a minute, and then he nodded, taking a mouthful of beer. "Okay, okay. Here's a silly one. You know how we have those books about how to raise everything from bearded dragons to pythons? Well, this one woman brought in her parrot and headed right for the books. Beautiful bird; bright green mostly—I think it was a Yellow-collared Macaw—nodding its head up and down and looking all around like it was taking everything in. She had it on her shoulder, and it was tethered to this leash she was holding, and you know our policy about having your pets on a leash being okay. So in she comes. She's saying, 'Einstein, don't you remember being here last time? That nice young girl gave you a treat, remember?' I think she was talking about last summer, when Martha was working. You remember her, Paul?"

I nodded; I'd worked in the store for the first time last summer, and I sure remembered Martha. She was about to head off to college in the fall. Long dark hair, deep brown eyes, and a body that wouldn't quit.

"Anyway, as you know, when one of the millet packets breaks open, we hold the stuff aside for the parakeets we sell. But Martha must have given Einstein some. So Einstein is back, bringing that lady with him." Dad chuckled at his own joke. "She marched right over to the books, looked through them for a minute, and then picked one up and opened it. She held it up to the bird. 'What do you think, Einstein? Is this the one you wanted?' He steps back and forth on her shoulder a few times, side to side, you know? Which she took for no!" He laughed and looked at Chris.

I looked at Chris, too. He seemed for all the world to be paying attention to Dad. Any casual observer would have been fooled. And I think Dad was fooled. But I wasn't. Dad went on.

"So she says, 'Okay, then, is this it?' And she picks another one up, and his head bobs up and down. And she says, 'Oh, good! We've found it.' And she marches right up to the checkout counter with it!" He was laughing too hard to take a swallow from the bottle he'd raised toward his face, and he slapped his thigh. I was still watching Chris, who was doing his best to smile. Dad took a swig at last and then said, "And do you know, that book wasn't about birds at all? It was about spiders!"

Now, personally, I thought this was the funniest part of the whole story, but Dad sank back into his recliner, satisfied. He sighed, shook his head, and drank some more beer.

After a bit Chris asked for another story, and Dad rambled on about a few things. I could tell he really wanted to hear more war stories, and I could also tell Chris was struggling with something. Maybe trying not to think about the war, like he'd said. It was a relief when Mom finally announced the turkey was ready to be carved, and Dad heaved himself up and went in to do his husbandly duty. I watched Chris until he realized I was looking at him.

"You okay, kid?" he asked.

"I was gonna ask you that."

He looked away, lifted his bottle and drank, and he didn't say anything else until we were called to the table.

Dinner was weird. That's the best word for it. Right from the start, when Mom made us all say grace. We hadn't done that since I was twelve, maybe? I was all ready to dig in, fork stabbed into a thick slice of white meat.

Her voice sounded almost eerie. "Let us bow our heads in a prayer of Thanksgiving."

From the blank look on everyone else's face, I was guessing she took all of us by surprise. But we bowed our heads, and she went on.

"Merciful Lord, thank you so much for allowing Chris to be home with us, even for a few days. Please watch over him and protect him as he leaves us again, even as he fights to protect the freedom we all enjoy. Thank you for this family and all the comforts you have given us. Thank you for the bounty of this meal and for your love. Amen."

We all mumbled something that sounded enough like "amen" to satisfy Mom, I guess, 'cause she was beaming this smile all around the table when I looked up. I'm sure her intentions were great, but I couldn't help feeling a little spooked. It didn't stop me from eating, but I think we all felt—I dunno, maybe constrained after that little display of religious fervor. I could tell Dad was holding himself back from what he wanted, which was to talk about the war. Chris, of course, had come to the table already in a weird mood, and maybe I had too, because of him. Mom obviously could tell something was wrong with Chris, but she didn't know what—or what to do about it. I was just trying to keep my head down. It felt like shooting of some kind was gonna happen sooner or later, at some point and for some reason I couldn't predict because I didn't know what was going on. But nothing happened.

Chris helped Mom clear the table, Dad went in the other room and turned on the TV, and I gathered the tablecloth and linen napkins together. I was on my way to the laundry room, all this cloth crumpled into my arms, when I saw Chris and Mom, alone together in the kitchen, get into this fierce hug. It was at that point that I decided the weirdness at the table must have been because Chris was leaving tomorrow, and everyone knew what that meant. It meant he had to go back to hell, and we had to stay here and worry about him. The reprieve of having him home had almost made things worse.

When I got back from the laundry room, Mom was alone in the kitchen, and no one was in with Dad. I debated: TV with Dad or cleanup duty with Mom? Wherever Chris was, I figured he'd probably come back to the kitchen. So that's where I went.

"Can I help?"

Mom didn't look at me right away; I think she was blinking tears out of her eyes. She turned a smile on me that was trying too hard to be a smile. "Sure, Paul. Why don't you help separate the things that go into the dishwasher from the things that don't? Watch out for those turkey skewers; they're vicious."

*As bad as punji sticks?*

Chris was gone a long time. At one point I peeked out to see if he'd gone into the living room too quietly for me to hear, but Dad was alone in front of the boob tube, watching some cop show. Finally I couldn't stand it. "Where's Chris?"

Mom took a deep breath. "He's in your father's den, dear. He said he had to make a phone call."

I scowled. "Who would he call?"

"Whom, Paul. Whom would he call. I'm sure I don't know. Maybe a girlfriend?" She kind of giggled; it sounded weird.

I blinked, feeling stupid. "Does he have a girlfriend?"

She stopped midway between counter and sink, her hands cupping bits of turkey she'd just wiped up. "I guess I don't know of anyone special." Her smile wobbled. "But you know he wouldn't be likely to tell his mother!" She tried a laugh, but it wasn't very convincing.

We finished our cleanup, the machine tethered to the faucet and churning away, and I had gone with Mom into the living room, pretending to watch Dad's show but really just waiting for Chris to make an appearance—his last one before tomorrow, the day he'd leave us again. It became more and more obvious that he wasn't with us, but nobody seemed like they dared say anything about it. *Shit. His last night, and he can't spend it with us? But then if he's gonna be all morose, like he was at dinner, do I want him out here?*

Yes, damn it; I did. I got up. I walked really quietly down the dark hall toward Dad's den. The door was closed and there was just a little light coming from underneath. Standing there, ears straining, I tried to figure out if Chris was talking or listening or not on the phone at all. Every so often I could hear this odd sound, almost like a sharp intake of breath, and then silence. And then there'd be a kind of strangled noise. And then silence. I lifted my hand maybe three times, wanting so much to knock or turn the handle, anything to get that door out from between us, but something held me back. Finally I tiptoed away and went back to the waiting room. I mean, living room.

I don't know what we were watching, because my eyes weren't focused on the screen and my ears were tuned to any noises behind me that weren't made by the dishwasher. It was an eternity, and in fact it was nearly ten o'clock, before Chris finally came in. He sat next to Mom on the couch, put his arm behind her shoulders, and leaned his head toward her. Nobody said anything. My throat started to get tight, and my eyes were burning. It was a minute before I recognized the signs for what they were and I focused on not crying. I wanted to look at Chris, to burn his features into my mind, but I didn't dare.

He went to bed before I did. He was gonna have to leave, as he put it, at oh-dawn-thirty tomorrow morning so he could get his transport back without being AWOL. I went upstairs maybe half an hour after him, brushed my teeth, and almost opened his door. It was all the way closed, and I wanted in. I wanted to see him, to hear him say nothing was wrong, to have him tell me he'd be back in no time at all. And I stood there maybe ten seconds before I admitted that I couldn't do that. I wasn't some eight-year-old kid needing to have his tears brushed away by big brother. I went to my room.

I lay there for a while, listening to the sounds of my folks getting into bed themselves, before I snapped off the light and turned onto my side. But I wasn't ready to fall asleep, so I turned onto my back again. Hands behind my head, I thought about jerking off, but I couldn't even work up the energy for that. It was like everything in me was focused on the room on the other side of this wall. Just beyond this very wall, the one behind my head, was Chris's bed, with Chris in it, the same Chris who might go over there and die before I ever saw him again.

Then I decided I was being morbid, and ridiculous. I nearly laughed; hell, maybe *he* was jerking off. This actually cheered me up a little, and I shifted my position so my head was closer to the wall. Again I almost laughed, because I could hear something. He was definitely doing something in there. I got onto my knees and pressed my ear to the wall.

He was crying. It sounded muffled, like he was sobbing into his pillow, but he was definitely crying. Gut-wrenching sobs. I pulled away and stared at the wall I couldn't really see in the dark. *What the fuck? Chris? The brave soldier, the guy who pulls his buddies out of punji pits, is in there sobbing like a baby?*

But no; it wasn't like a baby. There was way too much pain in it for that. He wasn't crying for his bottle. It sounded like he was crying for his life.

I threw myself onto my stomach and covered my head with a pillow. I didn't want to hear this. I couldn't stand the thought of him in there, crying like that. My mind reached back over the last week, going through his stories, trying to come up with something he'd said, or something he'd left unsaid, that might account for this. He hadn't overtold anything, hadn't made himself out to be this big hero, and nothing he'd described made him sound like a coward. He'd done some heroic things, he'd done some crazy things. He'd helped his friends, they'd helped him. He'd almost made some of it sound like fun, or at least like it made for stories that would be good in years to come. It sounded like he'd made some friends who would be his friends until he died.

*Until he died. Is that it? Is he afraid of dying?*

Would I be? Would I lie in there sobbing the night before I had to go back to a place that was hot and muggy and full of bugs and bullets and bombs and beer and koon sa? Would I go back to a place where I didn't know whether the Vietnamese girl I'd just met wanted to cut my throat? Or, really, when what I knew was that she did? Chris didn't talk like that, he didn't tell stories where the worst part was like some dark secret that could kill you, but I'd heard them, and I knew they were true.

*Why hadn't he told stories like that?*

Thinking back again, none of it had that fog of not-knowing about it. None of it except maybe that comment from Mason, about when something unexpected happens and you just don't know what to do. Sometimes in Chris's stories he wasn't sure *where* the enemy was, but he always knew *who* they were. There were no shades of gray. He didn't talk to us about killing villagers, or wondering who was a spy. But I heard about that stuff, on TV and in newspapers. Why was it just occurring to me now that Chris never talked about that part of it? Maybe we were all just so glad to see him that we took whatever he gave us and accepted it, face value. Like we believed what he wanted us to believe.

And here was the proof. I was willing to bet anything that if I went into my folks' room and told them their precious first-born was in his bed crying his eyes out, they'd tell me I was full of shit and to shut the hell up! Okay, that's a little dramatic, but essentially it was right; they wouldn't believe it. Or, they would refuse to believe it.

But it was real. I could hear it, or I imagined I could, right through my pillow. It was not the Chris that Chris wanted us to see, but it was real. I turned so that my feet were near the wall, my head toward the foot of the bed. I pulled my covers around until I'd made enough of a nest that I thought maybe I could sleep that way, not hear what was happening in Chris's room, not have to know what I didn't want to know. What he didn't want me to know.

But it was no good. Before I knew my feet had hit the floor, they had carried me into the hall and stopped in front of Chris's door. *Should I knock or just go in? Should I give him a chance to get himself together or ambush him in his disgrace?*

Was it disgrace?

*What else could it be? I mean, my God! If I ever acted like this, and Dad heard me? Man, I don't even want to think what he'd say, how he'd make me feel. But Chris gets away with it? After making us believe what a brave grunt he is?*

I didn't want to be angry with him. Really I didn't. This was his last night at home before going back to a place nobody in their right mind wanted to be, and I wanted to be nice to him. But I wanted him to be nice to me, too, and he was just holed up in there disgracing himself. Getting away with something I would catch hell for, just because nobody would believe it of Chris.

I opened the door and stepped in.

Then I shut it behind me quickly, afraid the sounds would get out. In my heart of hearts, I really didn't want to expose Chris, to do anything that would tarnish his image. I loved his image. Hell, I worshipped his image, and that's partly why I was angry. He was destroying it.

He didn't even know I was there. The light from the back-yard spotlight Dad insists on leaving on all night was just enough to let me see that Chris was huddled under the covers, and just as I had imagined, his head was under a pillow. His arms were clamped down on either side; it's a wonder he could breathe. I stood there as long as I could tolerate it, listening to something ugly and painful working its way up through his body until it came out in the vicinity of his face, and then I called his name.

"Chris?" It was softer than I'd expected, and he didn't hear me. I tried again.

I heard a gasp. His body jerked, and he lifted onto his elbows. He made another gasping noise. It was like he couldn't speak.

*Now that I'm here, what am I gonna do about it? What can I say? What do I want him to say?* I almost turned to leave.

He was breathing oddly, like you do when you've been crying so hard you can't breathe normally, but he managed to say, "Paul?"

"What is it?" It was all I could think of.

He worked his way into a sitting position and ran the fingers of one hand into his hair. I reached over to flick the bedside lamp on. He rasped, "No! No. Don't."

*Now what?* But he hadn't asked me to leave. So I felt my way across to where I knew his desk was, and I lifted the chair and walked it over near the bed. I sat down.

"What the hell's wrong?" I tried again, in a whisper. He ran a hand over his face and groped for the tissue box, blowing his nose as quietly as possible. I added, "I mean, besides the fact that you have to go back. Is that it?" I don't know what I was hoping. In the silence I thought, did I want that to be "it"? What would it mean, if that were it? And did I want to know what else it could be?

Finally he whispered, "No."

But then nothing. I felt a need to fill the gap. "So it's not that you're thinking the odds are stacking up against you? It isn't that the longer you're over there, the more likely something is to happen?" It was what I'd been thinking.

I could barely see him shaking his head. He snuffled a few times and then said, "No. That's not the way it works. It's not like the real world, the world where real people live. We aren't normal human beings over there. We live in the jungle, we go into the villages, and we kill people. Normal human beings don't do that. Normal human beings die over there. They're the ones in body bags." He snuffled almost violently.

"So you're not human anymore? Is that it?" I sounded sarcastic to my own ears. It wasn't what I wanted, but what the hell was he getting at?

"I thought I wasn't. I thought I was gonna make it." He took a deep breath, and it shook his whole body. "So, I guess you're partly right. Because I'm scared, Paul. I've been scared ever since I signed up, but tonight I'm scared shitless. I have nothing"— and his voice tightened so much it trailed away for a few seconds before he went on—"nothing to keep me alive anymore."

I shook my head at him. "That doesn't make any sense."

His whisper was angry, sharp. "I'm saying it's over! I've got nothing! There's nothing to hold on to anymore! And when that happens to you, you either lose your mind or your life or both. I've seen it happen, over and over."

"What's over? Nothing's changed, has it? The place is still there, the war's still going on, your squad is still . . ." I stopped when I heard him gasp again, like he was trying not to sob. "What? Will you tell me what you're talking about?"

He took a minute to recover. "You don't want to know."

I stood up, hovering over him. "Will you knock it off? You're in here sobbing like a baby, and now you're telling me you have nothing to live for, and I don't want to know?" I felt like suddenly our roles were reversed. He was the kid brother, and I was the one who had the right to make him account for himself. He covered his face with his hands, and I waited. I stood there, half bending over him, my eyes boring holes into his head so that maybe I could see what the fuck was going on in there.

But he didn't speak. I realized that probably he couldn't; the way he was breathing made it seem like if he spoke, he'd scream. So I sat down again.

*What's changed? If something really has changed, wouldn't it have to be sudden? Recent?* I said, "Who were you talking to? In the den? Who'd you call?"

He started breathing in and out really quickly, like he was hyperventilating. God, there was something really, really wrong. This was *so* not Chris. I was getting worried now. I got up and sat beside him on the bed, and when I put my hand on his shoulder he trembled, shuddering all through.

He said, "He's gone. He's gone, and I'm alone."

"Who? Who's gone?"

It was like he could barely say the name. "Mason."

"Mason, the guy in your squad?"

Chris pulled away from me and reached for more tissues. He grabbed a handful of them and held them over his face. He took several deep breaths and then said, "I loved him."

I wasn't sure what that meant—loved, past tense. "He's dead?"

Chris nodded. "It was his parents I called. He had asked me to, while I was stateside, and I put it off until tonight. And when I called them, they said"—and he had to get his breath under control again—"he'd been killed. While I've been home. He's gone."

Shit. Well, this would put the fear of God into a guy. But— Chris's reaction was still confusing me. All I could think of to say was, "That sucks."

We sat there for nearly a minute, me desperate to think of something helpful to say, him still trying to get himself in hand and not doing very well. Then, again, he said, "I loved him."

"You said that. I get it."

"I don't think you do."

Now I was getting angry again. "What's that supposed to mean?"

"Paul, I loved him. I mean, I really loved him. And he loved me. We—I'm . . . gay."

I didn't know I stood up. All I knew was I wasn't on the bed anymore. The three feet between us turned into thirty. My voice hoarse, I said, "You're shittin' me!" I wheeled away from him, paced across the room and back two, three times, I'm not sure. I was giving him time, time to take it back, time to say he was kidding, time to do anything that would undo what he'd just told me. I stopped in front of him, looked at the wall somewhere over his head, and asked, "What the fuck am I supposed to do with that?"

It wasn't a question for him. It wasn't a question he could answer. It was for me, but I couldn't answer it, either. I don't know where he was looking; I couldn't look at him. He took a ragged breath and said, "You hate me."

I backed up, nearly knocking the chair over. *Do I hate him? Do I hate Chris, my hero, my big brother? Do I hate the guy who's been the buffer between me and my dad's disappointment that I'm not like Chris?*

I walked toward the door. I wanted to get out, and I couldn't leave. Finally I leaned against the frame with both hands. Wasn't it just the other night I was lying in my room, wishing I could think of something bad Chris had done so I could be mad at him? Be careful what you wish for; isn't that how the warning goes? Well, here it was. Wasn't Chris *asking* me to hate him, really? Wasn't he giving me reasons with both hands? On one, there was the fact that he was sobbing and moaning in fear, and on the other was the fact that he—I couldn't even bring myself to *think* the word. But did I hate him? With something like fury, I realized I was about to cry. Me! I kept the tears at bay with words. I turned toward him.

"All my life, you've been the one. The good son. The shining boy. The one I was supposed to look up to. I've always come in second, always asking myself, 'Why can't I be more like Chris?' Should I be like you now? Should I want boys?"

"Stop it!"

I didn't want to stop it. I felt like I was on a roll, like I was about to say everything I'd wanted to say all my life, and finally he'd given me permission. Or at least an excuse. "I won't stop it. You're supposed to be the perfect son. And now I find out that not only are you a frightened sissy, but you're a queer! *This* is what I'm supposed to look up to? *You?* My God!"

I had walked away from the door toward the window, and what light there was shone on his face. For some reason I still don't understand, my knees buckled, and I fell onto the floor. And then I felt Chris's arms around me. Half of me didn't want him touching me. The other half, the half that won, reached my arms around him, too. But almost immediately, by some silent agreement, we let go. We sat cross-legged on the floor with him leaning his back against my shoulder.

"I'm so sorry," he said. "I didn't ask for this. I didn't want this. I can't help it."

"It's okay," I lied, wanting it to be true, knowing it wasn't.

We sat for a while in silence, and then he said, "Paul? I need to ask you . . . I need . . . Please, Paul. Please. Don't tell anyone."

I knew what he meant. I nodded. "Do you think you ever will? Tell?"

"I won't get a chance."

"What? Why not?"

About twenty heartbeats went by. "I don't think I'll be coming back."

"Bullshit. Bullshit, Chris. Goddamn it, don't talk like that. Just because Mason . . ." My voice trailed off. "Somebody else dying has nothing to do with whether you're coming back. You've lost other friends, right? Maybe they didn't mean the same to you, but lots of guys have died. That doesn't mean you will. Lots of other guys come home."

He didn't answer. And I didn't know what else to say. We sat there like that, maybe five more minutes. Then he said, "You've got school tomorrow."

"Fuck school."

"If you get a chance to do this, if the war's still going on? Don't join. Don't go. Do anything you have to do, but don't go over there." He pulled away and turned toward me. "Do you hear? And don't let Dad push you. Don't let his own frustrated ambitions force you into something like this. Don't try to live his life for him. Are you hearing me, Paul?"

I wasn't sure what to say. "Did he do that?"

"Just don't, okay? Don't do it. If you have to go to Canada, you go to Canada." His voice was getting louder, and I was afraid our folks would hear.

"Quiet!" I was already protecting his secret.

"This is important. Tell me you understand. Tell me you won't let him do that to you. Tell me—"

"All right, all right! I won't go."

He was quieter now. "I mean it, Paul. Don't let anything or anybody force you over there."

"I won't. I promise."

"And the other promise? Will you make that one, too?" I wanted to say what promise, but I knew. I must have waited too long, 'cause he said, "Will you?" I nodded. "Say it. Please."

"I won't tell Mom and Dad what you told me tonight." It was the only way I could say it. And there was no way not to say it.

He took a breath, like he had something else to say, but then he kind of deflated. Buried in my own thoughts, I didn't react. My brother was going away to die. My hero was already dead.

# Chapter 3

I can barely stand to remember what I felt the next day, when Chris left. I hadn't slept at all, I'd just lain there all night feeling like those SADEYE balls had all been shot directly at me. I had the pain in my chest and my gut to prove it.

I went over in my head all the things that might have happened to make Chris gay. Was Mom too affectionate toward him, and it hadn't happened to me because he was her favorite? Did Dad push him too hard, and Chris decided that being gay would be a quiet, internal way to fight back? Did it have anything to do with being over there with all those guys, girls hardly ever available, and being—you know—in his prime? Was it something Mason had talked him into, and it was better than nothing, and now Chris just thought he was gay because he'd—I don't know, done stuff with Mason and it had felt good?

It didn't make any sense. I had to hold myself back several times from running into his room and telling him to go AWOL, to go to Canada right now, I'd go with him, and we'd figure out how he could change back again. But I knew he'd never do that. He'd never back out, he'd never leave his squad like that, or go back on something Dad expected him to do.

Dad! This was all his fault. Chris had practically told me that

Dad had pressured him into signing up. But there was nothing for it now; it was done. And Chris wasn't about to undo it.

So that left me being mad at Chris for being such a goody-goody. But if he left here tomorrow, with me mad at him, and then he died . . . my mind wouldn't go there. So instead it went to a different place: Chris was wrong about being gay, and he wasn't going to die. Lots of guys came home! Some of them were missing limbs, and some of them were pretty crazy, but they came home. If only Chris could survive another few months, the war would end and he could come home for good and I could help him be normal again!

Through all of it, every imagined set of events, every possible outcome, his words echoed: "I don't think I'll be coming back."

My mind went round and round like this, all night. So in the morning, even though it was still dark, even though Chris was as quiet as he could be, I knew he was up. I knew he was in the bathroom. I watched all his motions in my mind's eye. Soaping his hair in the shower. Shaving as he stood by the sink, towel around his waist. I knew when he was back in his room, dressing—pulling on his underwear, his fatigues, his socks. Running a comb through still-damp hair. Such ordinary things. Such a fucking extraordinary day.

I lay in bed as long as I could, but when I heard him move toward the top of the stairs I sat up and swung my legs over the side of my mattress. Hands pressing on either side of me, I was ready to propel myself out there. To Chris. *Hold on to him! Hang on, don't let him go down those stairs!* My arms tensed, relaxed a little, tensed again.

And then I heard him start down, feet landing heavily with the weight of his duffle. Step. Step. Step.

*You could still get to him!*

Step. Step.

My entire face clenched, my hands tensed into tight balls. And I sat there. I sat there until the steps stopped, until I heard the duffle hit the floor downstairs.

I could smell breakfast; Mom must have got up incredibly

early, 'cause it was pancakes and bacon. Hurriedly I wet my hair, washed my face, and threw on some clothes.

As usual, I sat across the table from Chris. Dad wasn't down yet, so it was just the three of us. No joking today, though. No girlish silliness from Mom. No teasing from Chris. Every so often Mom would stand behind his chair and reach out a hand to touch his shoulder, his ear, the side of his face.

*Chris's last meal.*

It felt like we were going to a funeral. And in a way we were; but the deceased was here with us. All through the meal I threw glances at Chris. Mostly he was staring down at his plate, but I didn't dare really look at him for fear he'd raise his eyes and see me.

Dad showed up after Chris and I had finished. Or, after we had tried to finish. As good as it smelled, as good as Chris knew it would be compared to anything he'd get ever again, neither of us could get much down. Dad didn't even try. He just grabbed a mug of coffee and sat down. I think he was trying to sound cheerful, but the effect was startling and harsh.

"All set, son? Got yourself all put together for the trip?" His voice was too loud.

"Yes, sir." It was like Chris was getting into the habit again; he didn't usually call Dad "sir."

Dad saluted, and Chris did the same. He was gonna be himself, right to the end. Doing his best to keep everybody happy, to do what was expected of him. It nearly made me lose the little food I'd been able to swallow.

Chris had a cab pick him up. At first this made me mad; why couldn't Dad take a little extra time from work and drive him? But then I realized Chris probably wanted his last memories of us—and ours of him—to be here, at home, not in some crowded public place that had no meaning for him. As soon as the car arrived, Mom got Chris into this hug that I didn't think would ever end. When it did, Dad shook his hand and turned it into a kind of quick, hard hug that wasn't really a hug but was more a series of slaps on the back.

Chris and I looked at each other. He half smiled, and he

made a motion that made it seem like he was going to hug me. I stepped back quickly and my hand shot up in a salute. It was all I felt I could do. You know how in the service, even if you hate your commanding officer, or even if you think he's completely wrong about something, you still salute? It was like that. It was a sign of respect, but it felt like I was doing it at his funeral.

It was also a silent acknowledgment: I'll keep your fucking secrets, but I don't have to thank you for that honor.

His face went all stiff, and then he saluted back. Then he picked up his gear, turned, and walked out the door. I watched through the window as he got into the backseat. The slam of the car door was like a pistol shot.

For Thanksgiving, the one on the calendar, we had turkey leftovers. Mom had bought some wine, something we almost never have in the house, and she even let me have a glass of it. I can't say I liked it particularly, but I drank it; I think she was trying to pretend we could be cheerful. And Dad was doing his best, too. I was the lump. I was the one who knew Chris wasn't coming home. I was the one who knew he wasn't the man we'd all thought he was.

After dinner I went upstairs and threw the Ho Chi Minhs into the back of my closet. Then I stood in the doorway to Chris's room for maybe half an hour. Then I went into my room and pounded my pillow until I heard Mom calling up from downstairs.

"Paul? What are you doing up there? Aren't you going to come down and watch the movie with us?"

*A rerun of Peter Pan. Hell, why not? I could use a little fantasy right now.* But all the way through I kept making this connection between Wendy not being able to go home and Chris probably never coming home, and her problems seemed so pathetically unimportant compared to Chris's. Compared to mine. I just watched in glum silence. Didn't even want another piece of pie when Mom offered it.

\*   \*   \*

That Sunday, lying in bed listening to the sounds of Mom and Dad getting toast and coffee before they headed out to church, I almost got up to go with them. I felt really shitty about the way I'd let Chris leave—no hug, no handshake. So what if he was a fag? He was still my brother. And so what if he was afraid? Anyone in their right mind would be terrified of that place. Look at how I'd reacted to nothing more threatening than my own imagination that day in the basement. And here I'd let him slip away, back to the jungle to die, without even a real good-bye.

I was still thinking along those lines when I heard the car pull away from the house. Some little voice was whispering, *Get up! Go the window and watch them drive away, follow the car with your eyes as far as you can or they might never come back! If something happens it will be your fault for not being with them!*

Stupid, right? But my hands had to clench the sheet under me so that I couldn't dash to the window and watch the car disappear. Then there was silence, and this intense feeling of being completely alone.

*Damn Chris, anyway! Why did he have to burden me with his fucking secrets?* I'd had to listen to Dad for days, talking about how great Chris had looked, what a good soldier he was, with Mom adding what a handsome man he was growing into. Then Dad would go on about how bravely he was facing everything "over there." I'm surprised nobody noticed the blood dripping out of the corners of my mouth! I mean, I was biting my tongue so much, and so hard, to keep from telling them how wrong they had it. How they didn't know him at all. How I was the only one who really did.

So I lay there for a long time, feeling guilty about the way I'd treated Chris and wishing I'd gone with my folks to church, and feeling like the weight of what Chris had laid on me was what made me unable to get up and go with them.

*If I can't go to church and pray for your safety, big brother, it's your own goddamn fault.*

Like that made any sense. I pressed the heels of my hands against my eyes and held my breath to keep tears in. I missed him so much! So fucking much! And now I felt like I'd never have him back. Even if he was wrong about dying over there, if he couldn't go back to being normal I felt like he'd never be my brother again.

I tried to focus on what being gay was all about, tried to figure it out so maybe I could help undo it, but trying to think about that was like grabbing a fish underwater. I could sort of see it, and I could get close but not close enough. And sometimes I could feel it, but that was all.

What did come to mind clearly was the time Marty Kaufman and I had decided to teach this nerd a lesson. I couldn't figure out at first why my mind went there, but I guess it was an indirect way to think about something that was too uncomfortable for me to look at directly. Kind of like if you want to see a star in the sky, you have to look off to the side a little.

I was fourteen. Marty—who'd been held back in sixth grade—was fifteen, and the nerd, Anthony (a.k.a. Don't-Call-Me-Tony), was only thirteen because he'd been accelerated a grade at some point. This one year Anthony had seriously over-stepped his usual level of priggishness. He'd always been kind of a teacher's pet, always won prizes for things like spelling bees and giving the best speech, always got high marks for every-thing—especially math. And always lording it over us dummies. Or so it seemed like, anyway. Looking back, I think maybe he wasn't. I think maybe he was just trying to make us think he wasn't afraid of us, 'cause that would have been the worst.

Anyway, at the start of that school year, it didn't take him very long to let us all know that he'd been to this summer camp for math geniuses, and it became obvious real fast that this experi-ence had given him some superinflated idea of his own worth as a human being. Like because he was so smart, he was more important than the rest of us.

I suppose that if there were two kids in class who would take this the hardest, it was gonna be me, because of always feeling like the bad kid in the family, and Marty, who really was the bad kid in the family. He'd already run away like, three times? He'd been caught stealing records, he'd broken into the high school once with Kevin Dodge and they'd smashed as much glass in the chem lab as they could find, stuff like that.

Since my last name's Landon and Marty's is Kaufman, we've usually sat either next to each other or me behind him since sixth grade on. He was the sort of kid who's always thinking of new ways to get into trouble. You could usually tell when he was hatching something; his head would sink a little into his shoulders, and his light brown eyes would look at you sort of sideways from under the nothing-brown eyebrows. He wasn't too much of a threat in sixth grade—at least, not to me—but with each year he got taller and a little more threatening. And it always seemed as though his hair was just a little longer than it should be, like proving he was defying something. I sort of had to make friends with him, or it would have been hell. But I'd managed to avoid getting sucked into the worst of his schemes. Until Anthony came back from math camp.

And it was just too good. Too tempting. It was Marty's idea. I don't say that to get out of any of the blame, just to be clear that it was his genius. And it was genius.

You know that expression that goes, "It seemed like a good idea at the time"? Well, we literally kidnapped Anthony one Monday afternoon, on the way home from school. Marty had skipped out on his last class so he could go home and sneak off with his mom's car. She'd gone with a friend to a bridge party, or some such thing, and the car was there for the taking. He had a learner's permit, not the full license, but Marty wasn't one to let a thing like that stop him.

He picked me up at school, and we headed off in the direction Anthony would walk to get home. He was walking alone, par for the course; who'd walk with him? Marty slowed the car way down to roll alongside, and I rolled my window down to get his attention.

"Hey, Tony, wanna lift?"

He glared at me and then stared straight ahead. It took a few seconds, but finally he couldn't stand it, and he said, "Don't call me Tony."

"Aw, don't be so stiff. C'mon, let us give you a ride home. Whad'ya say?"

He looked hard at me, and I think we almost had him, but then he looked at who was driving. "No, thanks. I'm fine." He picked up his pace and moved ahead of us.

I fished a rope from the floor by my feet. One end was tied into a slipknot. And then I tried once more. "Anthony? You sure?"

He didn't even look at me this time. "I'm sure."

I could tell he was getting a little nervous. I rolled up my window and looked at Marty like it was now or never. He nodded and pulled a little ahead of Anthony, I jumped out and threw the rope over the kid, and then I shoved him into the back. He started screaming right away, and I almost didn't want to take the time to pick up his books, but I did. I threw them into the back, and one of them hit the side of his head. I looked to make sure he was okay, and he was staring at me, stark-raving terror on his face. At least it had shut him up.

Marty drove out to a dirt road and followed it to the edge of this field where there was a tree he was headed for. We tied each of Anthony's hands separately around the tree, and did the same with his feet. It made the rest of his body stand out, vulnerable, helpless.

Anthony was crying by this time. At first he tried pleading with us. "Please, don't. Don't do this. I never did anything to you. Please." Every so often he'd snuffle or sob. Marty and I just ignored him, and finally he gave up begging.

When we had him sufficiently trussed, we sat on the ground. Trying to look casual, I reached for a grass stalk and sucked on it. Marty looked at me and laughed. "Fuck that shit!" he said, and pulled a pack of Camels out of his shirt pocket; didn't offer me one, which was good 'cause I wouldn't have known what to do. He lit up, took a few puffs, then got up and went close enough to blow a lungful of smoke into Anthony's face. I was getting a little worried that I wouldn't be able to control Marty if he decided he wanted to do something really awful, so I tried to get him back to our program. I picked up my copy of our math book for that year.

"Hey Marty, you wanna start?"

Marty stood where he was, his nose inches from Anthony's

wet face, for another few seconds. "Yeah. Sure. Gimme the book."

He plopped down on the ground to my left and flipped the book open at random. "Okay, *Tony*, now here's the rules. I'm gonna ask you a question, and you answer. Only you won't know whether I want the right answer or a wrong answer. Paul here is gonna facilitate. Keep score. However you wanna look at it. See, before I ask you the question, I'm gonna write on this piece of paper here"—and he snapped his fingers at me so I'd give him the pen and the pad we'd brought—"either R or W. Then, if I wrote R and you give me the right answer, Paul's gonna cut through a little bit of rope with this." He leaned forward and lifted his pants leg, and strapped to his ankle was a leather sheath. He'd told me we'd have a knife, but I hadn't quite expected this lethal-looking thing. It was a dagger. As Marty lifted it out carelessly, using the same hand holding his cigarette, the late afternoon sun caught the metal and it sent this ray of light shooting toward me.

Marty went on. "If I wrote W and you give the right answer"—here he stood up and moved back over to Anthony— "I'm gonna cut away some part of your clothes." He put the cig between his lips and tossed the dagger into the air. Anthony's eyes followed it. Marty caught it and then plucked the cig out of his mouth. "In case you haven't got the full picture," he said, "if I wrote R and you give me the wrong answer, it's your clothes, not the rope. Got it?"

Anthony's eyes were locked on to Marty's. He nodded shakily, but he nodded.

Back on the ground next to me, Marty picked up the book. And he took his time browsing for just the right question. Cig back in his mouth, he ran the forefinger of his right hand down page after page, all the while toying with the dagger in his left hand. Finally he slammed the book shut and stabbed the dagger into dirt. "We don't need this," he mumbled. He picked up the pen, leaned over the pad where it rested between us on the ground, wrote "R," and asked Anthony, "What's one plus one?" He tossed the book aside.

Marty was right; we didn't need the book. The joke was going to be that Anthony had to guess whether Marty wanted the right answer or a wrong one. And, even more, it was a test to see if Anthony could bring himself to give a wrong answer to a math question.

Anthony was making a kind of squealing whining noise, like he couldn't stand the strain. Marty grabbed the dagger and stood in front of him again. "Is that calculation too tough for you, whiz kid? Y'know, my grandparents were German. There's a German word for kids like you. Wunderkind."

Anthony stopped whining. He took a couple of rasping breaths and said, "Wunderkind." He was correcting Marty's pronunciation, so the W sounded like a V, and the d on the end sounded like a t. "It's Wunderkind."

Did this kid have a death wish? Marty balanced the lit cigarette between his lips and tossed the dagger from one hand to the other a few times, dangerously close to Anthony's nose. Then, around the cigarette, he said, "That wasn't the question, asshole. Just for that, you lose a sleeve."

With his left hand he pinched up a layer of cloth at Anthony's left shoulder, sliced through it, and then started to carve through the cloth. He pulled Anthony forward so he could cut behind him, the ropes cutting into skin from the pressure. Then Marty sliced slowly down the sleeve, inch by inch, toward the hem. Thank God it was a short sleeve, or I'm not sure Anthony could have taken it. He kept squinting his eyes tight shut, and then opening them wide to watch Marty's progress, then squinting them shut again, all the while trying not to cough from Marty's smoke—probably terrified that a cough would cause Marty to cut skin.

Marty held the cut sleeve remnant in front of Anthony's face, then put it over his nose, and said, "Blow." There was panic on the poor kid's face by now, like he was afraid Marty was gonna suffocate him, and he just stared wildly.

"Blow your fucking nose, crybaby!"

Anthony did what he could, but he was having trouble getting his breath. When Marty was satisfied, he pulled the cloth away, laid it on top of Anthony's head, and rubbed the snot into his hair. Marty left the cloth there, a corner covering one of Anthony's eyes.

Back on the ground again, dagger stabbed into dirt and cigarette in his left hand, Marty resumed his role as inquisitor. "Now, Wunderkind," he said, pronouncing it the same way he had the first time, "what's the answer?"

Anthony whimpered, sobbed once or twice, and finally whispered, "Two."

"Eh? Speak up, Tony. I can't hear you. What was that you said?"

Anthony tried to take a deep breath and obviously failed, but he managed to say, "Two," a little louder.

Marty sat back, took another puff of the cig, observed Anthony for several seconds, and then slowly reached for the dagger. After he'd dragged out the suspense as long as he could, he handed the dagger to me. "You know what you have to do."

Now, Marty had written "R" before he asked this, so I knew I was to cut some rope. I also knew that Marty was trying to make Anthony think he'd made the wrong choice and that Marty had decided to give me the honor of cutting more clothing. But I wasn't in the mood for delaying agony, so I was going to cut Anthony's right hand loose.

Before I got close to the rope, though, Marty called to me, "Not all of it, Paul. Just cut maybe an eighth of the way through. After all," and his voice was silky, "we seem to have more clothing than we have ropes. We want to be fair, don't we?"

Marty had written "R" again before I sat down, and he called out, "What's one plus two?"

Anthony gritted his teeth, probably feeling a little encouraged that Marty had kept his word on that last one and had cut rope. But the secret wasn't in the right answer. It was in the right choice. "Five."

I looked at Marty, whose face was pursed into fake disappointment. "Oh, Tony. Too bad, kid." Marty stubbed his cig out in the dirt, reclaimed the dagger from me, and moved slowly over to the tree. Anthony looked anxious but not terrified, which was probably too bad for him. Marty stared at his face, then squatted down in front of him.

"No!" Anthony found his voice. His head jerked, and the snotty sleeve fell to the ground.

"Ha!" Marty shouted. "Wrong answer again!" He grabbed a handful of cloth right over Anthony's groin, and the gasp I heard told me that Marty had also grabbed a handful of flesh. Very, um, sensitive flesh. He pinched his fingers together hard, working the cloth slowly away from what was undoubtedly Anthony's dick, and then he lifted the dagger.

Anthony wasn't whimpering any longer. He was crying, now, crying out, sobbing and begging. "Please! Please don't! Stop it! What do you want?"

And to my surprise, Marty stopped. He let go of Anthony, lowered the arm with the dagger, and stood up. "You're hard as metal in there, Tony. Do you know that? Your puny little dick is all excited. I think it's enjoying this."

Anthony's eyes widened and his mouth hung open. "No!" was all he could say. "No!"

"Oh, but I think it is. Just look." Marty stepped back and to one side. "Paul, do you see that?"

And Marty was right. Anthony had a boner. There was no denying it. Marty leaned toward him. "Tony? Is there something you haven't told us?" Anthony just shook his head, desperate to understand, probably willing to do anything Marty said if it would get him out of this. "Oh, I think there is." Marty reached forward and with the flat side of the dagger he slapped a few times at Anthony's boner. Anthony flinched with every touch. Then Marty worked the blade up and down, sliding over the bulge and along the fly, then picked at the edge of the cloth with the metal point.

I can only imagine what Anthony was going through. But I'd had enough. "Look, Marty, I think we've got what we wanted." Marty turned to look at me, and I got a hint of what he'd been boring into Anthony. It scared the shit out of me. But I couldn't let this go on. "Just shove the snot rag down his back and we'll cut him loose. We can dump him someplace he can walk home from." I was having trouble breathing, praying it didn't show. Praying Marty wouldn't realize how scared I was.

"What was it we wanted, Paul? What have we got now?" I hated the tone of his voice.

I shrugged, trying once more to look casual. "Humiliate him. Take him down a peg. Show him that just because he's smart doesn't mean he's invincible. I think we've done that." I nearly added, "Don't you?" but I wasn't sure enough of the right answer.

Marty paced slowly back and forth in front of Anthony. At least I'd got him to stop pointing that dagger at the kid's groin. "I don't know. I'm not feeling quite—what's the word? I'm sure Tony here would know. What's the word I'm not quite feeling, Tony?"

Anthony closed his eyes and fought for breath.

"Mollified!" Marty shouted, and Anthony's eyes flew open again. "I'm not quite mollified." He started laughing. "Molli-fied. Like Molly, get it? Like Moll?" He laughed some more, looked at me like I should be getting the joke. I offered a weak smile, which was all I could muster; I wasn't getting it. "Molly. The gangster's Moll. You know, kid," and Marty stopped right in front of the tree, hands on hips and dagger dangling from one hand, "I don't think I'll call you Tony ever again. I know you don't like it. So I'm going to mollify you." He threw his head back and barked out one more guffaw. "From now on, you're Moll. You're my bitch, kid."

Marty moved forward again, dagger pointing upward now, directly under Anthony's nose. "Tell me that suits you. Go on. But don't nod, or you might lose a nostril."

Anthony's eyes were crossing so hard they must have hurt, trying to see the point of that dagger. He couldn't move, and he couldn't say anything, was my guess. Marty tilted the blade so that it was pointing toward the tip of Anthony's nose now, but he pulled his hand away about a foot.

"Come on, Moll. Say that suits you." He started moving the blade forward.

Anthony's squeal started again, and just before the blade point would have met skin he whimpered, "Okay."

Marty pulled the blade back an inch. "Okay, what? Come on, you little faggot, tell me it suits you. Tell me you liked having a guy's *dagger* so close to yours. Tell me you got hard because you're queer. Say that's why I can call you Moll."

Anthony was struggling to oblige him, I think, but he couldn't quite decide what words to start with. I got up and moved over to them.

"Anthony, just nod if it's okay for Marty to call you Moll." Anthony's eyes veered over to mine, and he nodded. "Nod that it's because you're queer." I couldn't let the kid off too easy, or Marty would keep at him. He nodded again.

Marty said, "Nod because you're my bitch, faggot."

Anthony squeezed his eyes shut and, once more, nodded.

Slowly Marty lowered his arm and slid the dagger back into its sheath. He punched my arm and said, "C'mon, Paul. Let's get outta here. This kid is pathetic." He moved toward the car.

"But . . . he's still tied up. And we have to take him home."

Marty was standing beside the open driver's door. He pounded a fist on the roof. "Leave him!" he shouted at me.

There was this tense moment when we stared at each other over the car roof, and then he pounded it once more, got in, roared the engine to life, and gunned it, shooting gravel in all directions. I watched until I couldn't see the car anymore, just dust hanging in the air over the dirt road. Then I turned to the tree.

Anthony's head was hanging down, and he was sobbing quietly. He knew the worst was over, but he also knew his life was going to be hell from now on. I didn't know what to say, so I just worked at the knots, cursing Marty for disappearing with the knife. And the car. How the hell were we going to get back? And Anthony's books were in the back of Marty's car. Come to that, so were mine.

When he was free of the ropes Anthony glared at me, still crying, and ran off down the road. I guess I didn't blame him, but I'd been thinking we ought to work together to figure out the best way to get home. On the other hand, I sure as hell didn't know what to say to him.

I picked up the ropes, my math book, the pen, and the pad of paper we'd been using, and walked down the road until I found enough scrub along the side to shove all but my book into a spot where they'd be hard to see. A lot of the plants were the kind with dark, dusky green, flat leaves that smell sort of sweet and sort of sour when you touch them. I think it's called sweet fern, but I've never liked it, and now I stunk of it all up my arms.

Five minutes later I heard an engine coming up behind me. I turned and saw a light blue pickup, some guy who looked like a farmer behind the wheel. He slowed down when he came alongside me. There was a dog in the truck bed.

"Need a ride, kid?"

Hadn't I just offered a ride to Anthony? I almost said no, but I really didn't want to walk all the way home. Plus, the guy looked harmless. "Thanks," I said as I slid onto the seat and pulled the door shut.

"What're you doin' out this way, and on foot?" he asked.

I shrugged. "Horsing around with a friend. Wheelies, you know. But he got pissed about something and took off."

The guy nodded, like he'd probably done stuff like that himself. Then he jerked his chin toward the road ahead and said, "That your friend, by any chance?"

I looked up the road, and there was Anthony, shuffling along, head hanging down. Christ, I was thinking; don't stop! Please don't stop! All I said was, "My friend drove off in his car."

"His shirt's ripped." The driver pulled a little ahead of Anthony, who didn't even look up. The farmer stopped the truck, got out, and went over to him. "You okay, kid? Need a lift?"

Anthony's head came up to look at the driver, then he turned to look at the truck and saw me. He shook his head violently and shoved past the guy.

"Hey! Kid!"

Anthony started running, but he stayed on the road. The guy got back in the truck, pulled forward so he was a ways ahead of

Anthony, and got out again. I turned to watch as he took Anthony's shoulders in his hands, shook him a little, and finally threw an arm around his shoulders, propelling him toward the truck. Anthony looked as though he was trying like hell not to cry.

I was sure neither of us wanted to sit on this seat, thighs touching, after what had happened. After what I'd done. I got out. "I'll ride in the back," I said, knowing that there was a distinct possibility that Anthony would spill his guts to the farmer. I hopped into the bed and got as comfortable as I could on a burlap bag full of something, across from the dog, a Border collie, who was tied to a heavy piece of equipment.

The guy shut the passenger side door after Anthony climbed in, and then he leaned his arms on the side of the truck bed next to the dog, staring at me. "What's going on?"

*It was Marty who got me into this mess. This isn't really my problem.* "The kid's a jerk," I said, wondering even as I said it where I thought this was going to get me. "We were just teaching him a lesson. We didn't hurt him. He's fine." The guy stared at me until I had to drop my gaze. I felt heat flowing up my neck and into my face.

"Where do you live?" After I told him he said, "We're taking this kid home, and then we're taking you home. After that, you're on your own." He walked around the back of the truck to get to the driver's side, but before he opened his door he said to me, "You're a bully, you know that, kid? You can't sink much lower than that."

We bounced along the dirt road until the guy turned onto paved surface. There was another ten minutes, maybe, to Anthony's house. So I was stuck back here until then. And maybe I wouldn't even get into the cab after we dropped the kid off.

Then again, it would get me away from this dog. He kept staring at me. It was like he was saying, "Are you proud of yourself, you big, big boy?" I tried waving a hand in his face, but he barely flinched and just kept staring. In case you don't know, Border collies are about the most intelligent dogs there are. There's a joke that goes, How many Border collies does it take to change a lightbulb, and the answer is one, but he won't get to it until he's checked to make sure the wiring in the house is up to spec. Dad's joke.

It was my Dad who told me about Border collies. And German shepherds. And standard poodles. And Australian shepherds. He likes the intelligent dogs best, I think. And that one, in the truck with me, he was definitely one of the smart ones. Now he was saying, "Do you feel great? Did you get what you wanted? How are you gonna feel when you see that kid in school tomorrow? What if he's not even in school tomorrow? What will you think then? Will you be worried? How are you gonna tell your mom what you did? What will your dad do? Worse, what will Chris think?"

What will Chris think. That was the worst, the dog was right. I figured my dad would blow his top, probably lash me a few times with a belt, ground me for a month. Mom would cry and ask how could I have done such a thing. That's all same old, same old. But Chris . . .

By the time we pulled up to Anthony's the dog had read me the riot act, and I felt like a total shit. Anthony got out of the cab and ran pell-mell toward the front door of the house.

The driver called back to me, "You getting in?"

I wasn't going to. I really wasn't. But this dog was too much. It watched me as I scrambled over the side of the bed, turning its head as I went around the front where I was hoping it couldn't see me, but I had to get into the cab on the dog's side. He was looking right at me, and I could almost hear him clucking his tongue. I slammed the door and braced myself for a lecture from the dog's owner, but the guy was totally silent. He wasn't looking at me, but this silent treatment was at least as bad as the dog staring at me. Finally I couldn't take it.

"It wasn't my idea, you know." No response. "The kid isn't hurt. He's just scared. He had to be taken down a couple of pegs. He thinks he's God's gift to the world or something." Still nothing. I threw myself against the back of the seat and sulked for all I was worth.

When we got to my house he pulled into the end of the

driveway. I reached for my math book on the floor, and finally the guy broke his silence. "Whatever you bullies called him, you're worse." Maybe Anthony hadn't said much, then. But it was like this guy knew, anyway.

I slammed the cab door without looking around; that dog was probably glaring at me.

There was maybe an hour before dinner, and after I scrubbed my arms to get off as much of the sweet fern stink as possible, I spent about fifteen minutes sitting on the edge of my bed, head in my hands, trying to convince myself this wouldn't be so bad. That farmer couldn't be right. I mean, how could being a bully be worse than what we'd called Anthony? After all, it was actually illegal to be queer. Or, at least, to do anything about it. My dad had gone on at great lengths about it after that Stonewall incident in New York City, when all these homos attacked the police who had come to arrest them, or whatever it was that had happened. There was a riot, anyway.

"Of course they should be arrested!" Dad had bellowed at the time. "Disgusting people. Shouldn't be allowed. Thank the Lord *we* don't live in that modern-day Sodom."

Still, this whole episode was making me feel ashamed, and I guess I knew, really, that it was bad. Soon I was trying to calculate how long it would be before Anthony's parents called mine, and wondering whether it would be better if I told them about it first. Then I realized it would be better if Chris told them. So I went to find him.

The door to his room was shut, and I could hear he was playing this new album by Cat Stevens he'd bought recently. I knocked on the door. And waited. I knocked again, louder.

Chris's voice, sounding a little odd, yelled, "Who is it?"

"Me." *Who else would it be?* I reached for the knob and turned it, but it was locked.

"Just a minute!"

*What's he doing in there, masturbating? Would Chris* do *that?* I'd got as far in my thinking as *Don't be an idiot; of course he would. He's not dead,* when the door jerked partway open.

"What?" He looked flushed, or surprised, or something. I barely caught some motion behind him.

"I—who's in there?"

"What do you want?"

*Must be a girl! Chris has a girl in his bedroom! Oh well, sorry, brother, this can't wait.* "I really need to talk to you."

"Now?"

"Yeah. The shit's gonna hit the fan."

He kind of sighed, or something, cleared his throat, and said, "Great. Um . . . give me a minute, okay? I'll come get you in your room." He waited just long enough to be sure I'd heard him, and then he closed the door again. I headed toward my door, watching over my shoulder toward Chris's, wondering how he'd got a girl up to his room past Mom. I positioned myself where I would be technically in my room but still be able to see if anyone headed for the stairs.

I waited a good three or four minutes, but when someone did head for the stairs it wasn't a girl. It was Jim Waters, this friend of Chris's. I remembered him mostly because his family had moved here the year before, and I remembered thinking, *Who would move* to *this place?* So it wasn't a girl; too bad. But at least, I figured, I hadn't interrupted anything.

*Ha! I didn't know at the time how wrong I'd been.*

I scooted farther into my room and waited for Chris to show up. He took a couple more minutes, and I was pacing by the time he got there; I would have thought he'd just come right in when Jim left. But it gave me time to decide how to start.

"What's going on, Paul?" His voice was flat, and I could tell he was irritated.

Not having a clue at the time what had really been going on in there, I launched into my own problem. "I've done something real stupid. Really, really stupid. And I'm gonna catch hell for it. There's no way out of that."

"So . . ."

"So I need you to help me keep it from being worse than it needs to be. You know how Dad is."

"I guess you'd better tell me what it is, then." He sat down on my desk chair. And I told him. But it didn't turn out quite like I'd hoped. He sat there, silent, and at first I figured he was just letting me get the whole tale out. But the longer he didn't say anything, the more details I gave him. Finally I ran out of words.

Chris had this really awful look on his face, somewhere between "I can't believe what I'm hearing" and "I don't think I know who you are." He was silent for so long, just looking at me, that I couldn't take it. "Well?"

He stood up, and he left the room.

Dumbstruck, I followed him out and watched as he started to go back to his own room. "Hey, Chris! Are you gonna help me talk to Dad or what?"

He stood in his doorway about three seconds, looking at me, and then he closed the door. I slammed a fist against the door frame, and then I heard Dad's car pulling up. I stood at the top of the stairs, listening to the familiar phrases my folks almost always say to each other when he gets home. Tonight he added, "I've got to go back to the store after dinner, hon. Can we eat soon so I don't spend all night doing paperwork?"

I was edgy all during dinner, expecting the phone to ring any second, expecting to be hauled into the basement for a session with Dad's belt. Chris was nearly silent. He didn't speak to me at all.

At one point Mom asked him, "Chris, are you all right, dear?"

"Yeah. Just concentrating. Got a paper to write for school." But I knew he was lying. He was being quiet so it wouldn't be so obvious he wasn't speaking to me. Nobody seemed to notice that I wasn't exactly chatting up a storm, either.

No one called that night. Marty called in the morning to say he and his mom would pick me up, which I took to mean he was willing to let me have my books back. I took Anthony's as well; didn't even ask Marty. I put them in my locker until English, when I thought I might see Anthony. He was there, bruised where I'd flung his book at him, and I just set his stuff on the desk in front of him. He didn't even look at me.

No one called the next night, either. I was almost beginning to wish someone would, so I could get this over with. A couple of times I nearly told Dad myself, figuring it would be better that way, but the more time that went by, the harder that seemed. And judging from Chris's reaction I wasn't sure a lashing with the belt would be all I'd get from Dad. So I kept my mouth shut.

Chris spoke to me only when he had to. And that was another reason I almost wanted the other shoe to drop. Bad enough that this tension was going on and on, but Chris not talking to me? That was agony.

The third night, after dinner, I was sitting on my bed and trying to do some homework. The pages of my book kept swimming, and something wet fell onto my notes and blurred the ink. With kind of a shock I realized I was crying. Fourteen years old, and I was crying like some baby. I fell sideways onto my pillow and buried my face in it to muffle the sounds, and I cried. Don't know how long I was at it before I felt a hand on my arm.

It was Chris. He sat on the edge of the bed, I sat up, and he held me while I dripped all over his shoulder. "I hate myself," I stuttered. "I hate myself."

"No you don't, little brother. If you were bad enough to hate yourself, you wouldn't know you felt this bad."

I'm not really sure that made any sense, but it made me feel better. I snuffled and pulled away. Chris reached for a box of tissues and I blew my nose. Then he said, "You need to tell Anthony you're sorry."

"I can't do that. He won't even look at me."

"Write him a note, then."

"What about Marty?"

"What about him?" I was about to protest that it had been his idea, but that hadn't got me anywhere so far. When I didn't answer, Chris said, "Marty will do whatever it is Marty needs to do. It's you I care about. And you need to do this. Not for Anthony. It might help Anthony, or it might not. Do it for you."

I snuffled a few times. "I guess he didn't rat. No one's said anything."

"I guess not."

I never did tell Anthony I was sorry. After Christmas holiday that year, he didn't come back. We heard he'd gone to another school, a private school with an advanced math curriculum. That seemed best, really; he got away from me and from Marty, and he would be with other kids like him. Maybe he'd even have to admit that he wasn't the smartest kid in the world; small fish in a big pond now.

Thinking back on this whole incident, I'm amazed it didn't occur to me that Chris's reaction was probably worse than Dad's would have been.

December ninth. That was the day the colonel, along with a lieutenant, showed up. Hats in hands, just like I'd pictured. It was a Saturday, so I was home. I'd taken to spending as much time as I could stand to at home, expecting this. But sometimes I'd just about go crazy waiting, and I'd have to get out, and the whole time I'd be gone I would wonder if they were at the house *right now*, that I'd get home to find Mom lying on her bed in hysterics and a doctor giving her a sedative, while Dad limped through the house punching things. I'd been noticing his limp a lot more these last couple of weeks. And I was angrier with him every day for putting us through this, for putting Chris through hell to make up for his own shortcomings, and almost certainly for getting Chris killed.

And now it had happened.

Dad wasn't home; he was at the store, which he usually was on Saturdays. I was in Chris's room, sitting on his bed, looking around at his things. The dumb things kids tend to collect had collected in spades in here. Chris was a bit of a pack rat, and even this stupid little fake mother-of-pearl handled jackknife he'd won at some fair when he was maybe nine was still in the drawer of the bedside table. I was in his room even though Mom had caught me in there several times since Thanksgiving and had told me to stay out. *Damn it, I will not stay out. He's my brother, after all, not just her son.*

So I was sitting on his bed when the doorbell rang, and I

jumped, which was what usually happened these days when that thing went off, or when the phone rang, anything that might tell us Chris was gone. So it rang, and I jumped and then sat still. Frozen, more like. *It's the mailman, and there's a package he needs a signature for. Or it's kids selling candy for some school project.* My ears hurt, I was straining so hard to hear.

Mom was in the kitchen, and as I heard her footsteps I pictured her wiping her hands on her apron as she moved through the living room toward the front door. I heard the heavy wooden inside door open, knowing she could now see through the storm door to whoever might be there. I held my breath. And I heard my mom cry, "Oh! No! No!"

I took the stairs two at a time, and when I got to the door everyone was just standing there like they'd been waiting for me to make my entrance before the action could continue. Mom was staring at the two officers, hands to her face. They looked businesslike but contrite, as sympathetic as they could, I suppose. But they were messengers from hell.

I remember going all cold. Something clicked off, and something else clicked on. I took Mom gently by the shoulders and guided her away from the door so that I could open it and let the evil in. Still speechless, she kind of fell into the easy chair I led her to. I gestured toward the couch, and the two men sat while I fetched a box of tissues for Mom. Standing next to her chair, I held her hand while the colonel spoke.

"I'm very sorry to bring you this news, Mrs. Landon. Your son, Private First Class Christopher Landon, was killed two days ago while serving his country in Vietnam."

*What the fuck are they doing? Do they think we don't know where he is?* Mom gasped and then sobbed and covered her face completely.

He went on. "He died a hero. His squadron was ambushed, and everyone but Private Landon and four other men were killed very quickly. Those four men were wounded. Your son found cover for them. He got three of them under cover and was almost back with the fourth man when he was killed. All of the men he rescued survived, so we know how brave your son was. We know his story."

*You know nothing! You don't know anything about him!* I was blinking like crazy and breathing oddly, but I would *not* cry. I nodded at them so they would know they'd done what they needed to do and they could leave now. And that's just what they did. They stood, and the lieutenant said, "Please accept our sincere condolences. We'll be in touch again soon. And remember that there was much honor in his death."

As if that would help. *He's dead! He's gone, he's fucking dead!* I gritted my teeth.

The colonel saluted Mom, not that she noticed, and said, "We'll see ourselves out."

She was trying to say something, but she was crying so hard I almost couldn't make it out. "I have to call your father."

"Oh, Ma, no. Not over the phone." I felt oddly calm, and somehow I knew that was the wrong thing to do. I didn't have my full license yet, but this was no time to quibble over details like that. I said, "I'll take your car and go to the store."

"No! Don't leave me alone."

"Then come with me. We can't tell him on the phone, Mom. That's all there is to it."

She did her best not to sob too much in the car, and I could tell the effort was costing her. She barely breathed all the way. Despite how calm I felt, my vision kept blurring, but I clenched my jaw and blinked a lot. *It isn't like I hadn't known. It isn't like Chris hadn't told me this would happen.*

When we got to the store Mom made me park away from the door, away from the other parked cars. "I can't go in like this, Paul, and I don't want anyone to see me in the car, either."

So I parked where Mom could see the front of the store, facing that sunshine yellow sign that read LANDON'S PET SUPPLY. I trudged alone across the pavement, barely aware of how far I had to walk between the car and the store—it's a big lot. Something in my mind was focusing hard on stupid details like avoiding icy puddles where I might slip, noticing all the wrinkly edges where the water had seeped between bits of pavement grit before it froze. I was in some kind of low gear, some survival mode I couldn't remember having experienced before. I tried to come up with an opening sentence for telling Dad, but there was no right way to say what I had to say.

Dad was standing near the registers, in an animated discussion with some man whose small dog was wrapping the guy's legs in the lead it was on. Dad stepped out of the way so the dog wouldn't get him, too. I stood off to the side until I could get Dad's attention, and then I jerked my head to the right, toward his office, and headed that way.

Carol was in there doing some paperwork. "Hey, Paul!"

"Hi."

"How are you?"

*Does anyone ever really want to know the answer to that question?* "I'm just waiting for my dad to come in. I have to talk to him about something."

"Oh. Do you need me to leave?"

I've always liked Carol. For an old person, maybe even older than Dad, she always seemed pretty with it. But how could I answer that? I was looking at her, feeling helpless, when Dad came in. He took one look at me and asked Carol if we could have a moment. It was an eternity before she shut the door from the other side.

"Paul?"

"It's Chris." I didn't need to say anything else.

He walked slowly around his desk, limping heavily, touching everything solid he could reach, everything that wouldn't move if he leaned on it, and sat in his chair. That calm I'd had was disappearing like so much fake fog in a horror flick. A few tears came out of nowhere and ran down my face.

"Where's your mother?"

"Outside in the car. She didn't want to stay at home alone, and she didn't want to come in." I swiped at my traitor eyes.

"Who drove?"

*Who cares?* "I did."

He took a few deep breaths, rubbed his face, and then asked me how we'd found out. And I started bawling for real. It was almost like now that he knew, the burden was shifting onto him. When it had been just Mom and me, I'd had to be strong.

I'm not sure whether I couldn't carry the weight anymore or whether Dad had done something to take it off me and now I could let go. I've wondered about that a lot.

So I told him how Chris had rescued those other guys, how he was a hero. To keep myself from losing it too badly, I pictured Dean Pendleton's blue wool hat, thinking that at last Chris had made up for letting him down. I told Dad everything Chris would want him to know.

What I wanted to tell him was that this was his fault, that Chris was dead because of him. I wanted to tell him that Chris had known he'd die, that he'd been really scared before he went back. I wanted to tell him why Chris felt he had nothing to keep him alive anymore, tell him about Mason. Maybe that's why I was crying—because of what I couldn't say.

I don't think any of us slept all night. The room next to me, Chris's room, seemed more than empty. More than hollow. I should have been used to not having anyone in it. It had been like that since Chris had signed up, but suddenly it was different. It was a black hole, and it was sucking all the light inside and devouring it.

In the morning I heard Mom get up, and I expected to hear Dad as well, since he'd been going to church with her for weeks. But it was only her.

I went downstairs and found her standing at the counter, watching the toaster. It was a cloudy day, and the light over the stove was on. I've always loved that light. Whenever the kitchen is dark and that light's on, it seems like all the world is somewhere else, doing whatever it has to do, and the light over the stove creates this haven, this zone of peace and security, just for me. That morning, seeing the light from across the room, shining down on nothing and Mom off to the side in the darkness, it didn't give me that feeling. Maybe it will again some day, when I can believe in peace again, when I can believe there are havens anywhere. That morning, seeing Mom's tired face with the skin sagging in odd places, it felt to me like that light was—I dunno, inadequate. Pathetic.

She lifted her head slowly when she knew I was there. Then she looked back at the toaster.

"You going to church?" I asked. She nodded. "Dad isn't up yet, you know."

"He's not going."

We stood there like that, her watching the toaster, me watching her. I jumped a foot when the toast popped, when that jarring metallic crunching slapping noise shot out into the room. I said, "I'll go with you."

She didn't say anything, didn't even nod. She started buttering her toast. I headed back upstairs to wash my face and put on some clothes that would do for church, and when I got back to the kitchen Mom had made me some toast with butter and jam. She had made coffee for two, out of habit maybe, and I poured some. I'd never had it before, and it tasted terrible. Mom smiled at the face I made, so at least that was good.

"You might like that better with cream and sugar," she suggested. She was right, but I still didn't think it would ever be my favorite drink. Even so, I decided that I would start drinking it. I would just start, that's all.

I drove. Chris used to drive her to church, and then Dad, and probably she liked that. We didn't speak all the way. It felt surreal to me. Like we'd crossed into another world somehow, just driving along, not many cars on the road, gray light and dead-looking trees all around us.

We sat in the same pew as my uncle Jeff, mom's brother, and his wife, Diane. Mom had called them last night, sobbing more than talking, and Aunt Diane had come over and they'd cried together. They nodded to me and smiled sadly, and Aunt Diane reached over and squeezed my arm. Probably Mom and Chris had always sat with them when he drove her. My aunt had had two miscarriages years ago and then I guess they'd decided against trying for any more, so at least there were no irritating cousins I'd have to deal with.

I'd forgotten about organ music. Don't know how I could have, it's so much a part of the experience. When I used to come here as a kid, the only parts I liked were singing the hymns and listening to the organ. Though it always made me a little crazy when the organist would try to do improv stuff on the last verse. I wanted the music to be familiar all the way through, damn it, and it was like they ruined the end for me.

Didn't take long for me to figure out that they were still up to their old tricks. Still ruining the end. In one way, I didn't mind; I mean, I hadn't been here in so long I couldn't exactly have anything to say about how things were done. On the other, I felt a real need for something—anything—to feel familiar. To feel like there was something that didn't get yanked out from under you. But the service felt familiar, anyway. Different minister from the one I remembered; had Mom mentioned that at some point? She must have. This guy seemed a little younger. And maybe a little more with it, but it was still a sermon.

It was Christmas season, so the readings were full of things anticipated, a coming birth, the dawning of a new hope. *Yeah, right.* I glanced at Mom to see how she was taking this. She was looking at me, her eyes moist, but she didn't look sad, exactly. She looked—wistful, maybe? Hopeful? *What do I have to do with hope?* I didn't feel like smiling, but I did anyway, just to give her a little encouragement; at least she wasn't sobbing, which I'd half thought she might do. I mean, there's nothing like everyone else sounding cheerful when you've been hit by a bus to make you feel even more like shit.

Several times as I sat there, I felt sure I was supposed to be praying or something. Was there really no place in the service where everyone just sat still and had a word with Jesus? But then I thought, what would I say? Besides, God had probably forgotten about me. So mostly I just sat there and let things wash over me.

During the last part of the service Mom took my hand. I couldn't quite remember the last time she did that. She held it until the final hymn was announced and we had to fumble in the hymnals, and I was thinking that maybe she and Chris used to do that. Hold hands.

*So I'm hope now? I'm the hand-holder?* One voice in my head said, "Oh, I don't think so." Another said, "Why not?" It was like that old comic book image where a devil was on one shoulder, and an angel on the other. "No way." "Why not?" "You can't take Chris's place." "Why not?" "Because even Chris failed at being the man she thought he was."

Well, that shut the angel voice up real fast.

When we got home, Dad was up and Mom made breakfast. She'd cried a little in church, and a little on the way home, and her eyes were red, but she wasn't moping as she moved around the kitchen or anything.

She made coffee and poured some for me. And then we sat there, the three of us, like lumps, carefully avoiding—or so it seemed to me—looking toward the fourth chair at the table. No one spoke, unless they wanted to ask for the jam or something. I don't know what my folks were thinking, but it was suddenly hitting me pretty hard that this was it now. This was everybody. There would never again be four of us.

I had sort of got used to it being just me and Mom and Dad while Chris was away, but it was always a temporary thing, you know? There was always that light at the end of the tunnel. But Chris was the light, and now he was gone.

# PART II

# A Question of Manhood

# Chapter 4

I spent as much time as I could that week in my room. Somehow it was less obvious, when everyone wasn't together, that the best part of the family wasn't part of the family anymore. I kind of expected that Mom and Dad would pull together, would help each other out. And I tried to convince myself that was happening, because otherwise I was gonna have to do something. I was gonna have to do what Chris would've done. And I didn't have a clue what that was.

So as long as I was in my room I didn't have to see that Dad was just plopped in front of the TV all night, sometimes well past midnight, or that Mom was on yet another cleaning frenzy. The only times she wasn't attacking any dirt that might be cringing in odd corners or polishing the silver candlesticks and candy dishes, she was in Chris's room.

The first time I saw her in there, I'd been in my room, door shut, supposedly doing homework. At one point I had to take a leak, and as I stepped into the hallway I realized the light on Chris's bedside table was on. With only socks on my feet I moved silently toward the door, which was almost but not quite closed. Mom was in there, kneeling on the floor and leaning on the side of the bed. It looked like she was praying. Like she was at some saint's shrine. I stood there maybe three minutes. She never moved.

When I came out of the bathroom, the door to Chris's room was shut and no light came from under it. I opened it carefully and peeked in; no one.

She was in there again when I got home from school the next day. I didn't see anyone downstairs, but her car was in the driveway. It was a bit of a relief not to have her see me come in, not to have her look at me with that face full of sad hope that I'd been seeing lately, and I didn't try to find her. Just headed up to my room. But Chris's door was open. And Mom was in there, standing near the bed and looking down at folded clothing. Some were shirts she'd sewed for him, and some were sweaters she'd knitted. I thought she might have heard me come upstairs, that she'd turn and say something, but she just stood there. Then she picked up a soft blue sweater, held it to her face, and inhaled.

I went into my room to drop my books, thinking I should probably go in there and talk to her, but not wanting to do that. I'd been concentrating on pulling some kind of psychological tarpaulin over my feelings, over what had happened, so I could put one foot in front of the other, shift my weight, repeat the process, and somehow keep moving forward in time away from how I would be feeling if I lifted that tarp. The alternative would have been hiding under the covers on my bed for who knew how long. So I sat at my desk, searching for motivation to pick up a book or a notebook, anything that would let me pretend to be busy, but all the while my mind was in the next room, watching Mom stand there and breathe Chris into herself. I got up.

From Chris's doorway I said, "Mom?"

She wheeled around like I'd frightened her. "Oh! Paul, I didn't hear you come home."

*Well, that says it all. Her thoughts are only on the son who won't come home, not the one who actually has.* I said, "What are you doing in here? Why are Chris's clothes all over the place?"

By now she was moving around quickly, picking up piles and putting them back into drawers. "Just reminiscing, that's all, dear. What would you like for a snack? What can I get you?"

I stood there silently, waiting to see if it would dawn on her that I hadn't responded. She finished putting the clothes away and turned a big smile on me. One that I didn't believe. Then she went around me and into the hallway, where she waited, smiling that fake smile. *Is she trying to pretend that she hadn't been acting like some forlorn lover? Or maybe pretending she was glad to see me? Or both?*

"Paul? Come. Let me close the door."

I stood where I was, which was definitely still in Chris's room. "You can close it. Maybe I'll reminisce some myself."

Her smile faded a little. "Come on, let me get you a snack. Would you like some soda?"

"I don't suppose you made any cookies today." She hadn't made cookies in weeks. She used to make them all the time. For both me and Chris, or so I'd always thought.

"No, dear, I didn't. Would you like that? Maybe I'll make some tomorrow. Come, now."

I moved toward the door, but I didn't step out of the room. Instead I took hold of the knob and started to close the door, leaving her in the hall. Suddenly there was a pressure from her side.

"Paul, what are you doing?"

I didn't let her pressure move the door. I couldn't see her face now. "I told you. I'm going to reminisce a little."

She pushed harder, but I held firm. "Paul, come out of there. Come have a snack."

"I don't want a snack. I want to spend a little time in here."

There was silence for a moment. When she spoke, her tone was sharp. "Paul! I want you to come out of there now. Leave your brother's things alone."

Suddenly it was a battle I had to win. I would not be forced out of Chris's room. But I couldn't exactly push my mother down the stairs. So I acted like I was leaving. I stepped into the hall, pulling the door closed behind me. She took this for obedience, but when I figured she was far enough away, toward the stairs, I whipped the door open and was inside with it closed and locked before she got to it.

"Paul!" She twisted the knob and then banged on the door. "Paul! Get out of there!"

"Why?"

"Because I don't want his things disturbed."

"You disturbed them."

"I'm his mother!"

"Was. You were his mother." This was cruel, I knew even then, but I couldn't help it. "And I was his brother. Don't I have any rights?"

She banged louder, shouted louder. "Paul! Please!"

I yanked the door open and glared at her. She looked panicked or something. I shouted, "He was no saint, you know!" And I was *so* close to adding, *He was a coward and a queer!*

She slapped me. I could hardly believe she'd done that. She'd never hit me. Not that I remembered, anyway. If my folks thought I needed physical punishment, it had always been Dad who'd delivered it.

I think she couldn't quite believe it, either. She stood there for a few seconds, hands over the lower part of her face, and then she wrapped herself around me.

"Paul! I'm so sorry. It's just that I want him to be in there still." She sobbed into my ear. "Can't you understand that?"

I pulled away from her. "Do you think I don't want that, too? Do you think I like that he's gone forever? Do you think I don't count?" I got into my room as quickly as I could and slammed the door. And I stayed in there, through the sounds of what must have been her throwing herself onto her own bed, through noises that convinced me she was sobbing, through hearing her go downstairs later, through hearing my dad's voice as he came home.

He was home maybe five minutes before I heard him coming up the stairs. He didn't knock, he just threw my door open. I turned in my desk chair to face him.

"Do you have any idea what your mother is going through?"

You know what went through my mind? It was this: *Dad's angry with me, and maybe I wasn't blameless, but he's gonna overreact. I need to get Chris involved.*

"Answer me!"

"Of course I do."

"I don't see how you could."

"Then why did you ask?"

"Don't talk back to me, young man. Now, you listen carefully. Your mother is going through hell. She's just lost a son. Until you're a parent yourself, you can't know what that means. So you need to take my word for it and behave as though you understand how much pain she's in."

"What about your pain?" By which I also meant, *What about mine?*

That stopped him in his tracks. But not for long. "I'm not here to talk about me. We need to straighten this thing out between you and your mother. Will you agree to be more sensitive and not cross her when she tells you she needs something?"

"Dad, y'know, I didn't chase her out of Chris's room. She chased me."

"And what did you do then? You locked her out! Out of her dead son's room."

"She was locking me out. She didn't want me in there."

"What are you talking about?"

"She didn't want me in there dirtying things. Messing things up. Spoiling the shrine." I lost it a little. I stood up. "What does she think, that I'm the dirty son, that Chris's room was, like, pristine? Holy? And that the bad son—that would be me—can't even breathe the air without ruining it?"

We stood there, practically nose to nose. I could hear the breath whistling in and out of his sinuses. Then he closed his eyes and stepped back, a small bob when he stepped with his bum leg. He looked at me, stern but quiet. "Paul, here's the thing. You and I cannot understand what a mother goes through at a time like this. What this family needs is calm. And when you rile your mother up like that, it's the wrong thing to do. I'm asking you to act like a man. You're not too young to understand that. Let your mother have her grief."

*And mine means nothing?* But I knew that he was making his own grief mean nothing, compared to my mom's, anyway, and if his meant nothing—or at least had to be buried—then so did mine. The big difference, of course, was that my grief included things they didn't even know about. Things they couldn't know about. I was already letting my mother have her grief by keeping her from the worst of it.

"Paul? Do you understand?" There was a threat in his voice.

"Yes." Chris would have said I'd have been stupid to say anything else at that point.

"All right, then." And he turned and limped out of the room. He didn't close the door. Without turning around, he said, "Dinner will be a little late tonight." Meaning, *That's your fault, Paul.*

I threw myself back into my desk chair and sat there, trying and failing to concentrate on schoolwork, until Dad called up that dinner was ready.

I'd just sat down at the table when Dad said, "Paul, don't you have something you need to say to your mother?"

We hadn't talked about this. Not anything specific, anyway. What did he expect? I looked at Mom. She was sitting there, eyes down, and she looked so sad.

"I'm sorry, Mom," I said. It's what Chris would have told me to do.

I could barely hear her reply. "That's all right, Paul. It's hard for all of us."

At least she acknowledged that. Maybe I had been a little hard on her. *But, damn it, I have grief, too. I have suffering. And on top of that, I've got Chris's secrets to carry.*

Midnight, and I was lying in bed, eyes wide open. I was almost dizzy from going back and forth between feeling like a shit for making things harder for Mom and feeling like I was being deprived of Chris a third time. The first had been when he'd told me the truth, about his fear and about his . . . well, you know. The second was when he'd died. And now I couldn't even go into his room! What I'd told Dad earlier? I really did feel like that. Like my just being in Chris's room would damage it somehow, dirty it, render it unworthy of the worship my mom seemed to think it deserved. Maybe I thought she'd gone a little too far, kneeling in prayer at the bed, laying out all his clothes, but I understood why she wanted to be in there. It was the most Chris-like place in the house.

And suddenly I needed to be in there. I stood in the door to my room and listened carefully: no sound from my folks' room. I would have felt better if I could've heard Dad snoring, but I would be quiet enough even if he wasn't quite asleep. I tiptoed to Chris's room and turned the knob slowly in case it squeaked. No sound. Once inside, I closed the door slowly so it wouldn't bump and make noise. Slowly and silently I released the knob.

I sat on the bed, facing the pillow, imagining Chris lying there. I reached out a hand and caressed the bedspread, imagining the surface was uneven as though his body lay asleep beneath it. When I felt my throat tighten I stood up and went over to the desk across the room. I sat in the chair sideways, facing his record collection, realizing with a slight shock that it hadn't even occurred to me to raid it. Mom wouldn't know, that's for sure. And he had lots of stuff I might want. I reached for the desk light, stopping myself just before I turned it on. Bad idea to advertise my presence, and there would be a chance to look through those platters by daylight at some point. So I just stared in their general direction through the dark.

For some reason the Cat Stevens album came to mind. The one he'd been playing when I got home after torturing Anthony. I'd been kept out in the hall then, too. There was some kind of disconnect going on in my head about that series of moments, when I'd knocked at his locked door. He'd had someone in here.

*He'd had a girl in here! So he couldn't be . . . No, wait. It had turned out to be Jim Waters. Right. So Jim Waters is a fag, too?*

I stood up, too quickly, and the chair bounced a little. In a panic I reached for it, and then I stood there leaning on it, my breath shaking with every inhale. Then I heard the door open.

"Paul?" Dad whispered.

I could barely see him move into the room and close the door. Silently he limped over to the bed and sat down. My head felt unnaturally light and my ears rang in the silence, which went on for maybe half a minute. It was like we were inhaling some life-giving essence that we couldn't get anywhere else. Then I heard a soft thudding sound as Dad's hand patted the bed beside him. I moved over and sat down.

More silence. Then, "Son, your mother and I both understand that this hurts you, too. Losing your brother. It's just that these things hit women harder. Maybe you're a little too young to understand this, but it's true. And what she needs right now is actually something that might help you, too. She needs you to be a man." He heaved a sigh, and then went on. "The thing is, you might need to grow up a little faster than you would have if this hadn't happened. If you were still a child, if you could really cry about this, then it would be different for her. She could hold you, and you could hold her, and both of you could cry together. But you're too old for that. So you need to take one more step into manhood. You need to be strong for her."

He shifted his weight on the bed and was quiet so long I wondered if he expected me to speak. And maybe he did, 'cause he said, "Do you understand what I'm telling you?"

*Do I? Well, maybe at the most superficial level. Be a man. I could get a sense of what that meant. But—be strong? Does that mean not having any feelings, or not showing them? And how can I just decide to grow up faster? What the hell does he want from me?*

I said, "Yes."

He laid a hand briefly on my leg. "Good. I knew I could count on you." Slowly he got to his feet. "Now, go back to bed. And tomorrow, let your mother know how much you'd love it if she did make cookies for you." He opened the door, and the hall nightlight created a silhouette out of him. He stood there, silently beckoning me out.

Back in my bed, I lay there, one minute thinking I knew what he wanted, the next having no fucking clue, and in between thinking that being a man meant letting your father force you to do something so stupid it got you killed.

*Cookies? What does being a man have to do with asking your mother to bake cookies for you? What the hell does he want from me?*

* * *

That week in school was hell. I wasn't planning to say anything about Chris, but there had been this newspaper article, going on about his heroism, his zest for life, his good grades in the past, all presided over by a shot taken of him in his uniform just before he went overseas the first time. Terry Cavanaugh seemed to be avoiding me, probably because his brother was safe in Canada and it made him feel guilty or something. Then for a day or so it looked like Bobby Darnell was my new best friend. His brother Ken was doing okay. In fact, they expected him home in January, for good.

Friday I flunked a history test. An important one. Badly. It was part multiple choice and part essay. I'd tried to study, sort of, but stuff just kept falling out of my brain. Mr. Treadwell, the history teacher, asked me to see him after school before I went home.

He looked all solemn when I got to his classroom. Solemn and sympathetic. Just what I didn't need.

"Paul, this isn't like you. Your grades have always been fine, and sometimes even great, so I know you can do better." He paused a minute to see if I had anything to say, but I didn't. I just trained my eyes on my own reflection in his eyeglasses, the black frames making it look like they were too far away from the pale skin of his face. "I know your family has had some devastating news. I was very sorry to hear about your brother, and I'm sure it has affected your ability to concentrate. So I think what I'll do is offer you a chance to improve on this one test by taking it home to work on it, open book, over the weekend. Christmas vacation starts next week, as I'm sure you're aware, but if you can meet with me on Monday with satisfactory answers—and by satisfactory, I mean you must correctly answer all the multiple choice, and the essays must demonstrate that you understand the issues involved—then we'll sit down again and decide on what grade you should get. Does that sound fair?"

I shrugged. "I guess so." And then I thought to say, "Thanks." What I really wanted to say was to screw the test, that I didn't give a fuck, anyway. But life at home was weird enough already. I didn't need to go adding Dad's wrath into the mix, and I wasn't sure I could predict his reaction to much of anything these days.

"Shall I come to your house?"

"No!" I hadn't intended it to come out sounding so sharp. "Um, can we meet for a soda, or coffee or something?" My folks could *not* find out about this, or they'd be watching me like hawks once school got under way again in January. "If it doesn't snow hard Monday, I could bike to the Burger King at Thompson and Rutledge. Say, two o'clock?"

He gave me this look like he was trying to see into my head. "You're trying not to let your folks find out, aren't you? And you're probably right. They have enough to worry about right now. So I'll do this one your way. But, Paul"—and he sort of looked at me over his glasses—"we need to get back at least to normal attention in January, or they will need to know. Understood?"

"Thanks," I said again.

Be a man. I had to be a man. Did men have to do history make-up exams? I guess if I thought about it seriously, men did have to fix their own mistakes. At least, the good ones did. So I holed up in my room on Saturday, coming out occasionally for cookies—which my mom was baking now too frequently for even me to keep up with her—and working on Mr. Treadwell's exam. It was the same one I'd failed in class, of course.

With free access to the book the multiple-choice questions were relatively easy, though there was always the possibility of some kind of tricky wording that would bite you in the ass. The essays scared me, though. Treadwell had said I'd have to demonstrate that I understood the issues. So I went back and forth between my class notes and the textbook, starting about five new pages every time I tried writing about one of the three topics on the test. When I got to the third one I noticed that there was a fourth topic. There'd been only three in class; what was this? Mr. Treadwell had scribbled in a fourth, with a note saying he'd added it because I was getting this opportunity the other students hadn't. *Joy.*

So I deciphered his handwriting, dreading what it might be. Here's what he'd written: "Describe briefly a day in the life of a medieval French farmer who had fled three weeks ago into the safety of his nobleman's hilltop castle to avoid an attacking army. Since that time, the castle has been under siege."

*Is he kidding me with this? What do I know about the life of a French farmer, now or a long time ago, under siege or not?* Okay, maybe we'd been studying the castles themselves, and we'd already had a pop quiz on the architectural parts of the typical fortified castle, but—even so. I threw my pen down and sat back hard in my chair, arms crossed. One of my legs started bouncing up and down, heel thudding against the floor. I got up, found my jacket, and went outside.

It wasn't fair. This wasn't something Mr. Treadwell had covered in class. We hadn't gone into the daily lives of anybody, really. Memorizing dates, who fought who ("You mean 'whom,' Paul," I could hear my mom's voice say), who won, who lost, and maybe how things might have been different if the other side had won instead.

Then I remembered he'd done something like this on the test at the end of October. "What if," the question had said, "Hitler had won World War II?" We weren't even studying twentieth-century history yet, so it had thrown me for a loop. But it had been included as extra credit. I'd ignored it at the time, but afterward it had got me thinking. Didn't do me any good, of course; too late to add any credit, days after the test. But this new one was like that question, in a way. It made me imagine things.

Okay, I thought, marching down block after block of my neighborhood, staring down at my feet, hands shoved into my pockets. Okay, so I'm a farmer in medieval France, and some army is attacking. They're burning houses and generally pillaging and raping. I hear they're on their way, so I take my wife and kids, maybe a cow or a pig, we each grab whatever food we can carry—we don't have anything else of value—and we head up the hill to the castle. It's hard going, uphill with all this stuff, and trying to keep the cow and the pig in line.

*Wait—why does it have to be uphill? Oh, right; if the castle is on the hilltop, it's harder to attack, and from inside you can see all around.*

But the question said "three weeks ago." What would I be doing now?

I turned a corner on my walk and had to slow down to get past some trash barrels that should have been taken into somebody's garage days ago. What would I be doing now? Probably not much. My family and I would be huddled into some corner of the lower bailey, maybe near the stables, maybe even with no roof over us. There aren't exactly going to be rooms at the inn for everyone who scrambled up that hill. There's no inn of any kind. Maybe I'd have fought with the blacksmith for a sheltered spot my family could live in for however long we'd be there. Every day one of my sons and I (I would have at least two, of course) would scour the grounds and any buildings we could get into for bits of food. We might have to frighten dogs away from garbage if our nobleman isn't generous or if food's just plain running out after three weeks. We wouldn't have anyone to send us care packages.

I pictured myself brandishing a stick in each hand, threatening the dogs, while my younger son threw stones at them and ran in to grab stuff while I kept the dogs at bay.

This was all pretty grim, and here in suburbia I was getting colder by the second. On my way out of the house I'd grabbed nothing but my jacket, and it was icy out. I picked up my pace and took another corner that would point me toward home.

I'd probably have to leave one son, the older one, with my wife and the daughter I'm sure I'd have, to protect them from unscrupulous men. Possibly even from the nobleman's guards or soldiers, who probably thought they had a right to take anything they wanted.

I was just pondering how badly everyone would stink, with no way to wash, when I got to my own front door again. And stopped.

I stood there, shivering by now, not really wanting to go in. If Dad was home, he'd be practically grafted onto his recliner, either watching TV or reading something. Mom would be attacking invisible bits of grime in obscure areas of the house or baking yet more cookies, in which case she'd expect me to ooh and aah and generally act like a little kid, all while I'm supposed to be acting like a man.

I opened the door as quietly as possible, sneaking into the warmth, wondering if I could get up to my room without being noticed. My eye fell on the door to the basement. That was closer than the staircase to the second floor, as long as my mom wasn't in a certain spot in the kitchen. I listened for any sounds she might be making and decided she was polishing the dining room table. So I made my move, successfully reaching the door without being detected, and tiptoed down the stairs. Some of them creaked, so I had to be careful. At the bottom I strained my ears again: nothing. No one knew where I was.

First thing I did was head for the furnace corner. I picked up Chris's old air rifle and sat on the ground with my back to the foundation wall, gun across my knees. Of course, my peasant farmer persona wouldn't have a gun. But would I be expected to help ward off attackers anyway? Very likely, really. And when you consider what the attacking army would do to me and my family if they got in, I guess I'd be motivated to do some warding.

I leaned my head against the stone foundation behind me and closed my eyes.

*I'm on the parapet. Is that the right word? I think so; it's the part you walk on that's just inside the . . . crenellations, I think they're called. There are soldiers wearing chain mail and a little body armor, maybe just helmets, shooting arrows at the other army below. I get pushed down the walkway to a group of men in a tag line, handling buckets of hot water to pour onto the attacking soldiers who'd got over the moat and are trying to scale the outer wall. The curtain wall, I think; yeah, that's right. I have to take a place in the line of bucket handlers, and I try to get into the line taking the empty buckets, but of course everyone wants that line; who wants to get their own hands scalded with splashes of boiling water and have to lift the heavy wooden buckets besides?*

*They take my son, the one who'd been throwing stones at the dogs, and put him to tending the fire where the water is being heated. Those of us in the bucket brigade take a break while we wait for more water to heat, and I look around. I hear a sound like "whack" and then a thud and then this large stone goes sailing overhead. They've got enough space in this particular castle for a catapult, and when it was peaceful they'd put away a huge supply of stones for just such a contingency. Maybe at some point the villagers—like me—were even forced to help gather the stones and bring them up to the castle.*

*Suddenly there's a hue and cry (see, I'm getting the hang of this) at the wall, where attackers were able to get a ladder up and are coming over the top at us. Our soldiers are too close to use their arrows now— no time to get the thing strung before an attacker is on them—and it's hand-to-hand, with swords and knives and, if you're lucky and skilled, maybe a mace. Not me, of course; I've got none of that. Just my two fists, and my feet, and my teeth, and anything else I can fight with. Though if I can get that knife that somebody just dropped . . . Got it! Okay, now I'm armed, at least, though I'll have to be careful where I thrust; I'll ruin the knife or hurt myself if I try to stab into mail or armor.*

*It's a weird feeling, pushing the metal blade into human flesh, and freaky when you hit bone. Plus you get somebody's blood all over you. The smell of fired iron meeting the wet iron of blood is mingled with an acrid smoke. Can't tell whether the smoke is coming from our own fire or if the attackers have set fire to something inside. No time to figure it out.*

*Suddenly a huge pain happens. That's the only way to describe it. It happens. At the base of my neck. And I can't move. I'm on the ground, and through a fog of pain I see legs and feet and the bodies of others who have fallen. Someone steps on my leg, but it doesn't hurt as much as my neck.*

*Someone has a hold on my other leg. They're pulling me, and I'm too out of it to fight. Feebly I try to dig my fingers into the grit I'm lying in, but it's no good. Then I see who's pulling me. It's my older son; he's found me!*

*He's just got me out of the worst of the fighting, I'm rolled onto my back, and behind him I see where another ladder has allowed attackers up, someplace where we don't have enough men to hold them. One of them lands, brings an arrow to his bow, and fires.*

*In slow motion I see my son's body arch backward, his mouth in a huge gasp, eyes wide and unseeing. He falls beside me.*

"Chris!"

*Who said that?!?*

My own eyes were wide, now. And unseeing. Or, what they saw wasn't our basement. It was my brother, brought down in the jungle as he tried to pull a comrade to safety.

I closed my eyes. And I just let the tears fall.

When I wrote this for my assignment, I left out Chris's name. I wrote it like I was remembering the day from my deathbed, as gangrene set in through a wound in my side I didn't even know I had.

# Chapter 5

That Sunday I went to church again. I wasn't going to. I mean, it occurred to me it would be a great way to "be a man," to take my mom to church and—you know—respect her grief, whatever. But I wasn't that great at being a man just yet. I still had a lot of the little brat in me.

This conflict was going round in my head on Saturday night, or Sunday early morning, whatever the hell time it was as I lay there wide awake. And I tried to imagine what it would be like if I told her. I'd sit her down at the kitchen table one day after school, before Dad got home. I'd say, "Mom, I know how much pain you're in. And I don't want to do anything to make it worse. But since you loved Chris so much, I think I owe it to you to make sure you really know who he was."

"Paul," she'd say, "whatever are you talking about? Do you think I didn't know my own son?"

"In most ways, I'm sure you did. But there was one thing. One very important thing. Something he told me the night before he went back to 'Nam. And he asked me not to tell you. But now I think that was wrong."

I'd wait until she asked for more. I'd laid two traps. One was the tantalizing nugget of information that was so important, that she didn't know, that he'd told me. Only me. I'd give up my sole proprietorship of this amazing confidence from him, but she'd have to beg. The other trap was that Saint Christopher had done something that was wrong.

So a number of heartbeats would go by, and then she'd say, "Wrong?" She'd start there because otherwise she'd have to face the fact that I knew something important about him she didn't. "What was wrong?"

"Not telling you himself." Another dig. He'd told me, but not you, so there.

"Paul, do I have to yank it out of you? What did he say?"

I'd heave a soulful sigh, blink a few times while looking down, then raise my head. "He told me he was gay."

There'd be this silence.

The thing was, my imagination had a hard time getting past the silence, because what seemed like the most likely reaction—though it might not be her immediate one—wasn't very satisfying. To me, anyway. I'm sure Chris would have loved it. It was that she'd accept it. She wouldn't like it, because she'd be sure it would mean he'd be unhappy trying to live like that, but his unhappiness would be the worst of it. He'd still be her sainted son.

So it would do only so much damage to tell her. On the other hand, though, I could never tell Dad. He'd punish me for just knowing it, though I'm not sure whether he'd want to hit me harder for telling him Chris was gay or telling him Chris was afraid.

The fact is, Chris shot himself in the foot, in a way, by insisting that Mom not know, because she would have loved him anyway. On the other hand, telling Mom would be like telling Dad. Chris would have known this, of course, so maybe he didn't shoot his foot after all but tried to keep me from the repercussions he knew would come from Dad. So why'd he tell me at all?

Under it all was the fact that I'd promised Chris. Practically on his deathbed. So I couldn't tell anyone, and there was no point in all this mental exercise.

Wait. I'd promised him I wouldn't tell our folks. Now, it's true that if I tell much of anybody else my folks are likely to find out. And in truth, I don't really want anyone to know. It's too shameful. But what about Jesus? What could it hurt? And isn't he supposed to know everything already? It would give me someone to talk to, and maybe it would even do Chris some good if I prayed for him. The church service I'd been to with Mom hadn't left a lot of space for that; maybe we were supposed to do it on our own. So I tried.

I felt like a retard, lying there in bed and talking to some guy who died like a couple thousand years ago. I'd done it as a kid, kneeling beside my bed. Should I try that? I got up and knelt on the floor, elbows on the mattress, head bent over folded hands. I felt like some kind of idiot. I whispered.

"Jesus, son of Mary and God . . ."

*Now what? Do I have his attention? How would I know?*

"If you know everything, then you know about Chris. So I'm not breaking my promise. I guess what I want to know is, can you help him? Is there really a heaven, and a hell, and what happened to Chris? Is he in, like, limbo, or purgatory, and should I even believe in those places, or are they just imaginary? Does it matter what we believe? It doesn't, does it. Because whatever we believe, we'll end up wherever you—or God, I never was too sure about the division of labor up there—think we're supposed to be. So it doesn't matter if I don't believe in hell. What matters is where Chris is now. And whether I can talk you into taking him into heaven with you.

"He was a really great brother, most of the time. But you know that already, don't you? So can't you weigh that against what he did with guys and get him off the wagon to hell?"

I waited, eyes clenched shut, my arms and belly shivering with cold.

Nothing.

I let my arms fall onto the bed and looked up at the ceiling. "Hello?"

Silence.

At first I thought, *Well, this is bullshit,* but then I remembered how long it had been since I even acknowledged that anyone was up there. So maybe it wasn't reasonable to expect an immediate response. But this wasn't about me. It was about Chris. In the end I decided to hope that not letting me know anything was punishing me for being such a delinquent when it came to praying and going to church. And maybe a little for being mean to my mom. I decided to believe that Jesus might be willing to help Chris.

When I heard Mom get up in the morning, I got up, too. I sat in the cold kitchen eating toast and jam, sipping sweet creamy coffee, and then I drove Mom to church.

The thing about church is that there are lots of boring parts. I think Mom and lot of others sort of get off on the sacrifice, giving up their time to the benefit of their immortal souls, or maybe of someone else's. Like I was doing for Chris, in a way; but if I was doing it, I wasn't getting off on it. I decided to use the time productively. I suppose some people would call it praying. I think mine was more like—well, somewhere between reasoning and begging.

*Jesus, if you really sacrificed yourself for us, then please make sure it counts for Chris. I mean, it would be one thing if he'd only thought he was gay and didn't do anything about it, but I know about Jim Waters, and then there was that guy Mason, so he probably did some things he really, really shouldn't have. The Bible does say that, right? That it's some kind of horrible sin? And I gotta tell ya, brother, it sure feels like it oughta be. Just the thought of it makes me want to retch. Kissing a guy? Man, no way! How could you want to do that? How could that ever seem like a good idea to another guy? What were you thinking, even to try it?*

I realized that I'd started talking to Chris instead of Jesus, so I sat back, closed my eyes a sec, and took a deep breath. And began again.

*Jesus, you can make it okay, right? I mean, if Chris repented? He knew he was gonna die. He told me so. And Mason was already dead when Chris got back there, so there wasn't any more—you know. Did he confess, or whatever he needed to do, and ask you for forgiveness? And could ya give me some kind of sign already?*

I waited. I tried to focus on what it might sound like if God or somebody like that spoke to me, but the minister's sermon started creeping in. At least, his words. The meaning of these little speeches always seemed pretty obscure to me. But he was making so much noise that if Jesus spoke, I missed it. Of course, if God or whoever wanted me to hear something, I'd hear it. If he can make a virgin pregnant, he can speak to me inside my head, or in a way so the only people who could hear it are the ones who should. Right? So was this still punishment for me? *And would somebody up there please help Chris?*

It didn't take me too long to realize I was starting to go around in circles again, just like last night. Maybe it had to do with sleep deprivation. I tried thinking of something totally un-related. My mind went to Martha, from last summer at the store.

Lovely Martha. Sweet smile. And that wasn't necessarily her best feature, pretty as it was, if you get my drift. I started imagining her in different places in the store, in different positions, bending over to stack things on the shelf where Dad kept aquarium water pumps, or reaching up with one arm to stock dried crickets while one of her boobs pressed against the rep-tile mite spray below—which would have had a hard time avoiding that boob. *And a hard time is what I'm gonna have if I didn't stop this line of reminiscing.*

So I started picturing Dad in the store. The goal was to stop going around in circles, right? But you know what I saw, in my head? That little dog. The one I'd seen December ninth, the day I'd gone to the store to tell Dad about Chris. A Yorkshire terrier, I think. It was running around its owner, round and round, its leash effectively hog-tying the guy. The dog had seemed desperate to be heard. To be noticed. To control some-thing. Anything.

Circles again. That was me, all over. And here's how I got out of it this time. That guy with the Yorkie? To have a dog like that, he'd have to be some kind of fag. Which put me right back into debate with myself about Chris.

I leaned forward and clutched my hair with both hands. Mom must have thought I'd found the sermon moving or something, because she reached over and stroked the back of my head. It felt so good I just stayed there as long as she went on doing it. And I started another prayer.

*God, I don't know why you made Chris die. Why you took him. Was it so he wouldn't get any farther into perdition than he already was? Was it that if he went when he was being a hero, saving other people, he would make it to heaven anyway? Whatever, I really need to know. So here's an idea. Maybe you don't want to talk to me directly, or even let Jesus do it, but what if you let Jesus give me some of what Chris had? I'm not talking about LPs, here. I'm talking about how good he was to Mom, how he convinced Dad to calm down. I'm talking about how everyone liked him, how he always knew what to say to make people happy. How he always knew what to say to me to make me feel better about myself. How about if somebody up there gives me just a little of that? It wouldn't have to be a lot, but it would sure help us down here. It would sure help get us through this time of missing Chris. It would mean that you've got him with you, and he isn't in hell after all. And it's only fair, since you took him. What d'you say?*

I knew better than to expect an answer right then. If I was gonna get any of Chris's qualities, it would show over time. And suddenly I had an amendment.

*Um, I don't want the part of him that made him want guys. I wanna be clear about that.*

Mom's hand stopped stroking. She patted my back lightly, and I turned and smiled at her. It felt good.

Was that my first sign?

School vacation is something I used to look forward to in a huge way. This year, though, it looked like this major downer, something to be got through alive if possible. It would be two weeks of trying to pretend that we can still have Christmas, that there's really some cheer in the world, some hope that someday things will approach a new kind of normal. It can't be the old normal, and I guessed the struggle we were going through was partly to figure out what the new one's gonna be. All I knew was we sure as hell weren't there yet, and those two weeks looked like no-man's-land.

There was a kind of slush falling from the sky on Monday. I'd told Mr. Treadwell that I'd meet him at two, and despite the crap on the streets I still intended to bicycle to the Burger King. So I put on a couple of layers—T-shirt, corduroy shirt, sweater— and then a windbreaker. My legs would get wet; not much I could do about it. Notebook and test papers in a backpack, I'd almost made it to my bike in the garage when I heard Mom call.

"Paul? I hope you're not going out in this weather!"

*Think fast . . .* "Got to, Ma. Library. Doing some research for a school paper on medieval French warfare." Ha! I sent a silent thank-you to Mr. Treadwell for the idea.

Mom appeared from the kitchen, hands wringing a dish-towel. "Why can't it wait until the weather isn't so dreadful? You've got the holiday."

"Well . . . I have to do the research first, then do the writing." I kept moving, maneuvering the bike out from where it was pinned behind Mom's car.

"Do you want me to drive you?"

"No! I mean, no thanks. Not sure how long I'll be. See you!" The sound of the garage door rattling up and overhead blocked whatever she said next, so I could pretend I didn't hear. I flipped the windbreaker hood over my head, shut the garage door, and cycled off.

It was nasty going, but the only other cars were people out shopping for gifts. I'd picked two o'clock to meet 'cause it's after lunch and before the time when mothers bring kiddies in to bribe them into good behavior with soft drinks and milk shakes and fries. I was already seated, chocolate milk shake in front of me, by the time Mr. Treadwell set a cup of steaming coffee on his side of the table. *Coffee. Maybe I should have got that. It's what men drink.*

As he shrugged out of his coat he said, "How are you, Paul?"

I was gonna just give him the pat answer, *Fine, and you?* But when I looked at him something about his expression said he really wanted to know.

"Okay, I guess." I let my tone of voice speak for me.

"Just okay?"

"Yeah." I didn't really know what else to say.

He nodded. "I can imagine things would be pretty dreadful for your family this season, under the circumstances. Please remember that if you want to talk about it, all you have to do is let me know. I'll meet you here, or wherever. My wife loves to meet my students, so we could even talk at my house. Just call, if you need to. Now," and he rubbed his hands together like they were cold, "what have you got for me? Did you finish everything?"

By way of response I dug into my pack and pulled out the test. He smiled and reached for it. I sucked on the straw in my milk shake while he read, going through the multiple choice like lightning, making just one mark with his pencil. He handed that page to me.

"Paul, read this question one more time, and let me know if you want to stick with this answer."

*Fuck. I knew there was gonna be something tricky in here.* But when I read it, there wasn't a trick. I must have just read it too quickly on Saturday. "I read it wrong the first time. Can I change the answer to B instead?"

"Considering all the others are correct, yes. And B is the correct choice." He put that section aside and started in on the essay questions. He wrote a couple of comments but didn't say anything. Then he started the fourth one, the one about the besieged castle.

Every once in a while, he pointed out something with his pencil and said, "What's that word?" I finally had to apologize for my penmanship. He grinned. "It kind of looks like you were rushing to get all the words onto the paper. This one engaged you, didn't it?" He looked down again, didn't wait for me to answer.

I was a little anxious about what his reaction would be to the ending. Since I'd written it from my supposed deathbed, the last sentence was incomplete, like I'd died before I could finish. I watched his eyes, which stopped moving when he got to the end, and he just stared. He didn't shift his gaze from that blank spot after my last written word for maybe half a minute. Then he set the paper down, his eyes still on it.

*He's gonna say something I don't want to hear. He didn't like it.* But when he looked up, what he said shocked me.

"Are you taking creative writing next semester, Paul?"

I blinked. "No. Why?"

"Even if you don't want to make a future out of it, writing can help cleanse your spirit. It can help you figure out what your priorities in life are. What's important to you." I shrugged; I wasn't sure what he meant. "Well, just think about it. Maybe for next year. Though I think you might find it helpful with what you're going through presently." He laid his hands flat on the table, on either side of the paper. "Now let's talk about your grade, shall we?"

He did all right by me. I ended up with a B overall for the semester, which was fine by me. Now all I had to worry about was whether I could meet with his concept of "normal attention," which I was supposed to get back to by January.

I wish I could say I used the time in the next couple of weeks constructively, though what that would have meant I'm not sure. I did accomplish getting gifts for Mom and Dad, anyway. I walked to the bus stop and rode into town, heading right for the largest department store there so I could just wander around until something inspired me. I didn't have a clue. It didn't help my mood any to realize that I wouldn't have to strain my brain trying to come up with something brilliant for Chris. A new album was the only thing that had occurred to me earlier, when it was still something I'd need to do, but I wouldn't even have known what he liked anymore. 'Nam changed people. *It sure changed Chris,* I thought, as I fingered men's leather wallets, contemplating getting one for Dad. *Changed him right into worm food.*

In the end I picked up a bath set for Mom—bubble bath, salts, powder, that sort of thing—and I left the department store to get what I'd decided on for Dad. But that was a bit of a problem, because at his smoke shop, when I'd found a gift selection of various pipe tobaccos, the old geezer of a clerk took one look at me and said, "ID?"

*Shit. Think fast.* "Is, um, is Mr. Chandler here?" He was the store owner, and I'd been in here a few times with Dad and had met him. I figured he'd be my only chance at getting out with this stuff. He was in the back office, where the clerk pointed me with one hand, keeping a firm grip on the gift pack with the other.

"Merry Christmas, Mr. Chandler," I said, hoping to set a friendly tone.

"Paul! Well, hello. You here with your father?"

"Actually, um, no. I was hoping to get a tobacco assortment for him for Christmas, but I have this problem."

He chuckled, which I took for a good sign, but he said, "You're quite right, young man. That is a problem. I wish I could help you, but the law has my hands tied."

I stood there shuffling my feet a minute and then said, "What about this. If I give you some money, you can buy it, right? And then, say, you step outside for a breath of fresh air, and we say Merry Christmas and all that stuff?" I held my breath. *Am I suggesting something illegal?*

He eyed me for a minute. "This gift pack you wanted. Is it the one with a pipe in it?"

"No. Just the packets." I'd thought about buying just a pipe, which wouldn't be illegal, but the idea felt like I was trying to do better than the one Chris had given him in November.

"And you aren't buying a pipe, or any papers, or anything like that, right?"

"Right." I saw where he was going, and I kept my mouth shut.

He thought about it for a minute and then winked at me. He stood up, draped an arm on my shoulder, and walked me slowly toward the door to the shop and stood there as I went through it. "It was really nice to see you, young man. Though I was very sorry to hear about your brother. Give my best to your father for me, will you?" He stood in the shop doorway, grinning at me, while I moved away from the windows. I went to the corner and waited. Very shortly afterward I saw him coming from around the block; must have gone out the back door, no coat even.

"You are a character, Paul. Here," and he handed me a bag. "Now you come back after Christmas with some money for me, and I want to hear how your dad liked these. Got it? And next time I see him, I'm going to ask how he liked them. If he just stares blankly at me, you're in a heap of trouble." He was grinning. "Got that?"

"Yes, sir. Thanks, Mr. Chandler. You don't want the money now?"

He slapped his hands against his arms in the cold. "You can't buy tobacco from me, young man. Whatever are you thinking?" And he turned and ran back the way he'd come.

So at least I got that errand done. But mostly I slept as late as anyone would let me, though Mom usually made me get up by eleven if I wasn't out of bed already. And I was jerking off all the time; it was about the only release I could think of that wouldn't get me into trouble. Mostly I did it in bed, and even though I tried to catch the mess in tissues my sheets got disgusting. One day, maybe the Thursday before Christmas, I ripped them off the bed and was just about to carry them downstairs to leave them in the laundry room when it occurred to me that I didn't really want my mom to see how bad they were, and I should wash them myself, but I didn't know how to run the washer. So I picked up a bunch of clothes and added them to the pile.

Downstairs I put the sheets into the machine and studied the controls, but I wasn't sure whether to use hot water or how much detergent or what else should go in there. I piled the other stuff—jeans, school clothes, socks, underwear—on the floor. This way it wouldn't look so much like I was just washing sheets, and maybe Mom wouldn't ask embarrassing questions. I went to find her.

"You're washing your own clothes?"

I shrugged. "Yeah. Thought it was about time I learned how."

She smiled kind of sadly and touched the side of my face. Then we went to the laundry room and I got a lecture on everything from water temperature to load limits. I washed everything I'd taken downstairs, and even though I already knew how to make my bed all this activity took me most of the afternoon. At least that was one way to kill time. And it must have met with Mom's approval, 'cause after Dad got home he came to my room, where I was reading some stupid science fiction book.

"Paul? Son, I just want to say that was a good thing you did today. Taking responsibility for your own laundry like that."

The only reply I could think of was, "Trying to make things easier for Mom."

He smiled, nodded, and limped off. *Now you've done it. You've managed to get your name attached to a new chore.* And I realized that what this must look like to Dad—instead of me hiding something from Mom—is my stepping up to being a man, like he'd told me I had to do. *Yeah, I'm a man, all right. And I've got the cum-stiff sheets to prove it. Just as long as I don't have to die like Chris, being the man you wanted to be.*

And then I felt like a shit. He was just trying to be nice to me. If only he hadn't got Chris killed.

On Saturday, after killing some time with a nasty bike ride through half-frozen puddles and lumpy mud, it occurred to me that Charlie, my friend with the baseball glove, would want to know about Chris. About what had happened to him, anyway; not everything. I started to get up and ask Mom if she had his address anyplace before I remembered she was at the grocery store.

Charlie and I had exchanged a couple of letters just after he'd moved, so I figured I had his grandmother's address, if I could just find the letters. I was pretty sure they were in a box in the back of my closet, so I went rummaging through all the junk in there. I located the box I wanted and tried to slide it forward, but it kept getting caught on something. Frustrated, I reached blindly into the dark and yanked at things. I'd littered the floor of my room with all kinds of crap from my closet before I figured out what the box had got stuck on. It was one of the Ho Chi Minhs. I fell backward onto my ass and sat there staring at it until I couldn't see it anymore for the tears in my eyes. I just let them run down my face for a minute, then I fell onto my belly, head on my arms, and sobbed.

I was still hiccupping when I sat at my desk and opened the top drawer, where I kept the five pellets from the SADEYE. *Sad eye. Yeah, that's about right.* I held them in my left hand, shifted books with my right to get to a notebook, reached for a pen, and began to write, sniffling frequently at first, then less and less as I wrote.

It started out as a letter to Charlie. It ended up as a letter to Chris. And it went round and round and round. Why this, why that, why the other. I'm keeping his secrets, I'm praying for him in church, I'm praying that I'll get some of the good parts of him so I can make life at home a little less shitty for everyone. How did he keep Dad happy, what did he do that Mom liked best. I put that I knew he couldn't answer but that I really needed to know, blah blah blah. And what in God's name, I asked, could I do to convince Dad I was acting like a man.

When I started to circle back again and ask some of the same questions I'd opened with, I sat back hard, slammed my left hand—pellets still clenched tight—down on the desk, and heaved a shaky sigh. I threw the pen down and crumpled all the pages I'd written on. They went into the wastebasket. And then I wrote to Charlie.

> *Dear Charlie,*
>
> *It's been some time, eh? I guess you and I aren't great letter writers. Hope everything's okay with you.*
>
> *I just thought you might want to know about Chris. He signed up with the army and was sent to Vietnam. He came back for a few days on leave last month, but when he went back, he got killed.*

I had to put the pen down and close my sad eyes for a minute while I got my breathing under control.

> *He was saving four guys in his platoon, getting them into cover under fire, when he got shot.*
> *Anyway, that's about it. Hope this gets to you, because all I have is your grandmother's address.*
> *Your friend,*
> *Paul Landon*

I'd just gone downstairs to find an envelope and a stamp when I heard my mom's car pulling in. As soon as I'd dashed upstairs I realized I should probably help her with the bags, so I shoved the letter into my top drawer and headed down again. Afterward, back in my room, I stood in front of the desk, watching dusk get duskier outside, wondering why I'd felt it was necessary to hide the letter. It's not like I shouldn't write it, and it's not like I'd said anything my parents shouldn't see. I figured maybe it was because I'd cried; a man wouldn't do that, right? Or maybe because a man wouldn't do anything to remind Mom how sad she was, so he wouldn't want her to see the letter?

Plus, there was that crumpled ball of what I'd written to Chris, in the wastebasket right beside the desk. I bent over and retrieved it. Turning around in circles, I scoured the room for a good place to hide it until I could figure out what to do with it. I settled on a spot under the mattress, since I'd probably be changing my own sheets again in a day or so, what with the mess I was still making of them. One arm stuffed between mattress and box spring, it occurred to me that if I did the trash myself, I could sneak it in then and no one would ever see it. My job had always been taking the trash outside, but Mom had always collected it. I'd have to do both, which could be a good thing; if my folks had liked my doing my own laundry, even though it was for the wrong reasons, they'd probably feel the same about the trash. Also for the wrong reasons.

*Is deceit part of being a man?*

As quickly as I could, I found Charlie's letters in the box I'd pulled out of the closet. Then I sat at my desk, addressed and stamped the envelope, and stowed it and the SADEYE pellets back in the drawer; I'd get the letter mailed somehow, probably on another bike ride. Next I threw everything except the Ho Chi Minhs back into the closet. The sandals went under my bed; I didn't want to lose track of where they were.

Sunday I drove Mom to church again. I was beginning to wonder why Dad never went with her anymore, but I knew better than to ask a question like that if I wasn't real sure I wanted to hear the answer. Don't stir things up, is what Dad had told me; we need calm. So I didn't ask.

It was the service before Christmas, and the place was fairly glowing with expectation. The sermon was all about the love God has for the world, the hope Jesus represents, and the lesson was that what we need most will always be provided.

So I prayed for all I was worth. I figured I'd built up a little equity by now, and maybe someone would at least let me know they'd heard me, even if maybe I couldn't have everything I thought I needed just yet. So I prayed for the protection of Chris's soul, for life to find a new "normal" soon, and for me to figure out what Dad wanted beyond laundry and trash collection. As I prayed, silently of course, I got this really intense feeling all through me and a kind of warmth in the general vicinity of my throat. My eyes watered, but this time they didn't feel like sad eyes. I took it as a sign that I'd been heard.

Toward the end of the service the minister announced that the midnight service would begin at eleven tonight, which seemed odd to me; why was that a midnight service? *Never mind; don't ask stupid questions. Just ask Mom if she wants to go to it.*

On the drive home, that's what I did. We were about halfway there, and the sun was trying to make us believe it was really up there someplace. I took a turn, careful to put on the blinker and slow down, pretending there was a cup of water on the dashboard. When he'd taught me to drive, Dad had told me that's the way to handle turns with Mom in the car, so that's how I did it.

Then I said, "Mom? Is that midnight service something you'd like to do?"

She didn't answer right away. I waited. Finally, "I don't know how you knew that, Paul. I haven't done that since I was a girl, but I was thinking during the announcement that it would be a wonderful thing to do. I just didn't want to ask you to go to church twice in one day, and I don't really want to go alone. My brother won't go, I'm pretty sure."

"That's okay. I don't mind, really." And in truth, I was hoping to feel that intense feeling again in this "midnight" service, maybe even get something by way of an answer.

We had fried chicken for dinner, which I really like. I chose to take it as a sign that I was doing what Jesus wanted. During the meal, Mom mentioned to Dad that I was taking her to the midnight service. His reaction was not what I would have expected.

Fork frozen halfway to his mouth, he said, "You don't usually go to that." And then he looked at me and scowled for a second before he put the fork into his mouth.

"It's kind of a special year, dear." Mom's voice sounded odd. I couldn't tell whether she was trying not to cry or if she was irritated with Dad.

We all watched a little TV, and when Dad went into his den about ten, I went upstairs to change. I kept picking out clothes and putting them back and pulling them out again, not concentrating very well, until finally I realized that what I wanted to do was ask Dad to come. Maybe he'd been pissed that he'd be all alone in the house on Christmas Eve. So I went downstairs and stared at the door to the den. It felt a little like a lion's den; I wasn't in the habit of going in there. That had been Chris's right. Chris's duty. But it wasn't like I was gonna say anything bad, right? Finally I knocked on the door.

"Come in."

He'd been reading one of his historical novels about British ships at war, and he looked over the tops of his glasses at me. I closed the door. If he said no, I didn't want Mom to know. "Um, Dad, I don't know if this is a good idea or not, but—well . . ."

"What is it Paul?" He sounded irritated.

"Okay, um, I was wondering if you might want to go with us. To the Christmas Eve service. We have to leave really soon, so . . . I don't know. I just thought I'd ask."

His eyes went back to the book, still open in front of him. "You know your mother is going to want to go to church again tomorrow, don't you?"

I blinked. *Is he serious? Will she really? Again? Well . . .* "It's Christmas." I shrugged. And what kind of an answer was that to give me, anyway?

"I was going to go with her tomorrow. I can't say I put any stock in all this praying, myself, but if she wants to go tomorrow I'll go with her. Give you a break."

So I wouldn't have to go tomorrow? Or was it that he didn't want me to? I nodded to show I understood he wouldn't go tonight, but then I asked, "So you don't think I should go to-morrow?"

He closed his book, holding a finger in the page to keep his place. "I don't care whether you go or not. I'm not altogether sure I like this churchgoing business, but I don't see how I can discourage your mother when you keep taking her."

"Oh. But didn't you go with her for a while before . . ." Before Chris died, was what I'd been going to say.

He opened his book a little sharply. "And what good did it do?" He glared at me while I tried to figure out how, or whether, to answer that. He sighed. "I honestly don't care, Chris. You know very well how I feel about it. Do what you want on this score."

Chris. He'd called me Chris. I was so dumbfounded I didn't know how to respond. *Should I point it out? No, that would proba-bly be a dumb-ass thing to do. It would only make him mad at both of us.* All I said was, "Okay. I'll go tonight. I'll think about going tomorrow."

*Did his comment to "Chris" mean he hadn't liked that Chris kept taking Mom to church? And did he think he was talking to Chris when he'd said that I knew how he felt? Because I really don't.*

As I was backing out of the den he said, "I doubt I'll be up when you get back, so I'll say good night now."

"Okay. Good night, Dad."

In a daze I dressed in whatever came to hand and was standing at the door, coat over my arm and keys in my hand, when Mom came downstairs. She looked sweet and happy and maybe a little sad, too.

"Shall we go?" And she smiled at me.

I did my best to smile back, and thank God I remembered to hold all the doors at the right times, and that we got to the church without hitting anything. All my attention was on what Dad had said to Chris. To me, but to Chris.

It was an effort to pay attention during the service, too. I'd hoped that I'd get some tiny feeling of hope that things would get better and that Chris's soul would be taken to heaven, but I was numb. I kept losing track of what verse we were on in the hymns, and I barely noticed the organist making a mess of the endings of all those familiar carols. Mom held my hand a lot, and one time I forgot she had a hold on it and I tried to reach up to scratch my ear. Embarrassment hauled me back to the present, but only for a few minutes. Then I was back into fog again.

*Had Dad resented it when Chris kept going with Mom to church when Dad wouldn't? And when Dad had started going again, after Chris had been home on leave, was he trying to be Chris for Mom? Had he been trying to do what he'd been telling me to do lately, to be a man and make things easier for her? And is he now getting me to do what he can't, just like he'd sent Chris to war for him?*

My breath stopped, and I had to take in a really sharp gasp to get it going again. Once I did, the fog was gone. Or, not gone, but it had a different quality to it. Now it was a sort of red haze, like anger. Like fury. I was breathing again, that's for sure. Too quickly. In, out, in, out, round and round, setting up a whirlpool. It was an effort to calm myself enough to be a sane person by the time everyone stood for the final hymn, "Hark the Herald Angels Sing." This time the fancy organ crap on the last verse really burned me, and I sang through gritted teeth.

I'd just shut the passenger side door for Mom and was walking around the back of the car to get in when I realized I hadn't spent any time at all praying. Not for Chris, not for me, not for anything. I stood frozen with my gloved fingers on the door handle; would this, like, cancel out all the praying I'd done up to now? I closed my eyes and took just a second to send up a silent plea. *Please, God; don't punish me—or Chris—for this.*

# Chapter 6

Christmas morning was a bust. It started out fine, with Mom making cocoa just like always, just as if Chris were there. She'd even done a stocking for me—candies, silly little trinkets, and a tangerine in the toe—which surprised me, 'cause I hadn't had a stocking in years. In fact, it confused me; it's kids who want Christmas stockings, not men, so I wasn't sure how to act. If I didn't get excited at all, it would hurt her feelings, but did I want to look like a kid in front of Dad? I walked a very uncomfortable line, and I don't think it made either of them happy.

Mom liked the bath set, or said she did, adding something about treating herself to some relaxing times. Then she handed Dad my gift to him where he sat in his favorite chair.

He stopped when the wrapping paper was partway off; he could already see what it was. He held it in both hands, propped it on his legs, and scowled at it. "Paul, just how did you manage to buy this? Did your mother do it for you?"

She was probably anxious to give me all the credit, 'cause she answered him herself, sounding cheerful. "Not a bit! He took care of these gifts all on his own." She smiled at me.

But there was thunder brewing; I was surprised she couldn't tell. Dad's eyes flicked from her back to me. "Young man, bring me your wallet."

I blinked stupidly. "What? Why?"

"Do as I say!"

"Andy?" Mom's voice was worried.

I tried to play casual. I shrugged and went upstairs, fetched it, and brought it back to where Mom and Dad were talking in hushed tones. He nearly snatched it from me and then emptied it completely, picking up every scrap of paper and examining every object.

"Dad, um, what exactly are you looking for?" I just stood there and watched, worried by his behavior, though I couldn't imagine what he thought I'd done.

Finally he threw the wallet onto the floor. "Where do you keep it?"

"Keep what? What are you talking about?"

"Don't you pretend with me. You know very well."

I threw a glance at Mom, silently pleading for her to come to my rescue, but she was looking at the floor. She obviously knew what this was all about.

*Time to be a man.* "Dad, if you want me to answer you, ask me a question I *can* answer."

He stood, paper and bows and tobacco packets falling in cascades. His voice was dark. "Where is the false ID you used?"

*ID? ID* . . . And suddenly it dawned on me. I let out an exasperated sigh. "I don't have a false ID. Mr. Chandler and I made an arrangement. He carried the tobacco out of the shop, gave it to me outside, and told me to come back after Christmas"— my voice started to rise—"to pay him for the stuff and to tell him how much you liked it!" We stood there, nearly toe to toe, and I realized for the first time that I was now just a little taller than him. My voice took on a sarcastic note. "So, Dad, how much do you like it? Please tell me so that I can report back to Mr. Chandler, since both of you don't trust me."

"This isn't a question of trust. Selling tobacco to you is illegal."

"Who do you think you are, a cop or something?" *That oughta hurt.*

He just stood there, breathing noisily through his nose, and then he said, "You talked Mr. Chandler into jeopardizing his store by breaking the law for you."

"Yeah. Sure. Whatever. You're welcome." I turned and stomped upstairs to my room.

My parents' voices drifted up from downstairs, and my ears strained for recognizable words and angry tones. When I could hear neither, I took it as a good sign; maybe Mom would calm him down for me this time. I half expected someone to come knocking on my door, and after an hour I heard first Mom and then Dad come upstairs, but I guess all they did was dress for church. *Will anyone ask me if I'm going?*

The answer was no. They just went downstairs again, got in the car, and drove off.

*What the fuck?* Had Dad told Mom I didn't want to go? Or was this their way of telling me how out of line I was and that I was only marginally in the family at the moment?

Would they have just walked out on Chris?

*Hell, no!*

I threw my door open and nearly ran downstairs. Mom had put my wallet back together and had already dealt with most of the wrappings and bows and crap, though it looked like she'd stopped partway through. But my stocking, all neatly re-stuffed, was in a pile with the wallet and the other things I'd been given. There was a new light for my bicycle, biking gloves, a new parka, and *Seven Separate Fools,* the latest Three Dog Night album. I wrapped my arms around all of it, hiked back upstairs, and tossed it all onto my bed. Then I went into Chris's room and pulled out about ten albums from his collection that I wanted and added them to the pile in my room. I stood there, panting more from fury than exertion, and ran a hand through my hair. Then I wheeled around and went back into Chris's room.

One of these days Mom was gonna put a special lock on this door and hide the key, and I wouldn't be able to come in here anymore. Would I still care? What difference would it make? I stood there, looking around at everything, turning in place, and getting angrier with each revolution.

"FUCK!"

I yelled it again, just to hear it, just for the satisfaction of doing it. Then, "Fuck you, Chris!"

*Fuck you. Fuck you for signing up. Fuck you for trying to do what Dad wanted you to do. Fuck you for going over there. Fuck you for getting killed. Fuck you for being gay. And fuck you for making me love you.*

*Oh, yeah; and fuck you for leaving me this legacy to remember you by. This legacy of secrets. This burden I have to carry for you the rest of my fucking life.*

I slammed the door on my way back to my room, where I nearly threw the mattress off the bed looking for the pages I'd written to him. The albums slid off of each other and onto the floor, but I didn't care. Crumpled papers in hand, I thundered downstairs, grabbed Dad's pipe lighter, and set fire to a corner of the wad. Too late I realized I needed to move the fireplace screen before I could toss the flaming mass in, and by the time I managed that with my one free hand, a bit of smoldering paper had separated itself and landed on some paper Mom hadn't picked up yet. Guess what happened.

Some indeterminate amount of time later, with the legs of the wooden table nearest the fireplace scorched and the carpet on that side of the hearth burned and stinking, the flames were out. My papers were gone, mission accomplished; but I had to come up with some reason why this had happened. I stood there, looking around, and my gaze landed on the pile of wrapping paper that Mom had left. So I crumpled it, tossed it all into the fireplace, and set fire to it. If I was going to catch hell—and there didn't seem any way out of that—I needed a better reason than "I was trying to get rid of some stuff I didn't want you to see." I contemplated disappearing for a while, but I knew that if Dad got home and I'd skipped out it would be worse. So I went back to Chris's room and knelt by the bed, thinking I'd wait there. And I prayed.

*Jesus, it wasn't my fault I didn't get to church this morning. I was going to go, you know that. If you're fair, you won't let this relapse affect what I've been asking for. Which, as you know, is for Chris to be in heaven, and for things here on earth to be calm enough for us to figure out how we can go on from here. So please don't blame me because my dad thinks I did something I shouldn't have. He's wrong. Mr. Chandler wouldn't have done something that would jeopardize his store, and Dad just couldn't back down from his high horse. So he tried to make it my fault anyway, which you know very well it wasn't. So don't take it out on me, or Chris. Please. Thank you. Amen.*

I sat on the bed, but that didn't seem right. I sat at the desk. But the walls started closing in on me, so I went into the basement and stayed there until I heard the car.

Predictably, Dad blew his stack. "What in God's name were you thinking?"

For a few minutes Mom stood in the doorway to the kitchen looking worried, but she must have figured she couldn't help because she disappeared into that housewife's haven.

"I was trying to help, I told you. I was getting rid of some of this stuff. Cleaning up."

"You sure cleaned up, all right. Just look at this mess! This table belonged to your grandmother, and now it's ruined. And the carpet!"

*Yeah, I can see that. Did you think that got by me?* I said nothing aloud but waited for the steam to rise a little higher, which I knew it would; he wasn't played out. But I wasn't gonna do anything, if I could help it, to make things worse. I kept my mouth shut.

"What do you think ought to happen next, hmmm? What's the next step here?"

"I don't know, Dad. I've said I'm sorry, I've admitted it was stupid. What else can I say?"

It escalated from there with him shouting about what a child I was until I'd about had it. I started fighting back. "It wouldn't have happened if you guys hadn't just left on me. Why didn't you ask me to go with you? I asked you to go with us last night."

"Don't you try to make this anyone's fault but yours, young man."

"You tried to make it my fault that you were wrong about my nonexistent fake ID."

Silence. Always a bad sign. It's the point in one of these arguments where Dad gives up on words and resorts to physical bashing. His arm shot out and pointed in the direction of the basement door.

Now we'd reached the point at which our family script says I'm to turn and walk in front of him to the door and down the steps, anticipating the strike of a leather strap against my ass all the way. But this time I didn't turn.

"What are you waiting for?" he nearly shouted.

"I'm waiting for an apology." I guess I had a death wish or something. "You accused me of having an illegal ID this morning, in case you've forgotten, and I had no such thing. The only thing I did wrong was to get you something I knew you'd like for Christmas. And now you're gonna whip my ass? I don't think so."

He stepped forward, nearly onto my toes, and looked up at me. "What are you gonna do about it?"

"Andy!" It was Mom's voice. She was in the fray now, and she pushed me away and faced Dad herself. "It's Christmas Day!"

I wanted more. I wanted her to point out that he'd been wrong to accuse me earlier, that they'd both been wrong not to ask me to go with them, and that the burned wood and carpet just evened today's score. But she evidently wanted all of us to live to see another day and just stood between us. It reminded me of that time Mom had told me I wasn't taking Laura to any party the weekend that Chris would be home. *Jeez, was that only five weeks ago?* Then, and now, she was stone. She was ice. She was something that would not be moved.

So in the end it took a woman to stare down two men who were bent on damaging each other. Because I swear, if he'd come at me with that belt, I'd have taken it away from him, and he'd be lucky if I didn't use it on him. I think Mom knew that. I think she knew the time when I'd let him do that to me was over.

Dinner that night was about as glum as it's possible to imagine. I was civil to Mom, but I didn't speak to Dad. He spoke to no one.

She cried as she did the dishes. I felt like a shit, but I didn't see what I could have done differently. Dad just landed in his precious recliner, and I went upstairs to my room. Mom went into Chris's room and shut the door.

*Happy Birthday, Jesus.*

The next morning, after Dad was safely at work, I sat at the desk in his den, with the door shut. I'd looked up Mr. Treadwell's home number and had even written it on a piece of green-lined paper. It was in front of me now, staring up at me. Three times, maybe four, I picked up the telephone handset and dialed a few of the numbers before I hung up again. The thing was, I didn't know what I'd say to him. What I had was a laundry list of complaints against my dad, and a few against Chris that I couldn't talk about. And what was Mr. Treadwell gonna be able to do about any of that? What could anyone do?

In the end I called Marty Kaufman. I could have called Bobby, or Terry, or a couple other guys, but I called Marty, probably because he's the one my parents liked the least. It had been a while since we'd talked outside of necessity, but we weren't enemies or anything. So we decided to hook up. He had his license by now.

"Let's cruise, kid," he said. "I'll let you drive some."

When I saw his car from my bedroom window I headed downstairs, shrugging into a jean jacket as I went. I called to Mom that I was going out for a while, not stopping long enough to hear if she had anything to say to that, or if she wanted any more information.

Marty had a five-year-old Mustang, dark green, standard transmission. We spent some time in a nearly empty parking lot while he let me practically strip his gears figuring out how to work the clutch, and finally I got it. Then he took the wheel back and gunned the car over icy patches, spinning around as many times as possible before the tires caught pavement again. At one point something went a little screwy under the hood, and Marty had to get this mondo toolbox, bright shiny red, out of the trunk.

"Jeepers, creepers," I said, faking amazement. "Anything you don't have in that box?"

"Not much. You never know what you'll need, eh?"

He had no trouble setting things to rights, and we were off. I drove some on the highway—license laws be damned—and we stopped for burgers and sodas around three o'clock. After that he just drove around, honking at other cars and whistling at girls, sometimes with the windows down so they'd hear. Marty made so many comments about one girl's body or another's that I finally asked him, "How much have you done, anyway? How far have you gone with a girl?"

"Christ, Landon. What haven't I done?" He laughed like a hyena and slapped the steering wheel. "You name it. Or just name a girl! Ha, ha!" He sniffed as though that punctuated the expertise he was claiming. "What about you? Popped anyone's cherry yet? Nothin' like it."

I hadn't even popped my own, truth be told. Not with any body parts other than my own hand. I decided against answering; Marty's question had sounded nearly rhetorical, anyway. But he wasn't through.

"Seriously. You done it yet?"

He kept glancing at me and back at the road. Finally I had to own up. "Not yet."

He nodded like he wasn't surprised. "Got anyone in mind?"

"No one I've seen yet." I tried to make it sound like no one I'd met was worth it.

"This is gonna be your year, kid. I'll see to it."

The conversation, what there was of it, ranged over various topics after that. Conversation is not what Marty does best. At one point he rolled his window down out of necessity—not just to whistle at girls. He'd let go of a whopper fart. I was sure he'd blame me, like, *Christ, Landon. What're they feeding you, rotten eggs?* But he cackled insanely and then rolled down the window frantically as he said, "Shit! Even I didn't like that one!"

Back at my house, he said, "Give me a little more advance notice next time, champ. I'll have a chilled six-pack in the trunk."

My dad was already home, which I thought was probably a

bad sign for me. It might mean they'd been waiting dinner for me. That wasn't the case. Something else was waiting for me, though. Dad was at the kitchen table facing the door, a beer in front of him, with no sign of Mom, or dinner, anywhere. We hadn't talked, Dad and I, since we'd nearly come to blows the day before. I stopped just inside the door to the kitchen, wary. He glared at me.

Then he said, "Do you know where your mother is?"

*How could I? I just got here. And why are you always asking me questions I can't answer?* I said, "No."

"She's upstairs. Crying her eyes out. And do you know why?" I took a deep breath as several wise-ass retorts played themselves out in my head. It must have been too long. "Do you know why?" he shouted at me.

"I'm sure you're about to tell me." *What does he expect?*

He stood, leaning his fingers on the tabletop. I was trying to get a sense of how drunk he was. His voice seemed steady enough when he growled, "She's been trying so hard not to cry. She's been trying to be here, in the present as she puts it, for you. And what do you do?" He waited; I couldn't tell if it was just for dramatic effect or if he expected me to say something.

I decided to answer him. "I take her to church and let her hold my hand during the service. I learn to do laundry. I work during my vacation on school stuff to keep my grades up. I pray for God to make me a little like Chris so I can—"

"Like Chris? You think you want to be like Chris?" His voice rose as he went on. "Whatever Chris was, at least he would never have left his Vietnamese sandals under his bed where his mother would find them while she's cleaning his room for him."

So many things went through my head I didn't know where to start. All I said in the end was, "Those aren't his sandals. They're mine."

He moved from behind the table while he did his best to terrify me. It would have worked once upon a time. "They represent your brother. They remind your mother of what she lost."

"I lost him, too. And so did you, even if you called me by his name the other night. And I'm sorry if seeing those sandals upset her, but they're mine, and they're in my room, and I'm not gonna pretend he wasn't my brother."

"No one's asking you to. But I'll tell you this: You're not going to be like him."

He advanced on me, but I was determined to hold this ground. Through gritted teeth I told him, "And he was nothing like you." That took him by surprise, and I leaned into the weakness I sensed. "Why couldn't it have been you who died over there instead of him?"

I was hoping to see more surprise. I wanted shock and awe. What I got instead was delivered in dead tones. "Do you think I haven't wished that every day for nearly a month?"

*At least we agree on something.* I turned on my heel and left him standing there. Upstairs, I stopped outside Mom and Dad's room, thinking I might go in and apologize to her, but I was still so angry I didn't trust my tone. Plus, what did I have to apologize *for?* It wasn't my fault Chris had given me those sandals, and I certainly didn't leave them under the bed so anyone would find them and weep. Maybe I should leave the SADEYE pellets out and see what effect *they* had.

I fell onto my bed, feet on the pillow, head toward the foot. *Is this how they'd bury someone they were ashamed of, rather than the right way around in the grave?* And then I cursed God. I damned Jesus. Why couldn't even *they* do something right? Here we had a houseful of people, all mourning the loss of the best member of the family—at least we agreed on that point—and we couldn't even get along? We couldn't even comfort each other? We couldn't even talk to each other in normal voices, have normal conversations? We had to be at each other's throat? And Dad even had to rub it in. "You're not going to be like him." It had almost sounded like he should have added, "If I have anything to say about it."

It would be one thing, I chastised the Almighty, if I hadn't been asking—begging, praying!—for help. Did this mean God was equally incompetent at saving Chris's soul? Was my brother turned over to Satan to be tortured forever because he'd had a few misguided intimate moments with guys, and God Himself was powerless to do anything about it?

If Jesus was the son of God, then it was the same way I was the son of my father. All four of us mean-spirited and useless.

As if we needed any more drama, Thursday the twenty-eighth was the day of Chris's funeral. I have to say I don't remember much about it. Mom had told me to invite anyone I wanted, so I'd asked Bobby Darnell. I wanted to ask Terry, 'cause I knew him better, but I knew Dad would throw a fit and Terry would feel weird. Bobby would understand.

So that was the next time I was in church. I sat next to Mom on the far side of Dad, and Bobby sat next to me with his parents beside him. I think if Ken had come home already it would have been impossible, but he was still over there, so Bobby and his folks were the right choice, even if it was a little tough on them. At least I did something right.

I'd expected to be, like, totally numb. And for the most part I was. Two things freaked me out, though. One was walking past the casket. It was closed, of course, and as we approached it I was thinking that was better. I'd seen it at the funeral parlor, but I'd stayed pretty far away from it. The thing had seemed so unrelated to Chris, anyway. And everyone there had kept coming up to me and saying how sorry they were and all, so it was pretty distracting, and it was easy to ignore the thing. But in the church, as it lay there looking imposing and dark and—I don't know, maybe ominous, I couldn't take my eyes off it. Like it was the last I'd ever see of Chris. But it wasn't Chris, and the last I'd seen of Chris was him getting into that cab and slamming the door. In a way the coffin was no more related to him there in the church than it had been at the funeral parlor, but in another way it felt even more him than the cab that had taken him away, even though I'd actually seen him then. None of it made any sense. My brain felt like it was retreating from the insides of my skull, and I started breathing really quickly. As we approached it, I tried focusing on Dad's limp; he was ahead of

Mom, who was ahead of me. That helped for about seven paces but no more.

I wanted to shout that Chris wasn't in there. That everyone was mistaken. They were just as wrong about this as they were that he'd been a brave soldier who would one day marry some sweet girl and have kids. But I was the only one who knew the truth, and all they'd do is lock me up. So I clenched my jaw shut and put one foot in front of the other.

The other freaky part was at the cemetery. They had Mom and Dad each throw a handful of earth onto the top of the coffin once it was in the hole, and of course Mom was sobbing the whole time. I couldn't blame her; I kind of wanted to do that, too. What got to me was the sound when the dirt clods hit the top of the casket and made this thud. Dad's was worse, 'cause his hand could hold more dirt than Mom's. And it was almost like Chris was knocking, banging on the other side of the lid to be let out.

They ushered us out after that; didn't let us stay and watch the rest of the dirt get piled onto him. Probably just as well. So we walked back to the big black car while the occasional piece of frozen rain bounced off someone's black-clad shoulder. At least that didn't make any sound.

I didn't go to church that Sunday. Neither did Dad. Uncle Jeff and Aunt Diane came to pick Mom up.

So 1973 started out with a kind of armed truce going on in our house. Dad and I barely spoke. Mom gave up on trying to turn me into Sunday Chris, which was fine by me because I'd decided God/Jesus/Whoever was full of shit, anyway. Mom started going regularly with my uncle and aunt. She stopped making cookies, and I didn't much care.

Charlie's letter, which I'd finally managed to get into the mail, came back "Addressee Unknown." The boomerang landed on a day when I'd gone to the library after school, and I got home just before Dad. I walked into the kitchen and Mom stopped what she was doing, wiped her hands on her apron, and picked up this envelope, looking sadly at me as she held it out. I took it and read the official stamped message.

"You wrote to your friend Charlie?" Her voice was soft, and I felt I needed to answer.

"I thought he might wanna know about Chris. I guess he's moved again."

"Oh, sweetie." She wrapped her arms around me and got me into this hug that reminded me of the way she used to hug Chris. She seemed oblivious of the hissing and spitting of whatever it was she'd been cooking on the stovetop.

We were still standing like that when Dad walked in. And he froze. From over Mom's shoulder I could see his face. It was like he'd seen a ghost.

# Chapter 7

The second week of January I stopped in at the Burger King one afternoon and applied for an after-school job. Without something to keep me out of the house, all I could see stretching out into the infinite future was sulking in my room, trying to beat Mom out of getting into Chris's room, and avoiding Dad generally. I started at Burger King that weekend without telling anyone what I was doing until Saturday morning. I had to let Mom know I was going out, and of course she wanted to know where. She just blinked in surprise at the news, so I headed out quickly.

They put me in the kitchen, which was fine by me; I didn't want to have to wait on some of those idiots who came to the counter and asked stupid questions and wanted special orders placed. My first duties involved getting utensils, condiment trays, and any other loose items into the dishwasher, cleaned, and put back where they could be used again. Some of the stuff had to be washed by hand, and I had these thick gloves to wear that made my hands smell funny and made my skin feel odd if I wore them for a long time, so I tried to vary the tasks so I could take the gloves off sometimes.

I got home about five-thirty, having done a shift from eleven to five, exhausted and reeking of an odd combination of kitchen grease and disinfectant soap. When I got out of the shower Mom said Dad was waiting in his den and wanted to talk to me.

*Fuck. Just what I don't need. Well, he's not going to get to me.* I knocked and opened the door without waiting for a response.

"Mom said you were looking for me."

"Sit down, Paul." I sat, hoping I didn't look quite as belligerent as I felt. "Your mother tells me you're working at the Burger King."

"That's right."

"Is this because your mother and I felt we couldn't increase your allowance when you asked last fall?"

*Was it? Maybe. Sort of.* "I guess that's part of it."

"You could have come to work at the store." He meant his store.

Actually, I hadn't even thought of that, but I wouldn't have done it, anyway. "I figured we could use a break from each other."

He sighed, and it sounded almost sad. "You're probably right." He sat forward in his chair. "I hope you're planning to put part of your earnings into your bank account for college expenses."

There had always been this sort of assumption, I suppose, in the back of everyone's mind, that I would go to college. With Chris it had been a big deal, 'cause he would be the first. Plus his grades were always high, while mine were mediocre. So the assumption hadn't been so strong in my own mind. But Dad had just laid it out in the open.

I told him the truth, as far as it went. "I hadn't thought of that."

"Then think of it. And do something about it. Your mother and I have some money put away for your schooling, just like we had for Chris. But even if we add his to yours it won't be quite enough to cover everything. You'll need to help. It will be better for you this way, too; you'll be less likely to take money for granted if you have to work for it. The Burger King is all right for now, though I would rather you had come to the store, but you should put away as much as you can."

I was still back on the phrase "if we add his to yours." And I must have looked as confused as I felt, because he spoke again.

"Paul, I'm not hearing agreement from you. Do we need to go over your salary together to decide how much . . ."

"No. Um, no. I—that won't be necessary. I was just surprised about the money you've put away, that's all."

"Then let's leave it like this. We'll review your bank account in a couple of months and see if it looks good or if some changes need to be made."

I would have been an idiot to tell him it was none of his business, even though I wanted to. Besides, I was confused as hell. Chris's college money was going to be mine? Dad had said "if." Did that mean anything? Did I have to do something, prove something, act in some particular way for that money to come to me? And at some point would he stop bouncing me back and forth between making me feel like he hated my guts and letting me feel like maybe I was a real member of the family after all?

At least he hadn't yelled at me for not telling him I was going to apply for the job. I racked my brains for why he hadn't, because it would have been like him, but the only thing I could come up with was that he thought it was another one of those "acting like a man" moments. But since I still wasn't clear what my being a man meant to him, all I could do was guess. I felt like I'd been guessing, trying, failing, occasionally succeeding although more by accident than anything else, for weeks. So the things I'd done trying to be a man had got me into trouble, and I'd been praised—or at least treated decently—when I'd done something that turned out to meet with Dad's approval without any such intent from me. And sometimes it was something I'd done to cover up something else.

*I can't wait to get out of this house for good.*

At first, in the Burger King kitchen, I didn't really know anybody so all I did was work. But it didn't take long to make the acquaintance of the different guys who flipped the burgers and dumped the fry baskets into the hot oil. This one guy named Tim was there only on weekends, and sometimes we had the same shift. He was a senior at my school, and I'd seen him around, but mostly that crowd won't mix down unless they have to. Tim and I kind of had to mix at the Burger King. I didn't like him right away, and he probably didn't like me, either. But pretty soon we figured out that we had this one thing in common. We both thought life sucked. It's amazing how strong glue like that can be between people who otherwise might not get along too well.

Every so often we'd take a break at the same time. We'd sit on the step out back beside the Dumpster, which didn't smell too bad in the cold weather, and we looked pretty funny with our jackets on over our stained white aprons. Usually he'd smoke a cigarette and bitch about the manager, David. I was getting along okay with David, so I just listened and did my best to sympathize without contradicting Tim at all, and that seemed to work. It also helped that I never repeated anything Tim said about David. And by then David had me learning to flip burgers and do the fries, too, which would mean I wouldn't always have to be dishwasher, so I didn't want to piss anybody off.

Sometimes Tim and I also chatted about the girls who worked the counter. Most of them were girls who had plenty of time to work because they probably couldn't get dates, but a couple of them were cute. Tim did a lot of speculating about how attractive the parts of them were that he couldn't see for their clothing.

One day when we had the same shift I was out back already, alone, just sitting there, when Tim came out. He plopped down next to me, reached for his pack of cigs, tapped it so the ends of a few of them poked out, and held it toward me.

I took one. I don't know why. It wasn't something I'd been thinking about, at least not seriously, and I'd never tried one. I think maybe it was because Chris never did. But—hell, he'd traded cookies for cigs, and he'd been over there smoking marijuana, and he wasn't around anymore, anyway. So I took one. I put it in my mouth like I'd seen other kids do so many times and leaned over to where Tim had flicked his lighter on. Somehow I knew that I should get the thing going by pulling only from my mouth, not my lungs, and that's what I did. Given the coughing fit that hit me just doing it that way made me real glad I hadn't actually inhaled that first bit.

Tim laughed and slapped my back. When I'd recovered a little he said, "I thought so. About time, though, don't you think?"

"Yeah," I said, my voice barely able to make its way out of me, "that's why I took it."

"Good man."

We didn't say much else. He gave me a few pointers about how to get the most enjoyment out of the cig, but we weren't big talkers, either of us. Which left me plenty of time to wonder if Tim's idea of "good man" and my dad's would be anything alike. Somehow I didn't think Dad would agree that my starting to smoke would be one of the ways he wanted me to prove my manhood. I felt a little ill after that first smoke, but I knew that wasn't guilt; that was just me losing my virginity.

After that I bought packs off of Tim, offered him a cig occasionally, and smoked them only on my breaks. But I did look forward to those breaks.

I was real careful with those first few paychecks. I didn't want to put away so much that I set up standards that would make future deposits look puny, but I expected Dad would remember that he wanted to see my bank account. My plan was to make the first examination meet at least minimal standards in the hopes that he'd see I was doing what he wanted and would then leave me alone. So by the end of February, even though I'd bought a few new albums, lots of cigs, and had taken Jenny—the cuter of the two counter girls—out once, I had socked away enough to at least barely satisfy my dad's expectations when he asked to see my statement. "I think you can do better, Paul, but this is a good start." He didn't say anything about wanting to see it again.

I was also doing okay in school. If I was getting Chris's money, I was gonna need decent grades. I knew it would be the school that'd get the money, but it would get me out of the house and into a culture where I could be myself for the first time in my life. That's how I thought of it. And since I was doing all right, even Mr. Treadwell—who'd told me he'd be keeping an eye on me—didn't feel it was necessary to call my folks in for some kind of parent–teacher conference, like he'd threatened in December.

In March, after my seventeenth birthday, I passed my full driver's exam, which meant I could now drive without one of my folks in the car. Jenny had been pretty disdainful that we'd had to take a bus for that date I'd taken her on, and I was determined to do it right next time. She was no Laura Holmes, but I figured she'd be good practice until I could get up the courage to ask Laura out again. Plus I'd been storing up brownie points, what with the finances and grades, so when I wanted to take Jenny out for a real date, it wasn't too hard to get Mom's car, even if it was only a boring old Ford.

We went to a movie—something she wanted to see, I don't remember what—and sat in the balcony. In the back. I took as much advantage as she'd let me, which was just enough to make me want more. Every so often she'd say, "I would like to see a little of the movie, please?" and I'd give her a few minutes when I just rested my arm behind her. But my hand kept creeping down almost on its own to find a boob, and sometimes it seemed like she was pretending not to notice. I know she did, though. I mean, I *know* she did. Because sometimes she'd groan a little and shift in her seat. The first time that happened I pulled my hand away fast, back to her shoulder, anyway, but before long she leaned against the seat in a way that encouraged me to let my fingers inch down again.

I had absolutely no idea what that movie was about. All I knew was how much I was loving the way my pants felt entirely too tight.

Afterward we went for a burger. Not to Burger King. I took her to this place with waiters and real booths. Our sodas got to the table ahead of the food, as usual. Jenny, sitting across from me, smiled this secret kind of smile and put her pocketbook in her lap. She opened it real carefully and pulled something out of it, still hidden from sight. Then she slid her own glass close to the edge of the table, looked around the room, brought her hand out from under the table, and poured something into the glass from a tiny bottle she had hidden in her hand. She pushed the soda over to me, and wiggled her fingers to indicate I should give mine to her. When I sipped from the glass she'd slid over, it was laced with rum.

Well, this was not the sort of date I was used to having. None of the girls I'd ever gone out with, or gone to parties with, would have carried the stuff in with her. I'd had a few drinks, sure; who hadn't? But this raised the bar. Jenny was opening a few doors for me that night.

We went parking before I took her home, though she kept a sharp eye on her watch. She told me, "As long as I meet their stupid deadline, they don't give me the third degree." Which I took to mean that Jenny and I were of the same mind; her approach to curfew was exactly like mine to financial planning.

We went out again the second week of April, and during the parking session she found ways to encourage me to touch a lot more female skin than I ever had before. It started with kissing, of course, and with me squeezing her boobs. But then she surprised me by poking at that straining seam in my pants, and I jumped.

She laughed. "Oh, so you can touch me, but I can't touch you? If that's what you think, forget it." And she dug into my crotch a little more with her fingers and then into my mouth with her tongue.

By the time we needed to leave she'd got my dick out of my pants, sucked on it, and kissed me as I came all over her leg. She used some tissues to wipe herself off and then she said, "Next time, lover boy, bring a condom. Then the messy part won't be so messy, and we can both enjoy it." And she took my hand and guided it under her skirt.

After I dropped her off I opened the trunk and got out a

towel I knew Mom kept back there for some reason, got back into the car, and jerked off into it all over again.

Condoms. Well, I guess she drew the line at liquor; she'd bring that, but the condoms were up to me. That seemed fair. But—how the hell was I supposed to get them? Just waltz into a drugstore and tell them I wanted to use them for water balloons?

As if in answer to my question, Marty Kaufman called me early on Sunday afternoon. Mom answered the phone, and I could tell she didn't really want to tell me who it was.

Marty needed a favor. His car was temporarily out of commission awaiting some repair, his parents wouldn't let him use one of theirs, and he had to pick something up. Could I drive him, he wanted to know.

"I'll have to tell Mom something about why I need the car," I replied. "What do you need to pick up?"

His laugh was a little sinister. "She doesn't want to know. Tell her I'm getting my mom a special present for Mother's Day. Secret."

I had a bad feeling about this. If my mom "didn't want to know," did I? Was it any worse than liquor? "Okay, so I won't specify, but just for my benefit, what is this 'Mother's Day' gift, anyway?"

"Tell you when I see you."

"How long?"

"Huh?"

"How long will we need the car?"

"Maybe three hours?"

"What? Where is this gift, anyway?"

"Kiddo, if I don't tell you, you won't have to tell anyone else. Right? So, can we go?"

"I'll call you right back."

It was not a fun conversation. First Mom pointed out that it was a little early to be shopping for Mother's Day. All I could do was repeat what Marty had said. Dad was at the store doing final tax prep, and Mom was suspicious enough that she wanted to check with him before letting me take the car for so long. Especially with Marty involved.

"Do you really want to disturb Dad today?" I asked. "Besides, it's better this way than if Marty were driving. At least I'm in control." To help convince her that I took her seriously, I was careful to say "were," which she always insisted went with "if." Some people have mothers who are drama queens. Mine is a grammar queen.

I'd given her a place to exert some control herself. "Well, you just make sure that boy doesn't drive my car! Do you understand?"

I did my best to look serious and obedient without overdoing it. A fine line. "I promise. I'll keep an eye on him. We won't get into any trouble." I almost added, *And it is for his mother.* But I think she already doubted that.

Marty was waiting outside when I got to his house, staring in the direction he knew I'd come from. He jumped in and started barking directions. After I'd executed the first few turns and got us on the highway, I asked, "And just where are we going, anyway?"

"West Virginia."

"You're shittin' me." My language had deteriorated, I'd noticed recently, with the advent of my supposed manhood. What with earning money, smoking cigarettes, and putting my fingers into that sweet well between Jenny's legs I'd broken a number of barriers this year. Language was just one more. I might have been saying things like "shit" and "fuck" in my head for a long time, but words like those were starting to find their way into my conversations with people like Tim and Marty.

"Straight up! And wait till you know why." And he sat back, like that was it.

"You gonna tell me?"

"You'll see. You'll shit your fuckin' pants."

"Fine. But you need to do something for me, too."

"Name it, kid."

"I need some condoms."

Marty slapped his thigh and leaned his head back and laughed. "No shit! I'll take you someplace you can get them."

"Fine. But you buy them today, and pay for gas, too."

He shrugged like that made no difference to him. Then he said, "Who you gonna do?"

"This girl I've been seeing."

"Virgin?"

"Seems unlikely. She told me to bring condoms next time I saw her."

"You?"

"What about me?"

"I mean, are you still a virgin?"

I must have delayed just a tiny bit too long before I said, "Hell, no."

"Liar. Liar! Ha, ha. Little Paulie's gonna get laid. Hey, if she's done it, you don't want her to be your first."

I figured it was pointless to protest my lack of experience again. "Why?"

"Duh. D'you wanna look like a total dork? Do you really wanna just shoot all over her boobs 'cause you can't predict the timing of things? Or not be able to come at all 'cause you're so nervous about what you should do?"

"Oh, believe me, I've done quite a few things already." I tried to sound as knowledgeable as possible. But he wasn't fooled.

"I don't give a fuck what you've done, if you haven't done *it*. We need to get you to a pro, and then you'll be able to handle yourself with your girl."

"Pro." All I could do was echo the word.

"Professional. When do you expect to see your girl again?"

"Maybe a couple of weeks. Nothing set up yet."

"So this weekend we'll take you out and let a real woman show you the ropes. Haven't done that in a while, myself; 'bout time I went again. She'll cost about fifty in cash."

Jesus Fucking Christ, he really was talking about what I'd thought he was talking about. A prostitute. "Isn't that a lot?"

He shrugged again. "Not for a little quality. The twenty-dollar ladies of the night won't be willing to take any time with you to

help you out. For fifty, you can get someone with a little sympa-
thy for your situation."

We were fairly quiet for the rest of the ride to the state line.
Part of the time I was racking my brains for a way to convince
Marty I didn't need that kind of assistance. Part of the time I
was thinking it was a really good idea but feeling scared shitless
about it. Never once did it occur to me that I might get caught.
That my folks might find out.

Once we hit the state line, Marty pulled out a piece of paper
and started issuing directions again. "Turn here. Look for a gas
station on the corner near a liquor store and pull in." Marty got
out and chatted with the guy pumping the gas. I couldn't really
hear them, so I rolled my window down a little, but they were
on the other side of the car. After the car was gassed up Marty
went inside, I assumed to pay. And he did. But when he got
back he had a wrinkled brown bag with him. He set it on the
floor under the seat.

"Away we go," he said. "Drive up this road until we get to a
place where they sell plants. Then look for a dirt road just past
it, across the street. No marker."

We turned onto the dirt road and followed it for maybe half
a mile. "Park here," Marty said when we'd rounded a couple of
huge piles of dirt, bigger than houses. He grabbed the bag and
got out, looking all around as he walked. I got out, pocketed
the keys just to be on the safe side, and followed. When he was
sure we were alone he sidled over to me, lifted the bag, reached
in and pulled his hand out.

It was a gun.

Marty had said I'd shit my pants, and I nearly did. He
opened his hand so it lay nestled there. It looked small but
mean. My voice barely a whisper, I asked, "What is it?"

"A snub-nose thirty-eight. Ain't it a beauty?" I reached toward it, but he pulled his hand away. "In a minute." He bent
over it, caressing it, and opened the chamber. There were bullets already in it. "I got more of these in the bag. Gonna use a
few of them today!" He looked up at me and grinned. "Let's go
shootin'."

I stood several feet behind him as he planted himself firmly, facing one of the dirt hills and about thirty feet from it. He held the gun in his right hand, steadied it with his left, aimed, and then there was a popping explosion. His arms rose with the recoil, and a spit of dirt on the hill flew into the air. He aimed again. With his third shot he hit what he'd been aiming at, which was a tuft of brown grass.

"Ha!" He raised both arms into the air and turned to face me. "Hot shit!" He bent over the gun, obviously entranced. Then he looked at me again. "Wanna try?"

I did, and I didn't. "Sure." And then he proceeded to tell me everything I was doing wrong as I aimed at that grass tuft.

"Left leg back a little. Hand higher on the grip. Hold it tighter. No, really hard. Aim with the front sight. It's going to buck, so stand firm and let your arms bounce up with it."

I missed the thing by several feet. So there was more correction.

"You milked it. Don't move any finger except the trigger finger. And pull it back smoothly, like you're rolling it. Don't worry about when it will fire, just be smooth so you don't pull the muzzle off target."

Much closer that time. I still hadn't hit it by the third bullet, though, and Marty took the gun back, reloaded, and fired all the rounds himself. I was itching for another try, but I didn't say anything. And when I looked at my watch, I realized I'd have to talk Marty out of doing any more himself, either, even though he was reloading.

"Gotta head out, Marty. We still have my errand, too, y'know."

He aimed again and fired, and I went to the car and started it up. He was aiming again. I put the car into gear and rolled slowly toward him as he shot, aimed again, shot again. I'd lost count. What I wanted was to get to him before he had a chance to reload.

Suddenly he wheeled around, gun pointed right at me. I braked and just stared at him. He fired. I jerked in the seat even though he'd pulled on an empty chamber. When I could breathe again I shouted at him, "You crazy fuck, knock off that shit and get in the car!"

He made some sound like a jackal might make, swept up the bag with the bullets in it, and clambered in, still laughing. Once he had the gun stashed away again I headed out, still breathing deeply to calm myself.

He made me stop at the plant nursery while he bought an azalea for his mom, "so it wouldn't be a total lie," he said. I had a brainstorm and bought one as well, and then we headed toward home.

"Where'd you learn all that shit about how to shoot? Milking the trigger, all that stuff?" I asked him.

"My dad shoots. But he keeps his gun locked up and won't let me near it except when he's with me, and I can't stand the stupid fuck. So I wanted my own gun."

"Why'd we have to come all the way here to get it?"

"State line makes a big difference when it comes to things like this, kiddo."

"And what are you gonna do with it, rob banks?"

"You're such a jerk, Landon. Why do you think I got a snub-nose? Maybe 'cause it takes up less room when you carry it around?" Which still didn't answer my question. I decided against pressing for more information. There were some things I just didn't need to know.

Close to home, and maybe twenty minutes late already, he had me pull into a drugstore in an area that I wouldn't want to walk through at night. At the counter there was a guy not much older than us.

His voice smooth and confident, Marty said, "I'll take a pack of Camels and two boxes of regular Trojans." He threw a twenty on the counter and then leaned his hands on either side of the bill. "We'll need a bag." The guy eyed him. Marty didn't actually look threatening, but he looked like it wouldn't take much to get him there. When the guy handed over the goods, Marty added, "Keep the change."

Back in the car Marty took the cigs and one box of Trojans from the bag and handed it to me. "Haven't seen that guy in there before. Next time he sees one of us, maybe he'll remember the change." Marty lit up and handed me the pack. He watched as I bounced one up, pulled it out, and lit up. I rolled the window down and blew the smoke smoothly outside the car.

"Well, I'll be," he said. "I woulda bet you hadn't done that yet, either."

"You need to roll down your window. If my mom smells smoke in here it'll be the last time I get the car."

He laughed, but he obliged me. "And you're gonna need it for your little girlie, aren't you?"

While we smoked, still parked, I asked him, "Who'd you call today, before you called me, for this favor?" I just wanted to know where I was in his pecking order.

He exhaled smoke, inhaled again on the cig, and smoke escaped as he spoke. "Couple a guys." He blew out the window. "Maybe you'll be higher on the list next time."

We stopped once more to fill up the gas tank, and again he paid. Afterward, as we pulled up to his house, Marty stuffed the gun into his pants belt under his jacket, set the bag of bullets on the dirt of one of the plants and picked it up, said, "Thanks, kid. See ya Saturday." He winked and headed up the driveway. He walked around back first, probably stashing the plant and the bullets out of sight.

On the way home I had all the windows open. As I drove, freezing cold, I kept feeling the jolt of that snub-nose in my palm, the warmth it gave off after a few shots.

Dad was home when I got there. Thank God Marty had said to put the Trojans in a bag. I held it as inconspicuously as possible. "You're late, Paul. Where have you been?"

"I told Mom when I borrowed the car. I'm not that late."

He got out of his chair and hitched up his pants. "Don't argue. Where did you go?"

"This special place where Marty wanted to get some fancy azalea plant."

"For over three hours?" I shrugged; it hadn't been my idea. "Did he put gas in the car?"

"He did."

His gaze told me he wasn't done. I was glad he'd already lit his pipe; that would make it harder to smell any smoke on me. I also noticed that it wasn't the one Chris had brought from 'Nam. "What color?"

"What?"

"The flowers. What color were they?"

"Dark pink. They weren't all the way out yet, though. But you can see for yourself."

"What?"

"I got one for Mom, too. It's in the backyard. I'm gonna surprise her with it before dessert tonight."

He made some harrumphing kind of noise, stuck his pipe into his mouth, picked up a section of newspaper, and plunked himself down into the recliner.

My approaching date with Marty, if you could call it that, sort of hovered over everything I thought about all week, and I made a special trip to the bank to make sure I had my fifty dollars in cash. And I practiced with my condoms, wasting as few of them as possible getting them on and, once loaded, off again. Good thing I'd taken over trash duty.

By the time I went to work on Friday I was a nervous wreck. Thank God Jenny wasn't working that night. It wasn't like she expected me to ask her out all the time; in fact, she'd made a point of saying she didn't want to be anybody's girl, and it didn't seem to bother her that I'd waited a few weeks to ask for the second date. But I didn't want to have to worry about how I was acting around her.

I was washing tonight, but I didn't much care. But before he left for the evening, David came up to me and told me I'd need to do the grill tomorrow night.

"Tomorrow night?" I echoed.

"That a problem?"

"It's just that I already have plans."

David shrugged. "Tim was gonna work, but he asked for the night off. He has seniority. So he's working early shift tomorrow, and you get late shift."

"So, how far in advance do I need to make sure I don't get called in on some particular Saturday night in the future?"

"Ahead of anyone who's been here longer."

On my break I called Marty. He wasn't there, of course, so I just left the message that I had to work Saturday night. He stopped by the Burger King around nine, ordered a soda and some fries, and waited till I could slip out to the back.

"What's up, Landon? You chickening out on me?"

"Hell, no! But I'm low man on the totem pole here, and I pulled this shift that I don't usually work 'cause someone else asked for the night off."

"What about next week? I'm itchin' for some action."

"Next week's okay. I'll let the manager know tonight."

"Don't screw it up, kid. You'll get the wrong sort of reputation." He jabbed me in the ribs and walked away.

I put in a request not to be assigned next Saturday night. And that next Friday night Tim was working, and I made sure he wasn't planning to dump Saturday night on me a second time.

"Sorry, Paul. Didn't mean to screw up your love life. Got big plans? Jenny again?"

"No, not Jenny. Someone else." Feeling like a big man, I added, "Gettin' some real action." Tim raised an eyebrow but said nothing.

The next Saturday, after dinner, I lied to my folks. I told them I was going over to Kevin's to work on a school project we'd been teamed up on. We weren't teamed up on any project, but when Dad asked what it was on I was ready. "The history of gun laws in the U.S."

This set him off on a monologue about the thirty-eight Special, the primary police pistol, and I let him rant for a while before saying I had to get over to Kevin's or we wouldn't have much time to work. I got the keys to Mom's car, grabbed condoms and cash, and drove to Marty's.

We took his Mustang for our expedition, and he drove into

an area of town I barely knew existed. There were X-rated movie houses and bars and all kinds of places we couldn't get into legally, but they sure set the stage for me. Marty pulled into a spot away from the lights but didn't turn off the motor. Instead, he reached under the seat and pulled out a brown bag. At first I thought it was going to be the gun, and I was a little freaked, but then he reached in and unscrewed a cap, raised the bag to his mouth, and took a few swigs from a bottle I couldn't see. He wiped the back of his hand over his mouth and handed the bag to me.

"Liquid courage, kid. Just in case you're nervous."

I was, but Marty knew I wouldn't want to admit that. I drank anyway; he had, after all, so maybe he needed a little courage, too. I think it was bourbon, not really sure. It tasted lousy, and it nearly made me cough, but I was smart enough to take just a small sip first to prepare myself, and then I took a bigger gulp, and then another. I handed it back.

Marty stashed the bag again and pulled into the street. "What we're gonna do," he told me, looking at people on the sidewalk, "is cruise around for a bit. Keep an eye out for women who look like they're advertising, and see if you like any of them. If so, tell me, and we'll see if she looks like a twenty or a fifty. The real high-priced ones won't be so obvious, so it's unlikely you'll pick up on one of those. When you see someone you want, we still drive around the block again before we say anything. If she's still there, and if she still looks like she's advertising, we make our move. And let me do the talking. Got it?"

I said, "Yeah," but I have to admit I was in a bit of a state. I had to keep reminding myself I was practicing so I'd be ready for Jenny, or I'm not sure I could have gone through with it. At first I couldn't tell which women were the working girls, but then I figured out that they were the ones who were walking slow, or not walking at all. And there weren't many other women around here, anyway. After that I saw a lot of women who looked like they were advertising, as Marty had put it, but none of them appealed to me. They all looked—I dunno, excessive or something. Over the top. Finally Marty started pointing some out. I just kept shrugging.

"What's the matter with you, Landon? Need another swig or two?"

"They just don't look like my type, that's all."

His guffaw nearly hurt my ears. "You idiot, of course they aren't. That's not the point. Just pick one that you can imagine putting it into, that's all. One that strikes you as maybe almost pretty, or maybe there's something about her that makes you hard. That's all we're here for. We aren't shopping for a wife, y'know."

I steeled myself and looked harder, finally noticing one woman, girl almost, who didn't seem quite as old as the rest. She was definitely older than me, but she didn't seem like some kind of demented aunt. "That one. With the tight pink vest."

"Good choice. Looks relatively clean. I got no problem doin' her."

"What?"

Marty started around the block again. "What did you think? That you'd be the only one getting any tonight? You do her first, and then it's my turn."

"Gross! I didn't think we'd be . . . um, with the same one."

Marty shook his head. "You are such a baby. Do you imagine for a second you'll be the first guy at her tonight? Or the last?" He drove on in silence, rounding the block, and she was still there. She looked almost sad. But she'd positioned herself near a hydrant, so it was easy for Marty to swing the car in closer to her. Something in my head clicked, and I realized she'd probably stood there deliberately, for just such an opportunity.

"Roll down the window," Marty said, and I did. He leaned toward it and let out a quiet whistle. The girl gazed our way and took us in for several seconds. Then she looked around her, and finally she moved over to the car, hips rolling.

"Hey, boys. Need some directions someplace?"

"How much?" is all Marty said.

She looked at him, then at me, and shrugged. After checking round once more she said, "One at a time, or together?"

"One at a time."

"Where?"

"You got a room we can go to?"

"Fifty. Each. Meet me around the corner." She turned to her right and walked slowly away.

"You called that one, Paulie. Right on the money. Keep your eye peeled for cops."

For some reason it hadn't occurred to me that that's why she'd kept looking around. Now it was my turn, and I looked very, very hard. We stayed put until it was clear which corner she'd meant, and then Marty drove forward.

In my careful observation of everyone I could see, I noticed our girl stop for about one second to say something to a guy in a doorway partway down the block. "She's getting another one," I said, straining to see him better, but it was too dark there. All I could see was that he was tall and broad.

"That's probably her pimp. He'll get a cut of her take."

"Why?"

He shrugged. "Protection?"

She was waiting in a dark spot. Marty pulled over and she leaned into my window, pointing a little ahead. A smell of something that must have been perfume wafted in. "Turn right into that alley. Leave the car in the loading zone. They don't ticket on Saturday night."

We parked and got out. I was having a little trouble breathing by this time. I shoved my right hand into my jeans pocket to stop the trembling, fingering the wrapped condoms, and then I checked in my left pocket for the cash. I hadn't brought anything else with me; I might not know a lot about pimps, but I do know that sometimes prostitutes rob their johns.

She led us down the sidewalk two doorways and up a dark stairway with no windows. It smelled of garbage and piss. I felt like I was in some stupid detective novel or something, the environment was so predictable. We walked a little way down a hall and she pulled out a key, and we went into a room not much bigger than the double bed, something that passed for linens all rumpled up on it. There was barely space beside it for a small table and a tiny lamp, which was already on, and a wooden chair. No frills, that's for sure. You can bet I recognized the smell in here.

She stood at the open door and looked at Marty. "You said one at a time. Who's first? The other waits in the hall."

He gave her a weird grin, I guess trying to look sexy, and stepped back out of the room. She shut the door.

"Cash?"

I reached into my left pocket, and the bills were out of my hand before I'd looked up, crumpled in a hand decorated with long, pointy fingernails painted some dark color I couldn't quite make out in the dim light. I almost couldn't see her eyes, there was that much makeup on them, and the room was so dark. But I could see her eyebrows were a lot darker than her hair. I didn't see where she put my money.

"Ever done this?" she asked as she unfastened her skirt. The way she was reaching behind made her boobs nearly pop out of the pink vest. She must have had a blouse on underneath, 'cause her arms were covered in some kind of lacy sleeves, but all I could see above the vest was skin. She set the skirt on the chair seat. No need to remove underwear; she wasn't wearing any.

There was no point in lying. "No."

"Thought so. Okay, here's the deal. No kissing. You do anything that hurts me and you're pulp. Just relax and do what I say. Can you work with that?" I nodded. "Condom?" I gave her both of the ones I had in my pocket, and she put one back. "Who d'you think you are? Superman? Take off your jacket, shoes, pants, and underwear. I don't care about the shirt or the socks."

She unbuttoned her vest, and there was a blouse underneath, the low neckline folded down so far that it hadn't shown above the pink. She lifted the blouse over her head and stood there, hands on hips, waiting for me. I'd been so intent on watching her boobs make an appearance that I hadn't done much. I rushed now, yanking things off and throwing them in the corner.

"Lie on your back," she told me, her voice a little gentler now. She reached down and removed the shiny black ankle boots she wore, and I watched her boobs sway and bounce. I was already hard. She got on the bed, her knees on either side of my thighs. I just stared at her boobs.

"You can touch them if you want," she said softly. "Just be nice."

I tried to touch them in a way that she might like, but it didn't seem as though she was even noticing. Her fingers ripped open the condom wrapper and pulled the thing out like she'd done it a billion times a day for years. I was still playing with her tits as she rolled the sheath over me. So much for my practicing. But, I told myself, I'd need to know how for Jenny. Then she pulled away where I couldn't reach her, and it worried me.

"Did I do something wrong?"

"Nope. Just want you to relax for a second. You wanna come while you're just wavin' in the wind?"

I made an effort to get my breathing under control again and closed my eyes. To my horror, I started to go a little soft. My eyes flew open.

She laughed softly. "Not to worry, little man," and she worked a hand under my balls and ran her fingernail gently along the ridge behind them. I stopped worrying.

As soon as I was filling out the condom again she lifted herself over me, held my dick, and pointed it under her. She lowered herself onto me, and I swear I nearly lost it right then. Thank God I didn't, or I'd have missed the rest of what it felt like to be hard and inside her. I tried not to think about what Marty had said, that other guys' dicks had already been here tonight, and after she'd plunged down hard onto me a few times I couldn't hold back anymore. All I can say is that it felt nothing like pulling on myself until I'd soiled my sheets at home.

By the time I was able to stand, she was already dressed again. She pulled a tin bucket lined with plastic out from under the table.

"Dump it in here."

I was glad I'd practiced getting a loaded condom off myself

without making a mess, and I did what she said. She stood at the door while I dressed.

"You did okay, kid. Welcome to manhood." She yanked open the door and jerked her head for me to exit. Marty was leaning against the opposite wall, but I knew better than to think he'd been there the whole time. I was sure he'd listened, but I didn't give a shit.

He punched my arm as he passed me, and the door closed behind him. I didn't want to listen, so I moved to where he'd been standing. I was just about to sink onto the floor when the door jerked open again. Marty stood there. "I need the rest."

"The rest of what?"

"The other fifty. I thought you'd already given it to her."

"I gave her fifty."

"Yeah, I get that, so now give me the other fifty."

I shook my head, confused. "What other fifty?"

I could see dark-tipped fingers reach round the edge of the door and try to pull it open, but Marty held it fast. He said, "I told you to bring enough for both of us."

"You said to bring fifty. That's what I brought."

He was struggling to hold the door by now. "We'll talk about this later."

Somehow he got the door closed. Now I could hear whether I wanted to or not. "I told you fifty each. Forty won't cut it. If that's all you got, then get out. You're wasting my time."

The door opened a crack and got pushed back hard against the jamb. This was getting ugly real fast; was he going to try to force her? I couldn't let that happen. No matter who had made what mistake, she'd been honest with us and good to me. I started toward the door, and then I heard her scream the name Eric.

*Who's Eric?*

I was about to reach for the doorknob when someone bounded up the hall toward me. It was a guy the same size and shape as the man she'd stopped to talk to on the sidewalk. The word "Protection" flashed through my mind.

"Marty!" I yelled. "Get out!"

Next thing I knew I was thrown so hard against the wall I

think the impression of my body must still be there. The door flew open and Marty bounded out.

"I'm gone!" he shouted. "I'm gone!" Eric did the same thing to him he'd done to me. I grabbed Marty and we stumbled down the hall, practically falling down the flight of stairs as he mumbled, "Why the fuck didn't I bring the gun?" We'd nearly made it when I heard Eric gaining on us. He must have stopped just long enough to find out from the girl what the problem was.

We headed toward the Mustang for all we were worth, but of course Marty had locked it. He fumbled for his keys, but Eric got there before he could unlock the door, and he slammed Marty against the car. I took one look at Eric and knew that even together Marty and I couldn't take him. I ran into the street and started shouting. I'm not sure now what I said, maybe "Help!" and "Police!" Who knows what I yelled. I could hear Eric working Marty over behind me, thudding sounds and grunts, and then nothing but footsteps.

I went back to Marty. He'd fallen on the ground, his face bleeding, conscious but unable to speak. Suddenly headlights shone full on him, and I could see that his face wasn't that bad. Probably his ribs took the worst of it.

The headlights belonged to a police car.

My first thought was *Thank God.* My second was *Shit.* Two cops walked slowly toward us, guns drawn. For all they knew, I'd been involved in getting Marty beat up. I'd never been so scared in my life.

"Hands on your head and stand up!" one of them shouted at me. I did, but my knees were shaking so hard I wasn't sure I could stay on my feet. One of the cops held his gun on me while the other felt around me for weapons, I guess. Or a wallet, which I didn't have on me. He made me lean against the car while he reached into my pockets.

"No ID? What's your name, kid?"

The rest of that evening is a bit of a blur. I managed to blurt out that a large man had beaten my friend. I tried like hell to avoid saying why, but in the search the cop had found my unused condom, and then of course Marty had some. He'd recovered well enough to be able to speak, but he kept insisting he wouldn't say anything.

At the station house, they took Marty and me to separate rooms and kept hammering me with questions. Finally they got out of me who I was. One guy left the room to call my folks, though I didn't know it yet. The only thing I can say for myself is that I didn't cave until my dad got there. Then it all came out. It felt kind of like the day I'd had to tell him about Chris getting killed, when I could be strong as long as Dad wasn't there. But once he was, it was like he uncorked something, like I'd been given sodium pentothal, and I spilled my guts. At least I didn't cry this time.

Marty wasn't seriously hurt, and amazingly I didn't get the belt as a result of this little adventure. But I also didn't get to ask Jenny out again. Dad made me quit my job at Burger King. He took my driver's license and my bank passbook away. And I got grounded for the rest of the school year, telephone privileges revoked, TV time severely curtailed. Plus, I had to work at the store on weekends. His store.

I spent a lot of time over the next couple of months feeling sorry for myself. Sometimes I blamed Marty, first for his bright idea, then for being idiot enough to think I'd pay for him even if he had told me to, which he hadn't, then for trying to cheat the prostitute. Sometimes I blamed Dad for making me feel like some stupid little kid when what I'd really done was become a man; even the prostitute had said so. Sometimes I blamed myself for being such an idiot, for not knowing that I could get into a shitload of trouble for something stupid when I could have just kept my head down and let Jenny be my first time. For letting Marty talk me into doing it in the first place.

Sometimes I blamed my mom, not so much because of what happened, but because of her reaction to it: "Your brother would *never* have done anything like this!" To which I nearly responded, *You bet your ass he wouldn't. He was queer. He'd have done something worse.* And in there someplace was more blame for her because she needed me to be Chris.

And sometimes I blamed Chris.

I'd sit at my desk, supposedly doing schoolwork, and stare out onto the street. I memorized the branch pattern of the tree in front of our house. I could tell you exactly what time the streetlights started to come on, predicting changes as the days got longer. And I'd think about Chris, and it seemed to me now that maybe once upon a time he'd had to be so good to make up for the bad things I did, and now I had to be a man to make up for him being queer. I blamed him for letting Dad force him into a situation where he ended up dead and leaving me to deal with the mess. And I blamed him for making me keep his secrets. Hell, for just *having* secrets.

And I blamed him for pretending to be the man Dad wanted me to be.

# PART III

# Initiation

# Chapter 8

Grade-wise, I scraped by. Mr. Treadwell and I had a couple of little talks, with him trying to find out what was wrong and me sure as hell I wasn't going to reveal anything. What business was it of his, anyway? Who was he to me? He wasn't even a guidance counselor. Sure, he'd been decent, but I'd *earned* that B in history last semester. Maybe I was barely earning a C now, but that was up to me. He kept trying to tell me that college would be— what were his words? an unfulfilled dream, I think—if I couldn't get my grades up. I made a bit of an effort toward the end and did well enough on finals to avoid disgracing myself altogether, but it was not gonna be Harvard or Princeton for me in a year. As long as I could go *someplace*. Get away from here.

Marty and I managed to recover our friendship, such as it was, at school. He finally agreed—much to my surprise—that maybe he hadn't been clear about my paying for his romp in the hay, and after trying to make it my fault that the police had shown up he admitted that I couldn't have known that we wouldn't end up needing any assistance, or that Eric would just get in a few licks and leave, so even though he caught hell at home for his part in our evening out, he was kind of used to that. Plus he liked making a show of how little it meant to him to have his father mad at him.

On weekends, at the store, Dad and I talked only as much as we had to. He told me to stack the dog food bags, and that's what I did. He told me to take inventory of the angelfish, and that's what I did. I got a tiny salary, which he put directly into the bank account I couldn't get at. I couldn't bring myself to speak much to him at home either, and I sure as hell wasn't gonna ride with him in his car to work and back, so I rode my bike, rain or shine.

Every once in a while Marty and Kevin would stop in, but unless they showed up on Sunday, Dad's day off, he usually sent them packing. Once I didn't know they were there until I heard Marty's voice shouting, "It's a free country!"

Just before school ended, Dad informed me that I'd have to work at the store all summer, and not just on weekends. I nearly threw a fit, but I was pretty beaten down by then and didn't really have the energy. He also told me I'd have to train the new guy, some kid named JJ O'Neil who'd just graduated high school with all kinds of honors and was headed to Cornell in the fall. Just my kind of guy. I'd seen kids streaming in and out of Dad's office, interviewing for summer jobs, but I hadn't paid much attention.

Sure enough, on the first Monday after school let out for the summer, when I got to work JJ was already there. Brownnoser, I thought to myself, showing up earlier than me on his first day, and it wasn't like I was late. He was already destined for greatness, according to my dad, so what did he have to prove? Worse still, Dad had made me come in on Monday, which was going to be my one day of the week off, just to train the guy.

I wheeled my bike through the rear entrance that leads into the stockroom, pushed through the heavy door into the store, braced myself for the wave of smells—bird shit, dog pee covered by antiseptic, fish algae, hamster cage, and two or three things I couldn't quite name and didn't really want to—and there he was, hunched over and labeling cans of cat food. All I could see was his back covered by a white short-sleeved shirt and really dark hair on his head. I ignored him.

First thing I did was try and scout Dad out and avoid him, so that as long as possible I could also avoid him telling me to work with the kid. I listened carefully outside the office door, near the front of the store, and it seemed Carol was in there on the phone. I peeked around the corner. She saw me and beckoned me in while she finished her conversation. I waited patiently. She'd kept on being decent to me, even though I'd bet anything Dad had told her exactly what had happened, why I was suddenly working at the store, and why there was so much dead air between us.

"Hey, Paul. Did you meet JJ yet?" I shook my head, afraid of what I was about to hear. "You're in for a treat. He's a great kid. Smart, too. Your dad's got him doing cat food at the moment, but he said if I saw you first—stop me if you've seen your dad—that you were to introduce yourself and show him how to clean the fish tanks. Do you want to go find JJ, or shall I come with you?"

*Oh well. Guess there's no avoiding the kid.* "No, I'll find him, thanks. Um, why are you in today? Don't you have Mondays off?"

"Just here for the morning, to get the paperwork for the summer help in order." She gestured toward a couple of folders on the desk. I knew they would contain whatever was needed by way of personnel records. "And you? Don't you have Mondays off, too? It's the slowest day of the week."

"Dad wanted me to be here for JJ's first day. Um, by the way, what's with the name?"

"Hmmm?"

"What does 'JJ' stand for?"

"I don't remember." She waved a hand, smiled, and then bent over something on the desk. It seemed kind of unlikely she'd have forgotten already—she was working with the personnel files, after all—but I turned and left, wondering what the big secret might be.

JJ was still where I'd seen him, whipping price tags onto the cans like he'd done it all his life. It wasn't a tough job, I don't mean that, but there's a rhythm you get into that takes a little practice. Practice he obviously didn't need.

I stood next to him a minute, waiting to see if he'd notice me. When he saw my sneaker he froze, almost like he was bracing himself for something. Slowly he stood, still looking wary. He tossed the gun into his left hand and looked up at me. He may have been a year older than me, but he was probably two inches shorter. His eyes were really dark, almond shaped, and his features were a little delicate. Almost pretty. Skin was slightly dark. It wasn't tanned, exactly, but it had color to it. He looked a little exotic, or something.

When I figured I'd left a little bit of an impression I held out my right hand, and we shook. "I'm Paul Landon."

"JJ O'Neil."

"Yeah, I know." I pointed to the labeler. "You used one of those before?"

He kept his eyes on my face, almost like he could read my intentions there and didn't want to miss anything. He nodded. "I've worked in food stores, supermarkets, most summers."

*Which explains* that, *anyway.* I nodded, barely making note of the slight lilt to his speech. "Dad asked me to show you how to clean fish tanks."

He smiled then, finally, and his face changed from wary to...I dunno, maybe bright? I couldn't help but smile back. He said, "Great! I want to learn about fish and amphibians. They're the animals I know least about. Is now okay with you, or should I go on with this for a while?"

At least he understood the pecking order here. Maybe I was in disgrace, but JJ wouldn't know that, and I was still the owner's son. "Why don't we go ahead and get started? I'll help you stack the cans you've labeled already."

As we walked toward the amphibian area he said, "Mr. Landon said you knew practically everything there is to know about the store. I hope you don't mind if I ask lots of questions."

It took me a few seconds to recover from JJ's first statement. Dad said something complimentary about me? And to someone else? Then I wondered why JJ was already so full of questions. "No problem. Are you planning to have a store one day yourself?"

He laughed, and it had a nice sound. "No, probably not. I want to work with animals. Maybe I'll be a vet someday. That would be my dream job."

"So why are you so interested in this store?"

"Oh, I'm interested in anything having to do with animals, and with people who love them. Your father seems like a real animal lover."

This took me a little aback. "This is your first day, right? How do you know how my dad feels about animals?" We were standing at the tanks by now, but I wanted to hear what JJ's answer would be, beyond the obvious; I mean, why would someone who didn't like animals have a pet supply store, anyway?

"Oh, we had a great talk when I was here for my interview a few weeks ago. I know he likes black Labradors best, even though some other breeds are smarter. And that he doesn't much like cats, which I think is too bad. It's just that they're different from dogs. People who like dogs often think cats are disloyal, but it's only that they aren't pack animals and don't develop bonds in the same way dogs do. Dogs live by social hierarchy. Cats live by rules and routines. I guess your mom is allergic, huh?"

I wanted to dislike the guy. He was showing off by getting here early, he'd already figured out that my dad's favorite dog was something other than what I thought it was, 'cause I'd assumed Dad liked the smarter dogs best, and he was giving me a lecture on animal behavior. Plus, he already knew something about my mom. Under normal circumstances, all this together would have more than wiped out how good I'd felt a few minutes ago when he'd passed on that compliment Dad had never seen fit to say directly to me, and I'd hate his guts. But he seemed so . . . I don't know, there was something about him that seemed beyond calm, almost removed, like even though he knew all this stuff, he didn't pretend it gave him some kind of edge. I would have had to talk myself into believing that he was trying to puff himself up even, let alone wanting to be on some kind of par with me. All I said was, "Yeah. She is. Listen, let's get started here."

I took him first to the schedule posted in the stockroom behind the tanks. "We don't try to do all the tanks at once. Each tank has a number, and it corresponds to this chart." I was about to go over what had been done last, but instead I asked, "Can you tell what we should be working on today?"

JJ took about five seconds to figure this out. "Number eleven today, right? Wait...eleven through fifteen."

I nodded. Didn't want to give him too much encouragement. "And can you tell what we need to do to them?" Ha. That will take a little more—

"Looks like we're cleaning these, and then we replace the filters in tanks one through five." He turned to face me. "Why is that? Why won't we—"

"Fish tanks have beneficial bacteria in them that do stuff like remove ammonia and other toxins the filters don't get all of. Some of this bacteria is in the filters. When we clean a tank, we replace about twenty percent of the water, which takes away some of the bacteria. So we wait to replace the filter—"

"...so you don't deplete the environment of the bacteria! Of course. And do you replace only part of the water for the same reason?"

I let a beat or two go by. I don't like being interrupted. "That, plus it's a lot of stress on the fish to change their entire environment all at once. And if we want another reason, it's so we don't have to take the fish out of the tank to clean it."

"Brilliant!" He beamed at me like it had been my idea. "Should the new water be warmed?"

I could tell it would be tough to keep this kid under control. I didn't want him thinking he was so smart that he'd go off half-cocked and ruin something. Dad prided himself in doing a better job than any other place he knew of to maintain the fish tanks; it's time-consuming work, and most places do the bare minimum. If JJ ruined something here, or killed fish, it would be my ass, not his. I said, "Let's go one step at a time. And just so you know, the freshwater fish are less fussy about water temperature than the tropicals, but they all prefer as little change as possible."

I cleaned tank eleven while he watched. I told him how important it was to avoid even a trace of soap, and how the cleaning tools we use are for glass. Acrylic tanks need different tools. At one point I asked him, "So, why this store and not a pet store? I mean, if it's the animals that interest you."

"This might sound strange, but you get to see more animals here. People don't usually bring their own pets into a pet store, so the only animals I'd see would be the ones for sale. They're often not in great health, and I can't do anything about that yet."

Good answers. I wondered if he had an answer for everything—it sure seemed like it so far—but I decided not to test things any further just yet.

We did tank twelve together, and JJ practically insisted on doing thirteen alone. It was nearly lunchtime, and I'd been thinking we'd break first. "You sure you wanna do that?" I asked him. "That's an unlucky number for your first solo."

He laughed. "Oh, I like the number thirteen. Maybe because so many other people don't."

I watched him like a hawk, and although I had to step in a couple of times, he did most everything exactly as I had. Partway through Dad showed up. He stood there a minute watching and then said, "Paul, you and JJ break for lunch after this one. And I need to talk to you in my office."

I didn't much like the tone of his voice. Had I done something wrong already? JJ and I finished up, and he didn't need to be told that everything had to go back into the stockroom. I said, "Did you bring lunch?" He nodded. "There's some picnic tables out back, if you want to eat outside." He smiled at me and nodded again, and I headed toward the office.

Dad was alone in there, and he launched right in. "Paul, what do you think you're doing, having JJ do a tank alone so soon? He could—"

"He got it, Dad. He was really sure of what he was doing, and he understood the process."

Dad was opening his mouth, a scowl on his face, about to scold me some more, when JJ spoke up from behind me. "I'm really sorry, Mr. Landon. I shouldn't have been so ambitious. It was my idea to do it on my own, not Paul's. He tried to discourage me. If there's a problem, it's my fault."

Dad stood there and blinked a few times. "Well. I guess we'll know there's a problem if the fish start going belly up." He didn't sound so fierce now, and for one eerie moment there it seemed almost like old times, with Chris talking Dad down off of whatever hill he'd climbed to throw stones at me. I snapped myself out of it by turning to look at JJ, confirming for myself that he wasn't anything like Chris.

Feeling irritated and not knowing why, I said, "I thought you'd gone to lunch."

"Oh, sorry. I thought Mr. Landon wanted to talk to both of us. I'll go now." And he did.

"Anything else?" I asked Dad, probably sounding a little belligerent.

Dad's jaw worked for a second or two. "We'd better not lose any of those fish. I'd like you to spot Alice on register three so she can have lunch now. You can go when she gets back. And tell JJ not to do any tanks without you. He can go back to cat food while you eat."

Dad's lunch was already on his desk. He ate in the office where he could keep an eye on the registers and watch how the cashiers treated customers. On one hand, I was pissed that I had to wait for lunch. On the other, it was a nice day, and I wanted to eat outside, but I wasn't sure I wanted JJ thinking of me as his best buddy, so I didn't want to set a lunch hour precedent and eat with him.

I sent Alice, who was probably fifteen and at least twice that many pounds overweight, to have lunch. It was fairly busy and I didn't pay a lot of attention to the time, but Alice returned in just under half an hour, right on time. JJ was with her. They were laughing like best friends. I gave JJ his orders and left.

Close call, I thought as I grabbed the lunch Mom had packed for me. I might have had to sit with *both* of them if Dad had taken the register, which he sometimes does. I chose a table and sat with my back to the door. I was mostly done with lunch when I saw two figures coming around the side of the building. Marty and Kevin.

"Hey, Landon!" Marty called in hushed tones. "They let you outside to eat? Aren't they afraid you'll make a break for it?" He and Kevin cackled.

Kevin stole one of my store-bought cookies and sat down across from me. Beside him, Marty lit a cigarette. Wishing I could bum one but knowing I'd be dead if Dad caught me, I pulled my food closer to my side of the table out of Kevin's reach. "What are you guys up to today? Dragging old ladies across the wrong intersections?"

Marty smiled expansively. "It's such a gorgeous day, we thought we'd go skinny-dipping at the woods end of Parson's Lake. Wanna come?"

"You know I would. Gotta stay here though, and you know that, too."

"Grumpy, isn't he?" Kevin asked Marty.

Marty made a face. "He's always like this at work, aren't you, Paul? Hey, here's a thought." He pointed with his cigarette to the side of the building, toward the garden hose that we kept wrapped around an old truck wheel, mounted on the wall, for cleaning the rodent cages, used dog kennels and cat carriers, that sort of thing. "How about if we just squirt you with that for a few minutes? You could even strip first!"

I decided against any reply to that ridiculousness, but I was ready to make a run for it if Marty showed signs of being serious. He didn't. We sat there a few more minutes trading barbs and generally saying nothing in particular, and then Marty, who was facing the building, looked up. His expression was weird, so I turned to look over my shoulder. It was JJ. He'd seen Marty, too, and had stopped in his tracks, eyes locked on him.

"What is it?" I called to him.

He stayed where he was, even though he had to raise his voice a little from that distance, and his eyes moved to me. "Your father wanted us to finish today's tank cleaning." And he waited.

In the back of my mind it occurred to me that he didn't say

anything like "Your dad sent me to get you" or "Your dad says lunchtime is over and to get back to work."

"Be right there." I watched him turn and head back inside, and when I was facing the remains of my lunch again I saw Marty's gaze was still on the door JJ had gone through. "What's with you?" I asked.

His eyes snapped to mine. "Nothin'. Just wondering if it might be time for a little mollification." He sucked on his cig as he gave me this significant look.

I turned again to look at the doorway—stupid, since there was nobody there—and back to Marty again. I knew he was referring to Anthony the math nerd and the time we'd made him tell us he was queer. "You're crazy. You think every guy who isn't like you is automatically a homo."

He flicked some ash and said, "Am I wrong about this one? You sure?" His voice told me he was sure of his own assessment. "And can you afford to make a mistake here?"

I knew what he meant, but I didn't want to admit it. Even from here you could tell that JJ had a sweet face, and he wasn't very big. Dressed right, he could pass for a girl. All I said was, "What's the worst that can happen?"

Marty inhaled on the cig, waited, exhaled at me, and said, "You don't wanna go and get painted with that brush, kid." And then laughed insanely. "Get it? You could get painted with the *pink* brush if you get painted with *his* brush!" and he jabbed with his cigarette toward the door JJ had gone through. Brush. Dagger. I knew what Marty was referring to. But I was still angry with myself for letting him talk me into our little escapade into the red-light district. Time to stand up to him, at least a little.

"Yeah, yeah. You're a real comic, Kaufman. I don't give a fuck whether the kid's a fag or not, and if you try painting me with *any* brush we'll have us a real conversation."

Marty raised an eyebrow. "Ooh, Kevin, did you hear that? Have I struck a nerve in our *pet* store boy?"

Kevin grinned at me like he didn't take Marty quite as seriously as I did. "I don't think we have to worry about Landon." He turned toward Marty. "After all, wasn't he the only one who did that hooker last spring? Seems to me you got some proving to do yourself."

Marty shoved Kevin sideways, nearly off the seat, and Kevin laughed.

I stood up, deciding not to give this conversation any more weight than it deserved. "I gotta get back in or my old man will have a shit fit. See you guys later."

Despite what I'd said to Marty? About not caring if JJ was a fag? I cared. I cared a lot. And I was a little shocked that it hadn't occurred to me. Now I was pretty sure Marty was right.

That afternoon, JJ and I worked on the last two tanks together so Dad wouldn't have any excuses to criticize, both of us talking as little as possible, and I held my hands carefully away from JJ's. Once they touched and I jerked back without really meaning to. I know he noticed, 'cause he froze for a second or two.

I had to talk more while I showed him how to change the filters on tanks one through five, but he said practically nothing. He caught on to the process just as fast as ever, but the brightness was gone. I couldn't say whether I missed his voice because the contrast with the morning was so obvious or because I'd started to like him. I had to watch that, though, didn't I? Wouldn't do to get painted.

That night I lay awake a long time. There were so many similarities between how I was feeling now and how I'd felt about torturing Anthony. I hadn't done anything to JJ, and neither had Marty, but the list of things that were alike was pretty impressive, anyway.

1. *Anthony had been afraid of Marty even before we tortured him. It sure looked like JJ was afraid of him, too; he'd stayed as far away from my lunch table as he could. In fact, he'd seemed afraid even of me at first this morning; when he'd seen my sneaker he'd gone as still as a rabbit hoping a hawk wouldn't see him.*
2. *It hadn't been my idea to treat Anthony like that, and I hadn't thought about JJ being gay. I guess I'll never know if Marty was*

*right about Anthony, but he's sure painting both of them with the same "pink" brush.*

3. *Both Anthony and JJ are smart and aren't afraid to show it, even if they are afraid of other things. That's a kind of courage.*

4. *Just like Anthony hadn't ever ratted on me, JJ didn't embarrass me in front of Marty by making it sound like my dad was yelling at me for taking too long at lunch.*

5. *I don't remember ever liking Anthony, but I sure didn't like what Marty and I did to him. Chris's reaction had certainly put the seal on my self-condemnation. If Marty tried to do something like that to JJ I'd feel even worse. I wouldn't need Chris around to make me feel like shit, but it would feel like he was watching anyway.*

6. *And now the sixty-four-million-dollar question. Had I gone along with Marty in torturing Anthony just so Marty wouldn't terrorize me? And what would I do if he decided to terrorize JJ?*

I had a nasty dream that night about this hideous skin disease. Chris was in the dream, and he had it, and every time I got near him it felt like some of it would show up on me, but I could never see it on myself.

JJ was there ahead of me again on Tuesday, even though I was a little early myself. He was helping Dad, who was up on a stool, stack the heavier bags of dry dog food in the stockroom.

"Paul, help JJ finish this lot. Then I want you both to man register four. Show JJ how to open it up. He already knows how to make change. I want him to work directly with customers today."

"Got it." I was taller than JJ, so when Dad got off the stool I got onto it. JJ didn't speak, and neither did I. After a few minutes of doing my best to make my part, which was harder than his, look easy, I felt like a stupid little kid; JJ didn't look like he was trying to prove anything.

Register four was the one closest to Dad's office. I took JJ through the opening routines, and it seemed to me that he was being real careful, in that cramped space where we both had to stand, not to touch me anyplace. It made me feel kind of guilty about the way I'd reacted yesterday when our hands touched, and it made me start to like him again.

Liking him lasted only about forty-five minutes. He was doing fine ringing things up and making change, and he was friendly with the customers without being inefficient. And then Mrs. Soper was there with that mutt of hers that looks like it's part wheaten terrier and part Chihuahua, it's so funny looking, and as usual it was yapping and jumping and generally ignoring anything she said to it.

"Lulu, please! Let Mommy get her wallet out so she can pay for the things she's bought for you."

"Lulu, hush. Don't be so impatient."

"Lulu, how many times do I have to tell you not to bark at everyone?"

It was always a challenge dealing with her, because even though Lulu paid no attention to her, Mrs. Soper paid all kinds of attention to Lulu and not enough to the business at hand. Plus she was probably in her sixties and did everything kind of slow, anyway. The two customers behind were getting irritated, and only one other register was open at the moment.

I had started to bag things, but Mrs. Soper still had items in her cart, so JJ couldn't ring them up. I might have reached for some of them myself, but JJ was in my way, just staring at the dog. Before I could move around the counter and start pulling things out of the cart, JJ reached into a bag I'd just loaded and pulled out a red strap leash.

He asked, "Is this leash for Lulu?" When Mrs. Soper said it was, he walked around the counter to where Lulu was still dancing on two legs, scratching at the side of the counter with her front paws, yipping hysterically. "Is it okay with you if I try to calm her down?"

"Oh, anything you can do!"

JJ ran the hook end of the leash through the circle of the handle so it made a kind of slipknot. He never spoke to the dog or petted it or anything. He leaned over and slipped the loop over Lulu's head. Then he released the other leash from the collar and handed it to Mrs. Soper, so the red one was the only one on Lulu. JJ positioned the loop just behind Lulu's ears, stepped a little away from the counter with the leash hanging loose from his hand to her neck, and he called her, slapping his leg. She eyed him a few seconds and then went to him. He let her sniff his legs but didn't touch her or speak to her, and then he moved his hand up along the leash until it was almost but not quite tight from Lulu's neck to his hand.

They stood like that for several seconds, and I walked around the counter to Mrs. Soper, who was watching JJ intently. I said, "I'm going to ring the rest of this up, if that's okay."

She said nothing, so I took over for JJ. I glanced up toward Dad's office, expecting that he'd be watching, and he was. But the other thing I'd expected—that he'd be disapproving of what JJ was doing and glad to see I'd taken initiative—wasn't how it looked. He was watching JJ as intently as Mrs. Soper was. *It won't be long before Dad comes to his senses.* I started ringing in the stuff I'd taken from the cart.

Meanwhile Lulu had got onto her hind legs and was beginning to paw at JJ's knees. He stepped away and yanked once on the leash, gently but noticeably, and he said, "Hey," really short and sharp. Lulu sat down at his feet. He waited, not looking at her. She jumped again, and again he jerked the leash and said, "Hey."

I'd finished ringing things up by now, and although the customers behind were undoubtedly glad Lulu wasn't making a fuss anymore, one of them was preparing to move to the other register, something Dad really hates to see, 'cause it means our customer service wasn't what it should have been.

Trying to get Mrs. Soper's attention so I could tell her the total, I saw her gaze turn to watch Dad, coming from his office. He was headed toward JJ, but he stopped at the end of my counter to watch.

Making an effort to keep from sounding annoyed, I said, "That's fourteen-oh-seven, Mrs. Soper."

"What? Oh, thank you, young man." She handed me a twenty, and I had to get her attention again so I could give her the change. But then she just stood there, watching JJ, the cart smack in the way of the next customer. I leaned over and pushed it along a little, and Mrs. Soper got the hint.

By the time I'd rung up the next customer's items, I had to get *his* attention, too; he was also watching the dog show. JJ had Lulu following him peacefully, not jumping, not yipping. He walked back and forth along the front of the store a few times, and when he headed back toward Mrs. Soper, several people applauded. JJ looked around, startled.

"Oh, young man!" Mrs. Soper oozed as JJ brought Lulu back to her. "You've worked a miracle!"

JJ, with Lulu sitting patiently at his feet, said, "Not really. It's very simple, actually. Part of the trick here is to have the leash in a loop up as high on her neck as you can. See how it keeps her head held high?" He pulled the leash upward gently to demonstrate. "If you've ever been to a dog show, you'd see that they walk the dogs on leashes like this. It makes them look proud, and it keeps their head looking forward. It also gives you a lot of control in case she starts looking around at things she wants to bark at. All you have to do, at the very first sign of distraction, is jerk the leash gently sideways, and her attention will come forward again, where you want it to be."

By now, I'd have thought it would have dawned on Dad that nothing was getting done in the store. Everyone was watching J J and Lulu, even Alice at register two.

And JJ wasn't done. "You need to remember, though, that a loop like this—which is essentially like using a choke chain— shouldn't stay on her neck. You should use it like this only when you're in situations where you need a lot of control. And never leave anything like this on her neck."

"Yes, yes. I see. Thank you so much!"

Dad and JJ stood watching Mrs. Soper's retreating back. She was already holding the leash wrong, and Lulu was back to her old tricks. Even so, Dad said, "JJ, that was remarkable. Where did you learn to do that?"

This really pissed me off. Here I'd done my best to try and keep things moving, to keep other customers from getting irritated and to keep up the cash flow, and it's JJ who gets praised.

JJ, who not only hadn't hurried Mrs. Soper up any but who'd actually slowed everything down even more. Where was Dad's appreciation for what *I'd* done?

JJ smiled and said, "It just comes of thinking like a dog when you need to. I'll get back to the register now."

So I stopped liking the guy again. The rest of our conversation was limited to business, even when there were no customers at our counter. During one lull, Dad came out of his office again.

"JJ, can you do that with other dogs?"

JJ shrugged. "Sure. The breed doesn't matter, except that some dogs are more powerful than others. The kind of behavior you want to correct can make a difference, like whether it's just distracted like Lulu or anxious and aggressive, and sometimes you have to be rougher with a dog. But once I get a dog to see me as the alpha, then—yes."

"Could you come into my office for a minute? Paul can cover for you here."

*So all of a sudden I'm "covering" for JJ?* I watched the door shut, fuming. When it opened again, several minutes and three customers later, there was no customer at my register. JJ just walked back and waited for me to step aside so he could take his place again. No comment, no explanation.

I couldn't stand it. I wanted to think Dad had read him the riot act, but Dad had seemed more interested in dog training than customer service. Finally, leaning against the counter and as far from JJ as I could get, I asked, "What did he want?"

"Your father wants me to lead a dog behavioral clinic on Saturday mornings. We'll start this weekend."

*What am I supposed to say to that?* "Great. Do you wanna take over at the register while I take a piss?" I didn't wait for his reply. He wouldn't need me unless he had to void an entire order, or unless the receipt paper ran out. I almost hoped both of those things would happen while I stood in the bathroom, not really needing to do anything, watching the puny dribble leave my dick and fall into the water, half tempted to just lift a leg and let go. I'd just needed to get away from JJ. Away from my dad's approval of him. *I'll bet Dad doesn't know he's gay. Wonder if I should tell him.*

That night at the dinner table, I had to listen to Dad rave on and on about JJ to Mom. "Irene, it was uncanny. It was like he had lifted all that little dog's worries right off her shoulders, and she had nothing else to yap about. She sat on the floor beside him, calm as you please, and waited for him to let her know what he wanted her to do. And when he walked her around, she trotted at his heel like she'd been raised just for that."

Mom asked, "What happened when Mrs. Soper took her again?"

"Oh, she went back to bouncing and yapping."

I couldn't help saying, "So he didn't cure Lulu. She's still a yappy little dog."

Dad waved his fork absentmindedly, gazing at nothing. "True. But I'll bet if Mrs. Soper treated her like JJ did, things would change. He'd just need to teach her how to do that."

Mom laughed. "So really, Andy, it isn't dog training. It's people training!"

Dad chuckled. "Maybe that's it." He was pretty quiet through the rest of the meal, thank goodness; no more raving about JJ the wonder boy. The Wunderkind. But he was thinking about him. You could tell.

The rest of that week, JJ and I spoke when necessary and not otherwise. So much for all the questions he had warned me he would ask. When he did speak I listened carefully—no, obsessively—to his tone, for condescension or superiority in it, in vain. There was one awkward day when we were both having lunch a little late, and he was alone at one table when I got outside. I sat at another empty table, my back to him. I felt almost mean. I didn't enjoy my lunch very much, wishing he would go in, but when he left it wasn't any better.

# Chapter 9

When I got to work Saturday morning before the store opened, as Dad insisted on weekends, JJ—per usual—was already there. But he wasn't inside, he was in a far corner of the parking lot in front of the store, right near where I'd parked on December ninth, leaving my mom in the car while I went to tell Dad his favorite son was dead.

JJ had used bricks he must have found out behind the building to mark off a corner of the parking lot, away from the store and in whatever shade he could find. By the time I saw him he was running a rope from brick to brick, wrapping it around one and running it along the tarmac to the next, some distance away. I rode my bike behind the store, wheeled it into the stockroom, and went to find Dad to see what chore he had in mind for me. What I really didn't want him to do was tell me to help JJ. I'd sooner stack kitty litter.

But guess what he said? It had nothing to do with litter. Dad was in the stockroom, leaning over a worktable and writing on a large piece of yellow poster board, a much brighter shade than our sign on the storefront. LANDON'S PET SUPPLY, it said on the first line in huge black letters, and underneath that was, DOG BEHAVIOR CLINIC and then 10–NOON SATURDAY MORNINGS, BARRING RAIN. I nearly said, *What, no line that says, "JJ O'Neil, Dog*

*Behaviorist*"? But I was afraid he'd put that on there, so I kept my mouth shut.

I didn't get out of the stockroom quick enough. "Paul," Dad called to me just before I got to the door, "I want you to help JJ this morning. Get the area set up. I took out an ad in the paper, and I'm hoping for a big turnout. Here"—and he handed me the sign he'd made—"take this outside. I've left a metal easel there for it to go on. And watch JJ; maybe you'll learn something."

The poster board almost ripped, I picked it up so roughly, but Dad didn't see. He was already on his way out of the room. As I carried the thing through the store I noticed Dad had already got two registers open, and he was explaining to Alice and Dave, this Korean War vet with a limp worse than Dad's from some war wound, that he was expecting lots of business. I'd never liked Dave. It seemed to me that he didn't pull his weight, that he was a real slacker. I was convinced that Dad hired him and kept him on just because Dad couldn't go to war, and this was some twisted way of compensating.

Carol was already on register one. And there were no customers in the store yet. It wouldn't even open for another ten minutes, for God's sake. What was all the fuss about?

Dad stopped me before I got outside. "Paul, I want you to come into the store from time to time and make sure everything's covered. Take a walk through, see if anything needs restocking, or if you need to open the last register. I'll be keeping an eye out, too, but it may take both of us."

I couldn't bring myself to speak. Just nodded and went outside. The easel was already set up, facing toward incoming traffic. I set the sign there and surveyed what JJ had done. It wasn't just a roped-off square. Around the square was a larger square, so there was maybe four feet between the inner and outer borders. JJ had a pile of stuff in the far corner of the outside square. I went to see what was there, and I saw leashes and collars, four opened bags of dog treats, plastic water bottles, an assortment of dog toys and rawhide chews, and some peculiar contraption made of leash straps and nylon fabric.

When JJ saw me and noticed the sign, he nodded. He didn't smile at me, didn't speak, nothing. I did a mental shrug. After all, did I especially want him being friendly? Maybe Kevin had been able to keep Marty at bay on Monday, but I really didn't need Marty even *acting* like he thought I was like JJ. Queer. And you never knew when Marty would pop in, despite Dad's insistence that he stay away. Like I'd told Dad Thursday afternoon, when he'd caught Marty and Kevin playing with the cat toys, I wasn't Marty's boss. I couldn't tell him what to do. And if I tried, he didn't have to listen.

So we stood there on the pavement, freckles of sun coming through the leaves of the trees that grew beside the tarmac, and waited. Silently. It seemed like there was nothing else to do until someone showed up, so I finally told JJ I'd be back in a minute and went to do a run-through in the store. I was determined to find something that needed doing, and as it turned out, that was stacking cat litter. Dad caught me at it. I say "caught" because that's how he acted.

"Paul, will you use your brain? If we're expecting lots of business because of a dog clinic, wouldn't you think we'd run out of dog supplies before we'd run out of cat supplies?"

"Fine," I retorted, wanting to accuse him of hating cats and not being quite stupid enough to do that, "I'll check on dog stuff."

"I just did. It's nearly ten. You go outside as soon as you've finished this stack." And he left me there.

*Jesus Fucking Christ. Is there* any*thing he thinks I can do right?*

By the time I got outside, not quite ten o'clock, there were already three people there, though there was only one dog. They must have just got there, though, 'cause I heard JJ saying, "While I'm working with Mrs. Thomas's beagle, there's bound to be some things that will apply to your dog as well. Where is your dog?"

The couple, evidently second in line, were the Carters, who used to bring their golden lab into the store before it got too old and had to be put to sleep. My dad had always liked them, because they rescued the lab when it was, like, ten. They'd res-

cued a few dogs other people wouldn't want. I once heard
Mom say that she thought it was because Mrs. Carter had been
adopted herself. That she'd been taken away from her real parents, who'd been really mean to her.

I stood next to JJ and said hi to them. Mr. Carter was telling
JJ about this dog they had rescued.

"Oh, we can't let her out of the van yet. We've had her about
a month, and she's still pretty cranky. Part shepherd, part collie, maybe four years old; we got her at a shelter. We were hoping to get here first so she wouldn't be tempted to attack other
dogs."

*Ha! JJ's in over his head already. This is gonna be fun.* But he
didn't look fazed. He just said, "That was very thoughtful of
you. What's her name?"

"We're calling her Gypsy; we don't know if she had a name
before or not."

"Is she aggressive all the time? Will she be a problem here,
do you think?"

"She's calmed down some since we got her, and she seems to
have bonded with my wife. We just didn't think Gypsy would be
patient and wait while you work with other dogs."

Meanwhile the look on Mrs. Thomas's face had changed a
little. She said, "Um, you know, I can go into the store with
Mozart and do some shopping first." She didn't wait for JJ to
finish saying, "That's so considerate. Thank you." Guess she
didn't want Mozart to be around a cranky dog that might attack.

JJ turned to the Carters. "What can you tell me about Gypsy?"

They talked about how she'd been mistreated, neglected,
how she didn't trust anyone yet except the Carters maybe a little. Finally JJ said, "Is she actually aggressive toward you, Mr.
Carter?"

He paused for a second and then said, "Yes. You're right, I
guess she is. It isn't just that she isn't bonding with me, it's that
she seems not to like me."

"It could be that most of her abuse in the past came from
men. You'll need to work hard to earn her trust, which will

mean you'll have to be painfully consistent with her. What do you want to accomplish today?"

"Nancy needs to be able to walk her when I'm at work. We walk her together at present, because she's so strong and aggressive. She just pulls Nancy everywhere and wants to attack other dogs, people, anything moving."

JJ turned to Mrs. Carter. "Can you control her well enough to bring her over here without having her get too aggressive?"

Mrs. Carter sighed. "We'll do our best."

I backed away from where I'd been standing, farther away from JJ, farther from where the dog would be brought. JJ must have thought I was still next to him, and he said, "She's not in her territory." He turned, surprised to see I'd moved. He raised his voice a little. "That could mean either that she'll be timid and anxious or that she'll be mean." He smiled at me, like he was patronizing my caution. "Why don't you stay where you are."

*Fuck you, too.*

But Gypsy was approaching calmly enough, looking scared, turning her head to see all around her. Mrs. Carter was behind her, holding the leash, trying to point her toward JJ with a tug here and there while the dog pulled in no specific direction.

I looked at JJ. He wasn't looking at the dog, he was gazing off to the side at nothing in particular, as far as I could tell. He said, "Keep hold of the leash, but let her approach me. She needs to sniff."

He didn't acknowledge the dog in any way. He just stood there, hands at his sides, while she walked around him, nosing his shoes, his knees, his ass, his groin, his fingers. Then it seemed like she was done, and she sat down beside him.

Very quietly, JJ said, "Good girl, Gypsy. Good girl." Then, to me, he said, "Paul, would you bring me the black leash from the pile in the corner, with the chain collar on it?"

*Are you kidding me with this? What am I, your hired help?* I eyed the dog. Mrs. Carter had a good hold, but there was slack. If Gypsy lunged, things could get ugly. As if on cue, the dog looked at me and growled.

JJ turned to look at me. "Don't look at the dog. You need to relax; don't act so nervous." He held out his hand for the leash. "Thanks." I backed off slowly, and I gotta say it took a lot out of me not to watch that dog.

JJ held a hand toward Gypsy, palm open and facing up. She sniffed it, and he reached toward her ear. She pulled her head away sharply, almost but not quite getting up. He said, "Okay, she probably won't let me put this on her." He handed the leash, choke chain in position, to Mrs. Carter. "Do you think she'd let you put this over her head while I hold the leash you have?"

"Yes, I think so."

"Make sure the chain is high on her head, behind the ears. That way it will be in the most sensitive spot, and it's where we can control her best." Mrs. Carter had just done that, and JJ had taken the end of the leash, when he said, "Paul, would you ask those people to stay in their car with their dog until we're done, or go into the store? Move casually and speak in relaxed tones."

I hadn't even noticed that there was another couple approaching with a medium-sized brown mutt. I kept JJ between me and Gypsy and did as he asked. The people took another look at Gypsy, saw how everyone was behaving, and they yanked their dog closer and headed for the store.

Too late; Gypsy had figured out the mutt was there, and she growled. I wheeled toward the training area and saw what I was afraid I would see. Gypsy was no longer sitting quietly on the ground. She was straining hard against the two leashes, JJ's and the one still attached to her collar that Mrs. Carter was hanging on to hard, and she was barking and trying to leap forward. JJ moved closer to her, which eased the tension on his leash. He yanked it sharply sideways, released and yanked again and then once more, each time with that low, sharp "Hey" I'd heard him use on Tuesday. And then Gypsy looked in his direction. One more "Hey" and another yank, and Gypsy stopped snarling, but she looked back toward the mutt.

To Mrs. Carter, JJ said, "Ease off. Tension now will just get her angry again." There was now slack on both leads. JJ yanked once again, and then you could've knocked me down, I was that surprised. Gypsy sat. Everyone breathed easier.

Suddenly Dad was beside me. I hadn't seen him leave the store. "Paul, you can go in. I want to watch this. I should be out here, anyway."

*Sure. Just when it's getting interesting, I have to leave.* To Mrs. Carter, JJ was saying, "What I'm going to do is walk her around the inside part of the square. Can you unhook your leash from her collar?"

Once I was back in the store I looked around. A few customers were in the aisles, and some at the checkout, but there was no need for me to do anything. If I followed Dad's instructions from earlier I'd take a tour through, but I was pissed at him. So I went to the plate glass windows in the front where I could watch the show.

Obviously there had been some progress just in the time it took me to get inside and make up my mind to disobey Dad. JJ was walking Gypsy around inside the two lines of rope. Every so often JJ yanked a little on the lead he held, and in my mind I heard him say, "Hey." Sharp. Quiet. Calm.

Standing outside the ropes, the Carters were talking quietly to Dad, watching JJ. I could imagine the praises they were heaping on him, getting Gypsy to behave so well. JJ held the leash with his hand really far down, closer to Gypsy's head than I'd ever want to get, but it wasn't tight. He looked relaxed, though his arm was a little stiff, and sometimes Gypsy would turn her head some. That's when he'd yank. At some point I became aware that Mrs. Thomas and Mozart were next to me, watching the scene as well.

JJ was walking Gypsy toward the edge of the tarmac, his back to the parking lot, when suddenly I noticed some other people headed toward them. There was a woman and a kid, probably her son, with a dog that was maybe a Weimaraner, soft gray with that anemic-looking nose. It started barking. Gypsy's head wheeled toward it and JJ gave a sharp yank, and another. The new people stopped moving and stayed where they were, trying to get their dog under control now. It was jumping up and down and making all kinds of noise, bits of foam spraying from its mouth.

JJ continued to face the trees along the edge and tried to get Gypsy to do the same, but finally it was obvious she wanted to attack. I couldn't believe what he did next. He grabbed the back of the collar, pushed down hard on it, forced Gypsy down onto the pavement, and rolled her onto her side. He crouched there, hanging on while she struggled and strained, and didn't let her up. She looked like she was trying to bite him but couldn't quite reach. He finally had to lean on her to keep her down. Mr. Carter started to help, but JJ said something to him and he moved a step or two away.

Maybe half a minute went by, and I would have thought JJ would give up. But he didn't. He didn't look angry or afraid, he just kept holding Gypsy down on her side until she finally gave up struggling and just lay there, chest heaving, tongue hanging far out of her mouth. JJ waited several more seconds and then he stood, letting her up but keeping the leash short. She tried to turn toward the other dog a few times, but now JJ's yanks had more effect. He turned her so her back was to the other dog again, pressed down on her rump with his hand, and she sat.

He handed his lead to Mrs. Carter, and she put her hand far down on it where his had been. And guess where JJ went. You got it, over to the Weimaraner. First, though, he picked up a leash with a choke collar on it from his pile. As he approached the group, he looked at the woman and said something I couldn't hear, but he didn't look at the dog. The woman could barely hold it, but it didn't want JJ. It wanted Gypsy. Then JJ grabbed the collar and slipped the choke chain he'd brought onto the dog. This time he managed to force the dog to turn its back on Gypsy without rolling it onto the ground. It didn't fight as hard, and it didn't try to bite him, and finally it stopped yelping and baring its teeth. Once it was quiet, he handed it to the woman, moved her hand down on it toward the dog, and said something else to her. She nodded, and then she and the kid and the dog went back to their car.

Mrs. Thomas's voice startled me; I'd forgotten she was there. "That boy is amazing. How on earth does he do that?"

I looked at Mozart, who seemed tame enough, sitting there between us. "What do you want him to do for you?"

"When I try to walk Mozart he just drags me. I know he doesn't look like a very big dog, but he's strong and very determined. My arm hurts a lot now, even when I'm not walking him."

After JJ's display out there, it didn't seem to me he'd have much trouble with Mozart. Maybe I wouldn't, either. "Do you mind if I hold his leash?"

Mrs. Thomas looked surprised, but she said, "I guess that's all right."

With my eyes I followed the strap from my hand down to the collar on Mozart's neck. Since we'd never had animals, I wasn't real used to handling dogs, though I'd been around them a lot in the store. I couldn't remember that I'd ever walked one, not beyond holding the leash kind of like this for a customer who needed an extra hand at one time or another.

On an impulse I crouched down and held on to the collar with one hand while I released the hook of the leash. Then I did what JJ had done with Lulu's red lead, running the hook through the loop handle at the other end and then putting the noose loop over Mozart, fitting it up behind his ears. I stood.

"What are you doing?" Mrs. Thomas asked. "That's going to choke him."

"It's what JJ does," I said. "Let's just give it a try."

Leash in hand, moving away from Mozart, I called him to me. He looked at me like I was crazy and turned back toward the window. This wasn't going well. I yanked a little on the leash and released, called again. Still nothing. So why had it worked for JJ, with Lulu? What had he done differently?

I went to the dog, Mrs. Thomas watching me closely, and I moved my hand down the lead so it was nearly taut. I yanked. Again.

Finally Mozart stood, but he just looked at me, like, "Now what?"

I jiggled the leash as I moved away, trying to get him to follow. At first I thought he was going to sit back down, but then he moved toward me, reluctantly, it seemed. I turned and walked, keeping the lead short, and he followed. I watched his head to see if he got distracted, and whenever he turned I yanked on the lead and said, "Hey." This seemed to work pretty well, and we went to the side of the store, past the shelves holding the lizards, and turned. But about halfway back to where Mrs. Thomas stood, he shook his head as if trying to shake the loop off, and he sat down. I couldn't get him to budge after that. Mrs. Thomas must have got worried I'd hurt him with the loop, because she came over and held her hand out. I gave her the leash, and she crouched down to hook it back the way it had been before. Mozart looked sideways at me, his eyes telling me, "Yeah. Who do you think you are, anyway? Get lost." Mrs. Thomas said nothing.

To her, I said, "Good luck." So much for learning something from JJ, as Dad had told me to do. And now I'd made an idiot of myself in front of a customer. *Thanks for nothing, JJ.* Part of me wanted to watch and see what JJ did with Mozart, but the part that won was determined to act like I didn't care. I didn't care what else JJ did, didn't care what Dad thought of JJ, didn't care that I was missing out on all the excitement. I decided to do some rounds.

Wandering around the store, I had to keep reminding myself to look for things that needed doing, supplies that were running low, things out of order or out of place on a shelf. In my mind I was still watching JJ hold that violent dog on its side. This was the kid who had frozen at the sight of my sneaker. Who had frozen under Marty's gaze. Out there, with the dogs and their owners, JJ did not look like that same cautious kid. Or like the kid who'd avoided talking to me most of the week. He was in command, and everyone out there was hanging on his every word.

More important, the dogs were his. He owned them. He was their lord.

As Dad had predicted, the store did get busy. I suspected that it was largely because he kept sending people inside to wait their turn with JJ, and obligingly they bought things for their dogs. Some of them came in, then went outside for their turn in the rope square, and then they came back in to buy choke chains. I was kept pretty busy making sure we didn't run out of anything on the shelves, and our supply of chains was so low by noon that I wondered if we would run out.

Every so often I couldn't help it. I'd go to the front of the store and watch. JJ kept the onlookers outside the outer perimeter of the larger square he'd roped off, and he worked with the dog and the owner in the center, leaving that four-foot buffer zone empty. From this distance, and with a small crowd gathering, the contrast between the tense or sloppy ways people handled their dogs and the calm confidence that radiated from JJ was even more evident. He looked almost holy out there. It was somewhere between the poem on the Statue of Liberty in New York—the one about offering refuge to the hungry, the tired, the poor, whatever—and a quiet little revival meeting where sins were carried into that square and left there, people and dogs leaving relieved of their burdens, the prospect of a happy life together showing on their glowing faces.

At the center of all of it was that small, sweet-faced kid with no real name. And on the sidelines stood my father, to all appearances a supplicant. A worshipper. At any rate, a believer.

Dad didn't come back into the store until twelve-thirty. He asked me for a report on supplies, and I pointed out the disappearing leashes and choke chains and then asked, "Where's JJ? Did some Doberman eat him alive?"

Dad didn't look up from his examination of rawhide chews. "You could learn a thing or two from that young man, Paul." Which didn't answer my question, and only tempted me to assure him that wasn't going to happen.

When JJ did come in, folded easel under one arm and yellow poster board under the other, I was watching for him. I expected him to look exuberant, triumphant, something. But he just looked like himself. Calm. Watchful, but calm.

Dad was watching for him, too, it seemed. "JJ, can you come into the office for a minute before you take your lunch break?"

*Lunch break? Am I gonna get one of those today?* I was bagging at register three, but I was dying to know what was going on in the office. As soon as I could I moved that way, but I didn't want Dad or JJ to see me. I hugged the wall just outside the door.

Dad was saying, "What was that, anyway? Why does that work?"

"It's called an alpha rollover. It's not something I would recommend people do, because it can be dangerous. I do it only sometimes, and only when the aggression has escalated beyond where I can control it another way. I do it with a dog that's already acknowledged my leadership, and Gypsy had done that. As I said, it's dangerous, so I don't teach most people how to do it."

"But why does it work?"

"If I remain calm, then I'm projecting leadership. Dogs want that. The rollover is a drastic way to demonstrate leadership, and like I said I use it only sometimes. It's... well, it's kind of intimidating to the dog." He chuckled. "Fortunately, they seem to forgive me pretty quickly."

"Intimidating. Doesn't sound like a great relationship. What about love? Dogs need love just like people do."

"If you give a dog what it needs, you *are* showing love, and they'll get that. Not through the rollover, that's not what I mean. But the first goal is to allow the dog to relax because she sees you as leader of the pack, even if she's the only animal in the pack. It won't do any good to yell at her or try to teach her tricks or commands. Sure, she can learn to obey commands. But first, you need her respect. And you'll get her respect only if you convince her you're in charge and it's safe for her to let her guard down.

"What a dog needs first, what will convince her you care about her, isn't hugs and kisses. It's allowing her to be calm by convincing her she doesn't need to be in charge. She doesn't need to understand all the complicated things around her, doesn't need to control everything. This is what a dog wants. You love her best when you treat her like a dog, because you're totally accepting her as she is. You aren't expecting her to be like a child or a human friend."

"I can't believe you wouldn't hug your dog."

JJ laughed softly. "I do hug my dog. I hug him a lot. But if I give him love when he's nervous or aggressive, it's like I'm telling him that's a good way to be."

"So, when? When do you hug him?"

"He lets me know when he's ready for affection. He approaches calmly, or he lies on his side or his back at my feet. Calm. Relaxed. That's when I pat him, massage his muscles with my fingers, and tell him what a good dog he is. And I love him for *what* he is. A dog."

It was more than I could stand there and listen to, Dad letting this kid tell him what was what. It wasn't so much that I didn't want JJ telling my dad the best way to behave. It was that Dad never listened to *me* about anything. JJ did everything right, and I do nothing right. It felt familiar in a very bad way. It was one thing when it was Chris being right and me being wrong. But—JJ? No. Sorry. *There's not enough room in this family for the both of us, JJ O'Neil.*

I went outside to dismantle the rope squares, partly to clear the parking area for cars again, but mostly to destroy the pedestal for JJ it represented. It wasn't until I'd piled the bricks under a tree and had looped the ropes and tied them that I realized I was also being JJ's cleaning crew. Fighting anger, I leaned one hand against a tree and rubbed my forehead with the other, squinting hard to try and keep myself from yelling.

After a minute or so I took a shaky breath and turned toward the store to see JJ headed toward me, a couple of shopping bags in his hand. I watched him approach, trying to come up with some smart remark that would let him know I didn't think he was God's gift to the canine world in general or to my father in particular. But I failed.

"Thanks," he said quietly when he was close enough for me to hear. "I'll gather the rest of this stuff."

*You bet your ass you will.* I was dying for him to say something, do something, even let his tone of voice make me believe that he felt superior, that he saw himself as some kind of star. But he just quietly picked up what was left of his supplies, put them into the bags, and went back into the store while I stood there like some kind of unarmed prison guard, hands on my hips, watching for infractions or insubordination to no avail.

Christ, but I wanted to hate him!

As if it weren't enough that I had to put up with JJ all day, my dad couldn't shut up about him over dinner that night. He seemed particularly impressed with something JJ had cobbled together and had used on this dog that was part boxer, part Saint Bernard.

Dad really got into the story. "Irene, you should have seen this guy who had the dog. A small guy, puny really. He got the dog thinking it would be good protection. And it is, but this guy is such a pip-squeak that he can't walk it. It was a riot watching this monster drag him over to JJ, who's not very big himself. So after JJ showed him what leash he should use and how to hold it, JJ could walk the dog, but this guy still couldn't. So JJ picked up this"—Dad held his hands in front of him like that would help him describe something—"this contraption he'd put together himself out of strap leashes and nylon material. It ties onto the dog's back, straps under the belly, and the nylon pockets hang on the sides. Then JJ has these bottles filled with water, and he puts them into the pockets."

Dad sat there a minute, gazing toward his dinner plate and shaking his head. "It was uncanny, I tell you. That dog settled right down. It's like so much of his attention went to carrying this load that he was easier to control."

Dad picked up his fork and stabbed something, but he didn't put it into his mouth. He wasn't quite done with his story. "He had a job to do. The dog. That's what JJ gave him. And the guy?" Dad chuckled. "He was nearly weeping, falling over himself thanking JJ." He ate the food from his fork without seeming to realize it, swallowed, and said, "You know, I think I'm gonna have to see if I can find some of those things already made. Or maybe I can commission someone to make them."

Mom asked, "Did JJ let him keep the . . . whatever?"

"He did. The guy wanted to pay him, and JJ said no. He said

to make a donation to an animal shelter instead. Can you believe it?"

I was gritting my teeth so hard it was difficult to eat my dinner. It was everything I could do not to fall on my knees, genuflect, and shout *Praise the Lord!* I kind of tuned out after that, not really caring to hear Dad complain about today's proceeds coming up noticeably short again, like had been happening from time to time.

On Monday, my one day of the week off, it rained. I wanted to sleep in, but my folks were having some intense conversation in the kitchen. So I stood at the top of the stairs, listening. Mom was saying, "I could talk to him and find out how he put it together. Maybe he even has a pattern, or instructions or something."

"That would be fantastic, Irene. You could even go and talk to him today. He's in the store."

Somehow I knew what they were talking about. Mom was gonna make JJ's doggie packs. She said, "Today? Didn't he work all week?"

"Yup. Said he wanted to be there on Sunday because it might be a day when folks would bring their dogs in. He's right, too. I'll try to get him to take a day off during the week."

*Try* to get him to?

As I told Marty and Kevin later that afternoon, hanging out at the Burger King, this kid was turning out to be a sort of King of the Canines. "He won't get mad at me even when I try to make him. He won't take money for something he bought the materials for and made himself. He wants to work all the time." I shoved a fistful of fries into my mouth and chewed furiously.

Kevin was intrigued. "So he's some kind of dog messiah, right? What's he like with other animals?"

I shrugged. "He talks about cat behavior, but we don't sell dogs or cats, and people don't bring cats in very often. But he did say he wanted to learn more about amphibians."

"That's not much help." Kevin took a bite of cheeseburger and then talked around it. "What's his story, d'you think?

Maybe his folks beat him and he just wants to be out of the house or something. Maybe they know he's a fag and he stays away 'cause he knows they hate him."

Marty was being too quiet. It worried me. I wanted to be able to gripe about JJ without having to hold Marty back from doing something like what he'd done to Anthony. What *we'd* done to Anthony. We sat there contemplating Kevin's theories for a minute, and then Marty said, "Well, unless he's Jesus Fucking Christ Almighty, he'll have a weak spot. Besides being queer, I mean. Or maybe related." He turned to me. "He's not afraid of the dogs, you say?"

"Not a bit. Shoved a ferocious, struggling shepherd mix right down onto the ground and held it there."

Marty nodded. "We'll see. We'll just see."

When I got home, Mom was at the kitchen table working with paper and scissors and a pencil. She was so intent on her project she barely acknowledged me when I spoke. "What's that?" I had time to pull a soda out of the fridge, pop it open, take a swig or two before she finally answered.

"I'm making a pattern for that dog pack JJ invented."

Terrific. I headed up to my room to listen to some music and sulk.

Tuesday it was still rainy, which for some reason tends to make people not go shopping. It was Dave's day off, like he deserved one. So it was Carol, Alice, me, and Dad in the store. Oh, and JJ, who evidently still wasn't taking a day off.

Sometime around eleven or so, Dad made me go with him into the stockroom to do some inventory and make a list of supplies to order. Choke collars would be at the top of the list, I knew already. We were done with cat food and had started hamster supplies when Dad realized he'd left some info he needed in a folder in the office. He was in the middle of counting something, so he sent me to get it. Kind of automatically I glanced around the store as I walked; almost no customers at the moment. Once I was in the office, though, Carol wasn't there, and the folder wasn't where Dad'd said it would be, so I had to paw through a couple of drawers. One of them contained personnel files.

I stood there looking down at the tabs, the white stickers with dark green borders standing out from the plain manila color. It took only a couple of seconds for my fingers to find the one on which "O'Neil" was written in Carol's neat script. I pushed the folder covers apart so I could read what was on the first paper in there. Head turned sideways, my eyes scoured the page for the field "Full Name." In it was hand-printed *José Jesus O'Neil.*

*Holy shit. Jesus! Kevin's going to love this. Messiah, indeed.* I pushed the drawer shut and opened another, where I found the folder Dad wanted. Just outside the office door I was about to turn right toward the stockroom when something on my left caught my attention. It was Kevin, standing not far from the front door, looking toward me. With his body toward the store, he shielded his right hand so Alice at the register wouldn't see, and he pointed my attention farther to my left. JJ was bent over, examining supplies for snakes or something, and behind him stood Marty. There was just enough noise coming from the air conditioning and the equipment needed to maintain the right environment for the amphibians nearby that JJ probably didn't know Marty was there.

In his hand, Marty held a small plastic container, the kind we use to hold the rose hair tarantulas when we need to get them in or out of their glass case. He was tipping it toward JJ's shoulder.

I froze. What the fuck was I supposed to do now? If I let the spider get lost or hurt, and especially if it was because of Marty, I'd catch hell. If I did anything to interfere with Marty's plan, it would be a different kind of hell, but it would still be hell. I snapped my head toward the stockroom; no sign of Dad. I stood where I could escape fully into the office and fake ignorance if all hell broke loose out there, and watched.

If you don't know anything about these tarantulas, they can't kill someone like JJ, unless he's allergic. Make him a little sick, maybe, and the bite is painful. But they move pretty slow most of the time; they're practically blind and feel their way along.

JJ was wearing a light blue shirt. I couldn't see him real well from there, but I could tell that the spider had crawled obligingly onto his back. Marty, looking crazed with silent hysterics, backed away on tiptoes. He set the plastic case on a shelf and went to where Kevin stood, both of them leaning over to watch JJ but also ready to split for the door in a microsecond.

JJ seemed oblivious at first, but after a few seconds, the spider had moved up toward the right side of his neck, and he must have felt something through the cloth. The spider's hairs are real prickly. Anyway, he started to straighten up. He turned his head a little toward the spider and then he froze. I expected a scream. Marty and Kevin no doubt expected a scream.

There was no scream. Maybe three seconds went by, and then JJ reached his left hand out for something I couldn't quite see, bent over a little, and the next thing I saw was the edge of a stiff spec sheet, maybe one on green lizards or something, that JJ was holding in front of the spider. Gently he poked at one hairy leg with the edge, and at first the spider retreated. But JJ just stood there, stiff paper resting on his shoulder, waiting.

Now, I've gotten used to these creatures. Over the years. It took a while, and even though I know they can't really hurt me and aren't likely to leap onto my head or anything...if that had been me? Surprised like that? I'd have been shaking like a leaf, and that sheet would have knocked the spider onto the floor. Then the spider would be sure to escape, and we'd have a tarantula loose. Not great for PR, in case there's any doubt about that.

But here's JJ, not particularly familiar with tarantulas, faced with finding one suddenly appearing on his back right near his head, and he's just as calm as he'd been with the dogs. He kept bending farther over until the spec sheet was the easiest place for the spider to go, and it went.

Several things happened in quick succession. JJ stood up, spider held on this makeshift platform in his left hand, and turned around, almost certainly to see what he could use to recapture the thing. I'm sure he heard Marty and Kevin cackling right before they shot out the front door. I stepped out of the office toward JJ, knowing where the plastic holder was, and Dad came out of the stockroom. I looked at Dad, he looked first at me and then at JJ, and then at the spider. He made a beeline toward JJ.

"What's going on here?"

There was nothing I felt safe saying, so I just headed for the plastic holder. But JJ knew what to say. "It seems the rose hair has found its way out of the spider tank."

"Stand still," I told him, setting down the folder I'd retrieved from the office. "Here's the container." Doing my best not to shudder, I planted the plastic cup over the ugly spider where it sat on the spec sheet, waving a front leg in the air. JJ put his hand over the cover before I'd got mine completely away and we touched, but there was no jerking away this time; the spider had all my attention.

Dad said, "Where's the other half of the container?"

I didn't know, so I started scouring the area. Dad and JJ went to the spider tank. I heard Dad say, "This is the only one of these we have at the moment, so it can go into the tank without the smaller container for now."

Finally I found the other half where Marty must have set it down before I'd seen him, and I picked up the folder again. As I walked toward the spider tank, Dad said, "Paul, how did that spider get out?"

"I didn't see how it got out. I had nothing to do with it." Which was true enough, technically, if not quite the whole story. "I didn't see it until it was on JJ, and he was coaxing it onto the paper."

Dad turned to JJ, but his eyes stayed on me for a second like he wasn't convinced. Before he could say anything else, JJ said, "I think I mentioned that I wanted to know more about amphibians and the other non-mammals. I had lifted the spider out in its container to get a closer look at it. Maybe I forgot to put it back."

Dad stepped away from both of us at this point. JJ's story was almost but not quite plausible. All Dad could say was, "Do you boys have any idea how bad it would be if customers thought there was a tarantula loose in the store? Do I need to remind you how important it is to treat *all* the animals with care?"

"No, sir," JJ said, hanging his head. "I'm very sorry. It won't happen again."

Dad turned to me. It was everything I could do not to shout, *I told you I had nothing to do with this!* But all I said was, "No, sir."

I could tell Dad was still sure he didn't have the truth, but there wasn't much he could do about it without calling JJ a liar. Maybe if it had been my lie, he would have pounced on it. He snatched the folder out of my hand and stormed off toward the stockroom. I knew he expected me to follow, but I turned to look at JJ. His face unreadable, he said, "You do know how that happened, right?"

"Yeah." I wanted to fake ignorance, but he'd just saved my neck.

"I don't like lying to your father. I don't like lying to anyone."

"No. I'm sure you don't."

"I won't do it again." And he turned and left me standing there.

Still putting off going into the stockroom, I headed outside to see if Marty and Kevin were hanging around hoping for amusement from whatever fallout their little prank might have caused. I'd just stepped outside, still under the overhang where I wouldn't get rained on, when I heard an engine rev and saw Marty's Mustang coming my way. Kevin's side was to me, and when the car was close he rolled his window down.

"Hey, Paul! What's that guy made of, stone?"

I took a deep breath, looked around me for some reason I'm not sure of, and walked through the drizzle to the car. "Look," I said, trying to sound stern, expecting Marty to ridicule me for it, "you guys have got to stop pulling these stunts. I'm already in deep shit here, and you're making it worse."

Marty leaned in my direction. "I suppose the kid squealed."

"You suppose wrong. He took the blame himself, though Dad seems to know better, and he suspects me of being involved somehow. Just knock if off, will you?" I slapped the side of the car door for emphasis and loped back to the store before either of them could say anything. But I heard Marty's sarcastic scorn in the sound of his tires as he peeled off.

Back in the storeroom, helping Dad again in that over-lit room that just emphasized how gloomy it was outside today, I realized almost with a shock that I wasn't going to tell Kevin or Marty what "JJ" stood for.

# Chapter 10

Thursday, after JJ was convinced to take Wednesday off, everyone was back, and Dad had JJ and me back at the fish tanks. JJ could work without supervision now, so it went twice as fast as when I did it alone. I decided to try to break some of the conversational ice I'd put in place.

"JJ, um, about Tuesday. Just to be clear, I didn't know they were gonna do that. With the spider."

"Okay. I believe you."

Well, that was fine, as far as it went. But it wasn't very satisfying. So I added, "I'm sorry they did it. I mean, they're my friends and all. I told them to knock it off."

"Thanks."

Okay, so now there were some shards of ice chipped off the surface, but I wanted at least to see some of the freezing water underneath. Something moving. "Could I ask you something about the dog stuff?"

He stood up straight, stretched, and glanced at me. "Dog stuff?"

"Yeah. What you were doing on Saturday. When Dad came out he sent me back into the store, and Mrs. Thomas and Mozart were watching with me for a bit. She said he dragged her around when she tried to walk him. So I tried to do what you'd done with Lulu, and he followed me a little, but then he just sat down and wouldn't budge."

JJ went back to scouring a tank. "Were you holding the leash way down near his head, and was it high up right behind his ears?"

"Yeah."

"Were you relaxed and assertive?"

*Was I?* "I can't remember."

"Dogs won't follow you just because you want them to. They need to respect you first. And if you don't take charge in a way that's clear to them, they aren't going to follow you the way you want."

"How do I do that?"

"Do what? Be relaxed and assertive?"

"Yeah. Where does that come from?"

He glanced at me and then back at the tank. "Inside you."

*Inside* me? *Oh, I don't think so. That isn't likely.* But it made sense that JJ had it inside him. All I had to do was remember how he'd acted when he realized the tarantula was almost in his ear. This seemed like a dead-end line of questioning. So I waited awhile and then tried another. "Do you mind if I ask what your initials stand for?" I already knew, of course. Maybe I wanted to know if he would lie to *me*.

He stopped moving. Frozen, like when he'd seen my sneaker beside him on his first day. "Why?"

*Whoa. Hit a nerve or something.* I shrugged. "No reason. Just curious."

After about a minute and a half of scouring in silence, he said, "JJ stands for José Jesus." Only he said it like it was pronounced something like Hossay Hayssoos. "But nobody around here seems to pronounce José correctly, so I shortened it years ago."

"Hozay," I ventured.

"No. You need to make the 'h' sound a little harder, and there's no 'z' sound. It's more like a double 's.' Plus you're adding a diphthong to the o and the e that shouldn't be there."

I tried again, and it sound even funnier. JJ smiled, though it looked like he was trying not to. He said, "Just stick to 'JJ.' It's better all around."

Tempted to say "Wunderkind" the way Anthony had said it when he corrected Marty, I opted instead for, "What is that? Spanish?"

"Sort of. Mexican. My mother is from Mexico."

*So that's why he seems a little exotic.* "So, is Jesus a name the Mexicans use a lot?"

"It's not uncommon. And I suppose the fact that it's almost unheard of around here is another reason I went to JJ. Not that anyone gets called by their middle name, necessarily. Unless someone who's cruel finds out what it is and abuses it."

Well, that sounded like a warning. I nearly replied, *What d'you think, I would do that?* But then I remembered that the moment I'd found out, I'd thought about telling Kevin. I wouldn't. Not now. I was on the verge of doing something really stupid and asking him if he was gay, when suddenly there was this woman beside him.

"Hello," she said, "are you JJ?"

He stopped working, wiped his hands off on a towel, and extended his right hand to her. Very grown-up. Very professional. "Yes, ma'am. What can I do for you?"

"I'm Mrs. Denneghy. My friend brought her dog here last Saturday, and she said you worked wonders. She has that mixed breed that's possessive about toys."

"Ah, yes. Tucker. I think we got your friend onto the right track, anyway. It's going to take some work."

"I have a Dalmatian that's almost two years old. He was a wonderful puppy, but for a few months now he's been getting more and more aggressive. I was afraid to bring him to the clinic, because he's really awful around other dogs. Do you think you could help him?"

"Have you had him checked out by a vet to make sure he isn't in some kind of pain, or if he has a neurological condition?"

"Oh, his vet is very well aware of the problem, believe me. He hasn't suggested any medical causes."

"I see. Well, certainly you're welcome to bring him on Saturday. I'd just suggest you leave him in the car at first, since we already know he's aggressive around other dogs, and we'll try to set things up the best we can."

"Oh, good. Thank you so much!"

We stood there, he and I, watching as she walked away. Almost under his breath, JJ said, "I had a feeling this would happen."

"What?"

"I knew people would start bringing their dogs during the week, not just on Saturdays. I told your father I expected it, but he said he was willing to take the risk. But if they start bringing in aggressive dogs . . ." His voice trailed off.

"She didn't bring him in."

"No, but someone else will. I'll finish this tank and then let your father know she was here, and that she'll probably be back on Saturday."

So I was saved from making an idiot of myself and asking JJ a question I shouldn't. I was pretty sure I knew the answer, anyway.

And he was right about the dogs. Later that same day someone I knew—my friend Mr. Treadwell—showed up. JJ and I were restocking dog collars. "Hello, Paul," he opened. "Hope the summer's going well for you." He turned toward JJ. "Are you JJ?"

Mr. Treadwell had brought in his English sheepdog because she was chewing all the fur off of one flank. Again, JJ suggested a trip to the vet first.

"Oh, I did that. The vet says if Ophelia were allergic to something, it wouldn't be just the one spot. We tried antihistamines, anyway, but they didn't help. And he couldn't find any other cause for it." He looked down at the dog and then back up to JJ. "We tried topical ointments. When that failed, my vet recommended sedatives, but I'm reluctant to do that. Do you have any ideas?"

JJ glanced toward the office, probably wondering what Dad would say about this. I spoke up. "I'll just go let Dad know you're working with a customer."

It was obvious Dad would have to make a decision about this—phenomenon, this situation, whatever it was turning into. When I got back with Dad, JJ had already taken the leash off Ophelia's collar and had put it on her neck like he'd done with every dog.

"She's obsessing," he said to Mr. Treadwell. "A dog needs to know who's in charge, and if no one seems to be, she'll take that role on whether she wants it or not. So she thinks she needs to control things, but she doesn't know how. She might think this activity she's doing, this chewing, is all she can control, or she might be using it to keep her mind off of all the stuff she doesn't understand. How often do you walk her?"

"I try to walk her every afternoon. I have to be in school early during the year, and I don't want to change the routine in the summer when I'm not in classes."

Dad and I just stood there. Neither of us knew what to say, that was for sure. JJ looked like he was hunting for the right words, but he didn't look like he didn't know what to say.

Finally, "This is a big dog, a herding dog. She needs activity, and she needs direction. If you can't walk her consistently at the start of her day, perhaps you could find someone else who could. She needs to have a way to spend her energy in the morning, and then she needs to know someone is in charge, so that her mind can relax. Then you should walk her as well, so she recognizes you as a leader. And then on weekends, or during the week if you can, it would be best for her if you could find someplace where she could run around in an open area. That could be at the end of the day, but she still needs to be walked in the morning. And she needs to be walked in a way that lets her know who the boss is." He handed the leash to Mr. Treadwell. "Can you show me what you do?"

Ophelia was sitting there, gnawing at the sore spot just like Mr. Treadwell had said. He took the leash and started to pull on it. "Come on, girl," he said. She looked at him, and for a second it looked like she was going to ignore him, but she stood and began to move. Her head hung down, and she just kind of loped along after him. He did a circle and came back to JJ.

JJ asked, "Is that sort of how it goes?"

"Sometimes she pulls me. It varies."

JJ nodded and reached for the leash. "May I?" First he moved the loop up under her ears, then he waited for her to start chewing. He yanked slightly and said, "Hey." Waited. More chewing, another yank. Once more, and then she didn't go back to chewing. She sat there and looked up at JJ.

He let the leash fall and moved away a little, and then called her. She got up and went to him immediately. Then he took the leash, and she walked behind him just like it was what she'd wanted to do all along. Her head was up, proud, and he walked her quickly to the front, then back and forth. Still walking, he signaled to Mr. Treadwell to come up. JJ handed the leash to the teacher, corrected his hold, and guided him on how to walk.

I watched intently. What had I done wrong with Mozart? JJ had said "relaxed and assertive." Certainly he was both those things. And Ophelia responded to it. She looked great. She looked happy, even once Mr. Treadwell had the leash again, because he'd picked up on what JJ was doing. He was beaming.

JJ said, "Okay, now stop, and see if she sits." She didn't. "Gently and quickly, squeeze your fingers on her back, just above the tail, push down a little, and let go." She sat. "Now wait to see if she chews. If she does, you give a gentle yank and make some quiet but sudden noise."

It was working. Everything worked. Everything JJ tried with that dog worked, just like everything else I'd seen him do had worked. Dogs, fish tanks, spiders—it didn't matter. He was charmed. And now Mr. Treadwell had fallen victim to his charms.

Mr. Treadwell and Ophelia both looked very happy when they left, a new collar for Ophelia already on her. Dad asked JJ and me to come into the office. The first thing he said was to me.

"Thanks for coming to get me, Paul. That was the right thing to do." Coulda knocked me over with a cat toy. "We need to decide how we're going to handle this situation, because it's sure to arise again. JJ, I know you predicted this. Dalmatian this morning, sheepdog this afternoon, and tomorrow it could be a Doberman with a mean streak that takes a bite out of somebody. We can't have that, and not everyone will be as thoughtful as Mrs. Denneghy, who knew better than to bring her dog in. Any ideas?"

"You could change your policy," I suggested. "Not let any dogs in at all."

Dad shook his head. "I really don't want to do that."

We all stood there in silence until JJ said, "We can insist that people bring the dogs for help only on Saturday. If someone like this fellow comes during the week, and if I think I can help, then I tell them briefly what I'll do and suggest they come back during the Saturday workshop. Kind of a triage."

"Doesn't solve the problem of the Doberman," I pointed out.

Dad was thinking and talking at the same time. "No, but if someone brings in a dog that looks dangerous...JJ, you'd be able to tell that pretty quickly, right? So you could ask the customer and the dog to step outside with you for an assessment. Maybe you can't really help, anyway; maybe the dog is too far gone. But you could do the triage you mentioned, away from the door. Maybe you should just go outside with anyone who brings in a dog that needs help. What do you think?"

"It's probably the best approach," JJ said. "We can see how it goes and make changes if we have to."

"Check in with me at lunch and at the end of the day, and give me a rundown of any dogs people brought in."

We all nodded, but I still had my doubts that this was going to work. For sure I wasn't getting near that imaginary Doberman. I decided not to ask what would happen on the days when JJ wasn't at work; I didn't want to get shot down again.

Friday another customer brought a dog in. It was a little yippy thing, a Pekinese maybe, and JJ took the owner outside. I went out, too, just to hear what he said, curious to see if it would be any different from what he might have said about Lulu. But I got distracted by Jack.

Jack was this homeless guy who moved around from storefront to storefront, finding shady spots in the summer and warm spots in the winter, and sometimes he hung out at the far corner here, near the trees on the edge, probably hoping no one would see him. Anytime Dad saw him, he chased him off. But I didn't quite have what it took to do that, so I just tried to pretend he wasn't there, which made it difficult to listen to JJ. But Jack was listening. He looked like he was fascinated.

When Dad got home that night, a couple of hours after I did, Mom had done some weird redecorating in the kitchen. She had strung up about four of those doggie packs she'd made during the week. She was nearly giggling when Dad came in and saw them.

"Irene, this is great. We'll have them for the workshop tomorrow. Paul, I want you to go to the grocer's before you go to the store and get bottles of water, or something we can put water into, like JJ had. Make sure you get some that will fit into these pockets. We could give workshop customers the water bottles to go with the packs they buy!"

"On my bike?"

Mom said, "Take my car, dear. I have enough materials to keep me sewing all day."

Dad chimed in. "You can drive your mother's car home at lunch and bike back to work. Irene, what do you think your production speed will be, now that you've done a few?"

"Oh, goodness. Maybe five a week? How many do you think you'll sell?"

They talked supply and demand for a while, and I contemplated how I was turning into JJ's helper again. But there was a bonus. My mom looked happier than I'd seen her since Chris was home.

Saturday was overcast, threatening rain, but Dad decided to do the workshop, anyway. JJ had the parking lot all partitioned off before I got there with the water bottles.

"Your father said for you to go inside when you got here. I

think he wants to be out here again, to make sure things go all right."

"Shit." It was out before I knew I'd said it.

"What? Is there a problem?"

Not one I really wanted to admit to JJ. "No. Everything's peachy." I went to find Dad, who was doing a last-minute examination of dog supplies. I spoke before he could. "Dad, I was hoping to watch from outside this time."

"I need you in here, Paul. And I need to be out there in case anything happens. Liability. I'm sorry, but that's the way it has to be."

All I could do was grit my teeth and walk away. But I spent as much time as I could at the front of the store, watching JJ. So I saw what happened when Mrs. Denneghy's Dalmatian and some other customer's English bulldog got into it. JJ had been walking the Dalmatian around the inner square, and several people were watching—most of them having left their dogs in their cars—from outside the outer perimeter, and it was going pretty well. Maybe JJ had wanted to challenge the Dalmatian or something, because it didn't look like he'd asked the bulldog owner to take her dog to her car or into the store. Dad was standing next to her, and he looked nervous.

"That bulldog is trouble." The voice startled me, and I turned to see Dave, the war vet, standing next to me, watching.

I was tempted to tell him to get back to his register. But for now, I just replied, "So is the Dalmatian."

"This should be interesting."

As he said that, the Dalmatian was coming closer to the bulldog, and damn if that little tank on paws didn't lunge. Bulldogs are really strong, and this one pulled the lady holding his leash, which was attached to a regular buckled collar, right along with him. So there they were, the bulldog's underbite firmly attached to the Dalmatian's hind leg, the Dalmatian wheeling around, not sure whether it should put more energy into biting or trying to escape, and Mrs. Denneghy screaming, not knowing what to do.

I didn't really think; I just ran outside. By the time I got to the dogs, Dad had grabbed the bulldog's leash and was trying to pull him away, but it wasn't having much effect, and JJ was trying to get the Dalmatian to hold still. He saw me approach.

"Paul! Quick, get me a rawhide chew and then take this leash and hold it."

No time to be scared or irritated. I did what he said. JJ bent over the bulldog, jabbed the chew into the side of its mouth until the jaws separated, grabbed the back of its neck, and yanked it down to the ground on its side. The Dalmatian yelped and pulled away, and I was stuck trying to keep it from running anyplace. I grabbed the collar and held on, letting the dog pull me away from that bulldog and not wanting to tug too hard on the choke chain.

You know how they say when you think you're about to die your life flashes before your eyes in a split second? Well, I was scared, but even though I didn't expect to die that day my mind flashed a scene in that same microsecond. When Chris had told us the story about being driven along this dirt road and seeing farmers' tools but no farmers and they knew something was really wrong, he'd said the spookiest part of being in a situation like that was that no one really knew what to do. You had no guidance, so all anyone could do was look to the ranking officer and pray like hell that he had a good head on his shoulders. I realized with a bit of a shock that I didn't feel quite like that. Maybe I didn't know what to do, but JJ did. I wanted him to do more of it soon, though; the Dalmatian was lunging and jumping around, trying to get away.

Mrs. Denneghy came running over to me and was about to wrap her arms around her dog.

"No!" JJ nearly shouted from where he was straining to hold the canine tank down. "Let him calm down. He might bite even you right now." She froze, this frantic look on her face.

*What, it's okay if he bites me?* I looked toward JJ, and he was showing Dad how to keep the bulldog on the ground. Then he came over to me and did the same thing with the Dalmatian— down on its side, just holding it there while it panted and heaved.

JJ's voice was quieter now. "Paul, go and hold the bulldog's leash so it can't get over here if it manages to get up."

So I stood there hanging on, watching Dad put all his weight into fighting that bulldog's determination to get up and charge again, wondering if it could pull me as easily as it had its owner. The bulldog was still struggling when JJ let the Dalmatian up. He handed the leash to Mrs. Denneghy while he examined the leg.

"It doesn't look too bad. I don't think the bone is broken, but you should get to the vet right away." He turned to the bull-dog owner. "You'll need to provide proof of rabies vaccination, or they'll have to quarantine the dog."

Mrs. Denneghy kept her limping dog far from the bulldog. She had a few words for the bulldog's owner, however. "He told you to take that dog away! And look what it's done!" She was near tears, and I didn't blame her.

So I guess JJ had said the bulldog shouldn't be there after all; maybe that's why Dad was so close to it, and looking anxious, when the fight started.

JJ joined Dad at the bulldog with a leash and choke chain in his hand. The dog was much calmer now, really just panting. JJ got the choke collar on him and said, "Mr. Landon, you can let go now."

Dad stood and backed away, and JJ stood there alone over the dog, leash relaxed and partly on the ground. The bulldog just lay there, almost like it was relieved it didn't have to do anything more. Dad decided to talk dog business with the owner. "About the rabies. Is the dog vaccinated?"

The owner seemed ashamed. "Yes. A few months ago. It's stamped on the tag there on his collar."

We all stood there, watching the dog's breathing slow for a minute or so, and then JJ yanked up on the leash and the dog stood. He said, "I'm going to walk him around the parking lot to make sure he understands his position and calm him down a little more. Paul, could you come with me and make sure no one approaches with another dog?"

I walked with JJ between me and the canine attack vehicle. It looked calm enough at the moment, and it followed JJ like it had been born to do that. "So the owner ignored your warning?" I asked him.

He kind of gritted his teeth. "Yes."

"Who'll be in the most trouble, d'you think?"

"I'm afraid it'll be your father, for having the clinic in the first place. It's not fair, and I warned him this might happen. I blame myself, though. I thought I could keep things under control. I should have insisted."

"But Mrs. Denneghy won't press charges or anything, will she?"

JJ took a deep breath. "I hope not. She understands what happened. But who knows what her friends, her husband, anyone might encourage her to do? At least the bulldog's had shots, though I'm going to verify that once I've walked him around a bit."

"Why does that help? Walking?"

JJ relaxed a little, talking about dogs in general as opposed to problem dogs in particular. "For one thing, it tires them at least a little. But more important, if you can get the dog to follow you, to believe that it *should* follow you, then it will accept you as the alpha. The leader. From that point on, though, it's like—well, if you'll pardon the inappropriate analogy, it's like riding the tiger. Once you get on you can't get off. If I do something that makes this bulldog think it sees a chink in my leadership, it will challenge me openly. Putting it onto its side, into a submissive position, was the start. Walking it now, making it follow me, is cementing the deal."

"For now."

"Yeah." He laughed, but it sounded unhappy. "For now."

We'd made an entire circumference of the lot, and the bulldog's owner was looking toward us, no doubt expecting JJ to return her dog. But he kept going.

"When will you give it back?" I asked.

Silence for about ten human steps, several more of the dog's waddles. "If I had my way? I wouldn't. That woman's personality makes this a dangerous dog, and he'll probably be the one that suffers. She isn't prepared to manage a powerful dog with a huge sense of self-importance. A warrior. She doesn't know how to be the alpha with a dog like this. Maybe not with any dog, but it would be less dangerous with a Chihuahua or a Pekinese."

"So . . . what are you gonna do?"

He sighed. "I'll have to give him back to her. I just wish I didn't. But I want to tire him out a little first. Though tiring this dog would take more than a couple of spins around the parking lot."

People were starting to leave the roped-off area, most heading for their cars. Only a few went into the store.

"Looks like your father has decided to call it quits. I expect he won't host another of these sessions."

"Will you still take dogs outside if customers bring them in?"

"I'll have to ask your father what he wants to do."

The lady who'd brought the bulldog was alone now, except for Dad, who was starting to roll up the ropes. JJ stopped some distance away. The dog stopped immediately and sat down.

"That's good," JJ said. "I want to check the tag here, away from his owner. Once he's near her again, things could fall apart. Will you hold the leash?" He didn't wait for an answer but just bent over the dog and twisted the collar to bring the tag onto its back. "At least she was right about this. He was vaccinated this year."

He stood up and took a step back where he could look at the dog. It looked up at him, tongue out, eyes soulful. JJ's voice made me look at him. "Poor fellow." His eyes were filling up with tears. He bent over the dog and stroked his head, then massaged his ears and jowls. The dog seemed like all its worries were gone. He'd turned them all over to JJ. JJ reached for the leash. "Paul, would you ask the owner to go to her car? I'll walk the dog to it once she has the door open."

As soon as I got close, the lady said, "Is he all right? He isn't hurt, is he?"

"The dog?" I blinked. "No, he's fine. He's very happy at the moment. Um, JJ asked if you would meet him at your car. He'll bring the dog when you have the door open."

"Oh. I guess that's all right." She left, and I turned to look at JJ again. He was still showering affection on that now submissive, sweet-faced demon.

Beside me, Dad said, "Well, I'll be damned."

We both watched JJ and the dog. I said, "Will you stop the sessions?"

Dad took a few seconds. "I hate to. These people need so much help, and their dogs need them to get it. But I don't see that I have a choice. Can't afford a lawsuit, and what if this had been worse? Was the dog vaccinated?"

"Yeah. JJ checked the tag."

JJ stood up and hitched the leash tight enough to signal the dog to move. They walked together toward the lady's car, and from JJ's face I could tell every step hurt him. It seemed like it took a huge effort not to start jogging in the other direction, tank in tow.

I said, "What if you set up specific times for each dog? You know, 'By Appointment Only,' that kind of thing. Could you do it then?"

Dad turned to me. "Paul, that's genius. It might just work. I think I'll give it a rest next week, and I'll talk to JJ about that idea."

Ridiculously, I felt as happy as the bulldog. If only I could be as dangerous as he was when I was out of sorts, maybe I could get someone to take my worries away, too.

The rest of that day I spent trying to catalog my worries. What were they, exactly? They hadn't changed much, I decided. My mom was still mourning Chris and seemed to have forgotten he wasn't her only son. My dad wouldn't let me have even pocket money. Marty and Kevin were sure to get me into deep shit at some point. I hated the idea that I had to go back to school in the fall and toe somebody's idea of where the line should be. I hadn't had a date since my evening with the prostitute, if that even counted as a date.

Oh, and I was supposed to be a man. Was that all?

Just before five, I was headed to the stockroom for some-thing. Once inside I stood there, scratching my head like some old geezer, unable to remember what I was supposed to be doing. And I heard a voice. Quiet, unhappy, upset.

"I wanted so much to take him with me! It was awful. I just know something's going to happen, and he'll have to be killed. Why don't they make people prove they know what a dog needs before they're allowed to own them?"

It was JJ's voice, but I couldn't make out who he was talking to. I moved quietly to where I could see the back door, which stood open. I could see part of JJ from the side, his shoulder and his back. And then I heard another voice. Another male voice.

"I know, love. I know. But you can't take the whole world on yourself. You did a lot for that dog today. And maybe the owner will get the message and change her ways, or give the dog to someone who can handle it. You do so much. But, sweetie, you can't do it all."

*Love? Sweetie?*

An arm wound its way around JJ's neck, and then he and the invisible man were hugging. The other guy leaned in, and then I could see the side of his face. I didn't know the guy, but he looked a little older than JJ. Taller, so he kind of bent over and wrapped JJ's body with his.

A brother? A good friend? I didn't want to focus on the obvi-ous. But then they pulled a little apart, just enough for them to kiss. I watched, horrified, as the other guy put his mouth right over JJ's and stayed there. And stayed there. This was no light peck. This was a *kiss*.

I hightailed it out of the stockroom to where I didn't have to see that. Where I didn't have to decide what to do about it. I just knew it was wrong. It *had* to be wrong.

All the way home on my bike in the afternoon, barely ahead of the raindrops that had been threatening since the morning, I grew more and more determined about what I had to do to shake that kiss. To get it out of my mind's eye. And what I had to do was be with a girl. It was the only way to exorcise this creepy feeling, and anyway I had some recreation coming to me. I wanted to see *The Day of the Jackal,* and I was going to take a girl. I'd take Laura if she'd go with me; I hadn't asked her out since Mom had made me cancel last November, but she'd been on my mind. Especially lately, when the only girl I saw regularly was Alice. But first I had to get some money.

My plan was to ask Dad over dinner, in front of Mom, after finding a way to remind him about my genius idea this morning. And I didn't have to wait long. Dad launched into the story of the battling canines, playing up his part in it for Mom— though to be fair, he did jump right in there.

Mom had the grace to ask, "Paul, you weren't anywhere near that scene, were you?"

"Well, yeah, I was. JJ needed my help. It took three of us…"

Dad interrupted. "It did, indeed! It took every ounce of my strength to hold that bulldog on the ground, I tell you."

So I let him have the floor, puffing himself up. And again Mom asked the right question. "You're not doing any more of these, are you?"

"I talked with JJ about a different arrangement," Dad said, like it had been his idea. He was going to go on, but I interrupted this time.

"I suggested doing it by appointment, so only one dog would be there at a time."

They both looked at me, Mom horrified that there might be more sessions, Dad like I'd stolen his thunder. I shoved a fork-ful of broccoli into my mouth, telling myself to wait this out in silence. And finally Dad was talked out. Evidently he and JJ had decided to give things a bit of a rest, and then Dad would put signs up in the store. Customers could call ahead for a specific appointment time on any day when JJ was working—not just Saturday—and they would work outside. Barring rain.

Every time JJ's name was mentioned, an image of that guy kissing him nearly made me lose my dinner. It didn't help that Dad's worship of the guy didn't seem to have lessened any.

When the tale of the day's doings seemed ground to a halt, I let just a smidge of silence go by. Then, "I was thinking of going to see *The Day of the Jackal.* It's got really good reviews, and it's rated PG."

Mom looked interested, and she was about to say something when Dad chimed in. "Where will you get the money?"

"Well, you know, I was kind of thinking it wouldn't be too much to ask. I'd like to ask Laura Holmes to go with me."

Dad wouldn't even look at me. "You know how that stands, Paul."

"Andy"—Mom spoke up like I'd been hoping she would if it came to this—"don't you think the boy's earned a little R&R? He finished the school year with decent grades, and he's been very responsible—"

"Irene, I don't need you going soft on me. We set the rules after that prank"—he looked at me here and scowled—"and I don't see any reason to change them now."

Fury made it real hard to keep my voice even. "So when will they change? What do I have to do to be treated like a human being again instead of a dog?"

*Whoa. Where did that come from?*

"Young man, don't you raise your voice to me. And you know full well why things are the way they are right now. It wasn't my choice to get you into so much trouble. You did that all on your own."

"But that was weeks ago! And I've done everything you wanted."

Dad picked up a chicken bone and stared at it. "And you'll go on doing so. I'll let you know when it's time for you to have some running room. For now, you're still in the doghouse, since that's how you want to think of it."

I stood and pushed my chair back hard, threw my napkin down on the table, and muttered, "May I be excused." Not a question.

Dad said, "You may not."

I ignored him and stomped out of the room with him calling my name behind me. I could hear Mom's voice, though not the words, and I left it to her to calm him down. *Where the fuck is*

*Chris when I need him? Young man, Dad called me? Man? Like hell. Not in his eyes.*

Sunday morning, after Mom left for church, Dad acted like there was nothing wrong between us. Maybe he couldn't really tell, or didn't care, that my opinion of him was particularly shitty; maybe he didn't take enough notice of me to know. I was glad to leave him behind, to enjoy his day off, when I rode to the store.

The weather was better than yesterday, at least a little sun. I'd had lunch at home since we don't open until one o'clock on Sundays, and I took a break around three-thirty after everyone else had been outside. I hadn't been out there more than a couple of minutes when I saw Marty strolling toward me. No Kevin in tow; Marty must have come by out of boredom.

He sat down without a greeting and lit a cigarette, then lit another and handed it to me. We sat there a minute in relatively companionable silence, and then he said, "Heard about the fracas here yesterday."

"Oh?" *God, but this cig tastes great.* Fracas. I was almost hoping it would be bad enough to shut Dad down. Or make him sell out to that chain after all.

"Mrs. Denneghy lives next door to us. My mom saw the dog's leg, all swaddled in bandages, and asked her about it." I just nodded. "Gonna call it quits with JJ's little therapy sessions?"

I chuckled. Therapy sessions; I liked that. "For now. Then it'll be by appointment only."

"Mrs. Denneghy was pretty upset. Wonder if your dad'll get sued."

"I don't give a fuck." I blew smoke into the air over Marty's head.

Marty sat up a little. "Trouble in paradise?"

"Nothing but trouble, and no paradise in sight. He still won't give me any of the money I've been earning, and I want to take a date to see a movie."

"Hoping to show off your newly acquired education?" He grinned salaciously.

What I really wanted to do was dispel the image of JJ's kiss, but I didn't want Marty to know that. Not only did I not want him to think I couldn't get that sight out of my mind, but on some weird level I also didn't want Marty to possess that information about JJ. I was keeping his secret, in a way, not that it was much of a secret. I shrugged.

Marty leaned back a little, his cigarette hand resting on the tabletop. "What if I lend you some money?"

My eyes jerked toward his. "Would you do that?"

He knocked some ash from his cig. "I'm not a charitable organization. May be a tiny bit of interest involved."

"I always knew you'd be a loan shark when you grew up. Starting early?"

"Early?"

"I said, when you grew up."

"Better be nice to me, kid. Do you want some moola or not?"

"So if I borrow, say, twenty-five bucks and can't pay you back until September, how much would that turn into?"

"You'd owe me thirty."

"Usury!"

"Want it or not?"

Oh, I wanted it. I wanted more than that, but at Marty's rates I couldn't afford more. "I guess so. But only if I get until the end of October. I don't really know how long this thing with Dad will go on."

He shrugged and we had a deal. I don't know where he got his money, but he always seemed to have some. He pulled a ten and three fives from his wallet and flipped them onto the table.

"Thanks."

Marty finished his cig, ground it under his foot, and we both got up. I decided to walk him around the front to make sure he left without getting into any trouble, or getting me into any trouble. Before we rounded the corner to the front, I could hear the excited yaps of somebody's small dog, almost certainly there for an unscheduled therapy session. I positioned myself between Marty and whoever would be out there. Like JJ.

I was right. The "by appointment only" hadn't started yet,

and Dad wasn't there to turn people away in the meantime; I couldn't see JJ doing that. And here some lady with an over-excited dachshund was trying to talk to JJ while the dog went round and round in circles, sometimes around the lady, sometimes just in place. JJ was listening intently to the woman, though I couldn't imagine why; I knew what he was going to do, almost no matter what she said. Marty came to a halt.

"What?" I asked him. He jerked his chin toward the scene. "Yeah? So? He does this all the time. C'mon."

He ignored me and stood there watching. I wasn't about to leave him to his own devious devices, so even though I was probably gonna be late back from my break, I stayed where I was. And anyway, Dad wasn't there to check up on me. We stood there and watched JJ go through his usual motions, my homeless buddy Jack watching the show from the opposite front corner, until JJ had got the dog under control. Then JJ headed out into the lot, dog and lady walking sedately beside him.

"See you," Marty threw at me as he started to walk away.

"Marty!" He turned. "Listen, don't you do anything. Leave them alone."

He made his face go all sad and disappointed. "Paul, my boy, what do you take me for? I wouldn't do anything that hurts your dad's business. Otherwise you'll never be able to pay me back!" He cackled and headed toward his car, and I watched him until he'd driven all the way out of the lot.

As I turned to go back into the store, my gaze fell on Jack, grinning at me. He was missing quite a few teeth, though his long stringy hair was still pretty dark so it probably wasn't that he was old. What with the dirt and the crappy clothes, it was hard to tell his age. He grinned, mouth hanging open, nodding at me. Maybe telling Marty to behave had given me a little confidence or something, and I decided to tell Jack to get lost. But when I got close to him, he spoke first.

"Takes all their burdens. Calms those dogs right down. A little Jesus, that's what he is. Just lifts all their problems right off of them." His stringy hair bobbed as he nodded wildly at me, a huge grin on his face. "Not like Bible Jesus, though. People can turn all their decisions over to that one. And they say, 'Thank you, Jesus!'" He pointed out in JJ's general direction and then right at me. "But here? Little Jesus puts the burdens smack-dab onto the people!" As he raised his filthy hands into the air he shouted, "Hallelujah, praise the Lord!" And then he cackled, kind of like Marty, but really insane.

*Yeah, Jack, you praise anybody you want. I've had my fill of Jesus, both Church Jesus and Dog Jesus.* Instead of sending the bum packing like I'd intended, I turned and opened the door back into the air conditioning and the smells of the store. *"Little Jesus." And Jack can't even know what "JJ" stands for.*

I spent the rest of that afternoon working out how I was gonna convince my mom to let me borrow her car without Dad knowing about it. In the end the only thing I worked out for sure was that he'd have to be nowhere around when I asked her.

My chance came that same night after dinner when Dad went into his den and closed the door. I offered to help Mom clean up, and she seemed a little surprised but not suspicious. Just before she attached the dishwasher to the faucet I made my move.

"Mom, I really appreciate how you stood up for me last night. I mean, I know what Dad's point is, but it seems like he's carrying it awfully far."

Mom was quiet for a few seconds before she replied. "Well, that was a pretty dreadful thing you did."

"I know. And I'm real sorry."

"Say 'really,' Paul. Use an adverb there."

"Really sorry. And I wouldn't do it again. But the point's been made. I'm not asking for a lot, here, just a single night out."

"I know, dear, but you heard your father."

"Well, I do happen to have just about enough money to see a movie with someone. A girl, I mean. There's this really sweet girl, very pretty, that had agreed—"

"Who, Paul. People shouldn't be referred to as 'that.'"

I took a breath. "Who had agreed to go out with me last fall, but I had to cancel." I decided against reminding Mom of all the details; they involved Chris, and they involved an unpleasant scene between me and Mom. I just wanted to make it clear I was trying to right a wrong, sort of. "But I'd need a car."

I waited. Finally Mom said, "That's a problem, Paul."

"Could I borrow yours?"

She waited until the attachment had the faucet solidly in its grip, and until she'd loaded soap into the dishwasher, before she answered. "I think you know the answer to that."

No good would come of pressing at this point. My fallback plan was to ask Marty if I could borrow his, and if I made Mom mad or suspicious it would be impossible for me to get out of the house at all. I mumbled, "Thanks anyway," and headed upstairs.

Monday, my day off, with Dad away at the store and Mom busy sewing doggie backpacks, I shut myself in Dad's den and phoned Marty in the morning, before he'd be likely to have left on one of his mysterious outings. He answered, as luck would have it.

"Landon? Why aren't you busy stocking cat food or counting pretty rocks for aquariums or something?"

"Day off. Listen, I'm in a bit of a bind on this date thing. It's what I borrowed the money for."

"Yeah? So?"

"I know better than to ask my dad for his car, but since my mom stood up for me when I asked for money I was hoping I could get hers. I can't."

"Well, well."

"So, I was kinda hoping I might borrow yours."

Silence. Then, "Interesting situation, Landon. You know what that car means to me." His voice was silky, and I knew he had something up his sleeve, so I just waited, wishing I had another friend who had a car to call his own. Marty made a sucking kind of noise and then said, "Here's the proposition. You can keep the money until December for the same fee *and* borrow the car for this one date, if you promise you'll do the deed."

"The deed." I knew what he meant, but I needed to stall for time.

"The deed, Landon. We know you're capable of it, remember?"

"Marty, the girl I wanna ask out is no prostitute. She's probably still a virgin."

"So much the better! If you could nab yourself one of them it'd do your rep a world of good."

"What rep?"

"C'mon, Paul. We both know that falling out of the social scene the way you have is a sure way to make people start wondering about you."

"WHAT?" *Calm down; he's just trying to rile me.* "It's not like I have any control over this, y'know."

"Oh, but you do. You have some control right now. You have money, and I'm offering you wheels. You just gotta pop the lady's cherry."

My mind raced. *I could lie. I could take Laura out and just tell Marty I'd done it. It would be easy enough to plant a used condom on the floor of his car.* But another voice chimed in. *Laura's a sweet girl. Do you think Marty's gonna keep this a secret?*

Was there somebody else I could ask out? Would it be worth the risk? I might not get another chance for a while; I was going to have to lie as it was, to fool my parents into thinking I was someplace they wouldn't mind.

No; I wanted to see Laura. And I did *not* want to "pop her cherry" and report to Marty about it; I liked her way too much for that.

"Marty, just lend me the car, will you? There must be some other way you'd like to torture me. I know—what if I pay you thirty-*five* dollars in December?"

"Nope. You got my terms. Nonnegotiable."

"That sucks, Kaufman. I'm not gonna do it." I wanted to tell him what I thought of him that he would even ask, but it was everything I could do just to say no to him.

"If you think that sucks, wait till you hear what everyone's gonna be saying about you."

"What are you talking about?"

"Well, what would you make of a guy who refused to have sex with a girl? Maybe you'd call him Moll."

My knuckles hurt from clenching the handset. I had to keep my voice low, but I said, "Fuck off. D'you hear me? Just fuck off!" I slammed the phone down.

It was several minutes before I felt like I could stop shaking and leave the den. Even then, I didn't want my mom to see me. It'd be just like her to notice me only when I didn't want her to. I avoided her work area and went to find my bike. Riding hard was the only way I could think of to recover.

Guess where I rode. I leaned my bike against that tree, the one Marty and I had tied Anthony to just a couple of years ago. I sat on the ground, leaning against the rough bark, head back and gazing up through the leaves. What if I had been Anthony that day? What would it feel like to have the Martys of the world believe I was gay, or even just treat me like they did? What if people thought I wasn't really a man?

*Hell, my dad already thinks I'm not. He barely treats me like a boy, let alone like the man he's told me I have to be.*

My eyes closed slowly, and what flashed across the insides of my lids was that kiss. That goddamned kiss that I just couldn't seem to forget about. I pushed it aside, and what replaced it was JJ's eyes filling with tears as he talked to me about having to turn the bulldog back over to the lady who owned him. That bulldog was a man, no doubt about that; he was all male.

*But he'd submitted to JJ.*

What the hell is a man, anyway? Is someone who's been in the army a man? I was pretty sure my dad thought he knew what a man was, but somehow it seemed likely that he and I would have different definitions. I toyed with that idea: *Dad, take this piece of paper and write down on it what the word "man" means to you. I'll do the same, and then we'll compare.*

But what would I put down? Strong. Brave. Stoic. A fighter, a winner. Where did that leave me? Where did it leave my dad?

He was stoic, all right. With stubborn attached to it. Did you have to be stubborn to be a man? Some women were stubborn. For that matter, some women were strong and brave.

Out of nowhere my mind went to that medieval French castle I was supposed to be helping to defend. I'd imagined myself there with my wife and family, and one of my sons saved my life up on the parapet. But then he got killed. Would that have made him less than a man, because he didn't win? And if my son had been JJ, would he still have been able to save my life? Somehow I knew he would. So was JJ a man?

*Am I?*

I'd stood up to Marty today. That took courage. Did that make me a man? And would Marty do things that made it seem like I wasn't? Things that made me look like a queer? Like Anthony? Like JJ?

Even if JJ, as my son in the castle, had been brave and strong, I expected that anyone I knew today wouldn't think he was much of a man if they knew the truth about him. Not even all those people who'd been singing his praises for getting their dogs to behave.

*My dad doesn't know the truth. Does he think JJ is a man?*

This was getting me nowhere, going round and round in circles just like some yappy little dog. I rubbed my face. When I opened my eyes again, I wasn't alone.

Remember that Border collie that had read me the riot act in the back of the farmer's pickup? Well, I was pretty sure that same dog was standing right in front of me, staring at me yet again.

He sat, his pink tongue dangling and dripping, his tail slowly sweeping the ground behind him. With his eyes he said, "So you think you're a man, now?"

"I don't know," I told him. "I don't know what that means."

"Was Chris a man?"

Now, there was something to ponder. Was he? He'd been strong and brave, and not stubborn. He'd killed other men, he'd saved other men's lives.

*He kissed other men. And he'd cried and cried.*

I closed my eyes. But then the dog said, "What makes a man not a man?"

Eyes open, I said, "Kissing another man."

"Why?"

"*Why?*"

"Yeah. Is there something unkissable about a man?"

I smirked at the black and white furry face. "No, stupid. Women kiss men."

"Was Chris a man?"

That again. I slammed a fist onto my leg. "I don't know! How should I know?"

"You knew him better than you know anyone else. What's so hard about this question?"

Through gritted teeth I told the dog, "If my father knew the whole truth, *he* wouldn't think Chris was a man!"

"We're not talking about your father." I picked up a pebble and threw it at the dog. It bounced off his shoulder. "Seems to me," the dog said, disdain in his voice, "that a man would have a better response than throwing things." And he got up and trotted away from me, up the road in the direction the pickup had come from that day that now seemed so long ago. And yet seemed like last week.

*He'd cried. Chris had cried big-time, when he'd told me he wasn't really a man.*

Suddenly I remembered another time Chris had cried. It was a distant memory, something I'd just about forgotten. Probably deliberately. I'd been, maybe, eight? Seven? I can't remember now what it was Chris had done, but whatever it was it had made Dad practically insane. And, as far as I know, that was the first and only time Dad used a belt on Chris. He'd used it on me once by then, and I'd yelled and screamed, so that's what I expected when Dad took Chris to the basement. I listened real hard. But all I heard was the belt landing.

Afterward, Chris holed up in his room. For days. Two or three, at least. He wouldn't come out, he wouldn't eat. He stayed in there and cried. I don't even think he came out to take a leak. If anyone but Mom tried to go in, he screamed and threw things at them. Finally she coaxed him out one day when Dad was at the store.

Whenever Dad was home, for maybe a couple of weeks afterward, Chris wouldn't come out of his room. It felt to me like there was this storm front always hovering, the kind that could break out any second into a tornado. And one night it did.

From where I was hunched into a tight ball on the upper landing, holding for dear life on to the balusters in front of me, I was torn between wanting to hear what Mom and Dad were yelling at each other and not wanting to know what it meant. Or maybe it was the other way around. But whichever, what I heard was that Mom was going to leave Dad and take Chris with her if he ever did anything like that again. To Chris. No one mentioned me.

How could I have forgotten that?

# Chapter 11

Evidently Dad and JJ had spent part of Monday making a few signs, which were hanging in various parts of the store when I got there on Tuesday—one at each register, one on the wall beside the office, and a few scattered in the dog supply section. It said that instead of the free-for-all clinic (not how the signs phrased it) on Saturdays, dog owners who would like to request JJ's services should call the office and set up a private appointment for any day except Sunday or Wednesday. Wednesday was going to be JJ's day off, I guessed, and maybe since Dad wasn't here on Sunday, he didn't want to risk something happening. I couldn't wait for the first time someone came in with a dog on Sunday and JJ had to turn them away; I wondered if he'd have the balls. He was Lord of the Dogs, maybe, but would he send the people packing, especially if they brought their delinquent dogs with them?

It didn't take long for me to find out what would happen if someone came in without an appointment on a day Dad *was* in the store. Before lunch that same day, there was this fortyish guy in ratty jeans and a sleeveless once-white undershirt, tattoos on both arms, dirty and thinning hair pulled into a messy ponytail, stubble on his jaw, who came in practically dragging this German shepherd by a chain attached to a body harness, a muzzle around its snout. They made their way past the door to the office. I was bagging for Dave at register two, and I saw Dad look up as the show passed his office. The dog was hunkered down, looking ready to snap at imaginary threats the whole time the guy was pulling him along.

Dad got up and stood in the office doorway, watching as the guy headed toward dog supplies. I knew JJ was cleaning tank filters at the moment and wondered if Dad would go and get him. By the time the guy stopped all I could see from where I stood was his head, but I could hear the dog's nails clicking; it must have been pacing over there.

I finished up with the customer I was bagging for and said to Dave, "I'm going over there. It might get ugly." I was kind of hoping it would.

"What d'you think you're gonna be able to do?"

I ignored Dave's question and looked toward Dad, who was now on his way across the floor. "Get JJ," was all he said to me.

He was at the tanks, as I'd expected. "JJ, there's a guy with a muzzled shepherd in dog supplies. The guy looks mean, and the dog looks meaner. Dad wanted me to get you. I'll finish this filter for you."

Wiping his hands on a towel, JJ asked, "Did it look like trouble?"

"Couldn't really tell. Maybe he just needs a new muzzle or something."

JJ left me there, finishing his job and considering the possibilities of what might happen. The guy himself hadn't looked like the type who wanted to learn any new tricks. As quickly as possible I finished cleaning the filter and replaced it in the tank. Then I headed toward dog supplies, listening as I went. The guy was talking.

"And he keeps chewin' through these leather things. I want a metal one, and I brung him in here to prove to you that I need it." I was close enough now to see he was talking to Dad. JJ stood a little to one side, watching the dog pace on its lead. Suddenly the guy yanked on the leash, which was really a metal chain attached with a large hook to the body harness. "Sit still, damn it!" The dog snapped its jaw as much as it could, shook its head, and stopped moving. But only momentarily.

Dad said, "We can certainly sell you another muzzle, but I don't carry metal ones. And if he's chewing through the leather, then a metal one would damage his teeth."

There was a quiet moment where everyone seemed to consider this, and I saw JJ take a breath. "How much time does he spend with the muzzle on?"

The guy looked at JJ like he hadn't known he was there and scowled. For sure, he wasn't there for a session with the behaviorist. Then he shrugged. "Most of the time. I keep him at my shop. Welding. But during the day I don't want him chewing on my customers, or me." He looked back at Dad as though he couldn't quite bring himself to have a conversation with someone as insubstantial looking as JJ. "I take it off him at night and when he gets fed. He guards the lot."

Dad was nodding like he understood, but JJ was far from through. He said, "So he never leaves the shop yard? How does he get exercise?"

The guy turned to JJ again, and the look on his face was like he couldn't quite believe this child was still pestering him. "I have him on a run. He can go back and forth as much as he likes."

"Then no wonder he's pacing in here." And JJ was right; the dog was at it again.

The guy put his free hand on his hip and glared. "What d'you know about it?"

I thought JJ looked a little scared, but he stood his ground. "If the only exercise this dog gets is going back and forth on a run, that's not anywhere near what he needs. But it's all he knows. So since he needs more, he'll do it whenever he has a chance."

The guy snorted and looked at Dad. "What am I supposed to do, take him to a doggie park?" He laughed and threw his head back. "He'd eat every other mutt in the place!"

JJ went on like he hadn't been interrupted. "He should be walked. Twice a day would be best, for at least forty-five minutes each time. Once he's calmer, he wouldn't need the muzzle. And then, yes, eventually you could take him to a dog park." Any second now I expected JJ to tell the guy how to pronounce Wunderkind correctly.

Dad was getting nervous, but I could tell he didn't want to let on. He was working hard at looking casual. The guy turned his whole body toward JJ this time and said, "What are you, some kind of dog expert?"

"Yes." Simple. True. Confident. Unbelievable.

"So, you wanna take him for a walk?" He held the leash out toward JJ, but JJ turned toward our supply display, picked out a metal prong collar and two thick leather leads, and he attached the collar to one lead. The guy laughed again. "You're gonna be lunch, kid. That muzzle he has on is nearly chewed through."

JJ was pretty much ignoring the guy now. He stood directly in the path of the dog, who was headed his way in his pacing routine. JJ didn't move, and he didn't look at the dog. The dog stopped and growled. JJ didn't budge. The dog barked and growled again. JJ stood. I was thinking that it took a man to do that. Or someone very, very stupid. Maybe the guy agreed, 'cause he stopped making comments.

The dog turned and headed back the way he had come. The guy got this "told you so" look on his face. JJ moved forward so the dog would have to stop sooner on his next turn.

The dog was really unhappy about having his pacing space reduced again. Lots more growling, and barking, head lowered, shoulders hunched, ready to spring. But JJ stood there, not even looking at the dog. I glanced at the guy; he looked worried. Then at my dad; so did he. Then at JJ.

Calm, but present. Present in a big way. It's hard to describe how he looked. Kind of like nothing could hurt him. Very quietly he said, "Don't pull back on him unless he knocks me down." He turned his back on the dog.

*Unless he knocks you down?*

Jesus Christ! I mean, José Jesus! The kid was brave, I'll give him that. He stood there, the dog ready to pounce, for several seconds. And then the dog relaxed a little. He moved toward JJ, definitely on guard but not threatening. He sniffed everywhere he could reach, and then he turned and paced back the other way again. JJ turned and moved forward again, so now the dog had very little pacing room. The shepherd made one more pace, which was really more of a circle by this time, and then sat down with his back to his owner and his side to JJ, maybe three feet away.

"Well, I'll be," the guy said.

JJ slapped his thigh and, finally, looked at the dog, who got up and went to him, and then when JJ pressed down with stiff fingertips on the dog's rump, he sat again. Then JJ slipped the prong collar onto the dog's neck and positioned it where I knew he would, high behind the ears, one leather leash attached to it. Now, at last, he took the chain away from the owner. He took it off the harness and attached the second leather leash instead, grabbed both in one hand, and handed the chain to the owner.

"Paul?" JJ said without looking at me. I didn't even think he knew I was there. "Would you hold the harness leash as backup?" He held it in my direction.

*ME?* I just looked at him.

The guy couldn't take it. "Look, I'll do it. I know how to handle him."

JJ's arm retracted so the guy couldn't take the lead. He said, "Please don't be offended. It's just that you and the dog have a dynamic setup that's based on force and competition, and I'd like to avoid those factors if I can. Paul?"

Dad was looking at me hard. I couldn't tell what he wanted me to do. I mean, here was this customer who didn't really want—or, certainly, hadn't asked for—JJ's demonstration of what a good dog this could be. But Dad didn't say anything to JJ, or even look at him. In the end I decided to do the thing that made me look like I wasn't a coward. I swallowed and stepped forward, taking the leash like it was a snake.

"You're just backup, Paul. You stay on that side of him, and I'll stay on this one. Don't pull on the leash or hold it tight unless he attacks. It would be best if the dog isn't even aware of it. Now, I'm going to walk him to the side of the store where I don't see anyone at the moment, and then we're going out the front door and around the lot outside. Ready?"

If I hadn't been so scared, I'd love to have seen the look on the owner's face. Maybe even Dad's face would have a little less worship and a little more anxiety than it usually did around JJ.

JJ positioned himself beside the dog, looked forward, took one step, and tugged gently on the leash attached to the prong collar. The dog got up and followed him. What I was thinking was that I'd turned my back on the church just a few months too soon. At that moment, I wanted to pray and believe someone would help me. And as if I really had asked for help, as soon as we were far enough away from the owner, JJ started to talk.

"I'm not going to tell you that this dog isn't dangerous, Paul." *No shit.* "But he'll be far less dangerous away from his owner, and even less if both of us are calm. It could help if you think of yourself as another member of the pack, and pretend you've accepted me as the leader. That will make it easier for the dog to do that. We'll all be better off in that case. So just be calm and stay beside the dog. I'm going to move a little ahead of him so he's actually following me."

He didn't look at me or even seem to wonder if I was listening, or if I would obey. The dog turned his head and tried to stall a few times, and JJ had to keep yanking sharply on the leash and doing that quick "Hey" of his. But he also kept talking to me.

"Ordinarily I would encourage you to take a position equivalent with mine, because the dog needs to see humans as leaders, but this dog is pretty far gone. And right now I just want to see how bad he is."

Finally I felt calm enough to speak. "Why? D'you think that guy in there is open to learning anything new about how to treat his dog?"

"Can I trust you to keep a confidence?"

So many things ran through my mind at this point. Mentally I tallied up all the secrets I was already keeping, including one or two for JJ. Finally, "Yes." *What's one more?*

He didn't say anything right away. We headed toward the

door that opened into the parking lot, and when we got to it JJ stopped. There was no one outside.

I asked, "D'you want me to open the door?"

"No. Just be still and act like one of the pack. I'm going to lead."

I would have shrugged, but my arms were too tense from nervousness. The dog had stopped when JJ did, and JJ pressed his rump to get him to sit. Then JJ pushed the door open and the dog stood.

"Hey." JJ let the door shut and pressed the dog's rump again. We did this two or three times until the dog didn't respond to the open door. JJ let a little slack into the leash, stepped outside holding the door with one hand, and then he tugged gently on the leash. The dog and I followed him outside.

JJ said, "I'm considering reporting the owner. If I do that, I want to be able to provide some information about the dog."

"Reporting him?"

"He's abusing the dog. I want to know if the shepherd can be recovered or if he's beyond reach."

So we walked around the perimeter of the lot two, three times? The dog was tense for the first circuit, and when someone drove in and got out of their car with a dog JJ had to yank the leash hard to get the shepherd to look the other way, but the dog did it. JJ sat him down again and we waited until the other dog was inside before we went on with our walk. As we started moving again, I had to pry my fingers open, I'd held on to the leash so hard. Muzzle or no muzzle, this dog was Trouble.

Trouble might be his name. I said, "You didn't ask the guy what the dog's name was."

"I don't really care. And neither does the dog."

"That makes no sense. You can't tell me dogs don't know their names."

"They don't know that they *are* names. To the dog, his name is just a noise that always sounds the same, and the dog knows it's associated with him, but that's it."

"Wouldn't it help you control him, though?"

"No. Control comes through leadership."

"And that guy in there with the tattoos? He doesn't supply it?"

"That guy in there is most likely seen by the dog as competition at best, and possibly a tormentor. He couldn't lead the way out of his own backyard, and he's given the dog no reason to follow him."

*No reason to follow him. So why is the dog following JJ?* "What are you giving him?"

"Well, for one thing I've given him a natural walking pattern, treating him like a dog rather than a robot or a block of concrete. But first I let him know who was boss. I ignored his threats without growling back, like that guy does. I mean, he growls back. In a funny way, the dog and the owner are a lot alike. They both put on this tough-guy posture, they talk rough, they act mean. I can only guess what the guy needs, but this fellow here just wanted someone to take control in a way that lets him be a dog. That's what I gave him."

"Can you give the guy anything?"

JJ chuckled. "I gave him a shock. I'll bet he didn't expect a puny little kid like me to stand up to his killer shepherd. I gave him an example of how the dog should be treated, of how to get the dog to take me seriously. More seriously than he takes the guy. Men like him usually think the tougher their dog is, the tougher the man is. I've shown him his dog can be just a dog, which that guy might see as making him seem less tough as a result. And so I've probably also given the man a reason to hate me."

"As if he needed another one."

"What?"

*Shit. Did I say that out loud? And can I recover from this?* What I'd been thinking was that the last thing a guy like that would tolerate would be to get shown up by a gay kid. A gay man. A gay anybody. "Nothing."

Maybe fifteen steps later JJ said, "Is there something you want to say to me?"

I cleared my throat. "Well...I mean, you know. What you said. You're not that big."

"You said '*another* reason.' I'd already pointed that one out."

He had me. He knew, I was sure, exactly what I'd been thinking. I took a deep breath. "Well, okay, if you insist. He probably thinks you're gay or something."

JJ's steps didn't waver, his hand didn't jerk or shake, his shoulders didn't hunch. He didn't miss a beat. "I am."

*Okay. There it is.* I took a deep breath. "So do you really want to report that guy?"

Calmly, JJ came to a stop, and the dog sat. JJ smiled down at him and stroked the top of his head, scratched his ears. Then he turned toward me. "What are you talking about?"

"It's illegal."

"What is?"

"Being gay."

I almost didn't hear it. He said, "You idiot." He bent over again and rubbed the dog's shoulders between the harness straps. "I'll tell you what, Paul. If you catch me in the act, then you can call the cops. And yeah, I suppose if I'm still in that position when they get there, I'll be arrested. You think that's going to happen?" He straightened up and looked right into my eyes.

*Well that's an image I don't need in my head, thank you very much.* My face twitched into a few different shapes and I dropped my eyes. "Probably not."

"Probably not. You bet your ass, probably not."

I shrugged. "I'm not trying to start a fight, here."

He laughed. "I think if you did, this dog would take your arm off, muzzle notwithstanding." Another pat to the dog's head and he turned and took a step, the dog right with him.

Neither of us spoke until we got to the door. JJ unhooked my leash from the harness and handed it to me. "I'm going around once more with him. You take that back inside and tell them I'll be in shortly." He didn't even look at me. Just like he treated the dogs.

The guy and Dad were watching from inside the door. I tried

to pass them without speaking, thinking I'd just put away the leash, but no.

"What's that kid doing to my dog?"

My jaw clenched. "You can see what he's doing. He's treating him like a dog instead of like somebody's bad temper." *Stupid. That was stupid. And why am I standing up for JJ, anyway?*

Dad tried placating the guy. "The dog seems to be enjoying the walk."

The guy's head snapped toward Dad. "He's had enough enjoyment. You don't have what I need, so we're outta here." He practically flung the door open and strode toward JJ, fists clenched. Dad followed, but I stayed where I was.

Dave, with no customers at the moment, stood next to me. He said, "You did say this might get ugly."

It was almost funny. There was JJ in the distance, his back to the store in ignorance that this tough, tattooed guy was striding angrily his way, Dad limping along behind and struggling to hurry. Just before the guy caught up to them, JJ and the dog turned a corner. JJ looked toward the guy, and even from this distance I could see the dog's hackles rise. His head went down, and when the guy reached for the leash the dog lunged. I dropped the leash and ran out the door and across the lot, watching as JJ tried to turn the dog away, but it was doing its damnedest to get at the guy's arm, despite the muzzle. The guy kicked the dog's belly and the dog backed off; probably it couldn't get ahold, anyway. JJ grabbed the back of the harness and struggled with the dog, trying to get it down on its side probably, but it was too powerful and too focused on the guy. All JJ could really do was get in between the dog and the man.

"Bastard!" I heard the guy shout. "You shithead!" He was flailing his arms around, and he nearly hit Dad as Dad got to him, just ahead of me. I don't think anyone knew what to say, but it didn't stop the guy yelling. He pointed an arm toward JJ, finger extended and stabbing with the words. "You asshole! You turned my dog against me!"

Suddenly I had something to say, between pants, anyway.

"You're the asshole! You turned him against you all by yourself."

Dad tried to calm things down. "Are you hurt? Do you need to see a doctor?"

The guy glared at me but spoke to Dad. "You've just bought yourself a dog, mister. I paid two hundred dollars for him, and that's what you owe me."

"Look, I'm sure the dog—"

JJ, gripping the harness, had to shout to be heard over the noises the dog was making. "You'll leave here right now, without the dog, and without any money, or I will report you for animal abuse. You'll be fined *and* you'll lose the dog."

The guy wheeled toward JJ, but the dog was going ballistic again so he backed off. With one more "Fucker!" he lurched in the direction of his truck. The dog grew calmer right away, and we all stood there and watched as the truck tires left black marks on the pavement. And we kept standing there, looking into the distance that the truck disappeared into, until JJ said, "I've got to walk him some more."

"And then what?" Dad said, obviously pissed off. "What do you plan to do with him?"

"I don't know yet." JJ turned his back on us and led the dog away.

*This would be the time to tell Dad the truth about JJ. To tell Dad that he's gay. Maybe I can't tell him about Chris, but I can tell him about JJ if I do it now. I may never get a better chance, and Dad's already pissed at him.*

But I didn't. Dad and I just looked at each other, then at the dog again. Finally I said, "Maybe he can be our mascot."

"He's a ferocious animal!"

"He's not, really. He was protecting JJ. And you know he had to have a grudge against that guy in particular. He didn't threaten you or me."

"We didn't get close enough! Paul, are you out of your mind?"

I shrugged. "It was just an idea. JJ will know better whether he can be recovered or not. Otherwise I guess he'll have to go to the pound, and they'll probably put him down."

Dad ran a hand through his hair. I could tell that was not an idea he liked. "All right, you and JJ talk it over and tell me what you think. Then we'll decide." He turned and limped back into the store, and I could tell his hip was hurting, probably from trying to get out here so fast. I almost felt sorry for him.

Great. Now I had to talk to JJ about this, and I didn't really know if he was mad at me. *Why did I open my big mouth?*

I decided to wait at least until boy and dog had had a few minutes alone to re-establish their relationship; JJ was the only hope of people not being devoured by the nameless terror. When they'd come full circle again, I fell into step with them.

JJ was not in his usual chipper mood. "What do you want?"

"As a matter of fact, I'm trying to help you. And the dog."

"Convince me."

*I guess I deserve that.* "Well, first of all, I think we need to give him a name. We can't just go on referring to him as the dog."

"If we give him a name it will be harder to let him go."

"Go where?"

JJ practically snorted. "Are *you* planning to take him home?"

"No, but—"

"Do you think I am?"

"I thought he could live here."

JJ stopped short this time, not so calm, but the dog sat anyway. "Here?"

"I'm not suggesting we tie him up the way that guy did, but if you worked with him couldn't you recover him enough for other people to walk him? There's somebody here every day. We could give him a doghouse out back and a spot someplace in the stockroom for when it was too cold or whatever."

"You're serious."

"Dad will take some convincing, but I mentioned it to him, and he knows we're talking about it. We'd just need to be really clear how it would work." JJ just blinked at me a couple of times. I said, "I was thinking Trouble."

"What?"

"For a name. Trouble."

JJ looked at the dog. "He's had enough of it, that's for sure." I'd been thinking it's what he was rather than what he'd had, but JJ wasn't wrong. "But it would be too bad if that stayed with him. I'm thinking Dante. He's been through hell, after all."

"Dante?"

"You know. Dante's *Inferno.*"

I nodded. "That's not too bad. So what would we need to do?"

"Well, first I'm walking him into the trees to see if he'll lift his leg." All three of us headed that way. "Then maybe we could take him into the stockroom and see if there's a good place to lay out a bed for him. Do you know of anyplace out back where he could be tied? We should probably set up a run for him when we can. It would be familiar to him, and he could still move around outside if he wanted to."

We stood there watching the dog relieve himself, chatting like the best of friends working out the details of some project we were actually excited about. The dog did a little of everything, then scraped up some dirt, and we walked around back and in through the stockroom door. The last thing he said to me before I followed the dog inside was, "You're going to have to learn to walk him, you know."

"Me? Why me?"

"Today, in fact. You need to be able to walk him tomorrow on my day off." He turned to look at me, a smile twisting up one side of his face. I just stared at him, mouth hanging open, and then he started to laugh. "Paul, I'm teasing you. I'll come over in the morning and walk him tomorrow. We'll do it together, and take turns. I think he'll tolerate it. You will need to be able to do it, though, maybe even tomorrow afternoon. With any luck, he'll be around here a lot longer than I will." So I'd sold JJ on the idea, at least.

In the stockroom, we tied Dante's leash to a set of metal shelves that were bolted into the concrete side of the building and sat him down. Then Dante lay down fully, and JJ stood for a few seconds looking at him, smiling, his eyes misting like they had for the bulldog.

He bent over the dog, stroking his head. "Good boy, Dante. Good dog." He stood up, wiped his eyes, and said, "Paul, it would be great if you got him some water. If you start giving him nourishment, he'll remember that."

By the time I got back with a new water bowl filled from the faucet in the corner of the stockroom, JJ had begun clearing a small area. "We'll need a bed for him in here. Is your dad ready to let us start using things from the store, do you think?"

Maybe it was just because I'd suggested this arrangement, but I was kind of getting into it. "If not, I'll pay for them. I'll talk to him." I had Marty's money if I needed it, and no sign of a date with Laura in my immediate future. So I just fetched whatever JJ and I decided Dante would need.

We worked together on Dante's spot while he watched. He'd drunk a little water and had lain back down, and there he was, paws crossed casually in front of him.

I said, "What if that guy comes back here to get him?"

"I suppose it's a possibility, but my guess is that if he came back, it would be to shoot him. Dante turned on him, don't forget."

"Shoot him?" I was about to ask why JJ thought the guy might even have a gun, but then I remembered Marty's.

JJ shrugged. "It's not out of the question. When someone's as insecure about his own masculinity as that guy is, it doesn't take much to push him over the edge. He's likely to strike out at anything that reminds him that he's still trying to prove he's a man. But he doesn't understand why he's insecure, so that makes him afraid. And unstable. So he lashes out. Especially since we kind of made a fool of him."

"You mean *you* did."

"Dante and I. And you, in case you've forgotten. You called him an asshole." JJ had that sideways grin again. "Couple a kids, getting his dog to act better than he could, nearly getting him bitten, and calling him names into the bargain? Yup, I'd say he's feeling pretty violent about now."

"Why does that make him insecure?" It was not a word I would have come up with in regards to that guy.

"Well, Paul, think about it. He has this dog that's so mean, the guy has to muzzle it and drag it around by a chain. He comes in here for even tougher equipment and this pip-squeak kid—me, in case there's any question—takes his dog and makes friends with it. It's like I've challenged the guy himself. Like I've sneered at him, 'You're not such a tough guy. You haven't even proved you're a man.' And I'm gay!" He laughed again like that was the best joke of all.

"Do you think he knew that?"

Another shrug. "Sometimes people look at me and guess. I think your friend did, my first day, when your dad sent me to find you."

"Yeah, he did." I was pulling a huge box full of cat litter bags out of Dante's spot, and JJ was pushing it. "Um, does my dad know?"

"Not unless you told him, or he guessed." He grunted and pushed harder. "I didn't say anything. I don't exactly walk up to people, shake their hand, and say, "Hi, I'm José Jesus O'Neil, and I'm gay.'"

I stopped pulling and looked at him, and he stopped pushing and looked at me. This was a whole new side of JJ. One I'd never seen. Plus, he was being so open about this thing that I'd always thought would be shameful. I was sure as hell ashamed of Chris for it, and Chris had acted like it was shameful, too. So how could JJ act so devil-may-care?

Almost wishing I could have asked Chris a few things, I challenged JJ instead. "But, don't you ever, like, think maybe you should be different?"

"Why? So people like that guy, and your friend, won't get their masculinity punctured when they see me having the nerve to be alive?"

"Well, I was thinking more like maybe your own life would be easier."

"Could you be gay, Paul?" I blinked and backed away a step. "I didn't think so. And guess what. I'm not going to pretend I can be straight, I'm not going to live a lie, just so you can feel more comfortable around me."

"I didn't say I was uncomfortable!"

His laugh was more like a bark this time. "You didn't have to say it. I've seen you back away. Are you saying you don't think I should be honest about who I am?"

"Maybe I'm saying that, if what you are is bad. If you were a murderer, would you be, like, all open and honest about that?"

"You're telling me you think what I am is as bad as being a murderer?"

"I didn't say that!" *How did I get on the defensive end of this conversation?*

"Look, maybe this is something you want—wishing there were no such thing as homosexuality. But being who I am is something I *need*. That's stronger than wanting. And it's more important than your comfort."

"So you'll make dogs feel comfortable but not people?" I felt like Jack's mouthpiece.

"Animals are at our mercy. It's our job to give them as much of what they need as we can. But people aren't pets. And as for making you comfortable? That's *your* job."

I was feeling a little threatened, like I had to stand up for my position in the world. "It's not just me, though, is it? It's not just what *I* want."

JJ's voice took on an edge. "Oh, are we going back to the illegal thing again?"

"No. What I was thinking is that it's ironical that your name is Jesus, since what you are is a sin. I was going to say that it's about what God wants. It says so in the Bible."

"First, you don't mean ironical, you mean ironic. And I don't happen to agree. And as for the Bible, are we talking about the God who made the earth in six days? If so, he made you, too. And he also made me. And he made me who I am. I guess I'd rather argue with the Bible than with God when there's a conflict. And by the way, there's a lot of stuff in that Bible of yours that *you* don't follow. How come you get to choose which things are sacred for you and which are not, and I don't?"

"What are you talking about?" My face must have been crimson; I was thinking of my few minutes with Lady Pink Vest. Plus I was irritated about being corrected; JJ wasn't my mother, after all.

JJ half smiled. "I can see you've got something in mind already. I don't pretend to know what it is, but I don't need to know. There are so many things I already know. Like I'll bet you didn't even know you weren't supposed to wear linen and wool together. Or plant two kinds of seeds in the same field. Do you have a sister?"

"What? No...."

"Too bad. Your father could sell her into slavery, as long as he took her far enough away, and maybe pay for part of your college education. Have you ever cursed your father? Because he would be expected to kill you for that." I just stared at him. "So, as I said, I'd rather argue with the Bible than with God. And if you think they're the same, then you'd better go and familiarize yourself with all the things in the book of Leviticus that will get you stoned to death by your neighbors."

If I'd been a little afraid of that tattooed guy's fury and curses earlier, that was superficial and quickly gone. This was different. JJ stood there, his face like stone, and maybe I wasn't actually afraid of him, but I felt bad in a way that I knew would stay with me. I couldn't decide if I was angry or ashamed. And I was having a hard time not thinking about Chris.

While I stood there like a dunce, JJ leaned against the box of litter again. Before he pushed, he said, "I am who I am, Paul. And so are you. And I don't think God wants us to lie about what he made us. Now, pull."

We got the box where we wanted it, and I tossed the dog bed I'd fetched into the cleared spot. JJ was watching me. Something in me wanted to shock him. It felt like he'd won something earlier, and I wanted some of that back. I said, "My brother was gay."

JJ blinked. *Ha! Surprise.*

"What brother? What do you mean, 'was'? You're not going to try and tell me he changed, are you?"

I took a breath. What an idiot I was; now I had to talk about Chris. My legs felt funny, and rather than have that show I sat down on what would be Dante's bed. I took another breath. "My dad doesn't know. Or my mom. I'm not sure I should be telling you. But since you're like him, maybe he wouldn't mind." I rubbed my face and then looked at JJ. I had his full attention.

"His name was Chris. He was in the army. He...he died last December. It was right after he'd been home on leave. The night before he went back to 'Nam, he told me. And he asked me not to tell our folks. *He* was ashamed." *Take that, JJ.* I didn't see any need to go into the relationship with Mason, or the crying, or the being afraid. This was more than enough.

But JJ didn't "take that." He sat on the concrete in front of me looking sad and said, "Oh, Paul, I'm so sorry. Were you close?"

All I could do was nod. I felt like crying, and I was *not* going to do that.

His voice was soft. "What a burden."

"Yeah." I pinched my nose to hide what I was feeling and stood up again. Sitting down was just going to encourage confidences, and I didn't want to exchange any more of those. In fact, I'd had enough of this entire conversation. "D'you want to come with me to talk to Dad about keeping Dante?" Maybe at least he could help with Dad. Like Chris.

He held out a hand to me to help him up. There was just a second or two of hesitation, and I reached for it. As he got to his feet it occurred to me that just as we hadn't known Dante's name when he got here, we never found out the owner's name, either. He would always be "the tattooed guy."

We managed to convince Dad that Dante would be okay there. We laid out a plan to get him walked and cared for, now and after JJ went away to school. Dad even mumbled something about needing to get more exercise himself, so it sounded like he might take some of the responsibility. For sure, he'd always wanted a dog. JJ pointed out that once we got Dante back to being a real dog again, if Dad felt he couldn't keep him here any longer he'd be the sort of dog someone would want to take, unlike now when he'd probably just be killed. In the end, JJ even worked things so Dad agreed that JJ could take Dante to a vet tomorrow, and Dad would pay for it.

But then we heard howling. Dad went with us back to the stockroom, and JJ tried to tell him he shouldn't go in first, but he didn't listen. Dante took one look at Dad and snarled. He was still tied to the shelves, but it was ugly, anyway.

"Mr. Landon, I think it might be best if you wait until I can introduce you in a way that won't upset him. Is that all right?"

Dad backed out of the room, his eyes on the dog, and said, "I guess so. This had better work out, and soon."

JJ and I went in, and he marched right over to the dog and clapped his hands sharply. "Hey!" he said and snapped his fingers toward the floor. Dante lay back down again. "Paul, come stand over him with me. He needs to see you as dominant, too."

*Well, he is still muzzled.* I went over as ordered, and the two of us stared down at Dante a minute.

"Now turn casually and walk away."

As I did, I asked him, "What kind of a dog do you have?" I was wondering if it had been a recovered dog, like this one.

"How do you know I have a dog?"

The answer to that would have given away that I'd eavesdropped on him and Dad that day, so I said, "How could you not?" I got to the door and turned to look at him.

"I do, as a matter of fact. He's a pit bull."

"Does he have a name?" I couldn't resist asking.

JJ chuckled. "Yes. Cain. He wasn't as far gone as Dante, but he had his problems. I think he's a great dog now. My mom loves him, too. She walks him a lot. She grew up with dogs, and what Cain didn't teach me, she did."

"Does she know?"

"Know what?"

"That you're gay?"

JJ took a deep breath. "Paul, I really hope you'll be able to stop focusing on that. It's just... well, I don't want to say it's not important, but it shouldn't keep coming up. You know?"

"Sorry." I wasn't sure exactly how I was supposed to just forget about it. I mean, it loomed huge between us. And between me and Chris. Between me and my folks.

"Yes, she knows. But I'm the youngest of four boys, and they've all gone off and gotten married and had kids, so she jokes that she doesn't need any more grandkids to spoil. And she likes that I'll be going to college. None of my brothers did."

"Are they cool with it? I'm asking only because of my brother."

"I guess mostly they don't know. It hasn't seemed important yet to tell them. My dad doesn't."

"So you do lie to some people." It was a challenge.

"No, if any of them asked me, I'd tell them. I told you."

Calm. He was so calm. It was like when he was dealing with unruly dogs. Should I, like, let him squeeze the small of my back to get me to sit at his feet or something? But I wasn't quite done. "I still don't understand why your mom is so okay with it."

"Well, Paul, first of all, you're assuming there's something wrong with being gay. Not everyone agrees with that. Me, for one. Plus, my mother believes everyone must be who they are. Maybe that's one reason she's so good with dogs; she accepts them for what they are and doesn't expect them to be something they're not. That works with people, too, y'know."

Half an hour before closing, JJ got Dad's permission for us to take Dante out for another few laps around the parking lot. JJ started things out, but he had me walk with him, ahead of Dante. At one point he told me he was gonna hand me the leash, reminding me how to hold it, and he passed it over. All three of us just kept going like nothing had happened.

After a couple of minutes JJ said, "At the next corner, come to a stop and see if Dante stops with you."

He did! The dog was right with me. He sat at my feet, and I felt this incredible high, like he had accepted me. Like he acknowledged my leadership.

Lying in bed that night, I couldn't sleep. Sometimes I'd feel overwhelmed by how fantastic it had felt to have Dante accept me, and sometimes it irritated the hell out of me that I hadn't been able to get JJ to admit he had a problem. Finally I decided my attempts at getting JJ to agree with me about the gay thing had been pretty wimpy, and I excused myself because I hadn't had any time to prepare. I'd been caught off-guard. JJ'd had lots of time to prepare; as long as he'd known he was gay, he must have been working out things to say to people like me. But that didn't make it right, and it was infuriating that he seemed to think it did.

I mean, my God, even Chris had thought it was wrong. Why else would he have apologized to me for it? "I'm so sorry," he'd said. "I didn't ask for this. I didn't want this. I can't help it." And who—oops, sorry, Mom—whom did I look up to more, Chris or JJ?

*Chris had been afraid. JJ isn't.*

*JJ didn't have to go to 'Nam, damn it!*

In fact, I'd bet that JJ wouldn't be allowed to go to 'Nam. All he'd have to do is show up at the draft board with his—what would the guy be called, JJ's boyfriend?—and he'd just waltz back out again. Chris had had more guts than that.

*Or maybe Chris just didn't have the guts to admit he was gay.*

*Christ! Will I ever stop going around in circles with this fucking thing?*

I pulled my pillow down around my ears to try to stop the voices in my head.

# Chapter 12

JJ showed up before me again the next day, despite the fact that it was his day off, to walk Dante with me. First JJ had me feed him, and then he put a new muzzle on him. He had me put the collar and leash on him, and he made sure I walked out the door ahead of the dog. We walked for about half an hour, around the lot first and then on the neighborhood streets behind the store.

We didn't talk much, except when JJ said Dante seemed to have been okay on his own overnight. For my part, I didn't want to start any conversations that might lead to the gay issue, because I wasn't ready to counter any of the things JJ had said or might say. I couldn't tell what was on JJ's mind. Maybe he needed some sign from me that we were gonna be friends, and if he didn't get that then he wasn't gonna push anything. Who knows.

Dante had a nasty moment when someone else out walking a dog got close, and another when Dante revealed a particular hatred of bicycles. JJ had to take him each time and get him back into control again, which didn't do much for my self-esteem.

Back at the lot, JJ took Dante's leash. "I'm going to walk him to my house, and then my mom and I will take him to our vet.

He's behaved himself very well, overall. D'you want to scratch his ears and massage his shoulders a little?"

I hadn't really touched him yet. But there didn't seem to be any reason not to. I reached down and dug my fingers into the folds of skin around his ears, and he looked up at me. If it hadn't been for the muzzle, I could have sworn he was smiling.

In the store I did a few fish tanks, and then I helped some lady with her kid decide which guinea pig to get and what supplies they would need. I never saw the point to guinea pigs, but the little girl was so thrilled she was squealing a lot like the pigs themselves. Should be a good match, I decided.

Around eleven JJ showed up again, with Dante. I wouldn't have known except that I was in the stockroom at the time, and they came in through the back door. Dante seemed exhausted. I asked, "How did it go?"

JJ sighed a little. "He doesn't like going to the vet. He proved that sufficiently today. I had to stay in the car with him while my mom waited inside until it was his turn. He was a holy terror in the waiting room with all those other dogs around, and I couldn't even just stay in the parking area with him, out of the car, because of course people kept bringing animals right past him and he went berserk every time. I'm a little concerned how he's going to do here, since people will bring dogs into the store."

"They won't come back here."

"No, but we need to get him socialized somehow. I'm thinking of bringing Cain in."

I gave a kind of snorted laugh. "I'd sell tickets to that one!"

"Paul, that's not funny. Too many people do exactly that. But it wouldn't be like that, anyway. I could keep Cain from attacking, and Dante would be harnessed and muzzled. I'm just a little worried that Dante will get too out of control."

"What about tranquilizers?"

"You are kidding, I hope. Anyway, that wouldn't socialize him. He needs to learn how to act around other dogs." He sighed again. "But that's a future project. Dante and I have both had all the training we can take for one day. Say, d'you think you could help me put up a run for him this afternoon?"

"Is he ready for that?"

"Probably not, but I have the time, and it's my time. So your dad would essentially be donating only your time. And then it would be there whenever Dante's ready."

I shrugged. "I guess."

JJ went and bought a few things at the hardware store, driving an old Chevy that was almost certainly his mom's car, and I had to admit he was pretty good with the tools. I guess I was feeling a little magnanimous or something, because I actually said so.

"My dad's a plumber," he told me, standing on a step stool and drilling a hole into one of the trees off to the side of the lunch area. "All his boys learned how to use tools. No option."

"I suppose otherwise you would have avoided this kind of work."

He stopped what he was doing and looked down at me. "Why?"

*Shit.* I tried to shrug it off. "Sorry; I know you asked me not to keep bringing it up."

"It? You mean, my being gay?" He shook his head and lifted the drill again. "Right. Everyone knows gay men hate power tools." The drill whined into the tree, and when JJ was satisfied with the hole he got off the stool, and then he looked at me again. "Stereotyping saves you a lot of time, doesn't it?"

We walked Dante again, and the dog was too tired to react as strongly to other dogs as he had that morning, so I was able to do the whole walk myself. Which was a good thing, since JJ was pissed at me and I was pissed at him.

When we got back JJ said, "Are you clear on what to feed him later? And how to get the muzzle off and back on again?"

"Oh, I know how to do it. I just don't know if he'll let me."

"Try it. Right now. He's tired, and he'll be better prepared for it later."

I looked down at the dog, who had accepted the bed we'd set up for him and was all stretched out on it, even though his harness lead was tied to the metal shelves. I was just about to walk to him when JJ said, "No. Call him. He needs to come to you.

The dogs in the pack are always expected to go toward the leader."

*Damn him, anyway. What makes him always right?* But I did it, and Dante came to me, exhausted or not. I scratched his ears again and then took the muzzle off.

"Now give him one of those treats."

We'd selected about four different kinds to see which one he'd like the best, but he seemed to like all of them. I gave him two of the biscuits, muzzled him again, and rubbed his shoulders. He smiled at me and went back to his bed.

"This is really good, Paul. He's accepted you. He follows you. Now we just need to get him used to your father. Maybe tomorrow. Don't forget to take the muzzle off again so he can drink water overnight. I'm heading out now. Listen"—and he went over to the worktable to find a scrap of paper and a pen—"if you have any problems this evening, call me here. It's not the number in my file."

"Oh? Where is it?"

He looked at me a second. "You don't want to know." And he left.

I stood there, frozen, looking after him. *You don't want to know.* It's what Chris had said to me when the answer was... well, you know what the answer was. So whether I wanted to know or not, I knew; it would be JJ's boyfriend.

I left Dante dozing and went back into the store, to fish tank filters and dried cricket restocking and occasionally bagging at one of the registers, most of the time speculating on the boyfriend. He'd seemed a little older than JJ. And if JJ was at his house, it seemed unlikely the guy lived with his parents. College student? It was a possibility. But I really didn't want to know.

Right?

I had a weird dream that night. Not about Chris, or JJ—not exactly, anyway. It was kind of like I was watching this training film or something, and the narrator kept talking me through this filmed scene where a small schooner, sails full open to the wind, is subjected to several different kinds of water disturbances. And no matter what the water is doing—head-on storm wave, rocking the boat sideways with the wake of a passing freighter, passed on one side and then the other by whale-watching ships—the schooner always reacts the same way. So each time the schooner gets tossed around in the water, it always recovers, and the narrator says, "This is the way a gay schooner will react in this situation." Then it's a different kind of turbulence, but again the narrator says, "This is the way a gay schooner will react in this situation." He said the same thing, no matter what. And, no matter what, the gay schooner always recovered.

After about the fifth time, I sat up in bed and shook myself awake. I thought of going into Chris's room, but somehow I didn't want to bring this weirdness in there. So I just took a leak and went back to bed.

By Friday afternoon Dante had made significant progress. JJ had gotten him to tolerate Dad going in and out of the stockroom, and he'd even spent a little time on his run. He was back in the stockroom because of an on-and-off drizzle, and I was bagging at one of the registers, and JJ was outside under the overhang with a customer and her dog, when I heard Dante explode.

First I looked around for Dad, praying he hadn't been the cause of the commotion. He was in his office, and he was at attention, too. I bolted toward the noise, throwing the door to the stockroom open. Dante was straining against his lead, barking and snarling viciously at a cowering Marty Kaufman, though he couldn't reach Marty because of being tied to the shelves. From where I stood in the doorway from the store, it was obvious Marty had come in from the back and had been surprised nearly to death when Dante jumped up and probably lunged. In Marty's haste to get back outside—or maybe he'd just fallen against them—he'd toppled a couple of stacks of bagged pine shavings for rabbit cages and was desperately trying to move them out of the way so he could open the door and escape.

Dad appeared at my elbow. "Well, this is something," he said.

"Dad, would you get JJ? He's out front. I'll see if I can calm Dante down."

Dad stood there another second or two, enjoying the sight, and then headed out. Now I had to deal with this dog. I didn't want to surprise him, so I moved around to get into his line of vision. He ignored me, focused on annihilating the intruder.

"Dante!" I yelled at him. "No! Stop!" I clapped my hands and pointed to his bed, and he proceeded to ignore me. I tried everything I could think of to get his attention. Meanwhile, Marty managed to kick enough of the bags aside so that he could open the door. He stepped outside and pulled the door mostly shut, still watching but obviously terrified.

Suddenly JJ was in the room. He marched right over and stood in front of Dante—blocking his view of Marty, which hadn't really occurred to me—clapped his hands and pointed. Dante ignored him, too, which did my heart good. But JJ was not going to repeat an ignored command. He moved to Dante's side, jerked the collar a couple of times without effect, and then put all his weight into forcing Dante down onto the concrete floor. Dante fought him for a minute, then just struggled a little.

"Should I shut the door?" I asked, thinking it might be good to get Marty out of the picture.

"No. Let him see that he has to submit even though his target is still in sight."

I looked over at Marty, whose eyes were bugged out watching this puny little gay kid manhandle a violent German shepherd. He was ready to run if necessary, but he was too fascinated to leave unless he had to. Eventually Dante stopped struggling and just lay there, panting and heaving like the bulldog, and like Gypsy, the Carters' dog.

JJ looked up at Marty for the first time. "Come back inside," he said.

"Fuck that shit!"

"Young man!" My dad's voice boomed from behind me. "We will have none of that language here. Now do as you're told and come back inside." I suspected Dad was secretly hoping Dante would take a chunk out of the terrified Mr. Kaufman. Truth be told, I would have found it amusing myself. Marty made a face and then shrugged, and gingerly he stepped back inside, leaving the door conspicuously open.

JJ said, "Come this way. He won't hurt you, I promise. Just approach casually. Don't look at him." JJ looked at Marty and chuckled. "And don't look so terrified. It will only enrage him again." I could hear ridicule hiding just behind his words; it seemed Marty was the only one in the room who didn't think it would be fun to see him lose a little skin.

So Marty moved slowly, cautiously toward the panting dog. "What am I supposed to do now?"

"Just stand there so he sees you're not afraid of him." There was that humor again. Then, "Okay, now turn casually like you don't care and walk back toward the door. I'm going to let him up."

I'm not sure Marty quite managed casual, but he made it to the door and turned around again, watching as Dante got to his feet. JJ, still holding the collar, jerked it once or twice toward Dante's bed and pushed the dog's side a little in that direction, using stiff fingers. Dante lay on his belly, head on his paws, and looked up from sad eyes.

To no one in particular Dad said, "He'll make a terrific guard dog, once we get him to obey a command to heel." Then, to Marty, "As for you, what do you mean by sneaking in here through the back door?"

Marty was trying to look cocky and wasn't carrying it off up to his usual standard. "I just went around back to see if Paul was out there on a break or something. He wasn't, so I came in. Didn't think it would be such a big deal."

*On a break? In the drizzle? Liar.*

"Next time, think again. You know I don't really like you in here, anyway."

Marty straightened up a little. "As a matter of fact, I'm here to get a few things for Mrs. Denneghy. You remember her? The one with the Dalmatian that got attacked at your clinic?"

Dad scowled. "What do you know about it?"

"His owners live next door to me." I knew this was true—or at least that Marty had said it before—but I had serious doubts about Marty's intentions to do anything useful for his neighbors or their dog. Even so, I said nothing.

All Dad could say was, "Paul, help him gather what he needs and see him out the door. The *front* door."

Marty gave Dante a wide margin as he moved toward the door that led into the main store area, and I followed him out.

"So what is it you need for the Dalmatian?"

"Not a fucking thing. What d'you take me for?"

"Oh, let's see . . . a thief, maybe? What did you think you were doing, coming in the back way like that?" I steered him toward dog supplies in case Dad was watching.

"Maybe I wanted to see how you and the queer kid are getting along."

I picked up a bag of dog treats and shoved them at his chest. "Eat shit, Marty. You don't scare me. Anybody questions me, I'll just point out how I was able to 'do the deed' with our prostitute, and you failed to perform."

"Like hell you will. Hey, what are these things for?"

"You're buying them, or you can face the possibility that my dad'll have you arrested for breaking and entering."

He held them up and stared at the bag. "Why these?"

Unbelievably, it seemed as though he was backing down. As though once he knew I would throw shit back at him, he wasn't heaving any more at me. All I said was, "They're Dante's favorites." Didn't matter that it wasn't quite true.

"Dante the monster in the back?"

"Yup. And he's my dog now. Got a problem with that?"

Marty slapped my shoulder. "Simmer down, boy!" He held the bag up, saluted me with it, and headed toward the registers. "See ya around."

I watched him go, and in my mind's eye I could see Dante the day his owner had brought him in. Pacing, threatening, snarling, until JJ had stood up to him. Until he realized that JJ had his number. I stood there just long enough to be sure

Marty wasn't going to avoid payment, and then I headed back to the stockroom.

Another surprise awaited me. There was Dad, crouched down over Dante, stroking his ears and saying, "Good dog, Dante. Good boy." JJ, standing a little away and watching, looked up at me as I came in.

Dad saw me. "That troublemaker gone?"

"Gone."

"What did he buy?"

"Some dog treats." *See, Marty? I was right to make you get something.*

"You boys clean up in here"—he pointed toward the mess Marty had made—"and then carry on with your work. I'm going back to the office." He started out the door but turned at the last minute. "Paul, maybe I'll walk Dante with you later."

*Well, well.* JJ beamed at me. "This is going to work, you know?"

JJ and I bent over our task. At one point we reached for the same packet; he backed off. I said, "Something about Marty reminded me of how Dante was pacing the day he showed up here."

A few seconds of silence, and then JJ said, "I can see why you'd say that. And maybe with retraining, Marty could be recovered, too. But right now he reminds me more of the guy who brought Dante in than he reminds me of Dante."

"The tattooed guy? Why d'you say that?"

"They both want you to think they're much tougher than they really are, and they'll walk all over anyone they can in their efforts to prove it."

"So, what, you just stand up to them and they back off?"

"Sometimes. It depends."

"On what?"

"On how cornered they feel and how much they think they might lose. On how scared they think you are. On how many buddies they have around them. Bullies don't want to be beaten; they can't afford it, because they'd lose too much status. So they won't start a fight they aren't sure they can win. They don't fight for principles; they fight for self-image."

"You sound like you know a lot about bullies."

JJ snorted. "With a name like mine, with a face like mine, and as short as I've always been, you bet I do."

I almost brought up being gay, but I didn't dare do that again. Guess I'm trainable. Instead, picking up a packet and throwing it onto the pile, I said, "You don't back down from dogs like Dante. Do you back down from bullies?"

He straightened up and brushed his hands off. "Did I back down from his owner?"

No; I had to admit he didn't. "I guess not. But you were scared of Marty the first time you saw him."

"I recognized him for what he is, just as he recognized me. And to be honest, I'm really, really tired of people like him, which is too bad because it seems like there are a lot of them. I just didn't feel like dealing with him."

"How would you deal with him?"

"Depends. When I was little, I would have just made myself too much trouble. A kid like me? I was always a target. But bullies really don't want to get caught. If they beat me up and I told on them, I'd be in even deeper trouble. But running away was a drag, and it didn't always work. So I fought back. I still got pulverized, but when the teacher or whoever came thundering toward us, I wasn't the only one with blood on him. And they knew better than to think I'd started anything. So the bully would get caught."

I just stared at him, wishing I could say I had that much guts, even to myself. I would have expected someone like JJ—especially if he was gay—to whimper and beg not to be hit anyplace it would show. But from what I knew about JJ by this point, how stupid was that assumption?

I bent over to pick up the last fallen package. "I had this weird dream last night." I didn't know I was going to say that; it just came out. The image of the boat had stayed with me all day long.

"Are you going to tell me what it was?"

I shrugged. And I told him about the gay schooner, and about what the narrator said. "I feel like it means something. But I can't think what."

"Are you asking what I think?"

"I guess so."

"A couple of things occur to me. It's like I said to you about stereotyping, when we were putting up Dante's run. Remember? But even more, I think it's like what my mom says when I have a dream that keeps repeating. Maybe you haven't had the dream more than once, but it's almost like you had it several times in one night. Anyway, she says it's because there's a lesson in it we haven't learned yet."

He stopped, like that was it, so I said, "Okay, so what's the lesson in this one for me?"

"What do *you* think? What is it you need to learn about people who are gay?" I guess he figured I wasn't about to answer that right here and now, so he said, "So, shall we get back to work, like your dad said?"

When we got back into the store, Mrs. Carter was waiting for JJ. She didn't have Gypsy with her, but she'd come for a consultation. As I was moving away, I heard Mrs. Carter saying something like how much better Gypsy was to walk, using JJ's techniques.

Walking Dante with Dad was interesting. JJ went with us, I guess just in case something happened, but he took the leash only once when Dante went a little insane seeing another dog. It wasn't a long walk, with Dad's leg, but other than the one crisis he held the leash the whole time. I'm a little ashamed to say I felt jealous.

One thing that Dante did for me was to take my mind off of the fact that I was very much still in a harness myself. On a tight leash. Penned in. However you want to look at it. Dealing with him, learning the best ways to handle him and maintain my position as alpha, took a lot of focus. I'd still rant and rave a little at night as I jerked off, but my days were less of a burden with Dante in the picture.

He got so that he loved spending time outside on the run, and we stopped needing the harness and the muzzle after a week or so. Sometimes I would look at him and think how happy he seemed, how I'd helped take away the awful life he'd been living, how his worries were gone. He seemed to think so, anyway. Oh, he was still difficult on the leash when he saw other dogs or bicycles, but not as bad as he had been. I could walk him alone with just a standard choke collar, no need for the prongs anymore. But I still had to fight pangs of jealousy when Dad took him for short walks, usually with JJ.

Things would have been at least decent, considering my virtual incarceration, if it hadn't been for Marty and Kevin. Marty must have decided I was okay or something after all, and the two of them started coming around when they knew I was likely to be on lunch break. Dante still hated Marty, and he stood staring at him the whole time Marty was around, but he didn't lunge. It was kind of like he just wanted Marty to know he shouldn't pull any funny stuff, whatever that would have meant to Dante. For his part, Marty tried to ignore the dog, but I noticed he always positioned himself as far away from Dante as he could before he fell into his studied casual pose.

I guess if I'd had any other friends I could see that summer, I would have told Marty—and Kevin, who was less of a trouble-maker but obviously under Marty's influence to some extent—to get lost. As it was, though, they were it. They were all I had. And I was still pissed enough at Dad for so many things that hanging with Marty was almost like a slap in the face to my dad, and I wanted that. Take that, Dad, for telling me to be a man and then making it impossible for me to do that. Take that, for overreacting to my little romp in the hay with Lady Pink Vest. Take that, for not letting me have any of my own fucking money. Take that, for not letting me go on one stinking date all summer.

And while you're at it, take THAT for making Chris die. For making him do what you couldn't, to be the man you couldn't be. For forcing him to go someplace he hated, and then to get

killed there before he had a chance to get back to being normal.

TAKE THAT!

That last one? That's what I wanted to shout every time I
came. Every time I shot cum. It was like I was shooting Dad with
the gun he was never given.

# Chapter 13

People kept bringing their dogs into the store to see JJ. The appointment thing worked pretty well, once customers caught on to it. But did Dad ever thank me? You know the answer to that. Instead he just kept piling praise onto JJ. It was, "Oh, JJ, you were so good with Mrs. So-and-so." And, "JJ, how did you learn how to do that?" And, "JJ, how did you manage to get that animal under control?" And, "JJ, I can't tell you how delighted I am to have you with us this summer." It made me grind my teeth.

JJ brought Cain in a few times on Wednesdays. I gotta say, that was one ugly dog. Little piggy eyes you couldn't see very well, ears clipped into tight curls that pointed toward each other over the top of his head. Didn't look like he had a wasted ounce of body space; there was no fat on him anywhere. Most of his short fur was charcoal, but there was a thin line of white down the center of his face and a blaze of it on his chest. I didn't know a lot about pit bulls except that they could be mean, and this one looked like he could live up to it if he wanted to. He wasn't a big dog, though. Not as big as Dante.

On the first few visits with Cain, JJ came in through the store only as far as the closed stockroom door, if Dante was inside, and I could hear Dante growling in there while Cain just hung out. Or JJ would take Cain into the stockroom, if Dante was outside. He said he was gradually introducing Dante to Cain's scent. It was funny to watch Dante in the stockroom, if he'd been outside and Cain had violated his sanctuary. He'd nose all around and growl a little. Once he lifted his leg, but I caught him before he could do much.

By sometime in July Dante stopped reacting very much at all, and JJ said it was time for them to meet. He and Dad, who was very interested to see this event, waited with Cain in the store, just inside the open door to the stockroom, and JJ asked me to bring Dante in from his run.

"Put the choke collar on first. Be sure you have a good grip on the leash, and be ready to yank him around so his back is to us if need be. I'll stand here where we can shut the door between the dogs if that becomes necessary."

Doing my best not to seem nervous, I grabbed Dante's choke collar and leash and went out, remembering to call him to me instead of going to him. Keeping the leash short and my grip tight, I made Dante follow me into the stockroom, but as soon as he was inside and saw Cain, he forgot who was boss. He lunged.

I did my best to yank him around; jerking on the collar wasn't going to do anything. So I kept him from getting to the doorway where Cain was, but I just couldn't get him to turn his back. Suddenly JJ was beside me. He grabbed the leash and literally lifted Dante's front end off the floor and turned him around. Dante wheeled again, and again JJ turned him. But when Dante wheeled yet again, JJ said to me, "Get him down. Push the collar down onto the floor."

I tried. Really, I tried. I knew what JJ had done, and I would have sworn I could do it, but I was just a little too scared to concentrate. Or maybe all those warnings I'd heard JJ give Dad earlier this summer, about how most people shouldn't try this, made me hesitate.

JJ did it. He waited until he was sure I couldn't, and then he did it.

"Help me hold him!" he shouted over Dante's noise. I managed to do that, though I was careful to watch where those jaws were snapping. I have to say, though, it didn't actually seem like he was trying to bite *us*.

Finally Dante stopped struggling, and both he and I were panting. I looked toward the door and there was Cain, Dad holding his leash, interested but calm as he sat watching the show.

"Sorry," I said to JJ. "I just couldn't—"

"It's tough the first time you have to do it. It's like you can't really believe you can. But you can. Not everyone has it in them, but you do. And next time, you'll be able to."

JJ stood, took Dante's leash, and gave it a slight tug. Dante stood, and JJ turned him so his back was to Cain and made him sit. At first Dante had a kind of beaten look on his face, but we all stayed where we were for a minute, and he seemed to feel better about himself, almost like he'd forgotten his humiliation. But he hadn't forgotten about Cain. He kept starting to snarl and trying to turn toward the pit bull, but JJ was still able to back him down and make him stay put, facing away from this threat to his dominion. They didn't get any closer to each other, but JJ made Dante just sit there, his back to Cain, for a couple of minutes. I couldn't help thinking Dante would get the better of Cain, if it came to it. He was a bigger dog, and he seemed so much more ferocious.

Finally JJ turned Dante and made him sit again. "Paul, you see how I turned him? I *allowed* him to turn. It was my decision, not his."

Dante, unbelievably, was not even looking at Cain anymore. Oh, he knew the other dog was there, and Cain knew Dante was, but they both just sat and looked around.

JJ said, "That's enough for a first meeting, I think. Maybe next week we'll let them get closer and actually sniff each other. That will help Dante learn how to be a dog with other dogs. But we don't want to push him too far today. Mr. Landon, will you lead Cain back into the store? I'll be right there." When Dad had left, JJ said, "Your father is very good with dogs."

For some reason this irritated me. Maybe because of how

jealous I'd been feeling when Dad walked Dante. Maybe because I knew that Dad would hate JJ if he knew the truth about
him. "I'll take Dante back outside," I said, wanting to exert
some control.

"No, I think he'd be more comfortable in here. He needs to
know the room he thinks of as home is safe. It's important that
he wasn't allowed to chase Cain out, so he wasn't able to claim
the space for his. It belongs to you, not him, and you let him
use it. But he needs to feel safe here again."

*What about me? Where can I go to feel safe?* I felt kind of like I'd
had the wind knocked out of me. I couldn't control Dante after
all. Puny little gay JJ had had to come to my rescue, and Dad
had seen that. *My room, like hell. Nothing here is mine. Every day
more and more of it belongs to JJ.*

It felt even worse a few minutes later, when I heard Dad talking to JJ, who was about to take Cain home. "JJ, that was phe-
nomenal. What an experience! You do amazing things with
these animals."

"Thanks, Mr. Landon. But it's just a matter of thinking like a
dog."

"Maybe, but so many people can't even learn to understand
other people, let alone manage to do something like this."

*Yeah. Try understanding me, Daddy-o.*

The Sunday after the first meeting of the dogs, Marty and
Kevin showed up around two o'clock. I was working on the goddamned fish tanks again, and they found me. We shot the
breeze for a couple of minutes, tales of conquests, sights seen
as they cruised in the Mustang, that sort of thing.

Then, "Where's the Wunderkind?"

My eyes flashed toward Marty. So he remembered that, too.
And it seemed he deliberately said it the way he wanted to say
it, not the way Anthony had.

"I think he's restocking bags of dog food."

Marty jerked his chin toward Kevin and they headed toward
the floor-to-ceiling shelves where we stack dry food for dogs, in
two aisles, and cats, in one. The shelves were open on both

sides to allow for maximum flexibility for whatever you might want to store on them, and for access from either side. I watched them go into the aisle where JJ was working. *Should I follow? What are they likely to do? What will JJ do? Will I get into trouble?* I decided I'd better follow slowly in the direction they'd gone, and I could hear Marty's slurred voice.

"How's it going?"

"Fine," from JJ. Quiet. Calm. Noncommittal.

"Those bags look kinda heavy." No response. "Aren't they heavy for you?"

"They're fine."

God, but he reminded me of Anthony, responding to my offers of a ride. *You're not exactly making yourself too much trouble now, Wunderkind.*

So here I am again, caught between Marty and someone I don't like but who doesn't really deserve the kind of attention Marty wants to lavish on him, and again I'm leaning in the direction of Marty. Again. Why? Was I still afraid of Marty or something?

Yeah. I guess I was.

From where I stood, a little hidden behind a low display case with ferrets in it, I saw Marty and Kevin go down the aisle past JJ's. Marty had that silent cackle expression on his face that told me he was up to no good, and in a few seconds I noticed the heavy bags on the shelf over JJ's head start to move. I was debating whether to shout, to warn JJ, when he seemed to hear something. He stood and moved to the side just as a thirty-pound bag came tumbling down. It thudded to the floor and split open, dried nuggets sliding along the aisle, under the shelves, all around.

I think if Dad had been in the store, Marty and Kevin would have dashed for the door, like the day they set the tarantula on JJ's back. But they knew he wasn't around. So instead they sauntered back to the end of JJ's aisle, Marty in the lead.

"Oh, my," Marty said, and clucked his tongue. "What a mess. That's too bad."

I had moved closer, and I could see that JJ wasn't even looking at Marty. It was as though he chose to believe the bag had fallen of its own accord, and Marty and Kevin didn't exist. He turned and walked out the other end of the aisle toward the stockroom, and for one crazy moment I thought he might be going to get Dante. But he came back with a broom, a piece of cardboard, and a trash bag, and he just started cleaning up.

Marty stood there a minute and then said, "Is it easier for you like that, just a few bits at a time? Not so heavy?" JJ still did nothing to acknowledge him. Marty punched Kevin's shoulder and the two of them headed casually for the front door, laughing loudly. I followed them with my eyes and then, to my horror, I saw Carol step out of the office. I headed back to the fish tanks, ready to deny any knowledge of anything.

JJ had said he wouldn't lie again to cover my friends' pranks, so I expected to hear about this. And sure enough, Carol came to find me.

"Paul, you've got to do something about those two friends of yours."

I kept working. I liked Carol, but what the hell did she expect me to do? But I couldn't just ignore her. I could, however, fake ignorance. "What did they do this time?"

"They're pushing those heavy bags of dog food off the shelves and onto the floor. Never mind that they've wasted the dog food. They could have hurt JJ seriously!"

Straightening up, I said, "That's awful. I'm sorry, Carol. He's okay though, right?"

"This time."

"Look, I'll pay for the dog food. Please don't tell Dad. He doesn't need anything more to worry about."

"True enough; these register tallies coming up short are plenty." And then she did what I was hoping she'd do. "Oh, never mind. But those boys are trouble, Paul. You should make it clear you don't want to hang around with them. Maybe they'll stay away."

"You may be right." I thought this was lame, especially as I had no intention of doing what she said, but it seemed to do the trick. And Dad never said anything about it to me.

In a kind of delayed reaction, I realized she'd made it sound like even more money was missing. It's no big deal, in a store like this, for the registers to be a little off at the end of a busy day, but there'd been talk of bigger sums lately. *Who would do that? Certainly not Alice, and certainly not JJ. But Dave...*

Tuesday, Mrs. Carter came in, still no dog in tow, and headed straight for JJ, who was restocking bird supplies. She looked upset, so I worked my way over to where I could hear. She was already into her story.

"I couldn't stop her." Mrs. Carter dug a tissue out of a pocket and blew her nose. She was crying, at least a little. "She ran right out into the street and tried to bite the tires." I heard a sob or two. "She always hated the trash truck."

*Gross. Gypsy's fur and guts are now stuck in the treads of trash truck tires?*

I peeked around the end of the aisle and saw that JJ had wrapped his arms around the now-weeping Mrs. Carter, and she was sobbing openly onto his shoulder. I expected he'd give her a couple of pats on the back and pull away, but they stood there like that, swaying a little, long enough for me to realize that JJ was crying, too. His eyes were closed, and there were tears making their way down his face. Finally they separated.

"I knew you'd understand," she said. "Of all the people I've told, most of them have just said, 'Oh, I'm sorry to hear that.' And then it's on to something else. Either they don't care very much or they don't want anything embarrassing to happen." She snuffled and blew her nose again, and JJ wiped his face.

He said, "In her whole life, the best times she had were the ones you gave her. She died a much happier dog than she would have if you hadn't taken her in."

Well, that was a stupid thing to say, 'cause now Mrs. Carter was sobbing all over again. Another hug, shorter this time, and he walked her out to her car. They stood out there talking for a few minutes, and when she drove off he didn't come back inside. He walked around the back.

Curious, I went into the stockroom and then peeked outside

where I knew Dante was on his run. He was lying in the shade, and JJ sat beside him, his face buried in the fur on Dante's neck.

*Some vet this kid is going to make if he falls apart every time some dog buys it.*

I didn't expect to see JJ on Wednesday. He didn't need to walk Dante, but he came in with Cain in tow. I was bagging at one of the registers, and I saw him and the dog go into Dad's office. They stood there chatting about nothing much, it seemed, and then Dad took Cain's leash and walked him back and forth in the front part of the store. Cain looked docile enough, like he knew what he was expected to do and didn't mind doing it. JJ stood there watching until a lady customer came up to him. It was his day off, and that's what he should have said, but there was a dog in the picture, and he probably couldn't resist. It was a big dog, some mixed breed, and the owner couldn't seem to get it to walk, just be dragged around.

"When he's off the leash, he moves. But when I try to walk him? Forget it."

Before you could have said, "Why should he follow you if you haven't convinced him he should," JJ was working with the dog. He went to get a choke chain, and he stopped and talked to Dad; it seemed he wanted to make sure Dad could keep Cain busy while JJ worked with the dog. But once JJ was outside, Carol called to Dad.

"Andy? That supplier of dog packs is on the phone."

Dad walked Cain toward the office. "Carol, can you take him while I talk to the guy?"

She looked scared. "That's a pit bull, Andy. I don't know..."

I have no idea why I did it. I said, "I'll take him." How bad could it be? He'd been—what was the word, recovered—hadn't he? So I took the leash from Dad almost without him having to slow down in his limping walk with Cain, and Cain and I kept going. Only I didn't just walk back and forth in the front. I turned and headed toward the stockroom.

I see now that I must have been out of my mind. But at the

time, all I was thinking was that it was my turn to rise to the top of the heap, to get some credit. I was sick of being ignored, dismissed, taken for granted, made to feel like I didn't matter. So I was going to introduce Cain to Dante. Alone. *Watch this, Wunderkind.*

Dante was out on his run, I knew. So I went through the stockroom with Cain and then out into the back. Dante, at the far end of the run, saw Cain and bristled. He got up and growled and then started barking. I thought it would be okay to move closer, but Cain almost seemed like he wanted to stay put, not go any closer. *Afraid of the big dog, you wimp?*

So I was looking at Cain, trying to get him to move forward without dragging him, when I heard the whine of Dante's run wire. It happened so fast. Cain's piggy eyes flicked toward Dante and without any other motion that I could see, he was airborne. The leash snapped out of my hand, and the two dogs collided with such force that I heard their heads crash together.

*Fuck!*

They were both on their hind legs, teeth flashing, forearms thrashing around. Desperately I tried to get hold of Cain's leash, but I was stark-raving terrified of getting close to those behemoths. I danced around for a few seconds, wondering how bad it could get, when I saw blood spurting from someplace.

"Help! Somebody, help!" I ran back into the stockroom and through the store, my eyes searching frantically for JJ. Was he really still out front? Hadn't he heard me? Christ! Where was he?

Carol came toward me. "Paul, what is it?"

"Where's JJ?"

She looked toward the front, but all either of us could see was the customer standing there holding her dog's leash, facing the side of the building.

"He's gone out back!" I turned and dashed back the way I'd come, wondering what on earth I could do to help. And there was JJ, aiming a hose full onto the dogs. He saw me.

"Paul! Get hold of Dante's lead, but don't pull him back until I can get Cain off of him."

Cain had managed to sink his teeth into the flesh on the side of Dante's neck, and he was not letting go. Dante was yelping and struggling, unable to get at Cain at all.

"He'll bite me!"

"Paul! Get in there. You did this, now you fucking undo it!"

I'd never heard JJ swear before. Maybe that was why I just did what he said. I grabbed Dante's lead and held it taut without pulling. JJ pointed the hose into Cain's mouth with one hand, hauling back on his collar with the other. I thought that pit bull would drown before he'd let go, but finally he opened his jaws. I yanked on Dante's lead, and JJ threw Cain onto his side. The dog was half overcome with water, and I'm positive that was a good thing for JJ.

Dante pulled me to the opposite end of his run and cowered there, which gave me a chance to assess the damage. He had lost part of an ear, and there was a bloody gap in the skin on his neck. He was whimpering.

I looked over to where JJ still had Cain on the ground and searched for any sign of damage. Couldn't see a fucking thing. It didn't look like Dante had done anything to that holy terror. JJ's head was down, like he was trying to get himself under control at the same time he was subduing his dog.

I decided to speak first. "Dante's hurt. We have to get him to—"

JJ's head snapped up, and his voice cut through me like knives. "Of course he's hurt, you stupid fool! What the hell were you thinking? That dog," and he jerked his chin toward Dante, "is no match for a pit bull in a fight."

I was mad now. "You're the one who brought that monster here! You're the one who wanted to socialize Dante with him! Don't you call me a stupid fool, you faggot!"

JJ stood, his foot on Cain's leash, and his eyes shot daggers at me. "If I were as much of a Neanderthal as you, I would sic my dog on you for that. You'd be cat food by the time he was done with you. And if you *ever* call me that name again, your father will know a lot more about you than he does now. None of it good. You're no better than that poor excuse for a human being that brought Dante in here to begin with. Now you stay put, and wait here until I can find someone to take you and Dante to the vet."

He tugged on Cain's collar, and damn if that death machine didn't get to his feet and trot after JJ. I stood there fuming, watching them go.

In the end, Dad drove Dante and me to get him patched up. Dante ended up with a big shaved area all around the gash Cain had taken out of him, several stitches holding him together. Dad didn't speak to me except when he had to. I don't know what JJ told him, but what I was wondering was what he *could* have told him. *None of it good? What the hell did that mean? What did he know? And what if I told Dad a few things, too?*

I stayed with Dante awhile in the stockroom while Dad and Carol went through the closing routine that evening. He was pretty groggy with something they'd given him, and he was drooling a little, lying on his side. I stroked his back from time to time and couldn't help feeling as whipped as he must have. All I'd wanted to do was what JJ had said, to introduce the dogs. After all, they'd managed to coexist the last time Cain was here, at least once JJ had done the rollover to Dante. What had gone so wrong? And why did that make me like the tattooed guy?

JJ had said some pretty unpleasant things about that guy. Couldn't lead the way out of his own backyard. He'd said the guy wanted to seem tough when he really wasn't. And that he'd had this thing about having a tough dog, like that made *him* tough, too. Like that proved something.

So what did it prove that this tough dog, who was now mine, had been practically ripped to shreds by JJ's? Did that make JJ tougher than me? Was he the man?

I'd been in there for some time when Carol opened the door. "Paul, your father and I are leaving. I see you've got your bike, so you can leave whenever you want. Just go out the stockroom door and make sure it's locked."

I nodded; didn't speak. Just sat there on the floor next to Dante. Maybe five minutes went by, and my ears rang in the silence. Then there was a knock at the back door. It was already locked, so who was that? God, if it was Marty, I'd—

I barely heard it. "Paul? Open the door, please. It's JJ."

*Marty would have been okay after all. What does that little . . . you-know-what want?* But I got up and went to the door. I opened it but stood in the way. "What?"

"How's Dante?"

"Like you give a shit."

"Paul, knock it off. You know very well I would never willingly hurt an animal. Now, how is he doing?"

I turned and looked toward my dog. *It's a powerful feeling to call him that—my dog.* JJ took advantage of the space I'd left and brushed past me, kneeling beside Dante.

"Poor fellow. I'm so sorry that had to happen. I know it's painful and scary." As he murmured, his fingers examined the shaved area, the stitches, the bandaged ear. Then he pressed gently all around the head.

"What are you doing?"

"The pit bull's head is denser bone than the shepherd's. Just making sure he's not bruised someplace—" And just as he said that, his fingers over Dante's left eye, the dog winced. "Thought so. I think you should avoid touching this spot. I'm sure he'll be fine, but in the meantime it's going to be very sore."

"You're touching it." Sulky. I sounded positively sulky.

"And he's medicated. Groggy. Once he's not, he'll react more sharply, don't you think?" He gave Dante one more gentle pat on his shoulders and stood up again. "We need to talk about what happened. You need to understand—"

"No, wonder boy, you need to understand something. You threatened to talk to my father about me. Well, listen up. All I have to do is tell him one thing about you—and you know damn well what that is—and you'll be out on your ear, dog messiah or no. He feels pretty strongly about what you are, and that feeling is not something you wanna deal with. Why d'you think my own brother swore me to secrecy, huh?" My voice had gotten loud, and Dante turned his head toward me, looking worried.

JJ seemed unfazed. "First, it might interest you to know that most men are much more sensitive about this issue when it's their own son in question. Second, this isn't about you or me. It's about Dante. Now, will you listen to what I have to say?"

I plopped myself down beside my dog and rubbed his shoulders and down his sides. "Why should I listen to you?"

"Well, gee. Maybe because you wouldn't even have this dog in your life if it weren't for me. How's that for a reason?" I didn't reply, so he went on. "What you need to understand is that Dante's a little like the lion in *The Wizard of Oz*. He makes a lot of noise so potential threats stay away. He'll even charge, and he's used to other creatures backing down when he does, so he's not good at fighting. He's had lots of practice making scary threats and not much practice living up to them.

"Now. The ideal way for them to have got close to each other would have been in a controlled way through something like a chain-link fence, like the one out past the trees on the side of the building. And one person would have been with one dog, while someone else was with the other one. What happened this afternoon was not only the wrong way to go about it, but also it may have set Dante back. He'll be even more fearful now, and fear is the place his bravado was coming from. He may resort back into aggression and be harder to control again."

He stopped, but I didn't say anything. I just stared down at Dante's fur and kept stroking.

"Paul, I'm telling you this for Dante's sake. Are you hearing me?"

"Sure. Everything I do is wrong. D'you think you're telling me something new?"

JJ moved toward me and sat down. "Where's that coming from?"

I wasn't about to spill my guts to him, so instead I said, "So how come your dog is so good at fighting, then? He didn't look like much. How was I supposed to know he was an attack dog?"

JJ took a breath and let it out slowly. "All right, I'll tell you. But first I have to make sure you understand that it didn't matter which other dog it was. Okay, with Cain Dante got ripped up a little, but that would have been the wrong way to introduce Dante to any dog. I was using Cain because I have him under such tight control that if it had been done right, nothing like this would have happened. So I want to make sure you won't try it like this again with another dog. Okay?"

"Fine. So why is your dog so mean?"

"Cain isn't mean. Cain is a pit bull. He's warrior through and through. He's not as big as Dante, but he's much more power-ful. His entire body is a dense mass of bone and muscle, and his temperament is the opposite of Dante's. He doesn't threaten. He doesn't bother. He just kills. That's the warrior in him. When he's under the influence of his alpha, his pack leader, he's much less likely to strike. And when he's really in my con-trol, that is when I have him on a lead, there's almost no danger at all."

"That doesn't explain why you have a dog like that in the first place. Who's trying to be the tough guy now?" I still sounded sulky, and I hated it. I wanted to sound calm, self-assured, confident. I wanted to sound like JJ.

"I didn't go looking for a dog like Cain. His story is a very sad one, and I haven't told very many people about this. I'd ask you to keep it confidential, but I know you're carrying a lot of se-crets already. So just use your judgment.

"He belonged to a neighbor who just didn't get dogs. It was a mistake for them to get pit bulls, but they took two that were brothers, and they named them Plato and Aristotle. Then one of them . . . well, Plato killed the other one. The owners blamed the dog, but really it was their own fault. They didn't do any-thing to provide the dogs with exercise, or leadership, or . . . But I don't want to get onto my soapbox. They were going to have Plato killed, but I'd made friends with him. So they asked me to take him."

"You have another killer dog named Plato?"

"Actually, no. My mom and I worked together to recover him, and even though we succeeded, she wanted to make sure I would never underestimate him. She renamed him. Now he's called Cain."

"Got it. Because he killed his brother. Would he really have killed Dante?"

"Once a dog has killed another dog, he never really gets rid of that. But now Cain's allowed to be a dog in a way that keeps the warrior part of him below the surface. I don't know what would have happened if he and Dante hadn't been interrupted, but it would have been very, very ugly. And Dante would not have come out of it well. Most dogs challenge each other for dominance, and if they can get dominance without fighting, they do. They fight only when their dominance is challenged, and usually only as long as it takes for them to prove their point or lose it. But with a pit bull, the fight is for the fight, in a way. Once a pit bull gets his jaws sunk into a perceived enemy, he won't let go. It's like a steel trap has snapped shut, and there's a very powerful, determined dog attached to it that believes it has nothing to lose."

"Doesn't answer my other question. Why do you want a dog like him, anyway? What are *you* trying to prove?"

JJ looked at me a minute. "What makes you think I'm trying to prove anything?"

"With a dog like that? You're the one who was so sure the tattooed guy was trying to prove something. Why are you exempt?"

"I took Cain so he wouldn't be killed, knowing my mother could help me learn what he needed. I keep him for the same reason. If I tried to give him away, I couldn't in good conscience do that without revealing his history. I'm telling you, a dog that has killed another dog has to be handled by someone who really knows what they're doing." He let a few heartbeats go by. "I do."

So fucking calm. So fucking self-confident. I felt pulled two ways. One was to beat the shit out of him. The other was to beg him to teach me how he did it. But at least I could challenge it. "You know what I don't like about you, José Jesus?" I didn't say his name very well, but I didn't care. "I don't like that you're so full of yourself you don't think you can make a mistake. I don't like that you're so calm all the time, like nothing can rattle you.

I don't like that you act like nobody can hurt you, nobody can touch you."

"Calm works for me. If I responded to your anger, or anyone else's, with my own? Let's be real: how much of a threat can I make? And you're wrong. I can be touched. I can be hurt. But not by someone who blusters and jumps around and is full of hate for reasons that have nothing to do with me. Not by someone who doesn't have the guts to get to know me because his friends would make fun of him. I can be hurt by someone I love."

He stood and looked down at me. "I came back hoping you were still here so we could talk about the dogs, so I could help you be as good a pack leader for Dante as possible. I still want that, and I'll still help in any way I can. But not for you. For Dante. And Paul, learn a lesson from Dante. It did him no good to bark and growl and snap when he came up against a dog that didn't bother with that." Again, the heartbeats. Dramatic effect. "I won't bother with that." He turned, walked out, and shut the door behind him. Quietly.

I got up, ran to the door, and threw it open. "Wait! What do you know about me? What would you tell my dad?"

JJ half turned back toward me, a lopsided grin on his face. "Nothing. Scared you though, didn't it?" He winked and walked away.

That night I had another dream about Chris. He and Mason were in the jungle, and all around them these booby traps kept going off. And after each explosion there was this high-pitched cackle that sounded just like Marty. At first the explosions frightened Chris and Mason when they went off, but when nothing ever happened except the noise and the cackling, the two soldiers smiled at each other and then hugged. And then they kissed.

Still half asleep, I sat up in bed. My head was churning. I had to do something to clear it, and the only thing I could think of was to go into Chris's room.

Sitting on his bed, the room felt different somehow. Different from how it usually felt when I went in there. It was almost like whatever part of Chris had still been in here had been leaking out. Maybe Mom and I had used it up between us.

I hadn't tried to stop him from going back. Oh, I'd thought about it. I'd yelled it in my head, begging him to go with me to Canada and become normal again. But I'd said nothing, just listened to him step down the stairs. And then I'd given him nothing but a fucking salute as he left. So maybe, like Cain, I had somehow killed my brother.

I fell sideways onto my dead brother's bed and bawled like a stupid kid.

# Chapter 14

Thursday JJ was back at work, talking to me the same as he always had. Which is to say not much, but like our little confrontation in the stockroom hadn't happened. I was tempted to act pissed off, but I decided it wasn't worth it. Plus, he kept going to check on Dante, make sure he was okay, and we kept meeting in there. So it was easier just to be ourselves.

Around eleven or so, I had reason to be glad I was playing well with others. I was just coming out of the stockroom when who should I see going into the office, undoubtedly for an appointment with JJ, but Laura Holmes. Remember Laura? The woman of my dreams? The one whose virtue I wouldn't let Marty force me to violate? There she was, long blond hair falling in cascades down her back, white short-shorts stopping the view of her tanned legs at just the right (or wrong, depending on your point of view) spot, a peppermint-candy-striped and body-hugging top with sleeves that just capped her shoulders. There was a woman with her, probably her mother, who had a yappy miniature schnauzer in her arms. You'll forgive me if I don't describe the mother. I barely noticed the dog. Needless to say, I made my way toward the office.

Fuck that; I ran.

Dad had just finished introducing Laura and Mrs. Holmes

(I'd been right) to JJ when I appeared in the doorway, doing my best not to let on how short of breath I was. Dad looked my way, irritated, and Laura and her mom turned toward me.

Laura, bless her heart, spoke first. "Oh, Paul! I didn't know you were here. Are you working in your dad's store for the summer?"

JJ went next, and when he was done I could have kissed him. Sort of. He moved over to me and said, "Paul has been helping me recover a violent dog—a German shepherd—and he's taken over the final stages. Perhaps he'd be interested in working with us on Truffles." He turned toward me. "Would that interest you, Paul?"

I was smiling like an idiot and barely got out, "Sure."

To Dad, JJ said, "Mr. Landon, I hope I haven't spoken out of turn, but Paul has shown a real interest in this process. Is this arrangement all right with you?"

Dad just stared at me like he didn't know who I was. Finally he said, "I suppose so."

Meanwhile the schnauzer was squirming, and Mrs. Holmes put it down. Truffles was wearing a powder blue collar with a matching leash attached to it, and she immediately started nosing all around the office. As it happened I was the first unknown person she approached. I raised my eyes away from her and just let her sniff.

To Mrs. Holmes, JJ said, "You see how Paul is essentially ignoring the dog and just letting her find out who he is through smell? A dog's most powerful sense is smell. Puppies can smell before they can hear or see, and they rely on that sense throughout life to provide critical information about their environments, including people. If Paul were to acknowledge her right away, it might lessen the position he hopes to attain as dominant over the dog." Truffles moved on to JJ. "Paul, would you mind getting the type of collar we've been working with? Obviously, Truffles will need the small size."

Suddenly I had no problem being JJ's assistant. In one giant step, he'd made me sound like an expert, a valued colleague, to Laura. And, really, to my dad as well. On my way back to the office, nearly dancing in fact, I sent up a silent prayer that I could remember everything I'd seen JJ do, or heard him say—like not looking at the dog right away—so that I didn't make an idiot of myself. Maybe I couldn't ask Laura out this week, and maybe not next week, either, but when I could she'd sure remember me.

The little group was on its way outside but still in the store, Truffles yipping and tugging out in front of Mrs. Holmes, and I joined them about ten feet from the door.

JJ said, "Now, here's an important lesson for Truffles to learn, and for you to learn as well. Paul is going to attach the leash to the collar he's brought, and then he'll show you how to handle the leash and the dog in a way that will give you the best control." I wasted no time getting the choke collar on Truffles and attaching the leash to it. Then I held the blue collar so the dog wouldn't dash forward and choke. "This is good for the dog for many reasons, which we'll go into in more detail outside. All set, Paul?"

Trying to sound calm and professional, I said, "Yes, I believe so. May I have the leash handle, Mrs. Holmes?" I held it just like I'd been holding Dante's, though with a smaller dog I had to make some adjustments.

JJ kept on saying things to the Holmes that he knew I knew but might forget, to make sure I looked as good as possible. "Paul is going to wait until Truffles is relaxed and ready to obey before he—"

"He's choking her!" Mrs. Holmes cried out.

"No, I assure you, that won't happen. What he's doing is giving gentle tugs on the leash to let Truffles know he is asking for her attention. This is the best way to convince her that he will be the leader and she will be the follower. If you let your dog pull you on the leash all the time, you have allowed yourself to be the follower. She's the leader."

Truffles kept starting up and trying to dash off, and I kept up with the "gentle" tugs, so JJ had plenty of time to reply to Mrs. Holmes, who wanted to know about the dog going to the bathroom, as she put it, or having fun smelling things.

"The leader decides when those things take place. I'll show you in more detail outside, but first we have to establish leadership." He glanced down at Truffles, who had finally decided to stand still. "Now Paul is going to show you how to get Truffles to sit and wait for her next instructions." I leaned over and pushed down just above her tail with pointed fingers. "This is the easiest way to communicate your intent. Truffles might learn to sit on verbal command, but unless you've established yourself as the leader she'll do that only when she wants to. What Paul just did is the way another dog would indicate what it wanted. Of course, it wouldn't use a hand. Paul's fingers acted like the gentle prod of the lead dog's mouth."

He looked at me. "I think we're ready. Do you agree?" I nodded and stepped toward the door, and Truffles trotted quietly beside me.

"Paul," Laura's sweet voice said, "that's fantastic! I can't wait to try it."

"Now Paul is going to use the same technique that he and I used on the German shepherd when we get to the door. Note that Paul is going to use the leash to make sure Truffles does not lead him out. He is going to lead her."

Thank you, JJ. I almost forgot that. And I nearly laughed; it was just like Jack had said: "Thank you, Jesus!"

I won't take you through the entire list of wonderful things I did with that dog. Dad watched just long enough to be satisfied that I wasn't going to make a mess of things, and JJ took over toward the end so he could demonstrate some things like the bit about how to "allow" the dog to have some loose-leash time for exploring, but he did it without making it obvious that I wasn't as good as he was at these things. For all Laura could tell, I was a star pupil and knew everything there was to know.

At the end of the session, which went on much longer than the scheduled thirty minutes (again, thank you, JJ), Mrs. Holmes knew how to walk Truffles the way she should, and so did Laura. Mrs. Holmes stood there gushing over JJ for a good three minutes, and I sent up one more silent Thank You when he carefully turned in a way that put Mrs. Holmes's back to me.

Which gave me some time with Laura. First we talked about school starting again soon, but then I asked her if she'd seen *The Day of the Jackal.*

"Ooh, no. But I'd love to. It's supposed to be really good."

I hedged as well as I could. "I'm kind of tied up here most evenings for a little while, what with the dog training and all. But can I call you after that? I'd love to take you."

She smiled. Smiled! "Sure. I guess that would be okay."

Mrs. Holmes interrupted us. "Laura, dear, why don't you walk Truffles to the car the way we've learned about? And JJ, oh—and Paul, please tell Mr. Landon how much I appreciate this service. I'm sure we'll be back."

JJ was all business professional. "We'd love to see you. And why don't you keep the collar with our compliments?"

"Oh! Yes, of course, that isn't ours. Thank you, young man. Thank you very much."

As the two of them walked away from us, I devoted just enough time to the retreating figure presented by Mrs. Holmes to get an idea where Laura got her looks. And I was still standing there like an idiot when JJ said, "I think that went well."

I held out my hand to him. "Thank you."

We shook and he grinned. "I had a feeling this young lady had caught your eye. Now, you see how much sense it makes that I'm gay? Otherwise I'd have had her fawning all over me." He punched my arm, winked, and started back toward the store.

He wasn't all bad, this kid. Quite a sense of humor, too. *Fawning all over him indeed.* But—he did have those deep brown, almond eyes. . . . Whatever, I was flying high all afternoon.

And over dinner, I was trying to figure out how to bring it up to Mom in a way that didn't sound like I was bragging—or that gave away how much it had meant to me to spend time with Laura—when Dad did it for me.

"You'd have been proud of your son today, Irene." To me, "Paul, I had no idea you'd picked up so much from JJ. I was watching from inside the store, and you were doing most of the work with the dog."

"Yeah, I've learned a lot watching him, and working with Dante."

"I had my doubts, after what happened with JJ's dog. But I guess you learned an important lesson from that mistake, didn't you?"

"What happened?" Mom wanted to know. I knew I hadn't told her, and although I hadn't picked up anything from her that indicated she knew what a problem I'd caused, I'd still sort of expected that Dad had told her.

Dad took a sip of water and leaned back in his chair. "Paul, why don't you tell your mother about it? I'd kind of like to hear what you have to say."

I took a deep breath. If I handled this right, I was planning to ask, sooner than I might have otherwise, about getting some of my money and some car keys for a date with Laura.

So I described the scene, "just the facts," mostly. I told how I hadn't known what JJ's idea was, with the fence in between, and I gave him credit for having the great idea to use the hose. By the time I was done I was really hoping I'd walked that line in a good way. The line between "I didn't know what the fuck I was doing and was just trying to show JJ up" and "I was an idiot and I'm sorry and I'll never do it again because JJ has told me everything I did wrong."

Mom was nodding, looking at Dad. "So that's what you wouldn't talk about last night. I knew there was something when Paul was so far behind you getting home, and the two of you didn't say one word during dinner." She turned to me. "Your father wouldn't say a word to me. I asked."

I looked at Dad, who was now tearing away at a corncob. *How d'ya like that? He didn't just come home and tell Mom what a bad boy I'd been.* I was so amazed at his discretion that I nearly forgot where I wanted this conversation to end up.

"So, anyway, Mom, do you remember the girl I'd been wanting to go out with? Laura Holmes? It was her, and her mother—"

"She, Paul. It was she."

*What the f . . . nobody says that. Never mind.* "It was she and her mother who brought in the dog that I worked with today. Her mom was really nice, and she couldn't say enough nice things about JJ." Ha! That ought to help my case. I'm not bragging.

And Mom, bless her heart, picked up on it. "Sounds like she should have said a few nice things about you, too, dear."

I shrugged. "The good news is that they both know a lot more about how to handle their dog now. I think they really got it. Don't you, Dad?"

He nodded. "I do. I do think so."

Mom said, "Well, that's a great story. Andy, if you're finished with your corn, Paul and I will clear for dessert."

But I didn't want things to get too far away from the topic. So once we were all spooning strawberry-covered vanilla ice cream out of our bowls, I opened.

"Dad, Laura is the girl I was hoping to take to see *The Day of the Jackal.* It's still playing, but it won't be around much longer, and I know she'd like to see it. What do you think?"

He let about two spoonfuls go by, chewing slowly. I knew he was dragging this out, but I also knew that was probably a good sign. Finally, "I suppose in the interest of customer service, we could allow this one event." He stabbed in my direction with his spoon. "But this doesn't mean you're off your own leash, young man. Just this once for now. Then we'll see."

Rather than press my luck, I opted to wait until later to ask Mom if I could borrow her car. But right after dinner I checked the movie times, and then I called Laura. And she said yes! The second time I'd ever asked her out, and she'd said yes both times. Never mind that it was nearly a year since the first time. I was just lucky she wasn't going steady with some guy. We agreed on the Saturday after next; she already had a date for this weekend. No surprise, I suppose; I was just gonna have to be that much better. I was up to that.

Thank you, JJ.

That Sunday afternoon, between appointments when customers brought their dogs in to work with JJ, the Carters came in. I'd gone to oversee Marty and Kevin, who were into the cat toys again. What was with that, anyway? I didn't want them getting me into any more trouble, or my date with Laura could be jeopardized. But when I saw the Carters head straight for the amphibian area where JJ was working, I couldn't say why but I made my way in that direction as casually as possible. Even from a distance I could tell they were excited, and as I got closer I heard Mrs. Carter talking.

"He's absolutely gorgeous! Oh, but JJ, he needs so much help. You know what these dogs are like, even when they've been treated well. They're huge, massive, and solid muscle. This one weighs probably a hundred pounds or more, and he's big even for a Rottweiler. And you should see the scars on him! My heart nearly broke."

JJ turned to Mr. Carter at this point. "You don't have him yet, do you?"

"No. We told the shelter we needed to consult with someone first." He chuckled. "That would be you."

"Because, you know," JJ went on, looking at Mrs. Carter again, "taking on a dog like this is going to be a lot tougher than working with Gypsy. You've just pointed out yourself how powerful he is. You won't be able to walk him. Not right away, anyway. Did he take to you, do you think?"

Mr. Carter shook his head. "Not exactly. I don't think he's likely to take to anyone in the immediate future. He's been too mistreated."

JJ stepped back and looked from one Carter to the other. And suddenly I was aware that Marty and Kevin were behind me, listening. I just hoped we were all out of sight.

JJ said, "It's very likely that no one will be able to walk him right away, if he's as bad as you say. How did they get him into the shelter?"

Mrs. Carter had the whole story. "He'd been kept in this tiny, narrow area, where all he could do was walk back and forth. The owner had—God, it makes me shudder—he had a cattle prod he was using when he wanted Geronimo to move, if the dog didn't want to. The poor thing was stepping in his own stools, and he's got sores on his legs and the biggest scar is on one flank. When the animal control people came to take him away, they had to shoot him with a tranquilizer dart. Then they cleaned him up and treated his wounds, but since he came to at the shelter he hasn't let anyone near him. They have a special doorway, just big enough for food and water dishes; they can't go in. He charges all the time. They were hoping he'd calm down once they got him away from where he was, but he's been in the shelter two weeks with no sign of improvement. So they were going to put him down."

"How old is he?"

"They're not sure. They think maybe three years?"

JJ's face was not radiating its usual optimism. "I don't know. I'm not sure this is a good idea. Much as I hate to say it, there are some dogs that can't be recovered because of how they've been treated. Because of what they've learned to do just to survive. They don't let go of their ferocity easily, because it's what's kept them alive."

"But they'll kill him!"

JJ's voice was soft. "Mrs. Carter, there are so many dogs who need good people like you to care for them. I'd hate to see you get hurt, either by the dog or by your own feelings of guilt when you can't help him and he has to be killed after all. Why don't you find a different dog to love?"

She pursed her lips. Mr. Carter said, "Honey, I told you he might say this." He looked like he was going to say something else, but Mrs. Carter wasn't done.

"JJ, we want to do this. And we're willing to pay for your help. Obviously we couldn't bring Geronimo in here, not like he is. But we want to pay for your consultation services and have you come to him. We want you to help us help him. Please. Please say you'll at least try. If it doesn't work, we won't blame you. We'll blame the people who did this to him. But we have to try!"

I could almost smell the wood burning, JJ was thinking so hard. What I was thinking was that the kid had recovered a goddamn pit bull that had killed its own brother. Why wouldn't he take this on?

Finally he offered an excuse. "Part of the problem is this is going to take some time. And it's August already. I'm leaving to go to college the last week of August. That wouldn't give us much time, and it might not be fair to Geronimo."

"Is it fair to just kill him without even trying?"

JJ let out a breath and rubbed his forehead a second. "Tell you what. Let me go with you to the shelter to see him. Maybe I can assess how serious the case is."

"Can you come now?"

"Now? I'm supposed to be working here."

"Until when?"

"At least five. The shelter will close by then, won't it?"

Mrs. Carter thought for a minute and then said, "Where's Mr. Landon?"

"He doesn't work on Sundays. You could speak to Carol. I think she's in the office. But please don't make it sound like it was my idea to leave."

"No. No, I won't. This is all on us. I'll be right back."

In the end Carol called Dad, and he gave permission for JJ to go with the Carters. Not only that, but he went with them. Leaving me at the store. At least Marty and Kevin left without doing anything they shouldn't, other than making a mess I had to clean up.

Dinner that night was all talk about the Rottweiler. And all, of course, from Dad, since he was the only one of us who'd seen it.

"I tell you, that kid has some kind of magic in him. He asked us all to stand at a distance, and from where we were we could see the Rottie, who did not like having anyone come anywhere near him, I can tell you! Snarling, drooling, foam spraying when he barked. JJ started walking toward the cage, slow and easy, very steady. The dog literally threw himself against the chain links, but JJ just kept moving forward. He had a bag of dog treats in one hand, but he didn't show them to the dog right away. He walked right up to that fence, inches from where it bulged every time the dog landed on it. Finally the dog jumped up, holding on to the fence with his paws, and made as much noise as he could to frighten JJ. But the kid wasn't scared. He stood there not moving, just staring at the dog, until the dog finally dropped to the ground. It stood there glowering, but at least it stopped trying to break through the fence.

"That's when JJ threw a treat over the top. It landed beside the Rottie, who ignored it. JJ threw another. The Rottie finally turned away from JJ enough to investigate, and he snarfed those treats right up. JJ threw another, farther back in the pen, and the dog went to find it. And another. And another, until the dog was all the way back in his pen. The dog waited, like he wanted more, but JJ just stood there. So the dog moved forward, but it wasn't charging. When it got to the fence, JJ threw another treat over. He sent the dog all around the pen by where he threw the treats until they were all gone, and the last one was right near JJ. Then JJ just turned and walked away, leaving the dog there.

"Well, the dog was not happy about that. He started yelping and snarling and pacing back and forth." Dad stopped long enough to eat something and take a drink. But he wasn't through.

"We all went into the shelter office to talk. JJ said that the Rottie was an extreme case and that he wasn't just charging out of fear. If that had been the case, when JJ walked up to the cage the dog would have kept barking but in higher tones, and it would have backed up and gotten a panicked look on his face. Geronimo didn't do that; he stayed right there, and he meant business. As JJ put it, his threats were not empty ones.

"But JJ was encouraged that the dog had allowed himself to be led around the pen, as it were, by JJ, throwing the treats, you know? So he would probably accept a leader at some point, if that leader were very strong-willed and had lots of patience. But he said it would take time and it would be dangerous. And he couldn't promise how far it would get before he had to leave."

"Leave?" Mom asked. "Oh, that's right. College."

"Cornell," Dad said, and I thought he'd look at me to rub that in, but he didn't.

"So, what are they going to do?"

"They're going to get as far as they can. The shelter will anesthetize the dog and bring it to the Carters', but they can't do it until Wednesday. Nancy and Don have that fenced-in backyard where he can move around more, and they'll also put a chain from his collar to a stake in the ground at least temporarily. The only other thing in the yard will be a shelter that he can't get behind, so the chain doesn't get wrapped around anything. JJ will go see him on Thursday after he's recovered from the drugs, and then he'll go every day and stand there with one or both of the Carters until he thinks the dog will let him come in, and then I guess we'll see. I only wish I could watch this unfold. What an adventure! I tell you, that kid is destined for something great. He's goddamned amazing."

"Andy, language! Please."

"Sorry, Irene, but this is great stuff, and that kid ... well, I just wish he weren't going away, that's all."

I got a weird feeling. It reminded me of when Chris had signed up, and Mom had wanted to hang on to him and keep him home, and Dad had been so proud that he was going. I had understood both of them. With JJ, it was like I wanted him to leave. But at the same time, I didn't.

Thursday came, and although it seemed the Carters did get their dog delivered, JJ didn't go over when he'd expected to. Instead, the Carters showed up at the store. Or, Mr. Carter did. I positioned myself where I could hear what he told JJ.

"It's Nancy's mother. We've just heard she may not live through the night, so we have to go now. This afternoon. The dog is in the yard, JJ, and he's healthy enough, but at least as violent as he was. We have neighbors who'll take care of him while we're gone. That is, they'll throw food over, and fill his bowl from a hose from outside the fence. It's awful, and I hate to do this to him. If we'd known, we'd have left him in the shelter until we got back. But as it is ..."

"So he won't see either of you for a few days at least?"

"Right."

"I should go over, anyway, maybe after dinner, even though you won't be there and I can't work with you. But he should see something, someone familiar. I'll bring him the same treats I gave him before. I'll go over each day like that, after work here, so at least he gets used to me, even if he can't get used to you yet. Is that all right?"

"Yes, yes. Of course."

"And please tell Mrs. Carter how sorry I am about her mother. I wouldn't say this to her, but I think I should tell you this may set us back a little. Not so much the few days you'll be gone, but if her mother dies, Mrs. Carter may not have the focus she needs, and she'll feel very vulnerable. The dog will sense that. We'll just have to see."

Mr. Carter nodded, squeezed JJ's shoulder, and left. JJ went into the office, I guess to tell Dad how things stood. I went back to work, thinking, *You mean her adoptive mother.* I couldn't help wondering if my mom was right, and Mrs. Carter kept identifying with these hard-luck cases because she'd been one herself.

Just before closing, Marty and Kevin made an entrance at the door of the stockroom. At least they hadn't come in through the back. I'd just got back from walking Dante, and he wasn't yet tied up to his metal shelves. Marty stood in the doorway, ready to head for the proverbial hills if necessary. Kevin disappeared back into the store.

"So, Paul. My man. Just checking. What did you decide to do about your date dilemma?"

"I'm taking her out, Marty, but that's it. I'm not doing anything to tarnish her virtue. And if you don't like it, you can have your money back now."

He sucked on his cheeks for a second. "And how will you pay for this pointless date? And with no car?"

"Oh, I'll have money. And wheels. I don't need you after all. Though"—I was feeling like I'd been a little harsh and wanted to soften it—"I do appreciate the loan. Do you want it back now?"

Marty shrugged. "A deal's a deal. You still owe me the extra five, but pay it back anytime between now and October."

I finished tying Dante up, but he didn't take his eyes off of Marty.

"Hey," Marty said, looking a little more relaxed now, "what happened with that Rottweiler? Did the Carters take it?"

"Yeah. It's quite the monster, by all accounts. Inside a fence *and* chained to a stake in the ground."

"And is the Wunderkind taming it?"

"Not yet. The Carters had to go out of town for a few days. Something to do with her mother." I edged Marty out of the room with me and shut the door. "Where's your partner in crime?"

"Scouting out the fag."

"Marty, don't you guys do anything to him, do you hear me? Every time you show up here I get into shit, and it's all your fault."

"Chill, Paul! Kevin's just hovering. Anyway, he never gets the brilliant ideas. It's always me." He laughed. "In fact, I'm gettin' one now. Let's go find Dodge."

It was the end of the day, and really there wasn't much more for me to do, and I wanted to know what the hell was up Marty's sleeve this time. We found Kevin leaning against the end of a display case. He was watching JJ clean out a hamster cage and, from what I could tell, trying his best to seem intimidating. Little did he know what types of bullies that kid could handle. Marty grinned and crooked his finger at Kevin to follow. We moved one aisle and several feet away, and Marty revealed his master plan.

"Okay, here's the picture. The Carters are away, right? And that monster dog is all alone, poor fellow. So I say we go and pay him a visit."

I hated the sound of this. "Kaufman, what the hell are you thinking? That thing would eat you alive."

"That's what everyone is saying. Let's see if they're right. Let's give the fellow a chance to show his stuff."

"Marty, I've heard about his 'stuff.' He's a killer. No joke. He's lots worse than Dante." Visions of what Cain could do to a teenage prankster flew through my mind, and they were ugly. And from Dad's description of Geronimo, he was even worse.

Kevin started making chicken noises, and it pissed me off. I came close to pointing out that Marty was already afraid of Dante, and he was half tame. "Look you guys, this is serious stuff. I'll tell you what's gonna happen. Either one or both of you will get mauled or worse, or that dog's gonna have to be killed, or both."

Marty's arm found its way across my shoulders. "Paul, boy-o, it ain't both of us. It's all of us. All three. We're all going." He slapped the back of my head and cackled, then looked toward the office, probably to see if Dad or Carol was bearing down on him. They weren't. "So we'll let you close up shop, and then just come out to the front. Kevin and me will be in the car, waiting for you."

"Marty! Wait!" But they were off. I stood there watching Marty's lope, calculated for a neat balance between belligerence and devil-may-care, wondering what the fuck I should do. If I didn't go with them, there'd be no hope for that dog. If I did, maybe I could keep them in check. And if I went to Dad and ratted...well, that would be the end of my life as a regular guy, as far as Marty was concerned. I'd become an Anthony-Don't-Call-Me-Tony faster than a pit bull could clamp its jaws on the neck of a German shepherd. And there'd be no Wunderkind attributes to salve my mangled self-image. I had nothing going for me, really.

I could tell JJ...but then what? How would he get there in time to do anything? Marty wasn't exactly gonna give him a lift to the scene of the proposed crime, and JJ wasn't planning to be there until after dinner. So, did I know enough about dogs yet to be any use? I'd learned an awful lot. I'd learned about Dante, and about Cain, and I was damned good with Truffles. I'd come a long way since Mozart had told me to get lost. My mind started to bring up the question of that Border collie, but—hell, those dogs are half human, anyway. They don't count for this tally.

So—maybe. Just maybe I could help.

Dad told me he was leaving, and I said I'd stay behind with Dante for a little bit. He reminded me to lock the back door, which he hardly needed to do, but I just agreed. I guess he couldn't help himself.

When I went into the stockroom to say good night to Dante, JJ was in there. He was kind of squatting across from Dante's bed, not really looking at the dog.

"What are you doing in here?" I asked, irritated. "I thought you'd left." He looked at me like he needed to say something, but he didn't. "Well?" I wanted him to go so I could make up my mind about what to do. I wanted a moment alone with Dante.

"Just thinking. Trying to figure something out." He gave me this intense look, and it gave me the willies. Like he was thinking about me. And I didn't really want a gay guy thinking about me.

"Look, um, JJ, I don't know what's going on here, but...you wouldn't, like, try anything, would you?"

He blinked. But he was still staring at me. "What?" He barked out a kind of laugh. "Just how appealing do you think you are? Or maybe you think that just because I'm gay I'm going to jump your bones."

"You don't have to sound like it's so weird." I felt really stupid saying everything I was saying. It was coming out of nowhere, and it made no sense, and I couldn't stop the babble falling out of my mouth. I just wanted to get rid of him. "It wouldn't be the first time a straight kid was...you know, seduced by a homosexual."

Now I *really* didn't like the look I was getting, but for a different reason. Hell, I liked this kid; he'd just done me this huge favor. Why was I saying all this crap to him?

He stood and started to walk past me into the store. But then he turned to face me again. "You know what? If I decide I want you, you'll know it. I'm out of here."

I closed my eyes and stood there a second, hating what I'd said, angry that I was in this position to begin with. I'd just wanted him out, that's all. It was as much for his good as mine.

It was for both of us. So I wouldn't have to help Marty tie him up to a tree someplace and torture him.

*Fuck Marty, anyway.* I crouched down in front of Dante and rubbed his good ear. "You be safe, old boy. I gotta go help another dog." I went out the back door, made sure it was locked, and trotted to the front of the building.

The Mustang was the only car out there, predictably. I wondered if Marty had been driving around the block to make sure my dad had left. Kevin got out and pushed the back of the passenger seat forward so I could clamber into the back—guess number three was my pecking order in this pack—and Marty gunned the engine. Marty, the leader. And I thought I could show him otherwise, talk him out of taunting the Rottweiler? What was I, crazy? I didn't have the balls for this. I nearly called to him to stop and let me out, but I didn't actually think he would. Then I would be in the even more awkward position of having lost my nerve without being allowed to back out of the mission.

All the way to the Carters' I prayed that Marty's reckless driving would cause us to be stopped by a cop, but that never happens when you need it to. So, much sooner than it would have seemed at any other time, we were there. The house was on a corner lot, and the side yard was parallel to Abbott Street with the chain-link fence right there. The door to the yard was at the corner of the fence near the house. Marty pulled up alongside the fence, turned the engine off, and the next thing we knew there was this *CLANG* from inside the yard. The dog—or rather, the canine monster—had literally thrown itself as hard as it could against the limits of the chain attached to the stake in the ground. All three of us jumped and leaned away from the fence side of the car, the side Kevin and I were on.

His voice low with a kind of awe, Kevin said, "Holy shit, Batman."

Marty, who had jumped right along with us, tried to pretend he wasn't fazed. "Aw, he's not so tough. C'mon." He got out and slammed his door just about in synch with the next *CLANG* from inside the fence. Marty stood there, the car between him and the fence, thumbs in his jeans belt loops, pretending he wasn't scared shitless. I was busy contrasting this sight with the picture my father had drawn of puny little JJ, walking right up to nearly this exact same scene without a tremor or a falter. Only JJ had gotten even closer to the dog; now, Geronimo was on a chain *and* inside a fence. JJ had stood within inches of a straining fence.

"He's not so tough," Marty repeated, probably trying to reassure himself, but the tone of his voice gave him away. "He doesn't even bark. What kind of a dog doesn't bark?"

It was time for me to use the little bit of knowledge I'd accrued over the summer from my own stupid moves. I leaned toward the open window beside Kevin and said, "I'll tell you what kind of a dog he is. A killer. A dog that doesn't even bother to bark isn't warning you. He isn't trying to chase you away. He just wants to rip out your guts. Get back in the car; we don't have anything to prove here."

*CLANG.*

"I think I like this dog."

*Shit.*

"Seriously. I can respect a dog like that. Kevin, Paul, get out of the car. Let's see what he's got to show us."

Kevin was with me. Almost. "Paul's right, Marty. We don't need to do this."

Marty turned swiftly toward the car and pounded the roof once with a fist.

*CLANG.*

I don't know what made Kevin jump more, but I was beyond jumping. I was terrified. But Kevin got out, and I knew that if I was going to have any influence here I needed to be seen as something other than the frightened kid I felt like. So I got out, too, and Marty led the way to the fence door. It was padlocked with a chain.

Now Geronimo was barking, and snarling, and just like Dad had said there was foam flying from his mouth. He'd reached the end of his chain and had stayed there, so maybe the *CLANG* was over, anyway.

"Stay put," Marty said, and headed to his trunk. He opened it and took out that huge toolbox he kept in there, setting it on the ground. He came back with a mallet.

I tried. I really, really tried to stop him. "Marty, this is getting way beyond dog baiting. You're into breaking and entering territory now." I could barely hear myself over the noise the dog was making, and then there was the noise of Marty's mallet hitting the lock. And again. *Please, please, somebody hear this racket, look at what's going on, and yell at us! Please! Why is it that that happens only when you don't want it to? Why does everything happen at the wrong fucking time?*

"This dog's got hold of me, Paul, my boy." Another mallet strike. "I've gotta get in there and test his mettle."

"Are you *crazy?* Marty, please! Stop this now!"

Even Kevin was worried again. "Marty, just hold on. What do you think you're gonna do, exactly?"

One final swing of the mallet broke through the chain the padlock was on, and both it and the chain fell to the ground. The door opened about an inch. Geronimo had stopped barking and was now just standing there, snarling and foaming. He was huge. And there was no doubt he wanted boy meat for dinner.

Marty pushed the door open and stepped into the yard.

Any thoughts I'd had about Marty not having the guts he'd pretended to vanished. He stood there, four feet inside the fence, staring at that monster, who was staring back at him from a mere ten or so feet away. Marty put his hands on his hips and turned to us.

"You fraidy cats coming in? What's the matter? Is the sky falling or something?"

Kevin looked at me and shrugged like he'd had his last meal on earth and couldn't afford to care, and then he followed Marty in and took his place at Marty's right hand.

"Paul? Chicken? And here I thought you'd been learning all about dogs this summer, from the Wunderkind. I would have thought you'd be the most fearless of all. Didn't the little faggot teach you anything after all?"

I took a deep breath and walked through the open fence door. I ignored Geronimo as best I could, and something in me said it would be better if the dog didn't associate me with the other two guys. So I stood next to Kevin, a little away from both of them. At first I didn't realize that what this did was to put me the farthest of the three of us from the door. But something brought that to my attention real quick.

Geronimo turned his back on us, trotted a little distance away, and just as Marty was saying, "See? We've got him on the defens..." the dog charged. The chain snapped away from the stake and trailed behind him.

At first the dog must have been as surprised as we were, which gave Marty and Kevin a chance to get to the door. In a kind of slow motion I watched them, knowing that by the time both of them got through the door Geronimo would be on top of them and I would be trapped. So I headed for the other corner of the fence along the road, thinking I would climb over— or even back in if the dog got out. It was a question of life or death, and I knew it.

But the dog didn't head for Marty and Kevin. He headed straight for me. I'm not sure what happened; I think he must have stepped on his own chain. Because instead of his jaws locking on to me someplace, he kind of stumbled against me. He knocked me down, and I fell into the corner of the fence on the ground and just covered my head with my arms.

*Jesus, oh God, anybody, help me. Please, please help me. Please. Please.*

Somewhere in the middle of my plea I realized that I wasn't being torn limb from limb. It took a lot out of me, but I peeked cautiously in the direction of the dog. And there he was. He was practically on top of me, or so it seemed. And he was huge, and staring, and drooling, and silent as Death itself.

I heard the Mustang's engine rev up and Kevin's voice calling, "Landon! Get up! Climb over the fence, man! Get out of there!"

*What would JJ do?*

I ventured a glance toward the car. Kevin was in the backseat, the passenger side door was open just a crack, and Marty was gunning the engine, ready to fly out of there.

I looked back toward the dog and slowly started to move an arm toward the fence.

"Don't even think about it." Geronimo said it with his snarl.

*Christ, a talking Border collie, a beagle, and now this?* I pulled my arm back, wondering how long he would stand guard like that if I just didn't move. Before I came to any conclusions there was motion outside the fence, and Kevin's voice from a little farther away than that, shouting.

"Marty! For God's sake, don't. You'll hit Paul!"

"Shut the fuck up! I know what I'm doing."

Growling from the dog. Another peek in the general direction of the car and I knew what Kevin had been shouting about. There stood Marty, perfect shooter's stance, hands gripping the snub-nose thirty-eight I'd taken him to get. *What irony. I'm going to be shot to death by a gun I helped procure.*

If Marty was gonna shoot the dog, he had to get the gun barrel positioned into an opening of the chain-link fence. But every time he moved toward the fence, the dog nearly went ballistic. When he backed off the dog did, too, but only a little. I figured, you know, my time had come; the only question was whether I'd get torn to bits by Geronimo's pearly whites or shot through the head by a snub-nose thirty-eight.

Then there was another sound, like someone getting off a bicycle in a hurry. Marty's voice said, "What the ..." and the next thing I knew JJ was there. The Jesus nut. The one your life depends on. *Where the hell did that come from?* I didn't see him, but I heard his voice.

"Paul." Calm. How could he sound so calm? He was ignoring Marty. "Paul, it's JJ. Listen carefully to me. Don't make eye contact with the dog. Look down. And stay still. He sees you as submissive at the moment. That's why he's not attacking. Don't try to take the lead with this dog, not at this time. Make a whimpering sound if you understand me, but don't speak."

*Like I could dominate this creature?* I whimpered, all right. It was all I could do.

"I'll try to get him to move far enough away from you so you can get up the fence. Watch where his feet are, but don't look at his face. Okay?"

Whimper. And I heard something land behind the dog. I think his ears twitched, but he didn't move, still drooling on me. Another treat, closer. And another. Obviously Geronimo wanted me more than treats.

JJ said, "It isn't working. I'm going to come in, and I'm going to be submissive as well. I'll try to get his attention away from you. Got that?"

Whimper.

I couldn't see what he was doing, and I didn't have a clue why he'd be any better off in here than I was, but I wasn't about to argue with him. Carefully not looking at the dog—though I did sneak a quick peek a few times—I could barely see that JJ was at the fence door now, and that he was getting down onto the ground. It was almost like he was in boot camp, doing grunt training and slithering across the ground to stay below enemy fire. He stopped moving when the dog growled, and he waited, and then he moved forward again. I glanced outside the fence toward Marty, who had lowered his arms but was still in shooter's stance, watching JJ like he was mesmerized by the stupidity in front of him.

When JJ was a few feet away from me, the dog's full attention on him, he curled into a ball on his side. I barely caught some motion, and something went flying into the air. It landed several feet behind the dog, who watched it but didn't move. JJ shot another so it landed a little closer to the dog. And then I got it. He was using the treats like he'd done at the shelter. Only from a much more precarious position.

Geronimo could get to the second treat without moving too far away from his prey—that would be me—and he gobbled it up. JJ shot out another. He was doing it from that curled position, and at first I couldn't figure why. But then it hit me that he didn't want the dog to see that there was a whole bag of the things. So JJ didn't want the dog attacking him for the treats, and since they were his only weapon, as it were, he didn't want to lose them all at once.

The dog moved toward the last treat and ate that. He looked back at me, but I stayed still. JJ shot again, farther away this time. The dog turned and followed the treat, and I saw my chance. Like lightning I shot up and scrambled up that fence. My phys ed teacher would have been proud.

Marty came over and grabbed my arm. "C'mon. Let's get outta here." He pulled me toward the car.

JJ was still in there with that killer. I yanked my arm away from Marty, stopped dead, and turned to look. JJ was still there, curled on his side in the dirt, watching me. I couldn't read his expression, but it didn't really matter.

"Paul! Get in the car!" Marty was half in already, and I could see Kevin's head in the back. I walked to the partly open passenger door, opened it a little, and slammed it shut.

"Paul, what the fuck!"

Behind the car, the bright red toolbox nestled in a clump of green grass. It was calling to me. I picked it up and headed for the door that led into Geronimo's den. Over my shoulder I said, "You can leave if you want. I'm not deserting JJ."

I stopped at the door to assess the situation inside. JJ hadn't moved, and Geronimo was about to make a dash toward me. I had to make my position clear to him quickly. I fell to the ground, pulling the door so that it looked closed, and he just trotted over to me, growling, slobbering, but not biting. He sniffed my hair and grabbed at my shoulder with his teeth but didn't sink them in. I whimpered.

Something landed just behind Geronimo. A treat. And he turned and ate it. As if it didn't matter, I heard the sound of the Mustang taking off.

JJ shot treat after treat, and gradually I crawled toward JJ, dragging the toolbox as quietly as possible, until the dog was far enough away that JJ felt he could speak.

He kept his voice low and even. "What we need to do is re-fasten his chain to the stake and then get out and fasten the chain on the fence door." He shot a treat. "You're doing great, by the way. You learn fast."

"Our lives would seem to depend on it."

"They do. And I'm not kidding. This is serious stuff. Just stay calm and don't give him any reason to think he's being challenged."

"He didn't bite me; just clamped on to my shoulder for a second. I whimpered, and he let go."

Some breath escaped JJ like he was relaxing a little. "That's good. That's very good. What you need to do is slowly make your way to the stake. Can you see where it is?"

I looked around. If I'd been standing, I probably would have missed it, especially since it was getting darker. Your perspective changes when you're crawling on the ground, though, like Chris could see something Mason hadn't, that night in the jungle. I saw the stake over near the shelter. "Yes."

"Go toward it, slowly, stopping every few feet to avoid getting his suspicions up. I've got to start reserving these things or I'll run out, so just go slow. Now here's the most important part. You need to go in a direction that will allow you to pick up the end of his chain. I'm going to try and keep him positioned so that he's within a radius of the stake that's shorter than the chain, but keep your wits about you and whatever you do, don't pull on the chain so that he feels it on his collar."

It was an eternity. I created a movie scene in my head. Or, it was a movie scene to me. It was real life for an awful lot of guys, and it had been real for Chris. I pretended I was making my way through a booby-trapped patch of jungle. It got my mind off the dog and helped me move slowly and carefully. And it worked.

I knew what I had to do next, but Geronimo wasn't getting with the program. As soon as I flipped open the box and started rummaging for the right tools, he came over and stood practically on top of me. I moved excruciatingly slowly, but even so he kept gripping one of my hands with his drooling muzzle. He never broke the skin, but each time he did this I had to hold still and whimper. Once he didn't let go, and I heard a treat land nearby. He went to fetch it.

It must have taken me—oh, I don't know, a lifetime?—to refasten that chain, but I did it. Between disciplinary bites from Geronimo, and the occasional lobbing of a treat it just took forever. Finally I had the tools back in the box and refastened the lid.

I could barely hear JJ say, "Curl onto your side for a minute and just hold still. Let him think you're not doing anything at all."

*I'm not doing anything at all. That's easy.*

After a minute or so, "Now, move toward the door, just as slowly as you moved toward the stake."

The occasional treat volley supported my escape, and I made it without setting off any booby traps. I was outside the fence, but I knew better than to do anything that would attract Geronimo's attention. I stayed on the ground. JJ started to move toward the door, and Geronimo seemed to figure out that something was up. He went to JJ and stood over him so that his front paws were on the ground on one side of JJ, and his hind paws were on the other. JJ stayed curled into a tight ball for maybe three minutes? Four? He didn't dare move even enough to shoot a treat out.

Then Geronimo figured out where the treats were. His huge head lowered itself toward JJ's stomach, where his hands were crushing the nearly empty bag, and the dog grabbed it. The head came up, bag in the jaws, and thrashed back and forth. What treats were left went flying, and Geronimo left JJ to go find some.

If I thought I'd moved fast to get up that fence, JJ was even faster. He shot up from the ground and lunged for the door. Behind him, Geronimo deserted his candy hunt and charged, but he was already pretty far out on the chain. It clanged, but it held.

JJ was safe.

I picked up the chain that had fallen when Marty had broken it, knowing that if Geronimo had figured out once how to break that chain he could do it again. Working as fast as possible, I managed to open a link and fasten the chain around the door.

JJ said, "I think you have enough chain to wrap another piece around."

I looked at him like he was crazy and, for the first time, noticed he was cradling his left hand. Blood was seeping between the fingers of his right hand where he was holding his left in it.

"My God. How bad are you hurt?"

"I'll live. Just get the second chain length on, will you?"

We left Geronimo snarling in frustrated fury, still on his chain, the door securely fastened. Only then did I notice that it was my bike that JJ had ridden to get here.

"C'mon," I said to him. "Let's knock on some doors and call your mom or someone to come get you and get that stitched or whatever."

He was oddly compliant, and he let me take over. I couldn't tell how bad the bite was, but if it subdued JJ I figured it had to be pretty awful. Two houses away someone was home and let us in. We phoned his mom, gave her the address, and then went to sit on the front steps to wait, after the neighbor ran cool water over JJ's hand and wrapped some gauze treated with antiseptic around it.

We sat there silently for a few minutes. Then I said, "I'm sorry."

JJ took a shaky breath. "For what?"

"For the things I said at the store earlier. It's just that I needed to be alone to think what to do, and you were looking at me so oddly."

He nodded. "I knew what they were planning. I heard them tell you. And I was trying to figure out whether you'd be open to...you know, betraying them. Working with me to stop them."

"I don't know what we could have done. I did my best to stop them. That's why I came." Silence for a few minutes. I asked, "Does that hurt real bad?"

"Yeah."

I wrapped my arm around JJ's shoulders. He leaned against me, and we stayed like that until his mom's car appeared.

For all I was worried about JJ's wound, I was distracted by his mom. Sure, she was in her forties probably, but she was gorgeous. Thick dark hair around her shoulders, nice build, and it must have been from her that JJ got his sweet face and those gorgeous eyes. But she was all business. She bundled JJ into the car and took off, leaving me there feeling like I'd swung at something and missed. If it hadn't been for Geronimo over there, lying down now but watchful and as close as he could get to the fence, I don't know how long it might have been before I snapped to and went to fetch my bicycle. Geronimo charged once as I approached the bike, but I got away as quickly as I could so he wouldn't break that fucking chain again. I was not, I mean *not,* going back in there to repair it.

I was kind of late for dinner. Given that, and given that JJ was going to show up at work the next day—if he even came to work the next day—with his hand all bandaged, I figured I'd better come clean to my folks. Or, as clean as I needed to. I figured they didn't need details like Marty's gun.

I was barely in the door when Dad's voice, originating from the kitchen table, thundered through the air. "Young man, where have you been?"

I didn't answer, not wanting to yell from a room away. I waited until I was in the kitchen and spoke calmly and quietly. I was not going to let Dad rile me. "JJ and I were trying to stop Marty and Kevin from taunting Geronimo. It got a little messy, and JJ got bit. His mom is taking him to get patched up now, but I imagine his left hand will be in bandages tomorrow. If he comes to work."

I almost fell into the silence that followed this pronouncement. Mom stopped between the table and the stove, where she was probably headed to get my dinner, and stared at me. Dad sat there, his jaw hanging a little open for a few seconds.

Finally, his voice rising in volume, Dad said, "What did you say?"

I pulled out my chair, willing myself not to rise to his challenge, not to try and shout him down. "Marty heard about the
Carters leaving town, and he thought it would be fun to see
how ferocious Geronimo was. He wanted me to go with them. I
wasn't going to, but then it occurred to me I might be able to
keep the problem to a dull roar."

Before I could get anything else out, Dad nearly shouted,
"And you failed! What's this about JJ's hand?"

I looked at him a second, let a few beats go by, gave Mom a
chance to sit down, and then said, "I'll tell you what happened
if you'll let me." I waited. He didn't say anything, so I went on
with the story, making sure that JJ's courage was noted, but so
was mine. I made it clear that I could have got away, that I could
have left JJ in there with the Rottie, but that I went back in to
help him. And I think I did it more or less like Chris had told
his war stories. Not glorifying myself, just telling it like it was.

When I was done, both my folks just looked at me. And
somewhere in there it occurred to me that I'd crossed some
line. I'd passed some test. I'd stood up to Dad in a way that was
my way. Not Chris's way, which had worked for Chris, but in my
way. And I felt a warm glow not unlike the one I'd felt in
church all those months ago. The time I'd felt as though Jesus,
or God, or somebody had heard me. Had taken me seriously.

I went to the stove and helped myself to some dinner.

# Chapter 15

JJ, of course, did come into work the next day, and his left hand was bandaged. Which meant that he wasn't going to be doing any cleaning of fish tanks, probably until he left to go to school in just a couple of weeks.

I managed to arrange things so that we had our lunch breaks at the same time, and not at the same time as Angela; I wanted to talk with JJ alone.

He was already at a table, doing his best to manage his lunch using his right hand and only a couple of free fingers on his left. I sat down across from him.

"Want some help?"

He grinned at me. "Sure."

I leaned over to extricate his sandwich from its wrapping. "So how many stitches?"

"Not too many. And no permanent damage. Mostly it's just a question of making sure there's no infection. The really good news is that rabies is very unlikely, since Geronimo hadn't come into contact with any other animals for so long. And he was at the shelter for long enough that he would start to show signs before treatment would be too late for me. The shelter had already vaccinated him while he was unconscious, of course, but that doesn't mean he wasn't already sick. We'll see, but I'm not worried."

"Will they put him down, do you think?"

JJ took a bite of sandwich and looked at me while he chewed for a few seconds. Then he said, "Kill him, Paul. You mean will they kill him. I don't like using those euphemisms. 'Put him down.' 'Put him to sleep.' 'Euthanize him.' No matter what they call it, it's killing. So that's what I say. And the answer is, I don't think so." He set his sandwich down and chuckled. "As a matter of fact, my mom is now interested. I think that even once I've left for school, she's going to try and convince the Carters to let her work with him." He smiled at me. "Maybe you'd like to help."

"Me?"

"Why not? You've learned a lot about handling dogs, and you sure showed that you aren't too afraid to be useful. Which reminds me. Thank you. I was a little too stressed out yesterday, after our adventure, to say that. But what you did took guts. Coming back in like that." He shook his head slowly. "I have to admit, I hadn't really thought out what I was going to do, once I got in there, other than give you a chance to get out. But thank God your friends left their toolbox! Anyway, that was really smart of you. And brave. So, thank you." He reached his right hand across the table toward me. As I took it in mine, I couldn't help remembering the time our hands had touched and I'd pulled back. Not this time.

Around midafternoon, working alone on fish tanks, I noticed Kevin Dodge roaming—or skulking, really—around the store, alone as far as I could tell. I let him look until he found me; I didn't feel like making anything easy for him.

"Hey, Paul." He stood there, hands in his pockets, glancing around, probably to see if my dad was bearing down on him. I looked up, caught his eye, and looked back at my work again. I said nothing. From him, "How's it going?"

Without even a glance at him I said, "Ducky."

He tried a snicker. "You, uh, you got out of that okay yesterday? Don't see any gaping wounds."

"Not on me." I still wouldn't look at him.

"That's good, then." He stood there awkwardly for maybe another thirty seconds before I decided to cut him a little slack. At least he'd come to find out if I was still alive, which is more than Mr. Kaufman had done, and it had been Marty's brilliant idea.

"There was someone else involved, you know. I mean, involved in a good way. Someone who did get hurt."

"So the dog got him? Bad?"

I stood up. "Do you care?"

Kevin shrugged and looked uncomfortable. "Look, Paul, I didn't want any of that to happen, y'know. I was with you, man. Trying to back Marty down. He just wouldn't do it."

"And you peeled off with him, leaving JJ and me in the lion's den. You're a real pal, Kevin."

His voice got kind of squeaky. "Look, man, I'm sorry about that. It was just that...aw, shit, I don't know what it was."

"I do. It's called cowardice. You were afraid of the dog, you were afraid of getting caught. And you're afraid of Marty." He turned away from me but didn't move off. "Are you always gonna be afraid of Marty?"

He wheeled back. "Aren't you? I didn't see you telling him off!"

"You didn't see me run away with him, either. And if he were here right now I'd tell him a thing or two. And if JJ had lost more than a chunk of his left hand, I'd have gone to the police. He's a menace, Kevin. Dump him. Or go down with him."

After another few seconds of shrinking into his own shoulders he asked, "So JJ's all right then? Mostly?"

"Mostly." I decided to take a chance. See if Kevin had anything salvageable in him. See if maybe he could be recovered. "He's doing inventory in the stockroom. Maybe if you pay him a quarter he'll let you see his stitches."

I bent back over my task to give Kevin some space to make his decision in. It felt really good to see him head toward the stockroom. I knew he was going in to apologize, or at least to approximate that intention.

Before I fell asleep that night, I thought again about taking JJ's hand over the picnic table. And about sitting with him to wait for his mom, when he'd leaned against me. If anyone had told me even a week earlier that those things wouldn't creep me out, I'd have thought they were nuts. But they didn't. They didn't creep me out at all.

In the darkness over my head, it seemed like that Border collie was there, mouth open in a grin. "See?" he said, tongue dangling wetly out of his mouth. "When you're not afraid of something, you don't have to strike out at it."

I blinked at him. "Are you telling me I was afraid of JJ?"

"Weren't you? Weren't you afraid to touch him? To have Marty even threaten to paint you with the same brush?"

*Marty.* "Are you telling me that Marty is afraid of JJ?"

"Terrified."

I grinned back at the dog. He was right. Just like Dante, and the tattooed guy, Marty was aggressive toward things he feared. Which seems to be life in general, but—for Marty, anyway—JJ in particular, and what he represented.

The dog asked, "So, are you still afraid of Chris?"

"That's different."

"Why?"

Why? Why was it different? I wasn't afraid of Chris, anyway; the dog was wrong about that. Okay, I hadn't wanted Chris to touch me just after he'd told me about himself. But that wasn't what I felt the strongest about. To the dog, I said, "Chris betrayed me. He lied to me, in effect, anyway. He made me think things about him that weren't true, and he hid what was real."

"He hid the part he knew you'd hate. And why do you suppose he did that? Do you think maybe he couldn't trust you to still love him?"

I opened my mouth to shout *I do so still love him!* But nothing came out.

I rolled my face into the pillow and refused to talk to the dog any longer. *I do love Chris. I do. I really do. He's my brother, and I love him. I hate that he never told me. I hate that he didn't trust me until it was too late. Until I didn't have time to get used to things. But I don't hate him.*

\* \* \*

My date with Laura was beyond great. I was such a gentleman, parking the car and going in to chat with her folks for a few minutes, which included a brief visit with Truffles as well, and some glory moments as Mrs. Holmes told her husband how marvelous I was with dogs.

I didn't try any funny stuff with Laura during the movie like I had with Jenny, though I did take her hand at one point. She let me hold it for a few minutes, which I took to mean that I could have a good-night kiss.

I got several. And thanks to all my experience with Jenny, and to the fact that I'm not some kid who's still tying his sweatshirt around his waist with the sleeves hanging in front to hide any unintentional activity, I was able to keep everything within the bounds of what I thought she'd approve of, with just a hint that there was more where that came from. And she agreed to see me again.

So on Sunday I made it a point to talk to JJ and thank him for setting me up the day we worked with Truffles. He asked about the date, and I told him it had been fantastic and would, I hoped, be the first of many.

JJ walked Dante with me late in the afternoon. At first I wasn't sure why; he had to keep his hand in a sling when he walked so it wouldn't just dangle, and at first it didn't even seem like he wanted to talk. But eventually he did.

"That's really great about Laura, Paul. I get the sense you've liked her for a while."

"Yuh. Like, over a year. I almost had a date with her last November, but then my brother came home at the wrong time and Mom made me stay home the whole time he was with us."

"Doesn't sound like you lost any serious ground. With Laura, I mean." Didn't seem to be much to say to that, so we took a few blocks in silence, except for a couple of times Dante tried to act up a little. Then JJ said, "This, um, this may be a little weird for you, and if you think so that's okay. But if you'd like to meet my friend, he's picking me up after work."

I tried stalling for time. "What's his name?"

"Ben. He's a freshman in the College of Humanities at Carnegie Mellon. He wants to be a social worker."

Okay, that was more than I'd asked. But I was still stalling. "Won't get to see much of him if you're at Cornell. That's gotta be . . ."

"It's about a six-hour car ride. We'll see how it goes."

Which I took to mean it probably wouldn't go very well, in terms of staying together. We walked along in more silence, and it occurred to me that maybe I could get used to the idea of JJ being gay. Maybe not even notice it, like I barely noticed my dad's limp anymore. We were almost back to the store when I finally said, "Anyway, sure. I'd like to meet him. You met Laura, after all, right?"

He beamed at me. "Right."

So I was settling Dante down for the night, and everyone else but Carol had left, when there was a rap on the stockroom door; someone was outside in the back. Dante growled just for a second, and I hushed him. When I opened the door, there was a guy who looked like he must have been the one who kissed JJ that day.

"You Ben?" I asked, thinking he didn't look gay, particularly. But then, I wouldn't have thought Chris did, either.

"Ben Sanborn." He held out his hand; second homosexual hand I'd shaken in only a few days. "You're Paul?"

"Yeah."

"It's great to meet you. Sorry to intrude back here, but the front door was locked already. I got here a little later than I'd hoped."

I heard JJ's voice behind me. "Looks like you two have met already. I saw your car, Ben. I figured you'd come around the back. I'm about ready to leave."

"Not so fast, there. I was kind of hoping I could meet this famous dog, too. Will you introduce us, please?"

For the first time since Ben had knocked, it occurred to me that Dante hadn't growled or anything. If that had been Marty, Dante would have been on his feet, making threatening noises. But with Ben? Nothing.

JJ walked toward the dog and Ben followed, not looking at Dante. Well schooled, evidently. JJ said, "This is a pop quiz, Paul. What are we doing right now?"

I almost chuckled. Teaching, even now. "You're letting him know you accept Ben, and you're letting Dante sniff and see who he is."

JJ smiled at me and then at Ben. "He's a good student."

"I can see that."

Eventually Ben and Dante got to the touching stage, and the dog let Ben scratch behind his ears, not that there was much left of one of them.

"This the ear Cain consumed?" Ben asked.

"It's healed pretty well, hasn't it?"

I said, "So you know the canine warrior, I guess. I'm not sure I ever want to see him again!"

JJ laughed. "Too bad. You will, if you work with my mom on Geronimo. She told me to ask if you wanted to. She'll probably use Cain to help socialize the Rottie."

Ben turned to me. "Do you think you'll do that? What a challenge, and what an experience. JJ will be so jealous he can't be a part of that."

The two of them hadn't touched since Ben had arrived, but now Ben crooked his arm around JJ's neck and pulled their heads together. They didn't kiss or anything, but the affection was obvious.

At that moment, the door from inside the store opened and Dad walked in. Everyone froze. The tension was so intense that Dante felt it and made some noise that was half-whine, half-growl. What the hell was Dad doing here, anyway? On Sunday afternoon?

JJ recovered first. "Ben Sanborn, this is the store owner and Paul's father, Mr. Landon." Ben stepped toward my dad, who was still just inside the door, and extended his hand. Dad looked at it, and at first I didn't think he was going to take it, but Ben was just standing there holding it out like he wasn't going anywhere. If my dad was going to refuse the handshake, he was gonna have to make it real obvious. Finally he took Ben's hand, but he let it go as soon as he could.

Again, JJ was the one who spoke. "We'd better get going. See you tomorrow, Mr. Landon." He and Ben threaded their way past me and out the back door.

Dante and I were still holding our breath when Dad said, "Like hell you will." Quiet. Under his breath, almost. Almost a growl. He stared at the now-closed door.

I was trying to make sense out of what I was feeling. I mean, JJ being gay was a piece of information I'd been holding myself back from telling Dad most of the summer. Sometimes it had been a major effort. But now? Now I didn't want him to know. I didn't want him to do or say any of the things I had once wanted him to do and say.

Dad turned to me. "Was that what I think it was?"

*How the hell do I respond to that?* "What do you mean?"

Still looking at me, Dad pointed his whole arm at the door. His voice louder now, he said, "Is that boy a faggot?"

JJ had reacted very badly the one time I'd used that word in his hearing. And now, to my ears, it sounded like an insult he didn't deserve. I could answer Dad's question. I knew the answer. I didn't want to answer. "What difference would it make if he were?"

"What difference? What kind of a dumb-ass question is that?" Louder still now. "I will not have a homosexual working in my store! Do you hear me? Now, tell me if you knew this about him!"

I couldn't have said whether my father reminded me more of Marty Kaufman or of Geronimo at that moment. Maybe somewhere between the two. Ranting and railing away at something that was absolutely no threat to him, shouting at me, showing aggression that had fear underneath it. Just like the Border collie had said.

"What are you afraid of?"

"WHAT?"

It was an effort, but I kept my voice at somewhere near normal pitch. "You look terrified."

That floored him, briefly. He blinked stupidly a few times and then marched, limped, right at me. I think he expected me to back away. I didn't. "I'll show you how terrified I am," he growled at me. "Now tell me what you know." Dad was Dante, pacing, the first day I saw him. And I was JJ. Not moving. Standing right in his path, and not moving.

It's amazing how fast your mind moves. Only split seconds went by, and yet so many things bounced around in my head. Like, *Maybe I'm standing up to Dad like JJ had stood up to Dante, but JJ is a dog expert.* Like, *Maybe I don't like how Dad is reacting, but my own reactions to JJ have been nothing to brag about so far.* I almost said, *What would be so bad if Chris were gay?* I came so close.

Instead, I said, "What would be so bad if JJ were gay?"

Dad made some loud noise of disgust and headed toward the office. "Carol is waiting. We'll talk about this later."

I watched him go and then followed. I hung around outside the office door, just out of sight. Carol's voice said, "It's over a hundred dollars this time. This is the most that's been gone all summer."

I heard papers being flipped, nondescript sounds, and then Dad said, "I know who's been doing it. I'll be firing him tomorrow."

*Is he going to fire JJ for the missing money? He knows as well as I do who took it!* I stepped into the doorway. "You can't do this! JJ isn't the one who's stealing."

They both looked at me. Then Dad reached for the door and tried to shut it, but I held it open. Dad said, "This doesn't concern you, Paul."

I was shouting now. "It does! It does concern me. That kid saved my ass, and you can't fire him for just being who he is!"

"Carol?" Dad said. "Why don't you go home. Thanks for calling me tonight; you did the right thing."

She made her way to the door, looking as nervous as I felt. I hoped I was hiding it better. As soon as I heard the door handle click into place, I said, "Dad, you can't do this."

"Be quiet and listen to me. I know JJ is not stealing."

"Then why are you going to fire him?"

Honest to God, I could not make any sense out of the expression on his face. Maybe profound sadness? He almost looked like he was going to cry. He sat down heavily into his chair and dropped his head into his hands. I stood watching him, hearing the wall clock tick the seconds by. Finally he looked up at me. "For your sake."

I'd have bet the expression on my own face was pretty inscrutable at this point. I reached for a chair, too, and plunked myself down into it. "What?"

"Did you know he was gay?"

I could feel my brain scrambling desperately for some way to answer that without feeling like I was ratting on JJ. My eyes bounced around the room, my hands raised and fell a couple of times. I'd wanted to say this all summer! But now...I took a shaky breath. "Yes."

"How long have you known?"

"Pretty much since he got here."

"How?"

"What?"

"How did you find out?" It sounded like someone else's voice. So quiet, so tentative.

I shrugged uncomfortably. "Marty pointed it out to me, and sometime later I asked JJ."

Dad's turn to take a shaky breath. "So he never...he never did anything? To you?"

"Good God, Dad! No! Of course not. Why would you think that of him?"

Dad rubbed his face. "I'd never forgive myself if I put you in harm's way."

This made no sense to me. "You put Chris in harm's way." *Shit.*

"What did you say?"

It was now or never. I'd brought him up, now let me finish him off. "Chris was gay, Dad." I expected explosions. I expected earthquakes. I expected to have to run for my life. What I didn't expect was what he said.

"How did you know?"

How *did* I know? That's very different from "How *do* you know?" or "What the hell are you talking about?" In a kind of daze, I said, "He told me. The night before he went back, last November. But...did you know? And does Mom?"

"Yes." He sat back in his chair, hands resting limply on the desk. "Why do you think I was trying so hard to make a man out of him?" I could feel my face kind of scrunching up with effort, trying to understand what was going on. In the end I just shook my head, a slow boil starting in my guts as it dawned on me what I'd been through in the last several months to keep from Dad information he already had.

He went on. "I've known, but hoped I could change things, since Chris was eleven. I caught him doing stuff with another boy—some redheaded kid—that I wouldn't even have wanted him doing with a girl at that age. And I used the belt on him for the first and only time."

"I remember that."

"You may also remember how he reacted."

"I do. And I know what Mom threatened."

He pinched the bridge of his nose and took a breath. "You told me once that I should have died instead of him. And I told you I'd been wishing that, too. Remember?" He waited for my nod. "The army was the only way I could think of to fix things. I still don't know what went wrong, why he ended up like that. For a while I thought it was because your mother babied him, but now I'm not so sure. Because I thought the way she treated him was what made him weak and afraid of things, and that's how I picture—those people. But when JJ works with those dogs, he's not weak. He's not afraid." He looked around the room and then back at me. "I would never have thought JJ was gay."

"What makes a man a man, Dad?"

"What?"

"You heard me. What is it?" He blubbered something incoherent, so I gave him a hint. "Is a man brave and strong? Does he live up to his commitments and keep his promises? Does he save lives? Is a hero a man? Because Chris was all those things."

"So it didn't help."

"What didn't help?"

"Being in the army."

I almost snorted. "You know, he found a...I don't know what he'd call it. Another man in his own squad. They were in love." Again with the face rubbing. "He thought you didn't know about him. He begged me not to tell you." My teeth ground together.

Now Dad bent his head onto his arms on the desk, and if it had been anyone else I might have thought he was crying. I didn't know what to say, so I just waited him out. It was painful; I'd been tortured for months, wanting to tell him, not wanting to tell him. Wanting to preserve Chris's image, desperate to destroy it so mine could improve.

Finally he sat up and looked at me. "I never let on to him that I knew. That felt important. I guess I felt that if I said the word, or if I confronted him, that would make it real. It would give him something to throw at me."

"Chris wouldn't have done that. He wouldn't have pushed back at you, ever." Even now, guts clenching to stifle fury over my pointless struggle, I couldn't let Chris down.

Dad shook his head. "You're wrong. What do you think he was doing when he locked himself in his room? At his age he didn't know it, but he was setting the stage. And letting only your mother into his room was a battle tactic. Got her on his side. It wasn't what a man would do, was what I thought. A man would react more like you. Come out yelling. So all I could do was try to put it behind us. I chose to act like he'd done the same. I've been so worried it would happen to you, too. Because I don't know where it comes from. So I've been pretty hard on you. Haven't let your mother coddle you. Haven't let you get away with things. At least I didn't fail with you."

My head started shaking on its own. Voices were sounding off in my brain. Like, *You got Chris killed!* And, *You think I react the way a man would? Then why all the "act like a man" lectures for the past several months?* And, *Is JJ a failure? Was Chris?* The only thing I could think of to say aloud was an echo of something JJ had said to me. "Could you be gay?"

His voice was weak, tired. "What?"

"Because I couldn't. And JJ can't be straight. He shouldn't have to live a lie, just so we can feel more comfortable around him."

"Paul, that's not the problem. It's illegal, and it's unnatural, and it's immoral."

"I don't agree."

"Son, you can't argue with the law...."

"I'm not gonna report him. Are you? And as for being unnatural, sure, it feels wrong to me. It *is* wrong for me. Because I'm not gay. But JJ, and Chris, probably feel exactly the same way when we try to force them to be with girls. I'll bet that turns *their* stomachs." I realized I was talking about Chris like he was still alive, but to tell the truth it kind of felt like he was in the room with me. It felt like he was smiling.

I thought Dad would bring up the Bible next, like I had with JJ that day, but he didn't. He just closed his eyes and put his head in his hands again. I wondered if he was thinking what I was thinking—that he'd gotten his own son killed in a misguided attempt to straighten him out. *And now he's about to fire J J to keep me safe?*

"You can't fire JJ, Dad."

He looked at me over his fingertips a minute and then dropped his hands. "You swear he hasn't touched you?"

I tried to smile, but it was a little wobbly. "Dad, he saved my life. He got me a date with a girl. What else can I tell you? No, he hasn't touched me. He's got a boyfriend, anyway. What does he want with me?"

He took a couple of shaky breaths and then surprised me again. "Think I'll go take Dante for a short walk. Why don't you go home and let your mother know I'll be along shortly."

I opened my mouth to tell him Dante had had his walk, but then I realized that wasn't the point. We left the office and walked toward the stockroom, me to get my bike and him to get Dante. Just before I opened the door I thought about the time

I couldn't get Dante to calm down. I'd tried and failed to do the alpha rollover, and JJ had said that I'd get it. In my head I heard his voice tell me, *Not everyone has it in them. But you do.* To my dad I said, "I'm going to help Mrs. O'Neil recover Geronimo."

Dad did the strangest thing. He hugged me.

That night, in bed, I thought I'd never get to sleep. My mind kept trying to line things up and make sense out of them, starting with the fact that my tortured silence had meant nothing. Dad had known long before I did. But Chris hadn't realized it.

If Dad had known Chris was gay for so long, then all those years when I thought Chris was calming Dad down...what was really going on? Was it that Dad just didn't want to deal with Chris so he backed down to get away from him, or was it more like Dad knew that if he didn't back down, Mom would leave?

Was I the only one in the family who thought of Chris as strong and brave? Was Dad unable to see those parts of him because he figured if Chris was a homo he couldn't be those things, too?

Had I always thought of Chris as Mom's favorite because she knew she had to protect him, and knew she couldn't protect me, too, and he needed it more? Or maybe because Dad would go ballistic if she got soft toward me?

Whatever the answers were, one thing kept rising to the surface. Dad had thought he was protecting me. He had thought he was keeping me safe from something he thought was dangerous. In his own weird way, in a way I don't know that I like, he was loving me. I think he was wrong about the danger, but I was wrong about the love. I didn't see that.

Now I do.

# Chapter 16

Monday, my day off, I went into the store. I got there real early, gave Dante a short walk and then put him on his run. I even beat JJ in. Dad asked what I was doing there, and I said that if he was about to lose one of his employees, maybe he could use me today. He squeezed my shoulder and asked me to let him know when Dave got there.

JJ was in before Dave, of course. I saw his mom's car in the front when she dropped him off. He looked kind of sideways toward the office like he wasn't sure whether he wanted my dad to see him. I was feeding the amphibians where I could see if Dave came in without being seen very well myself, but JJ spotted me and came over.

"How's the hand?" I asked as he approached.

He looked down at it like he'd forgotten it was bandaged. "Okay. Fine. Um..."

"If you're wondering about any fallout from yesterday?" I waited, and his expression told me I was right. "I think it'll be okay. Just keep a low profile maybe. Dad's got a bad day ahead of him for other reasons."

"That why you're here today?"

"Yeah. He might need me to be here." JJ smiled and nodded. I added, "Um, in fact, could you walk Dante for me? He only got a few minutes earlier, and I'm not sure how easy it'll be for me to get away for a little while. He's on his run."

"Sure. Happy to."

He was out with the dog when Dave got in. I didn't need to tell Dad he was there; Dad was watching for him.

Dave did not go quietly. There was ranting and railing I could hear right through the closed office door about how he'd served his country and this was the thanks he got and he'd sue and all kinds of crap. Thank God there were no customers in the store at the moment. Alice was there, and she looked frightened, so I stayed near her. On his way out, Dave knocked over as much stuff as he could reach, which fortunately didn't include anything with animals in it.

Dad came over to help me clean up the mess. I asked, "You okay?"

He reached for a fallen package of dry dog food that was on special and said, "I hated doing that. He's a vet."

"And a thief."

Dad sighed. "It's not like I didn't warn him. He's been doing this for months. I was going to look the other way, but he got greedy."

I stopped myself just in time before asking why he hadn't given Chris as much slack. But it wasn't going to get us anywhere to bring that up.

Tuesday night we had a surprise phone call. I answered.

This man's voice said, "Is this Paul Landon, by any chance?"

"Yes."

"My name's Dennis Halpert. I served with your brother. He saved my life."

Dennis came to see us that weekend, after a flurry of housecleaning that rivaled Mom's efforts before Chris's leave last fall. I ran to the door when I heard his car pull up, and I watched him get out. It took him a little while, and when he came into view, on crutches, I could see that the bottom half of his left leg was missing.

Mom fussed over him, making sure he was comfortable and

had anything he might possibly want. Dad and I just wanted him to talk. We wanted to hear about Chris.

Dennis talked. He told us how everyone in the squad looked to Chris for sanity, for clear thinking. How guys used to seek him out to tell him their problems, their worries about girlfriends back home, their fears about a mission coming up. And he told us about the day Chris died.

Mom cried quietly through most of the story of Chris's last day on earth. Dennis was the second man Chris had pulled to safety. He couldn't help with the others because of his leg, but he could see Chris coming back with the last guy. The thing I remember best was when he said, "I saw Chris get hit. He was half carrying Tim, who was barely conscious but not seriously hurt, and I saw the bullets hit from behind. All this red appeared on Chris's chest, and I looked at his face." Dennis had to stop for a second before he could go on. "He wasn't surprised. It was like he'd been expecting it. He grimaced, and—pardon the language, ma'am, but goddamn me if he didn't just keep moving. He got Tim to where Carl could grab him and drag him under cover, and then Chris just kept going. I guess he didn't want to give away where we were. He kept moving until we couldn't hear him anymore."

Dennis rubbed his face for a minute. "After all the firing stopped, Carl crawled out to find Chris. He was a good fifty feet away. I won't describe what Carl saw, but I'll just tell you I don't think I could've walked ten feet in that condition."

Mom was sobbing openly by now, and Dad and I kept lifting our glasses of iced tea to cover our faces. Dennis, unashamed, took out a handkerchief and blew his nose.

We gave this story some space, and probably nobody trusted their voices, anyway. But after a while, I said, "Can I ask you something that's been bothering me?"

"Sure, Paul. If it's bothering you, I'm sure Chris would want it to stop. He thought the world of you."

Okay, another second or two before I could trust my voice again. Then, "When he was home, he told us about some of the stuff that happened, but he never said anything like other stories I've heard. Like, not knowing who was an enemy and who wasn't. And who was even dangerous and who wasn't. Do you know why not?"

Dennis shrugged. "Maybe because that was one of the creepiest things about being over there. I remember just after I got there, it was a question I had. And what I was told was that if a Vietnamese person had a gun, they were the enemy. And if they were dead, they were the enemy, even if they had no gun. It could be a kid with a gun, or an old lady throwing a grenade. It could be anybody. And we didn't have the luxury of taking a lot of time to figure it out." He took a deep breath. "I think that's what will haunt me the worst. The rest of my life. And I know this is no consolation for you, but at least Chris will be spared those nightmares. The war is over for him."

When Dennis left, I walked him out to his car alone. I helped him get settled and then I had one more question for him. "Did you know Mason?"

Dennis looked up at me like he was trying to decide what to say. "Sure. Mason was one of the nicest guys you'd ever hope to meet." He laughed. "Though he did have a thing about snakes, and I'm afraid we were a little cruel about that a few times." We stared at each other a minute, and then he said, "Did Chris tell you how much Mason meant to him?"

I nodded. "Yeah. Did, um, did the other guys know?"

"We all knew. And we didn't care. We were kinda glad he had someone. Paul, everyone loved Chris. Admired him. He coulda had green hair and three arms and we would've loved him just as much. He was about the best friend a guy could have. And he loved you like you were his son."

"I loved him, too."

I watched the car drive away, and then I just stood there. And stood there.

Dad went into his study after dinner that night, a very quiet meal, and shut the door. I was really tempted to go in there and tell him the rest of what Dennis had said, how much the other soldiers didn't care about the part of Chris that Dad hated so much it got Chris killed. But that seemed like such a negative thing to do, and Dad probably already felt like shit, anyway. Maybe some solitary time-out would do him some good. If I wasn't—weren't (*that's for you, Mom*)—in front of him challenging him, maybe it would be easier for him to let himself admit he was wrong.

Instead, I decided I had two things to talk with Mom about. One was that I was sure she'd like to hear the other great things Dennis had said, now that I knew that she had known about Chris. And the other was that she knew about Chris.

I found her sitting on the back steps, swatting at the occasional mosquito and gazing into the darkening sky. It was a tough choice: leave her to her own thoughts or bring her some of mine?

I sat down beside her, knees up, arms crossed on them. Neither of us spoke for about a minute. Then I said, "Dennis told me the squad knew about Chris."

I wasn't watching her, but I could almost feel her stiffen beside me. A cautious glance sideways told me she was still looking out at nothing as she said quietly, "What do you mean?"

"He had a...a lover. In the squad. Did you know that?" I turned my head to see that she had covered her face with her hands. "It was Mason. Dennis says he was a terrific guy." She shook her head a little but kept her face covered. "Mason died while Chris was home last November. That phone call he made was to Mason's parents."

That got her attention. When she looked at me I could see a little light from the kitchen reflecting in the tears on her face. She looked like she was in agony. I wrapped my arm around her shoulder and she leaned against me and sobbed.

When she had about cried herself out, blowing her nose on a tissue from her apron pocket, I had something else I needed to say. Ask.

"Did you know how much Dad's being tough on me had to do with Chris?"

She nodded, and her breath caught a few times. Then she said, "I'm so sorry. I had to choose. Either I could keep Chris safe and let your father be the way he felt he needed to be toward you or I could try to protect you, too, which would have made things even worse. It didn't seem to me as though you needed my protection nearly as much as Chris did. I had to choose, Paul. Do you understand?"

I sort of did, and I sort of didn't. I said, "So just because you didn't think I was gay, and you knew Chris was, you thought he needed protection and I didn't? Is that what you're saying?"

Her sigh was shaky. "I suppose so."

I bit my tongue before I could point out what her protection had meant to Chris, what had happened to him because of it, in the end. If she had protected me, what would it have meant for me? Would things have been even worse for me? Probably.

I could barely hear my own voice. "I guess you made the right choice." But there was more to say. "Chris thought you and Dad didn't know."

"He knew I did. I let him believe his father didn't. I thought it would make living together as a family easier if they could at least try to act normal toward each other."

"But... he asked me not to tell you. Why would he say that?"

"Not to tell *me*? Or not to tell anyone?"

What had he said? It might have been "anyone," and I put my own interpretation on it. This was all so tangled. I shook my head to clear my brain and sat quietly, thinking. But then I realized that I wanted her to know that just because Chris was gay didn't mean he was a coward, or a sissy. "JJ is gay."

She pulled away from me. "What?"

"Yup. Dad knows. I've known all summer, but Dad just found out on Sunday night." I wanted to add that if there was one thing JJ didn't need, it was protection. But that might have made her feel like she'd done things all wrong with Chris, and what would be the point of that now?

*Is this what it means to be a man?*

We talked for a bit more about JJ, which seemed to ease the tension enough for me to say good night and not feel like I was leaving her in some emotional state. Up in my room I put on the Cat Stevens album that Chris had been playing the day he'd had Jim Waters in his room, and I stood at my desk gazing out into the odd shapes the streetlight made shining through the leaves on that tree I'd spent so much time staring at this year.

On its own, my hand opened the drawer where I kept the SAD-EYE pellets. I lifted one out and set it on the table beside my bed, propped up against my alarm clock so it wouldn't roll off.

I lay in bed for a while, picturing Chris and Mason and the guys in their squad laughing and joking and talking about home, wondering if the other guys resented that the two gay guys had their lovers right there and everyone else had only letters. But it hadn't sounded like that, from what Dennis had said. It had sounded like if it hadn't been for the jungle, and the bugs, and the bullets, that squad was actually the best place for my brother to be.

Mr. Treadwell and Ophelia, not a gnawed spot on her anywhere, came to the store on JJ's last day. We stood outside near the corner of the building, and after questions about the bandaged hand Mr. Treadwell asked JJ about his plans, what veterinary schools he might consider, where he thought he might like to practice. And then he turned to me.

"Have you been writing at all, Paul?"

"Writing?"

He looked at JJ. "You should have read this short story Paul submitted for extra credit. He told it from the perspective of a medieval French farmer who'd taken refuge with his family in a castle under siege. Blended history and family and emotional trauma together beautifully. It was gripping."

JJ tilted his head at me. "What's this? A secret talent? You should pursue that, you know."

I scuffed a sneaker against the ground. "I dunno. It's a lot of work."

Mr. Treadwell said, "JJ, I wish you all the best. Thank you so much for your help with Ophelia. You have a rare gift, and the world will be a better place because you share it." They shook hands, and Mr. Treadwell led Ophelia away as JJ and I watched.

"Look at her, will you?" he said. "Head up, proud, she's one happy dog."

At the end of the day, after everyone else had told JJ how much they'd miss him and how much they'd learned from him, he turned to me. "Paul, will you come with me while I say good-bye to Dante?"

We stood out back in the shade, with Dante tethered to his run and lying happily under his favorite tree. Out here was where Marty had revealed JJ's nature to me. This was the run that JJ and I had put up together. Where my ignorance, my misplaced anger at JJ and my father, had nearly cost Dante his life. Where I'd called JJ a faggot and he'd told me off. Where I'd asked him what he knew about me that my dad wouldn't like, and he'd said there was nothing and then winked at me.

He said, "This has been a pretty amazing summer."

"Ditto." I reached into my pocket and pulled out the SADEYE pellet I'd taken from my drawer after Dennis had been to see us, after I'd talked with Mom about Chris. I held my hand out.

"What's this?"

"A going-away present. It's a SADEYE pellet. From a cluster bomb. Chris gave it to me."

JJ's eyes moved from my palm to my eyes. After several seconds he looked down and held his right hand out, and I rolled the pellet onto it.

There was so much to say, and no way to say it. Finally we just looked at each other again, and the next thing I knew we were hugging. I hugged him as though I could hug Charlie again. I hugged him for the apology I never gave Anthony. I hugged him for the farewell I wouldn't give Chris. I would not make those mistakes again, and I would not lose this friend. I hugged him hard.

And then I watched him walk away. He turned once, smiled, and waved.

*What will his life be like? Will he go through it always fighting a war other people make for him? Will he become a veterinarian? Will he and Ben stay together, or will he meet some other guy and fall in love all over again? Will he have lots of dogs, and maybe a cat or two?*

When JJ was out of sight, I looked down at my dog, who was smiling up at me. With a small shock, I realized that Dante had never talked to me. Yet. I rubbed his good ear.

*Think maybe I'll take creative writing in the fall.*

# A Question of Manhood

## ROBIN REARDON

### ABOUT THIS GUIDE

The suggested questions are included to enhance
your group's reading of Robin Reardon's
A QUESTION OF MANHOOD.

# DISCUSSION QUESTIONS

1.  Paul's father has one leg that's shorter than the other. How does this physical limitation affect how he interacts with the world in general and with his sons in particular?

2.  In one of Chris's army stories about being in Vietnam, Chris says that sometimes the spookiest part of being in a difficult situation is when no one really knows what to do and they have to trust their commander to decide on the best course of action. How does this dynamic play out in Paul's life? Who should his commander be?

3.  You've probably heard the expression "Pray like hell, but row away from the rocks." When Paul goes with his mother to church, he prays like hell, but he feels as though he gets no answer. And, in fact, his life gets worse. When he finally figures out that he also has to row away from the rocks, how does he do that?

4.  Paul's father keeps telling him he needs to act like a man, but it seems the more Paul tries to do this, the more he misses the mark and angers his father. Ironically, there are other times when Paul stops worrying about meeting his father's expectations and then receives praise. Is it more Paul's inability to understand what his father wants or his father's inability to communicate it that causes the disconnect? Or is there another cause?

5.  JJ's ability to handle dogs is not limited to his demeanor and his tactics. He has an underlying strategy that applies equally well to humans interacting with humans.

At one point in the story, he describes it to Paul's father. Can you identify it?

6.  Jack, the homeless man who sometimes hangs out in front of the pet store, draws a comparison between "Bible Jesus" and "little Jesus," or JJ. He says people want to turn all their troubles over to Bible Jesus, but JJ puts the dogs' burdens onto the people. What do you think is at the heart of Jack's comment? What is he trying to say?

7.  As Paul tells his father about what happened with Geronimo, he doesn't resort to his usual rebellious behavior when his father challenges him. And when the conversation is over, Paul feels as though he's passed some test. What is that test? What rite of passage is he referring to?

8.  Toward the end of the story, Paul begins to feel that he could get to be as comfortable with the idea of JJ being gay as he is about his father's limp, which he doesn't even notice anymore. If it's possible that people who are uncomfortable with homosexuality could change their attitude if they were around gay people enough, what would that take? How could we make it happen?

9.  Does it seem to you that Paul's mother made the right decision regarding which son to protect? How did this decision shape the family dynamics?

10.  More than once, Paul is confronted by a Border collie, arguably the most intelligent breed of dog, and the collie asks him difficult, leading questions and tells him things he doesn't want to know. In whose voice is the collie really speaking?